CLEOPATRA GOLD

Also by William J. Caunitz

One Police Plaza
Suspects
Black Sand
Exceptional Clearance

CLEOPATRA GOLD

WILLIAM J. CAUNITZ

CROWN PUBLISHERS, INC., NEW YORK

CAUNTIZ, WILLIAM
CLEOPATRA GOLD

Published by Crown Publishers, Inc., 201 East 50th Street, New York, New York 10022. Member of the Crown Publishing Group.
Random House Inc. New York, Toronto, London, Sydney, Auckland.
CROWN is a trademark of Crown Publishers, Inc.

Manufactured in the United States of America

ISBN 0-517-57498-5

For my grandsons,
Joshua and Matthew

1

THE GHOSTS ARRIVED EARLY. Two of them got out of a taxi in front of the Savoy Hotel on Manhattan's Park Avenue. It was a little before ten in the morning as they quietly made their way through the lobby to the elevators. They were supposed to be businessmen, so they had dressed in lightweight suits appropriate for a humid New York summer. They clutched Louis Vuitton suitcases and wore watches with heavy gold bracelets.

They took the elevator to the eleventh floor and walked along the corridor to suite 1101. One of them inserted a plastic key card into the slot above the doorknob, and when the bulb glowed green he pushed the door open, and they went inside. Fifteen minutes later four more well-dressed Ghosts carrying Coach leather carryalls knocked softly on the door of suite 1103.

A short time later an aging, noticeably overweight female

Ghost with short gray hair outfitted in one of the hotel's maid uniforms appeared on the eleventh floor, pushing a service trolley. She stopped in front of the adjoining suite, 1102, and knocked. After getting no reply, she knocked again. Still there was no answer, so she took out her passkey and let herself in. The guest who had been staying in this suite was scheduled to have checked out at eight that morning in order to catch a ten A.M. flight to Los Angeles. She had to make sure he was gone. Stepping into the foyer, she called, "Hello? Housekeeping."

The small hall led into a large living room with a window that overlooked the jagged verticality of the city's mix of buildings new and grand, aged, low and humble. The bedroom and bathroom were to the left, off the living room. The Ghost went directly into the bathroom and picked up all the dirty towels scattered on the floor. Then she walked back into the hotel's corridor, tossed them into the trolley's cloth hamper, and, reaching into the middle shelf, slid out a stack of oversize bath towels. Back inside the suite, she nudged the door closed with her knee and went into the living room, where she put the stack on the sofa against the wall between 1102 and the bedroom of suite 1103. Leaning forward, she reached up, spread her arms, and lifted down the eighteen-inch-wide reproduction of an anonymous oil painting of a shepherd herding his flock over rolling hills and put it down on the floor. The woman pulled out an identical painting carefully concealed in a stack of towels and hung it in the empty space. Stepping back, she made sure the picture was straight and looked naturally in position. She picked up the other picture and walked into the bedroom, where she put it on the bed and wrapped it in dirty bed sheets. Back outside into the main corridor, she shoved the dirty linen into the hamper, slid out clean sheets, went back inside to the bedroom, and unfurled and spread the top sheet over the mattress.

*　*　*

The Ghosts in suite 1101 were unpacking their quite unbusiness-like equipment in the bedroom that adjoined the bedroom of suite 1102—two Uzi submachine guns were placed on the bed. The shorter of the two Ghosts opened another suitcase, turned the lid to face the wall, and clicked on a knob concealed in the suitcase's hinge. The flat television screen concealed in the inside of the suitcase's lid glowed, and a picture of the maid making the bed in the adjoining bedroom sprang into full color. The other Ghost was checking the reel-to-reel audio backup equipment inside the other suitcase. The rule was, when you stole sound and pictures, you made sure you really got at least one of the two.

In suite 1103 the other Ghosts opened their carryalls and took out three double-barreled shotguns and one Ingram MAC-10 machine pistol with sound suppressor. The oldest of the four had unkempt dirty blond hair; he keyed a number into his cellular telephone and asked the person on the other end, "You ready?"

"Yeah. You?"

"Yeah. Hang loose." The older Ghost switched off the phone and looked down at the video receiver in time to see the maid walking out of the living room of the adjacent suite with a satis-fied, somewhat nasty smile tugging at the corners of her mouth. He couldn't repress a grin at the thought, We get off on doin' this shit. After punching another number into his phone, he said in a low, suddenly intense voice, "Bring in the green."

A black Lincoln Town Car made a right-hand turn out of Sixty-third Street and drew up in front of the Savoy Hotel. Three burly men wearing obviously expensive jogging outfits got out and walked to the back of the car. One of them opened the trunk while another motioned to the bellhop to bring over his lug-gage cart.

A barrel-chested man wearing a loose-fitting Mexican-style white shirt with an embroidered floral design down the front climbed out of the passenger seat, clutching a nylon flight bag.

He joined the others and watched as four suitcases were taken out of the trunk and loaded onto the luggage cart.

Seven minutes later the four of them got off the elevator on the eleventh floor of the hotel and convoyed the luggage down the corridor to suite 1122. The one with the nylon flight bag handed the bellboy a five-dollar bill and said firmly, "We'll carry 'em inside."

Once inside the suite, the man with the flight bag took out a cellular telephone, keyed in a number, and said, "The green be here."

At three-thirty that beautiful June afternoon, undercover detectives Vito DiLeo and Jerry Levi let themselves into suite 1102 of the Savoy. They were swarthy, medium-size men both with black curly hair, although Levi's was starting to recede in front. Levi was closely shaven, his jowls a heavily shadowed bluish color that comes from a twice-a-day need to shave. Curly black hairs escaped from the confines of the cuffs of his light Sea Island cotton shirt. His long, narrow face had an ascetic cast, El Greco–like, especially because of his huge black eyes. Both men had grown up on the streets of Manhattan, DiLeo on Mulberry Street in Little Italy and Levi in the small Sephardic community clustered around Hester Street. Levi was fluent in Spanish and Ladino, the Judeo-Spanish language of the Sephardic Jew, while DiLeo spoke several Italian dialects. His face was open, friendly—a man quick to tell a joke and laugh heartily at his own punch line.

For the past eight months they had been working their way up the tangled branches of a narcotics-importing network that had uncovered and murdered an undercover detective ten months earlier. That cop's name was Tony Fermi, another officer of Sephardic heritage. DiLeo and Levi had been posing as big-time dopers who represented a retailing network operating in Brooklyn, Queens, and Staten Island.

Levi was wearing beige trousers, tasseled loafers, and a brown linen sports jacket over his white cotton shirt. DiLeo had on a gray summer suit and an open-necked blue button-down shirt. Both had .380 Beretta automatics jammed into their waistbands at the small of their backs.

DiLeo ambled over to the painting above the sofa, gave a "thumbs up" gesture, and said, "You receiving, Big Guy?"

One of the Ghosts in suite 1103 banged three times on the wall.

Levi reached into his jacket's left breast pocket and slid out what appeared to be a disposable plastic pen. Holding the instrument out in front of him, he tested, "One, two, three, four, I love the Marine Corps. All you Ghosts out there receiving me?"

Knocks resounded through the living room and bedroom walls.

"Is the money room set up?" Levi asked.

More knocks.

Looking carefully at the innocuous, cheap-looking pen, he said to DiLeo, "Incredible stuff Tech Services comes up with. The Job's come a long way since the days when a cop had to rap his nightstick on the sidewalk to summon help." He slid the transmitter pen back into the pocket of his jacket.

DiLeo went over to the window to admire the view of the city baking in the unusually hot June morning. "I love this town."

Levi flopped down on the sofa. Picking up the remote and flicking on the television, he said, "I hope this thing goes down today. David's Bar Mitzvah is in two weeks. I don't want to be still out there playing games with these scumbags. I need to devote some time to my family." Flipping channels, he looked over at DiLeo and laughed.

"What's so funny?"

"I can't wait to see you at the Bar Mitzvah wearing a yarmulke."

"Kiss my ass, you Rican half-breed."

Levi flipped to the in-house movie channel. *"Sea of Love."*

"Seen it. What's today's date?"

"The thirteenth."

"Lucky we ain't superstitious."

At five o'clock a well-dressed man carrying a gleaming black leather Gladstone bag walked into the Grill Room of the Savoy and asked the maître d' for a table in the no smoking section, one that had a view of Park Avenue. The maître d's practiced hand made a ten-dollar bill disappear magically as he escorted the guest over to a window table with a "Reserved" card on it. He let the maître d' pull out a chair for him, sat down, and casually pushed his bag under the table.

Two women in subdued but obviously expensive designer suits, one a strawberry blonde, the other a dark and quite voluptuous brunette, were chatting over tea and scones at one of the nearby tables. One of them laughed at something her friend said, picked up her napkin, and while dabbing her mouth whispered into the mike concealed in the right sleeve of her suit jacket, "The mule just arrived."

From his seat the man with the Gladstone bag had a view of the hotel's entrance and the entire restaurant. Nervously repositioning the bag up against the wall with his foot, he studied the menu. A waiter in a starched white jacket came over and asked, "Are you ready to order, sir?"

"Yes. I'd like the endive, watercress, and Bibb lettuce salad with the lemon vinaigrette on the side, and the Dover sole."

"Anything to drink, sir?"

"Just water, thank you."

As the waiter turned to leave, the man slid his jacket open and checked to see that his beeper was turned on. He looked out the window in time to see an attractive woman half turn her body around, lower herself into the rear seat of a taxi, and gracefully lift in her legs. He loved this time of year; the skirts got so short that they virtually disappeared.

Seventeen minutes later two casually dressed men got out of a taxi and stood under the hotel's canopy, looking around with the idle expressions of people waiting to meet someone. The stout one had a pug nose and small ears set close to his head. His companion was over six feet tall and built like a pro basketball player. The shorter man glanced inside the restaurant at the man sitting by the window nibbling at his salad. Their eyes met briefly, then the two men walked into the hotel and took the elevator up to the eleventh floor.

DiLeo and Levi lounged around the suite, not saying much or paying attention to the movie. They were suffering through the undercover doldrums, a mixture of anxiety over what was about to go down and boredom waiting for it to happen. It was during these periods that undercovers turned down their volume, conserving their energy while dreaming about such mundane things as cutting the lawn, strolling through the shopping mall with their family, and taking in a Saturday-night movie with the wife—anything but doing kilo deals with scumbag dope dealers.

Levi looked at his watch. "Five-twenty. They were supposed to be here at five."

"Dopers are always late, you know that." DiLeo pushed himself up off the sofa. "I gotta take a piss."

A few minutes later three slow knocks on the door made Levi jump up, his adrenaline surging. He took his Beretta out of the waistband of his trousers and went over to the door. "Yeah?"

"It's us, Ramón and Conrado."

Peering through the little glass lens in the middle of the door, Levi saw the magnified faces of the dopers. Conrado, the short one with the flattened nostrils and strong Indio features, came in and stood in the foyer, scanning the room. Tall Ramón came in behind him and closed and locked the door. He moved with an eerie mixture of silence and fluid grace.

Walking back into the living room, zipping up his fly, DiLeo saw the new arrivals and said, "Hey, you guys finally got here." Going over and grabbing Conrado by the shoulders, he added, "Good to see you, amigo."

Conrado's eyes turned to stare coldly at the undercover cop. "I don't like hotel rooms. They're too easy to bug."

"Hey, amigo, if it's not cool here, split. We'll deal another time, another place. Next time out, you pick the spot," DiLeo said, going over and flicking off the television.

Ramón seemed to take up a great deal of the air-conditioned space of the hotel room; his cruel face, with an ugly scar running down the chin, turned toward DiLeo. He folded his arms and said slowly, in a low, hoarse voice, "You always smelled like the man to me."

DiLeo assumed a pissed-off expression, jerked his thumb at the door, and said, "There's the fuckin' way out, amigo. We came here with a mil six to deal. You don't got trust . . . fuck you . . . we'll take our green somewhere else."

Conrado raised an eyebrow, staring into Ramón's cold gray eyes, and said, "My friend is overly cautious, sometimes."

Levi smiled. "There's no such thing as too much careful in our business."

Conrado put his overnight bag on top of the writing table in the front of the living room and said, "I wanna make sure you understand the fine print. We give you a franchise to peddle our produce with your commitment that it's not to be stepped on. You'll do nothing to adulterate its purity. In return, we guarantee you your supply, and that no one else hustles our stuff within your territory."

Ramón then broke in, "You use *only* our glassine envelopes, the ones that have our logo. On the crack vials you should charge a deposit; you recycle them and maximize your profits." Walking around the room, his fingers checking the moldings, looking for concealed microphones, he added, "As we agreed, the price is a hundred and sixty thousand a kilo, minimum first order, ten keys, payable on delivery. After we do business awhile, and we get to know each other better, credit terms can be arranged." Looking at the painting hanging over the sofa, he went on to ask, "Questions?"

The undercovers shook their heads.

"Then let's do it," Ramón said. "Your money's here, right?"

"Yeah," DiLeo said, "but before we go for it, we wanna taste."

"First the money," Conrado insisted.

DiLeo looked over at his partner and shrugged. Levi walked over to the door, opened it, and made a sweeping bow, throwing out his hand in a gesture of exaggerated courtesy. Conrado picked up his overnight bag from the writing table and followed the others out of the suite.

DiLeo knocked twice on the door of suite 1122, counted to five, and knocked twice more. The door was jerked open to reveal the unsmiling face of the man in the loose-fitting white shirt, pointing a MAC-10 directly up at Ramón's mean face.

The dopers strolled into the suite contemptuously and were greeted by stern faces and the menacing snouts of sawed-off shotguns. Two suitcases were on top of the writing table in the living room, and two more were on the floor. The dopers went over to them and opened the two on the desk. Conrado ran caressing fingers over the tightly packed stacks of bills. He looked over at the unsmiling Ghosts and the shotguns cradled in their arms, grinned, and said, "Loosen up, guys."

Ramón unzipped the overnight bag and took out an electronic currency counter and a penlight device called the Black Light, which exposed counterfeit money. Randomly pulling bills from several bundles, he brushed the penlight across them, checking.

Pretending to be offended, Levi lamented, "Ain't there no trust left in the world?"

"No," Ramón said without looking up from his task.

Conrado reached down into the suitcase, worked out a bundle of money, and began running it through the currency counter. Watching the bills spill through the machine, giving off an electronic buzz, DiLeo said, "Why don't I send down for a couple of bottles of DP to celebrate?"

Eyes fixed on the flashing red numbers, Conrado said, "We're not done yet; besides, Dom Pérignon gives me gas."

Ninety long, tense minutes later, Conrado looked up at Ramón and said, "It's all here."

Ramón nodded, reached back into the overnight, and took out a hand taping machine and three rolls of different-colored masking tape. After examining the rolls and deciding which color to use, he inserted the orange roll into the hand machine and proceeded to spread strands horizontally and vertically across the tops of the open suitcases, effectively color-coding the contents and preventing a switch. That done, he took out a Magic Marker and initialed each of the crisscrossing strands of tape. He did the same thing to the other three suitcases. When that was done, the dopers walked out of the money room, leaving the suitcases where they were. The undercovers followed them.

Downstairs in the Grill Room, the man who had ordered the endive, watercress, and Bibb lettuce salad with lemon vinaigrette on the side was sipping decaffeinated coffee when his beeper went off. He put down his cup, switched off the signal, and motioned to the waiter for his bill.

The two attractive women at the nearby table were still lingering over their tea. One of them turned sideways to get a tissue out of her pocketbook that she had hung over the back of her chair.

Opening the bag and reaching inside, she whispered into her sleeve microphone, "The mule's getting ready to leave."

His bill came; he paid in cash, then reached under the table, picked up his Gladstone bag, and left the restaurant. As he was walking across the lobby, he paused to admire the large floral arrangement on top of the Louis XV table, then saw that the elevator had arrived and stepped into it.

Ramón opened the door of suite 1102, took the Gladstone bag from the man, then turned and handed it to DiLeo. The undercover carried it over to the coffee table and sat down on the sofa, beneath the painting of a shepherd herding his flock across the peaceful, rolling hills.

After opening the Gladstone bag, DiLeo removed two kilos of white powder in sealed clear plastic bags, stacking them on the table. He put the bag on the floor, picked up his attaché case, put it down on the cushion next to him, and took out a red Swiss Army knife and a NIK test pack. From the bag he removed a thick plastic sack about six inches long and slid off the clip that sealed it across the top. Using the knife's widest blade, he sliced into one of the plastic bags and carefully withdrew a small amount of powder on the blade's flat side. He squeezed the sack open and dumped in the powder, tapping the sides to make sure all the material fell to the bottom. After refolding the pack across the original fold point on top, he slid back the clip, resealing the packet. Secured at the bottom of the plastic sack was a slender glass ampoule containing a reagent that identified opium alkaloids and heroin compounds. Using the tips of his thumb and forefinger, DiLeo squeezed the glass tube, crushing it and releasing the reagent on the powder. Gently agitating the packet, he watched the clear liquid turn a rapidly developing deep purple. "Up, up, up, and away," DiLeo murmured, under Conrado's and Ramón's satisfied smiles.

"How'd it test?" Levi asked.

"Looks like eighty-five percent pure," DiLeo said. After testing the remaining kilos, he looked up at the dopers and said, "Definitely quality stuff."

"Then we got a deal," Conrado said.

"Yeah," Levi answered, quickly adding, "But there's a problem. You've seen and marked our money, and all we've got are two keys that you've spoon-fed us. We gotta test the entire stash."

Conrado's lips drew back in an angry snarl, showing a lot of gold dental work. "We guarantee the quality."

Levi and DiLeo smiled at each other. "You guarantee?" Levi said. "Lemme tell you something. The people we represent guarantee . . . with our lives. So if we don't get to test the entire stash, we got no deal."

Conrado started to say something when his beeper went off. He made a bewildered shrug of his shoulders at the other doper, looked down at the number in the device's tiny display window, and, unfolding his cellular phone, walked over to the window, punching a number into the hand-held instrument. "Yeah?" His body tensed when he heard the voice on the other end. His back was to the others, or they would have seen his cheek twitch nervously. "Yes, sir. Yes, of course, Hector," he said, and switched off the phone. He stood with his back to the others, staring out at the city, not saying anything.

DiLeo glanced at his partner with questioning eyes. Who was Hector? What was that call all about? Any unexpected happenings during an undercover buy was not a good sign. Bad vibes began to creep down the undercover's spine.

Conrado turned, looked at Levi, and said, "We'll take you to the stuff."

On the way out of the suite, Levi looked at the painting over the sofa and shook his head, signaling he had no idea what was going down. Ramón and Conrado led them down the corridor toward the elevators. Conrado leaned in close to his partner and whispered something, then rushed ahead and held open the door to the stairwell and announced, "We'll walk."

It was a cold, silent place, with walls and stairs painted battleship gray and banisters colored a glaring cardinal red.

"What floor?" Levi asked, unable to ignore the bad vibes now surging through his body. Should they abort and collar the dopers or play it out? Who the hell was Hector? Whoever he was, Levi thought, he had to be someone *muy importante* for that stone killer Conrado to call "sir." "What floor we goin' to?" he repeated.

"Fifth," Conrado said.

They had just passed the ninth-floor landing when the exit door was quietly pushed open behind them. A man stepped out onto the landing, a tall, distinguished-looking Hispanic dressed in a beautifully tailored brown light woolen suit. A wide streak of white ran through the middle of his black hair, and his dark, searching eyes were set deep under his overhanging brow. His cheeks were badly pockmarked; he was wearing latex gloves, and his right hand was hidden inside a brown paper shopping bag. Looking down at his quarry, he raised the bag.

DiLeo, sensing danger, wheeled around, saw the stranger pointing the shopping bag at them, and started to scream a warning. The man standing on the landing squeezed off a short burst from his silenced weapon, sending a hail of .45-caliber slugs tearing into the undercover's chest, toppling him dead on the stairs.

His hand reaching frantically for the automatic in the small of his back, Levi spun to face the danger. He had just grabbed the Beretta's checkered grip when a burst of silenced automatic fire plowed into his body, lifting him up and slamming him into the wall, where he sank to a sitting position, his blood leaving a broad smear down the cinder block. "I'm not going to David's Bar Mitzvah," he said in a tone of utter weariness, and died.

The shredded shopping bag was thrown down the stairs.

Color drained from the dopers' faces as they watched the shooter move down the steps toward them, his expressionless eyes peering at them with chilling indifference.

Ramón raised his hands in a gesture of supplication when he saw the MAC-10 with the blunt silencer at the end pointing at them. "We were told they were okay," he pleaded.

"They were cops," Hector whispered, and shot Ramón and Conrado dead.

2

"TOO TALL PAULIE" KICKED the wastebasket across his ninth-floor office in One Police Plaza and gloated with malicious satisfaction as it bounced off the wall, spewing paper across the room. He stormed after it and kicked it again. This time the force of his blow broke through the thin plastic skin, impaling the basket on his shoe. "Goddammit!" Hobbling, he worked it off his foot and hurled it at the wall, knocking down a photograph of himself and former Police Commissioner Ben Ward.

Behind his desk once again, he slumped onto his chair and stared out the window at the Municipal Building's gingerbread cupola encased in scaffolding, wondering for the fiftieth time when the city would finish the apparently endless renovation.

Assistant Chief Inspector Paul Burke's lithe, six-foot-two-inch frame had long ago earned him the nickname "Too Tall Paulie."

For the last eight years he had commanded the NYPD's Narcotics Division. Most of his twenty-eight years in the Job had been spent working narcotics. Last night's murder of DiLeo and Levi had raised to three the number of undercovers killed in the past year and a half, three of the best in the Job, all murdered while trying to infiltrate the same network. How had their covers been blown? he kept asking himself. He pushed himself out of the chair, went over to the coat closet, and rolled out his dance board, a large square of three-quarter-inch hardwood. After wheeling it to the center of the room, he let it fall flat on the floor and went back to the closet. He took out his tap shoes and walked over to the couch, where he sat down and unlaced his street shoes.

Except for the bagel and coffee he had wolfed down when he got to One Police Plaza at nine-thirty, he had eaten nothing since early last night, but he didn't feel hungry. Just angry and puzzled.

Some people meditated; Too Tall Paulie danced. When he was on the board tapping, he was free, his body floating, his jumbled thoughts clearing, focusing. He had been at the crime scene for most of the night and had come directly to his office from there. He needed to clear his head, to focus on how their covers had been blown. Tossing aside his street shoes, he slipped his feet into his dance shoes and laced them up. After taking off his shirt and tie, he folded them carefully over the back of a chair, stood on the board, and began tap-dancing, his body loose, his arms moving in the same rhythm. He hit a triplet in swing time with his thoughts focusing on the mistakes that he might have made. Was there a leak in the office? Had the dopers bought one of his people? Was someone sleeping in the wrong bed, bragging to the wrong person?

After dancing for a while, beads of sweat glistened on his receding hairline. He had been at it for about fifteen minutes when Captain Dave Katz, his executive officer, walked in without knocking, carrying several brown manila file folders. Ignor-

ing the now familiar spectacle of his boss absorbed in a tap routine, something unlikely to be seen in any other police office
anywhere in the world, Katz went over to the television in the
corner of the room by the desk and popped a videocassette into
the VCR. He turned on the machine, stepped back, and lowered
himself onto the edge of the chief's desk. His short legs dangled
just above the floor. He was dressed in a gray suit that comple-
mented his fresh, almost boyish complexion. People tended to
assume he was younger than his actual age, which was forty-
seven.

Too Tall Paulie continued dancing, his eyes riveted on the
unfolding footage. DiLeo's grinning face appeared on the screen.
"You receiving, Big Guy?" Seeing the undercover caused Too
Tall Paulie to break his time signature and start noodling, the tap
dancer's way of humming to himself, as he intently watched the
four men leaving suite 1102. Katz got up off the desk, switched
off the VCR, and inserted an audiotape into the slot of a Japa-
nese-made high-quality audio playback unit. "Levi had a transmitter concealed in a pen," he said, pressing the Play button.

Burke stopped dancing and ran his fingers through his gray
hair as he listened to the sounds of shuffling feet going down
a staircase, then the chilling sound of the muffled puffs of a
MAC-10. A gasping sound was quickly followed by the thump
of a body hitting treads, and then came the desperate scraping of
feet, followed by the silenced bark of the MAC-10 and the thud
of an object colliding with another. A pleading voice: "We were
told they were okay."

Katz shut off the machine before the sounds of men shouting
frantically, "Get ambulances!" rolled off the tape. He looked at
his boss and said, "The shooter probably took the elevator down
to the lobby and then just calmly walked away."

Too Tall Paulie stepped off the board and went into the bathroom. While urinating, he called out through the open door,
"What about the Ghosts on surveillance outside the hotel?"

"I have them going over mug shots now. One of them might recognize the shooter as someone who left the hotel." After washing and toweling himself dry, Burke came out of the tiny bathroom, removed a clean undershirt from the side drawer of his desk, and pulled it over his head. He sat down on the couch and wearily looked around his office as he unlaced his dance shoes. "Ya know how you know you've made it in the Job? When they give you your own bathroom."

Katz grinned thinly.

"There's a great golf course down in Pebble Beach. Right at this moment I have an urge to dash upstairs to the Pension Bureau, throw in my papers, and retire to California to play golf and get reacquainted with my wife." Tugging off a shoe and casting it aside angrily, he added, "But I can't do that, because three of my people are homicide victims, and that's the kind of unfinished business I don't intend to leave behind when I go."

The XO looked at his boss with an expression of concern on his face. They had been friends a lot of years, through a lot of good and bad together, but never anything like this. He knew Burke well enough to know that he had the same searing frustration gnawing at his guts.

Getting up off the couch, Burke asked sadly, "How, Dave? How were they made?"

Katz screwed his face up and said softly, "I don't know, Paulie. I just can't figure it."

"Did we make any mistakes?"

"None that I can see. A CI made the introduction *after* Fermi's death and then got out of the picture. We figured DiLeo and Levi were totally convincing to the dopers, at least in the first two meets."

"Was the same confidential informant used to introduce Tony Fermi into the network?"

"Yes."

"Then that's our connection. Where is this CI now?"

Katz rubbed the bursitis pain in his left shoulder and said nervously, "Still out there working the street for us, Paulie. We're holding three counts of direct sale, all A-one felonies, over this guy's head. No way, no fucking way he's gonna roll on us. He'll do life plus fifty if we send him back inside."

Burke plucked his shirt and tie off the chair. Shoving an arm through one sleeve, he said, "If we didn't screw up, and the undercovers didn't, and the CI didn't roll over, then the only logical conclusion we can draw is that we have a problem at home."

Shaking his head in emphatic disagreement, Katz said, "No way. Our undercovers are too compartmentalized. Only a handful of our people even know who they are."

Buttoning his shirt, Burke paused and asked thoughtfully, "Remember JoAnn Banks? She fell in love with the network's honcho and ended up in his bed."

"I remember her all too well. I ran her. A three-year operation went into the toilet because of that bitch, not to mention a million dollars of taxpayers' money."

Burke sat at his desk and started making notes on a yellow legal pad. "One of our people might be dippin' their dicks into the wrong honeypot. Check around. And lean on that so-called confidential informant, make damn sure he didn't change camps, or isn't playing both sides of the street." He went over to the coat closet, pulled out his brown suit jacket, and slipped into it. Struck by a sudden thought, he looked across the room at his executive officer and asked, "Is Joey-the-G-Man still hanging around with those crazy Hasidim?"

3

SCHOOLBUSES LINED THE CURB in front of Yeshiva Beth Chaim. Passersby who bothered to look through any of the open first-floor windows would see Hasidic boys with yarmulkes and side curls studying at their desks.

The school, located on the northwest corner of West End Avenue and Ninety-sixth Street, had for more than fifty years been home to Public School 66. Eight years ago a new P.S. 66 was built on One Hundredth Street, and the city leased the old building to the yeshiva. It was a good deal for the religious group. The annual rent was only a thousand dollars, and the only other requirement, besides having to maintain the property, was to allow the Board of Education's Manhattan maintenance unit to occupy, and use, the row of attached one-story stone garages strung across the back of the school yard.

Too Tall Paulie parked his Department-leased Cadillac Sedan de Ville in a garage a block away from the yeshiva. Walking across West End Avenue toward the school yard, he saw a group of boys playing basketball, their arms, curls, and tsitsis flailing. He grinned, recalling Joey-the-G-Man's nickname for the Hasidim—Brownsville Detectives.

Deputy Chief Joe Romano had spent his entire thirty-three years in the Job working in the Land of Trick Mirrors, as the Intelligence Division was known in the Department. The NYPD's table of organization listed only two subunits for the division, the Criminal Section and the Public Security Section. Too Tall Paulie knew that there were unlisted units within the Land of Trick Mirrors that only his old friend Romano knew existed. Joey-the-G-Man was the CO of the Intelligence Division's nonexistent covert action unit—the Special Operations Section.

Walking across the school yard, Burke watched with interest as one of the players went up and jammed in the ball. At the string of garages, he made an oblique right, heading for the one with the plaque that read MAINTENANCE UNIT.

Pushing open the door and going inside, he saw a middle-aged woman in a cream-colored linen dress sitting behind an inch-and-a-half-thick glass wall. "May I help you, sir?" she asked through the microphone.

"I'm Chief Burke. I'm here to see Chief Romano."

"Identification," she asked, pushing out the steel depository drawer.

Too Tall Paulie took out his laminated identification card and plunked it into the cavity, then watched her pull the drawer closed and retrieve his card. Spinning around to the computer, she began scrolling the Force Record File to the B's. When she entered that bank, she pushed several keys, and Burke's picture rolled onto the screen. She compared the face on the other side of the glass with the one in front of her, dropped his identification card into the drawer, pushed it out, and, reaching under her desk, buzzed open the steel door.

Another woman appeared on the other side and led him through another door and down a corridor lined on both sides by closed doors with cipher locks. It was obvious to Burke that all the garages had been connected by a common corridor into one large suite of offices.

Romano was at the end of the hallway, waiting. The head of Special Operations hurried to meet his friend. Shaking hands, Romano said, "I'm not going to ask you how you feel, Paul. How are DiLeo's and Levi's families holding up?"

" 'Bout as expected," he said, following Romano into his Spartan office.

"The only thing keeping both widows on their feet is the Chaplain's Unit working with them on funeral arrangements. Levi's burial is first—you know they gotta plant him within twenty-four hours. Looks like DiLeo's requiem mass will be on Thursday."

Not one picture was on any of the walls, not one personal memento or remembrance anywhere to be seen, nothing that gave a clue as to the personality of the occupant. The top of the desk was bare, save for the telephone and one yellow pencil. Watching his friend going back behind his desk, Burke thought, Only phantoms work in the Land of Trick Mirrors.

Folding his hands on the desk in front of him, Romano smiled and said, "It was you who laid the moniker Joey-the-G-Man on me, wasn't it?"

"I'll cop a plea on that one. We were in the Academy. I never thought it would stick."

Romano's smile evaporated, leaving behind a bony face in a blank mask and a bald head. "What can I do for you, Paul?"

Burke tossed a glassine envelope on the desk. Romano picked it up and examined the logo of three golden horizontal stripes backgrounding the ancient face of a beautiful woman with taut braids across the top of her head. "What's this?"

"A dime bag of Cleopatra Gold, guaranteed to be eighty-five to ninety percent pure heroin."

Romano felt the tic invade his face. He sucked in a deep breath and rubbed his eyebrow, hoping the disturbance could not be seen. "Cleopatra?" he said wanly.

"The network that murdered my undercovers. It's been around for about two years, as far as we can determine. Designer drugs catering to upscale clientele. Before, heroin was never chic the way coke was, but AIDS made the hypodermic needle passé. This network is aggressive as hell; they market the shit out of their product. It's really caught on. Their stuff is so pure it can be snorted; it gives a quick high without coke's crash landing, and . . . no needles. They also peddle a line of high-voltage crack in the ghetto in these gold-sprayed vials—they collect a deposit on the fucking things and recycle. Environmentally concerned dopers, yet. We've been trying to work our way up the network; it's cost us three of our people."

Looking up, Romano asked, "How'd they make your undercovers?"

"We haven't a clue."

Romano sighed. He knew Burke wanted the kind of help he couldn't give to him.

Burke's voice took on a pleading edge. "They can't be allowed to walk away from three dead cops."

Romano very carefully scratched an itch on his Adam's apple, his eyes fixed on some distant spot. "Why come to me?"

Leaning forward, Burke said, "I want you to insert one of your deep undercovers into the Cleopatra network."

Romano's eyes flashed to the man sitting in front of him, and he said softly, "We don't have any undercovers."

"Joey, three dead cops . . ."

Romano held up a protesting palm. "Don't. Okay? The simple answer is, we don't have undercovers."

"Bullshit. It's an open secret in the Job that you run the deep ones."

"I don't know what you're talking about."

"Three dead cops, Joey."

Romano picked up a pencil and began tapping it on the desk, staring expressionlessly at the man in front of him. "I don't even know if there are any deep undercovers in the Job."

"Bullshit," Too Tall Paulie snapped, glaring directly into Romano's eyes.

"All your years in the Job and you haven't learned about the deep ones," said Joey-the-G-Man. "Your undercovers have homes, families. You set them up in apartments, provide them with phony ID, give them flash cars, plenty of money, but they get to go home on weekends or during the week. I understand it doesn't work that way with the deep ones. I've been told that they have given up their own identities for the ones we've provided them. None of them are married. There's no record of them ever being a member of this Department, they're trained by the CIA. They're cop clones without a life of their own."

"They're cops who take orders."

"Wrong. They're people with a mission. And if they were under my umbrella, you could bet your ass I'd never allow them to be used in a narcotics investigation, because in the dope business there are no good guys or bad guys, only the same untreated sewage squishing around the same slime pool. You can't trust anyone because there is no way of telling who is working what side of the street."

"I fucking resent that, Joey. My people are honest, dedicated professionals with a lousy job to do. Who the hell do you think you are, bad-mouthing my division? You . . . you . . . fucking spy."

Romano smiled; his tone softened. "Paul, I'm sorry. I shouldn't have said that. I know you and your people are a hundred percent. But the reality is that not a week goes by that some cop isn't locked up someplace for dealing drugs. It's become such a common occurrence in Miami that the newspapers there don't even bother to run the story anymore."

"It's not only cops," Burke said sadly.

"I know. It's also the bankers and brokerage houses that launder billions for the cartels, and the chemical manufacturers who sell them their products, and the fancy law firms who research the court transcripts of every major drug conspiracy trial, studying the mistakes other traffickers made, and then flying first class to Colombia to give seminars to the cartels on the pitfalls to be avoided." He let the pencil fall from his hand. "It's a slime pool I would never insert a deep one into, no matter what the motivation. But that's all academic, because, as I already told you, I don't control them, and I really don't know who does." He looked Burke directly in the eyes, put forth his most trustworthy expression, and added, "Honest, Paul, I don't know anything about the deep ones."

Shaking his head with disgust, Too Tall Paulie got up, leaned across the desk, and gave his friend a limp handshake, said, "See ya 'round," and left.

The Brownsville Detectives were still playing basketball in the mellow early-afternoon sunlight when Too Tall Paulie stalked across the school yard, cursing under his breath.

4

J OE ROMANO SAT FOR SEV-
eral minutes contemplating a
speck on the wall before he grabbed the telephone and dialed an
in-house number, saying to the person who answered, "Meet me
in the Room, now."

Romano left his office and walked down the long corridor of
locked doors until he reached one in the middle. There he
stopped, keyed the six-digit combination into the cipher lock's
keypad, and entered a cheerless room constructed of a foot of
concrete and lined with an inch and a half of steel plate. A walnut
table and four chairs, and floor fans in each corner, were the only
furniture. A round ceiling fixture locked inside a steel grille was
the only light in the gloomy room. Romano was inside the Special Ops conference room, known to the few who used it as
the Room.

Romano scraped back a chair and sat. From the table's only drawer he took out a package of cigarettes and a sardine can that served as an ashtray and lit up, blowing a stream of smoke at the fan and watching it dissipate into nothingness. Last year his wife had cajoled him into promising to stop smoking, and with his most trustworthy smile he had promised to give up the dirty habit, and he had, almost. Now whenever he was uptight, and in the Room, he would sneak one or two, but only when he was alone with Andy.

Lieutenant Andy Seaver's name had not appeared in any Department orders since Special Order 142, dated July 1, 1965, transferring him from a patrol precinct into the Detective Division. His transfer on December 1, 1971, from the Pickpocket and Confidence Squad to the Intelligence Division was accomplished by a telephone message direct from the police commissioner's office. He was still carried on P&C's roster, and his biweekly paycheck was still sent by the controller to P&C.

A medium-size, light-complexioned man with thinning blond hair and green eyes, he was seldom seen without a stubby Italian cigar stuck in his mouth. He'd never married, although he always wanted to. He was dating a woman who was the banquet manager at the Barrington Hotel, which meant she worked long hours. She thought he was a clerical patrolman assigned to Pickpocket and Confidence and that his boring, safe duties included typing roll calls and payroll records.

When Seaver walked into the Room and saw Romano tapping the pack end over end, he groaned softly, because he knew that was a sure sign of trouble. "What's up?" he asked, yanking back a chair.

"Has this place been swept?"

"This morning."

Romano took a quick drag on the cigarette and announced, "She's surfaced."

"Who?"

"Cleopatra."

Their eyes locked in the tense silence. Seaver's head began to shake as though he were trying to rid himself of a horrible memory. "You sure?"

Romano told him of Too Tall Paulie's visit and the Cleopatra Gold network.

" 'At's hardly proof positive. A lot of the shit peddled on the street has brand names. Makes the dopers feel important."

"It's her," Romano insisted.

"What do you want me to do?"

"Speak to him."

"Joey, he's been sheep-dipped for twelve years, longer than any of them. We can't keep him under forever. He doesn't know what a civilian is. He thinks the world is made up exclusively of bad guys, scumbags, and assholes. If we don't bring him out soon, he'll never be able to surface and have a normal life, never."

"It's her, Andy."

"Joey, we put these people deep, make them live phony lives for too long. It's against every law of human nature, and when we're done with them, we resurrect them back into the real world. Then we toss them into the garbage heap. They can't be cops, their personalities are too screwed up to deal with the public, so we retire them on a disability and wish them fucking adieu. This is Eamon's son, for chrissake. We owe him a shot at a normal life."

Joey-the-G-Man stared at him for a long minute. "No cop has a normal life. Not me, not you, not anyone. We owe him a shot at her. He'd never forgive us if he discovered she'd surfaced and we didn't tell him. He'd go bad on us. We owe him this final performance, and then we'll make him a civilian."

Seaver tossed his cigar stump into the sardine can and said, "Give me one of those cancer sticks of yours."

*   *   *

Assistant Chief Paul Burke parked his car in a garage on Eighteenth Street and walked. People in the Job who rated flash cars did not park them on the street. There was just too great a risk of their being stolen, which created the embarrassing possibility of their owners being exposed as cops. Members of the service who rated flash cars also rated credit cards in their names or in the names of dummy corporations.

A heavy weariness hung over Burke as he made his way along First Avenue thinking of Levi's funeral tomorrow and DiLeo's on Thursday. He would attend both and dutifully tell the widows how sorry he was, and he'd extol their husbands' heroism and dedication and promise the Department would always be there for them and their children any time they needed help, knowing full well that their husbands had already passed on into the Job's folklore and that the widows would be pensioned off and forgotten. He also knew that one question would haunt him for the rest of his life: How had the dopers known?

Too Tall Paulie entered the Thirteenth Precinct station house and walked past the high, imposing desk, flashing his shield to the uniformed lieutenant looking down at him and continuing to the rear of the sitting room. Then he went through the door that led into the lobby of the Police Academy. Past the elevators, he turned right into the corridor of trophies and flags and pushed his way through the double doors into the gymnasium. A class of recruits jogged around the perimeter track in cadence while another class parried nightsticks, practicing combat techniques.

Sergeant Jim Neary, the head physical education instructor at the Academy, had taught thousands of recruits the quickest and most effective way to disable a mutt. A well-built man in his late fifties, he was calling cadence when he saw Burke come in; he motioned to another cop to take over and walked across the gym. One of Neary's unlisted duties was to scour recruit classes for undercover candidates. After what had happened last night, he'd expected to see Too Tall Paulie sometime today.

Standing next to Burke, brushing his arm across his sweaty face, Neary watched the class work the track.

"They're babies," Burke said.

"How do you think I feel training them? Twice around and I need oxygen." He looked at Burke and said, "Sorry about your men. I remember both of them." They fell silent, old cops remembering lost partners, friends.

Burke lifted his chin at the recruits. "Anyone interesting?"

"Figured you'd be around today, so I pulled one folder for you. It's in my office."

The glass-fronted office was on the other side of the gym. They walked inside, and Neary opened one of the side drawers of his desk, lifted a stack of papers, and pulled out a folder, which he handed to Burke.

As he watched Too Tall Paulie reading the Character Investigation Report, a knowing smile creased Neary's face.

Burke looked up and asked, "What's your assessment?"

"Intelligent, and a lot of earned street smarts."

"This one is no virgin from Sunnyside."

"Inspector, if you want virgins, call a convent."

─── **5** ───

NVIRONMENT, THE LATEST
trendy club favored by the
city's leisure class, was located on Twenty-second Street in the
Chelsea district inside a nineteenth-century building that had
formerly served as a cloth factory's warehouse. When Seaver
arrived a little after midnight, a line of people snaked around
into Fifth Avenue waiting to get in, even this early in the evening.

Directly across from Environment, a sanitation truck was half
up on the sidewalk making a pickup, its compactor groaning as
the sanitation man beat a mangled refuse can across its lip before
tossing the can onto the sidewalk, strewing bits of garbage across
the street. A homeless woman squatted between parked cars,
relieving herself, heedless of the catcalls coming from some of the
people across the street. Up the street, a car alarm wailed.

Walking toward the four bouncer types funneling the "beauti-

ful people" through the iron gate, Andy Seaver lit up a stubby
Italian cigar and decided to go over to the meanest-looking one.
He slipped a ten into the goon's hand, confiding, "I'm looking
for my daughter. She's only fourteen. Mind if I duck inside for a
minute and look around?"

The doorman's paw gobbled up the ten, and a small nod of his
oversize head motioned Seaver through the gate.

Inside, Seaver joined the end of a line waiting to pass through
the metal detector. A flashing neon sign on top of the machine
blinked NO GUNS. PLEASE! Seaver had no problem with that
rule; he wore a plastic Glock nine-millimeter that didn't ring any
bells on these older metal detectors. After being cleared through
the detector, Seaver paid the twenty-five-dollar entrance fee, in
cash, and walked through large wooden doors with bas reliefs of
whales and into a huge room pulsing with earsplitting music. It
had a long bar on its left under a row of stained-glass windows
depicting a Rousseau-like jungle and animals.

Edging up to the bar, he called out to one of the bartenders, a
Chinese woman named Jasmine who always wore a yellow ribbon tied around her queue, "Johnny Black, rocks."

Jasmine took up a water glass, tossed in several ice cubes, and
poured in a long stream of scotch until the glass was filled to the
rim. Passing it out to him, she said, "Fifteen dollars."

Thrusting a twenty at her over the heads of other patrons,
Seaver said, "Keep it," and walked toward the darkened stage at
the rear of the long main room. An ornately carved stone pulpit
that once stood in a church was slightly to the right of the stage;
it had a life-size cutout of the secular Madonna standing there
preaching in her garter belt and bustier. Speakers, strapped to
iron columns that ran up into the tin-slated ceiling, boomed out
a wild samba-mambo beat, while a gyrating, humping mass
danced under the many-colored lightning of rotating strobe
lights.

Sipping his drink, Seaver watched a woman dressed in long

black bloomers, cowboy boots, a T-shirt with the logo FARM AID, and a black velvet ribbon pinned in back of her orange spiked hair. She was dancing with something whose gender Seaver could not determine; it was wearing a blue sailor's uniform sprinkled liberally with rhinestones. The ridiculous and the sublime, he thought. He turned away and spotted two Oriental men draped with heavy gold chains, medallions, and rings, headed in his direction. Here comes the Golden Triangle contingent, Seaver thought.

He brushed past the two men, making for the curving stone steps leading up to the balcony, a more exclusive retreat that overhung the dance floor and ran down one entire side of the main room. Long banquettes lined one wall, and cocktail tables were crammed around an inkwell-size dance floor. In the center of the wall was a busy, well-stocked bar. Scurrying waitresses wearing only black body stockings and high heels darted between tables.

Seaver immediately spotted Che-Che Morales, a heavy-duty Mexican doper, and his crew of four Latino scumbags lounging on the banquette, drinking champagne and partying with their girlfriends.

Unlike the other dopers, who were garishly dressed and bejeweled, Morales wore jeans, a dark *guayabera* shirt, and high-top sneakers. He was a thin man in his late fifties with a bony face that looked like stretched leather. His brazen black eyes, thick lips, flat nose, high cheekbones, and jet black straight hair that fell to his shoulders stamped him a full-blooded Indian, not a mestizo.

Morales was a major *traficante* about whom law enforcement knew all too little. His savage instinct for danger had enabled him to insulate himself from the best-laid traps the police could set for him. Ever since he had popped up in New York five years ago, he had been a key player in heavy drug commerce.

Sipping his drink and ignoring the dopers, Seaver weaved his way past tables and dancers over to the other end of the loft; slipping a foot onto the mahogany railing, he stared down at the spirited dancers. Soon his foot was tapping out the reggae-samba beat blaring from the speakers, and his shoulders swayed to the rhythm. In his peripheral vision he saw the two Oriental men he had spotted downstairs making their way over to Morales.

Suddenly the music stopped, and then the lights dimmed. The crowd below surged toward the stage, chanting, "Alejandro! Alejandro! Alejandro!"

The room sank into darkness, and still they chanted. An anxious stir of anticipation swept the club. A single spotlight beamed down onto the stage, revealing a man standing with his head bowed, his hands at his sides, a trademark long-stemmed rose in the right one.

A collective gasp escaped from many of the women, as the man remained motionless, controlling his audience, heightening their expectation. He was dressed in faded jeans, a black shirt with the three top buttons opened, and expensive Italian loafers, no socks. His wavy black hair, bronzed skin, piercing black eyes, and high flat cheekbones were pure Indian, while his straight nose and oval chin bore strong evidence of his gringo heritage. The crossing gene pool had given him an exotic and distinctive, magnetic appearance. Alejandro was the latest heartthrob to burst onto the club scene. He broke into a slow smile, his gleaming teeth a beacon. The women in the crowd squealed with delight as he raised his head and brought the rose up to his mouth, caressing it with his lips, kissing its petals. Holding the flower by the stem, he kissed it farewell and tossed it out into the blackness, where the women leaped to catch it. The winner pressed it to her well-displayed breasts and cried out, "We love you, Alejandro! We love you!"

From his perch Che-Che Morales looked down at the entertainer, and something resembling a smile crossed his lips. Then he turned and huddled with his Oriental guests.

Alejandro's hand rose up over his head and crashed down at the same instant the band behind him broke into "Cuidado Amor." His body began to sway, weaving in and out of the illumination of the single spotlight, caressing the darkness, his eyes closed. His light baritone was agreeable, but it was not his musical talent that had earned him a lead role at Environment. It was his ability to captivate his audience, the way he made every woman believe that he was singing only to her, the way his body and his eyes caused women to unleash secret fantasies, and, above all, because he and Che-Che Morales were *compañeros.*

For fifty minutes he sang to a rapt audience, concluding with his theme song, "Quierame Mucho"—"Love Me a Lot"—a song whose words he hoped to sing someday for an audience of one. Running off stage, he snapped a towel off a nail and dried himself, smiling contently at the sound of his audience's stamping feet, at the demands of "Encore! Encore!" He looked out at the marimba player, who gave him a thumbs-up.

The lights went up, and Alejandro ran on stage to his audience's thunderous approval. He moved about the stage throwing kisses, applauding his admirers downstairs and up in the balcony. He sang two encore songs and ran off stage into his makeshift dressing room made of five shower curtains strung across a corner of the rear stage. Inside, he took off his soaked shirt, dried himself with a towel, tugged on a clean T-shirt, and left, heading for the backstage exit with his audience still demanding, "Alejandro!"

Out in the muggy night, he walked across the tiny parking lot behind the club, motioning to the three bodyguard types protecting the cars that favored guests were allowed to park in the lot. One of the big men returned his wave and pulled back the steel gate that opened on the street.

Alejandro squeezed down into the black Porsche Turbocharge, turned the ignition, roaring the engine to life, and drove out into the unsleeping night.

He parked on Second Avenue, switched on the hidden toggle switch that killed the car's electrical system, and walked down Fifty-fifth to a five-story walk-up on the north side of the street. The building he entered was in the middle of the block, and its facade faced a glass tower cooperative with a curving driveway and a majestic fountain arching water into an ornate stone recycling pool.

He let himself into the vestibule with his key and climbed the steps to the third floor, where he rounded the banister and went up to the front apartment with a nameplate that read "J. McMahon."

He admitted himself with the key and stepped inside. Walking into the living room, Alejandro said to the man looking out the window, "It must be *mucho* important for you to make contact that way."

Seaver went over to the bar and poured in more Johnny Black. Looking at Alejandro, he asked, "How's your mother?"

"She opened a restaurant on La Playa Ropa, directly down from Martha's."

A warm glow of remembrance flowed over Seaver's face. "That's nice," he said, coming over and sitting next to him. "Would you like us to resurface you?"

Alejandro looked at him, astonished. He could sense that "Mother Hen" was stalling, wrestling with some inner conflict. He got up and went over to the bar, began tossing ice cubes into a rock glass. Pouring in scotch, he asked, "What kind of a question is that? You know I'm not going to finish until it's finished." He scoffed, "Can't you just see me being a cop, walking a beat or doing whatever it is that they do?"

"When we put you under all those years ago, we thought making you a singer in the *cuchifrito* joints was a perfect cover. We never thought that one day you'd be the new sensation. You have talent, you could break through into the big times, maybe. Have a good life, a family."

"Why you breaking my balls, Andy? I'm not going anyplace and you know it. As far as me being the next Julio, forget it. I was singing in rice-and-bean joints until Che-Che saw me and took an interest. We're both Indians from the same area. He's my friend. He trusts me."

"And you're working him for us, remember?" Seaver said with a sarcastic edge to his voice.

Sipping at his drink, Alejandro said bitterly, "In case *you've* forgotten, yes, that's what I do."

Regarding him sadly, Seaver said, "You've changed, Al. You're like a clenched fist. Hey, man, it's me. Lighten up."

Alejandro gulped his drink. "I've got another show to do, and Che-Che wants to party later, so why don't you tell me why you've come?"

"We've discovered a new network we want you to infiltrate."

"What about Che-Che? Do I drop him? He's a major player. Through him I might be able to work my way up to some of the top Colombians."

"This network is responsible for killing three Narcotics undercovers."

"So let Narcotics insert another undercover."

"Their entire unit might have been compromised."

"Andy, you know damn well Mexico is a major processing and distribution point for the cartels, and Che-Che controls a big piece of it. He's been giving up important information to me because we're both Tarascan Indians, and he considers us blood brothers. A few months back I introduced him to an Agency clown posing as a banker from the British Virgins. And now Che-Che is happily laundering some of his money through an Agency bank in Road Town." Pointing his glass at Seaver, he added, "They're giving us their money, and you want me to drop him? Get real, Andy, have the DEA insert one of theirs into this new network."

A mirthless laugh came from Seaver. "Federal Drug Enforcement no longer employs undercovers to infiltrate. The suits in Washington say it's too dangerous. So now they subcontract that work to informers. You should pardon the expression, but they actually call these guys 'subagents.' They're out there peddling their own shit and giving up the competition to the DEA."

"What about the big seizures I've been reading about?"

"They're angeling off, allowing the drugs into the States, then following them to their destination and arresting the schmucks who come to pick them up. It's great PR."

"That's really cozy," Alejandro said. "The DEA and the Agency 'angeled off' Noriega for years. Scarface would give up the competition's stuff coming into the States."

"It's great for the DEA stats. Keeps the old budget funded."

Seaver's eyes fell to his glass. "What makes this new network so important?"

Andy Seaver slid his hand into his sports coat, brought out a dime bag, and placed it on the cushion next to him.

Alejandro picked it up and examined the logo, the thin golden stripes behind what looked like an ancient etching of a beautiful woman with a jutting chin. As he lowered himself to the sofa, his face hardened, his mind flashing back involuntarily to unbearable memories. His hand contracted into a white-knuckled fist, crushing the envelope and sprinkling ten dollars' worth of heroin over his leg.

Sweat ringing his hairline, Alejandro took one more sweeping bow, threw out his last kiss, and ran off stage to the echoing demands for "More! More!"

Once back in his makeshift dressing room, he pulled off his shirt, tossed it into his overnight bag, and went over to the cruddy sink on the backstage wall. He turned on the tap and watched a steady trickle of rusty water turn clear, then soaked a washcloth and wiped the perspiration off his face and torso. Ever since leaving the safe house earlier that evening his mind had kept running continuously down the same worn highway. Cleopatra was not going to escape this time. Turning, he angrily threw the wet cloth on top of his crumpled shirt. He put on a clean paisley sport shirt, patted on some after-shave, combed his hair, and stepped outside the curtains. Alejandro moved easily, unrecognized, across the now pitch-dark dance floor, going over to the stone steps leading up to the loft. The flashing lights showed snapshots of frantic and indifferent faces.

Che-Che and his noisy entourage had turned their part of the balcony into their private playpen. Some of the cocktail tables had been pushed aside to enlarge the dance floor, where one of the dopers mambo-reggaed with his clinging girlfriend. Che-Che sat alone impassively, watching, his snakelike eyes taking it all in while bodyguards slouched nearby.

Alejandro was greeted with applause when he reached the balcony. Men rushed forward to shake his hands, pat his shoulder, while many of the women clutched him in an adoring embrace, some of them whispering in his ear.

Che-Che flashed a welcoming smile at the singer and with a flick of fingers ordered people next to him to make room for Alejandro. Dopers squeezed out, making room for him on the banquette. Sliding in next to Che-Che, Alejandro pulled a champagne bottle out of one of the buckets and poured himself a glass of the sparkling wine. Turning to face Che-Che, he toasted him: "*Salud.*"

Slipping easily into the dialect of the Tarascan Indians, a mixture of Tarascan and pidgin Spanish, Che-Che said, "You were great tonight."

Answering in kind, Alejandro said, "Thank you, my friend." He sipped wine, taking in the revelers, then added, "Why do you come to places like this? You hate them."

"To make sure my people don't get stupid on me."

"You can't be with them all twenty-four hours a day."

Che-Che's lips tugged slowly into a quick smile, then snapped back into their placid state. "My punishment for stupidity is swift and painful."

Alejandro grimaced disgust. "Yeah. I heard."

"You'll have to meet my pet one day."

"No, thank you."

Che-Che reached down and picked up an envelope from the cushion, slipped it onto Alejandro's lap. "A gift for your help with the banker."

Alejandro discreetly let his hand fall to his lap and slid the envelope inside his shirt, tucking it into his waistband.

"You should come with us, you'd make a lot of money."

Sipping wine, Alejandro said, "When I was a kid peddling trinkets to the *turistas* on La Playa Ropa, I dreamed one day I'd be a famous singer and that my mother and sisters would no longer have to spend their days hawking jewelry on the hot sand of Zihuatanejo's beaches, playing the dumb Indians to a bunch of gringos getting off on trying to talk their lousy Spanish. I was going to buy them houses in San Angel or Coyoácan. I still have that dream."

"When I was fifteen I started pimping for tourists in Ixtapa." Che-Che sipped his wine. "Do you remember the tale about who Las Gatas was named for?"

Alejandro smiled. "For the sharks that used to swim in the waters. They were supposed to have whiskers and be as playful as cats. And our King Caltzontzin, lord of innumerable people, ordered a stone barrier built out in the bay, so he and his daughter could enjoy the crystal waters without sharks. And today the great barrier remains, but the sharks are all gone."

"You remember well, my friend."

"My mother used to tell us many wonderful stories about our people, and their greatness before Cortez and the Mexican secretary of tourism discovered our beaches."

"And your father? You seldom talk about him," Che-Che said

thoughtfully, watching the ribbon of bubbles in his champagne glass.

"As you know, he was a gringo who was murdered by agents of the Federal Judicial Police."

"Yes, those devils. Did you ever find out why they had him killed?"

"No. He was retired U.S. Army, no threat to anyone in Mexico." Alejandro yanked the dripping bottle out of its bucket and poured wine into their glasses. After plunging the bottle back into the crackling ice, he turned to Che-Che and whispered, "When I'm a big star, I'm going to buy a jet to fly from concert to concert, and I'll let you load your coke and money, and I'll fly it all over the world for you. No gringo cop would ever think an international singing star was a dope courier for some Indian who still says 'Itzi Nejo.' "

Che-Che roared with laughter at Alejandro's use of the Indian name for Zihuatanejo. "That's a great idea; only problem is, coke isn't the great investment it used to be. Operating expenses have gotten out of hand." He leaned close to his friend to confide, "Heroin is making a big comeback. I think it's the drug of the future."

"Heroin means dealing with the pinky-rings."

Che-Che grinned his deadly grin. "The Chinese have taken over the heroin trade. They kicked out the Italians. The Wiseguys weren't so wise. They thought it was smart diluting the shit out of the dope, greedy bastards. They never learned that greater purity gives a better high—that insures loyal customers."

Staring out at the dancers, Alejandro asked, "What's caused coke's expenses to go up?"

"A lot of things. For example, two weeks ago a Delta Force strike team took out a processing plant in Bolivia that was producing over fifteen tons a week, and grabbed a lot of our people, turning them over to the locals. We had to bribe them all free, and build another plant. Very expensive. Our profit margin is dropping."

Alejandro shrugged, absentmindedly peeling the wet label off a champagne bottle. "If I were in your business, I'd play 'Let's Make a Deal' with Washington."

Che-Che fixed his eyes on a woman's very shapely gyrating ass, which seemed to have a mind of its own. "How would you do that?"

"The Medellín and Calí control the world's source of cocaine, and you're one of their major movers. . . ."

Che-Che's eyes turned cold; he sipped wine and did not respond.

"What I'd do is ask Washington for a farm subsidy, you know, just like they pay the farmers here not to grow crops. Say a billion or so a year for both cartels. In return they'd agree to halt all production. No cocaine problem, and Uncle Sam saves a fortune on enforcement, and is able to use that money to pay off the national debt. That way the cartels get what they want most, respectability, and living long, safe lives, free from the fear of being kidnapped to the States."

Che-Che toyed with his glass. "Medellín and Calí hate each other. They'd never sit at the same table."

Peeling off the rest of the label, Alejandro said, "That's why they would need someone great to put the deal together, someone who would walk away with a commission that would allow him to live the rest of his life like Caltzontzin—to swim where there are no sharks."

"I'd miss the excitement. Look, *compañero,* you're talking illusions, fairy stories."

Alejandro poured more sparkling wine, plunged the bottle back, and looked up to see a beautiful young woman making her way over to them. He marveled at how her lithe body slunk effortlessly through the crowd. She was wearing a plain white dress and was braless, and her only jewelry was a pair of earrings with jade drops dangling at the end of gold ropes. Alejandro's attention fixed on her eyes, large emerald pools, and they were riveted on him.

"Here comes one of your fans," Che-Che whispered. She stopped about a foot or so from their table and, staring directly into Alejandro's eyes, slid her hands up under her dress and slowly worked down her underpants. Stepping out of them, she tossed the skimpy undergarment on the table in front of the singer.

Alejandro picked them up, caressing the silk with his lips, his molten eyes fixed on hers.

Her lips parted, and her breasts rose with each audible breath.

He kissed the underpants and slid them into his shirt right next to Che-Che's envelope. She turned and walked back into the crowd, casting a single glance over her shoulder in time to see Alejandro sliding out of the banquette.

Her Fifth Avenue apartment's bedroom overlooked Central Park.

They stood by her bed, looking at each other, kissing, touching, each time longer, their tongues exploring. He unzipped her dress. She shrugged it free and pushed it off her shoulders, allowing it to gather at her feet. She was breathing hard, her face flushed, nipples hard. He undressed quickly, struggling out of his tight black jeans. They fell into an embrace, toppling onto the bed, kissing, touching, savoring foreplay. He wanted her because she wanted him, needed him, lusted for him. It was at these moments that he felt free, complete, only when he was working toward that shared magical moment, not hurrying, being considerate, aware of her rhythm, her need for him, and his need for her.

She broke away from him, moving downward, licking, kissing, taking his toes into her mouth and sucking them. He groaned, stirred by the erotic pleasure she was giving him. Her tongue delicately swept the back of his toes, and he loved her.

After moving up, kissing him all over, she spread her legs over his face, straddling him, commanding him to take her into his mouth, and as he did he loved her for the pleasure he was giving her.

Her spent body collapsed on top of him, her long brown hair fanned across his face. She moved her mouth down to his ear, licked it, and commanded softly, "Fuck me, Alejandro." He rolled her onto her stomach. She pushed her knees up and stuck up her rump, and he mounted her, thrusting himself deep inside of her. She spread out her arms and grabbed the headboard.

After, they lay in each other's arms, savoring the warm afterglow, catching their breath. "Whew," she sighed.

He leaned over and kissed her softly.

"Oh, by the way, my name is Ann."

They both laughed. "Hello, Ann."

She rolled onto her elbows and looked down into his eyes. "I hope you believe that I've never done anything like this before. I've always wanted to, but never had the nerve. When I saw you on stage tonight, I wanted you. I had to have you."

"I've always wanted to do something like that, too, but I could never muster the courage."

"What's your fantasy?" she asked, kissing his forehead.

"Seeing a beautiful woman walking down the street and going up to her and sliding my hand up her dress, and having her look at me and say, 'Thank you.'"

She laughed. "I don't suggest you ever try that." Her hand began roaming his body, and they made love again. After, they lay quietly in each other's arms, intimate yet distant.

"When I was a little girl I always wanted to be a ballerina. I used to fantasize that I would meet a prince and fall in love, and he'd carry me off to his castle and we would live happily ever after."

"And did you ever meet your prince?"

"Unfortunately he turned out to be an asshole."

"Sorry."

"I met him in graduate school. He was my professor in seventeenth-century English poetry. When I first saw him . . ."

Listening to her talk unguardedly, openly, about herself, he grew tense. He knew that there were no truths about himself that he could tell her. He lived a lie without friends or love, and in order to survive in this world he had long ago suppressed his emotions. They were now buried so deeply inside of him that he was not sure they existed anymore. Every time he was with a woman, Seaver's long-ago warning—"Be careful of entanglements with women; their knowledge is deadly"—echoed through his mind like a storm warning. The NYPD had made up a complete "legend," a totally bogus biography of Alejandro Monahan: an idyllic childhood, loving parents, puppy love, school, real love followed by heartbreak, his desire to become a singer, and his struggle to achieve that goal. He had learned to tell his lies so well that he almost believed them. As he pressed her close and told her about himself, he prayed that one day he would be able to reach deep inside, recover his feelings, and tell some woman how desperately alone and afraid he had been during his eternity of lies.

They lay in each other's arms, enjoying the moment, listening to the faint sounds of the night. Then, abruptly, he told her that he had to go home and walk his dog. He got dressed, took her phone number, said he would call her, and left. He went home and crawled into his empty bed. He didn't have a dog. In fact, he hardly had a real life.

The barge's purple sail billowed in the evening sky. From its deck, music spread across the Nile, causing people to flock down to the river bed in the hope of seeing their queen. On the barge, half-naked servants served Cleopatra and Che-Che Morales a banquet on gold plates.

On deck, Alejandro, dressed in a tunic and running sneakers, moved toward the pavilion carrying a platter of delicacies, his hands flat beneath the tray, concealing a dagger coated with cobra venom.

The head eunuch stood outside the pavilion, inspecting each platter, making sure that the tasters sampled all the food and drink before passing them into her presence. Moving forward, Alejandro saw the woman named Ann standing by the bow talking to other women with familiar faces. They were staring at him, whispering.

Alejandro's eyes flew open, his body was soaked with sweat. That damn dream. I always get close to her just before I wake up, he thought, aware of the ringing telephone. He reached out and snapped the receiver to his ear. "Yeah?"

"You sure you wanna go through with this?"

"Don't you ever sleep?" he asked Seaver.

"No."

"You already know the answer to that question, so why are you getting me up in the middle of the night?"

"It's nine A.M. And I wanted to make sure you remembered the time and place."

"I remember," he said, and fumbled the receiver back onto its cradle. He reached over the side, groping for the wastebasket full of old sneakers and shoes. He yanked one out and chucked it over the foot of his bed. He'd always had a problem remembering a nocturnal telephone call in the morning, so a while back he'd taken to keeping a basket of old footwear nearby and tossing one out every time he got a nighttime call. Somehow the sight of the shoe or sneaker jogged his sleep-time memory. He turned on his side, remembering the woman Ann. He could smell her lingering scent on his body and wished she were next to him now. But she was gone, pushed away like all the others. It just wasn't human not having feelings, and that scared him. Hell with it, get some sleep, he told himself, wishing away the irrational uneasiness churning up inside him. But it was no good; the dream and the call had left him wide awake.

The stinging lances of cold water washed away the memories of the dream and the woman. After shaving, he walked into the living room and went over to the music system inside the breakfront, turning on the compact disc player. The lilting sounds of the Clancy Brothers singing Irish ballads drifted throughout his apartment. He went back into his bedroom and dressed in the usual jeans, black sport shirt, black loafers, no socks. In the kitchen he made himself a cup of coffee, then walked out onto the terrace.

Looking down from his Fifth Avenue co-op at the Washington Arch, the marble gateway that presided over Washington Square Park at the foot of Fifth Avenue, he saw that the ravages of time and pollution had eaten away a good part of ol' George's face. The stonework on the arch had deteriorated a lot in the seven years since the Job had given him the money to purchase the apartment, he thought, taking another sip of coffee. He walked back inside, his attention falling onto the Aztec head on top of the breakfront. Looking around, he pursed his lips with satisfaction at the strong Mexican motif running through his apartment.

The Clancy Brothers were singing "Troubles," and he recalled his long-dead Irish grandfather telling him about the Great Hunger. And he remembered his mother's mother recounting stories of the Conquest and how the Spanish had destroyed their cities, burned their libraries, and slaughtered their priests. He wondered how his Irish grandfather and Tarascan grandmother would have gotten along. They would have been instant amigos, he decided, his lips pressed into a tight smile. Alejandro Monahan is a polyglot of misery, he thought, glancing at his watch. Seeing that it was almost ten-thirty, he gulped the remainder of his coffee and left the apartment.

Seaver would be waiting, but before going to the meet he

wanted to stop off at the bank and wire his mother nine thousand of the thirty thousand that Che-Che had given him. Undercovers didn't have insurance policies, so this way he could make sure that his family in Zihuatanejo was provided for if he vanished from the face of the earth, a strong possibility for someone in his line of work.

6

AT ELEVEN THAT MORNING Alejandro walked into the living room of the East Fifty-fifth Street safe house and tossed the envelope Che-Che had given him onto the cushion next to where Mother Hen was sitting. "A present from Che-Che for the intro to the banker," he said.

Seaver lifted the flap and peeked inside. "A lotta green."

"Twenty-one large. I took nine for the retirement fund. Make sure that's debited against my expenses. What do I do with the rest?"

"Use it as flash money. That way the doper'll be subsidizing you for a while instead of the taxpayers."

Alejandro picked up the envelope and tucked it inside his shirt. "What have you come up with on Cleopatra?"

Seaver pulled a folded sheet of paper out of his jacket pocket and, holding it between two fingers, responded, "One alphabet soup intelligence report for the DEA, DIA, and CIA's Narcotics Control Center." He opened it and read: "Cleopatra, a pseudonym used by one of the narco-cartel's top assassins. Real name unknown. Believed to be a female in her late twenties."

He looked at Alejandro. "This report was compiled in seventy-five. She'd be in her forties today." He continued reading: "Known to be fluent in English, Spanish, possibly French. Possible Mexican or U.S. citizen. Ran hit teams for Medellin and Calí in late sixties, early seventies. Known to be responsible for the murder of José Rodriguez, the police chief of Zihuatanejo, Mexico, on January 24, 1972. After that she disappeared, and is believed to have gone into the narcotics trade on her own."

"What about the dopers killed at the Savoy?"

Seaver read from another report: "Ramón and Conrado had no criminal record in this country. The Counter-Narcotics Center had them cross-referenced to Cleopatra."

"On what basis?"

"An informant in Bogotá dropped their names as two of her top shooters. That was in eighty-one."

"What about the mule who lugged the dope to the hotel?"

"Roberto Barrios, alias the Thin Man, a stone killer who'll run his own deal if the risks are minimal."

"Greed and caution can be a deadly combination. Can we find this guy?"

"He's findable. The Joint Task Force has a CI trying to score him."

"Lemme ask you something: Does anyone inside our Narcotics Bureau or the DEA or the Joint Task Force know that the Intelligence Division has deep undercovers roaming around the slime pool?"

"The powers atop Mount Everest want us deep and quiet."

"Like dividing your forces and losing the war?"

Seaver frowned. "Ever hear of Handschu?"

Alejandro shook his head.

"Handschu was an antiwar activist during Vietnam. Our Intelligence photographed her at several demonstrations and listed her in our files. A few years later she graduates from law school and applies for admission to the bar. The character committee of the bar does a round robin on her and comes up with our derogatory intelligence report. She's denied admission to the bar on the basis of our report, and sues. The result: the Handschu Authority, an intelligence oversight committee made up of the first deputy police commissioner, the chief of detectives, and one eminent civilian-type jurist. No, repeat, no, covert intelligence operations into noncriminal civilian activities can be commenced without the authority's imprimatur. Like we have a suspicion that a bank might be laundering narco-money, or a phony religious or civil rights group is extorting money from store owners or building contractors."

"But a deep undercover can go where others dare not tread."

"Something like that."

"What about the CI who made the intro for DiLeo and Levi?"

"Jordon Hayes, a dime bagger who sees himself as a mover and shaker instead of the putz he is. Every heavyweight deal he ever dealt went down with either a NYPD or a DEA undercover. We own his soul."

Alejandro walked over to the window and pushed aside the curtains. Peering past the venetian blinds, he watched women chatting with each other inside the vest-pocket park alongside the glass tower apartment across the street while their children played on a brightly colored Jungle Gym. Normal people, living normal lives, he thought, his eyes following the mailwoman as she pushed her cart past the cascading fountain. He turned and looked at Seaver, a shadow falling across his face. "Your stale intelligence report neglected to mention that when Cleopatra whacked the police chief she also slaughtered several others, including my father. It also neglected to say that I was there, and didn't raise a finger to help him."

"For chrissake, will you ever stop beating yourself? You were eleven years old. What the hell could you have done?"

"I should have done something."

"And you and your sister would both be dead now. It was over in seconds. You had no way of knowing what was going on inside La Perla."

Alejandro was silent for a long time, then said quietly, "I can't forget one single second of what happened. It was around one o'clock. Dad was playing dominoes in La Perla with Jefe Rodriguez. They'd play every day; it had become a ritual with them. Mom had sent Maria and me to get him to come home for lunch. We were walking through the parking lot in the rear of the restaurant when I heard the first rounds. I shoved Maria to the ground and fell on top of her." He sat on the ottoman, facing Seaver, folded his arms across his legs, and added, "I still have nightmares over it. I hear that bitch laughing as she ran for her car flanked by her shooters. She had on a long yellow dress, and the sun shone through it." He stared coldly at Seaver. "How come you never mention my dad?"

Seaver lit up a cheroot, tossed the match into the ashtray, and said, "Eamon Monahan was my friend and one of the best detectives this Job ever had. But one winter he goes to Zihuatanejo on vacation, meets your mom on the beach, and falls in love. He was thirty-eight and three years short of retirement. After that trip he started to take all his overtime in lost time instead of cash, and hook it onto his swings and fly to Zihuatanejo for long weekends. He'd spend every vacation with your mom. When he had his time in, he threw in his papers, got married, and went to live in Mexico." He dragged on the cheroot, looked over at Alejandro, and added, "Sometimes I wonder if your dad wasn't the target of that hit instead of Rodriguez."

"My parents knew that the local politico wouldn't take kindly to a retired gringo cop living among them, so they told everyone Dad was retired army."

"Your dad telephoned Joey-the-G-Man the week before he was killed, asking for the latest intelligence on the Medellin operating around Zihuatanejo and Ixtapa. The dopers were using an airstrip outside of town to transship their shit into Texas . . ."

"And the Federal Judicial Police were protecting the strip and charging the dopers a transit fee. I know all about that." He fell silent, staring at some spot over Seaver's left shoulder. "How long did Dad work for our intelligence people?"

"He spent most of his time in the Job working narcotics, but toward the end he transferred into the Land of Trick Mirrors."

"Why?"

"He'd been in the slime pool a lotta years. He wanted a change of scenery." He pondered the ash on his cigar, flicked it into the ashtray. "No way the Eamon Monahan I knew would sit by and let a bunch of scumbag dopers take over a town he was living in. He'd have given the locals the benefit of his considerable expertise."

"He was out of it, Andy. No way he'd get back into it. He promised Mom."

"But just suppose . . . he did get back into it."

Something glowed in Alejandro's eyes. "That would mean that Rodriguez or some of his people had their hands out, or someone in New York rolled over." He fell silent. "Twenty years is a lot of agos. Naw, no way he'd get back into that world."

Alejandro reached into his shirt pocket and came out with the crumpled glassine envelope that Mother Hen had given him the night before. He smoothed it out and studied the logo with the beautiful face backgrounded by the four golden stripes. "Why Cleopatra now, Andy? I figured she was history, vanished. Ever since my father's death I've done a lot of research on the real Cleopatra. There is not much about her that I don't know." He leaned his head back and closed his eyes, exhuming memories. "My grandmother was fond of telling us the Tarascan story of an ancient queen from a faraway land who sailed the great sea in straw boats containing a great treasure. She landed in the land of the Tarascan Indians, and married the great king Itzamna, and together they founded a mighty kingdom."

"An ancient myth."

"Myth usually has some truth in it, and in the case of Tarascan oral history, a lot of truth, believe me."

"What the hell are you trying to tell me?"

"I'm going to go back to the books on Cleopatra. I believe that there's a reason our doper, Cleopatra, assumed that name. And if we find that reason, we find her."

"She's probably just a fucking killer who gets off on using the name."

He looked at Mother Hen. "Would you like to know what problem consumed a lot of the real Cleopatra's time?"

"I'll bite."

"The establishment of a strong criminal justice system throughout her kingdom, particularly the police department in Alexandria, where there was a high crime rate. She established anticrime units to take on the street gangs on their own turf; she also set up intelligence units to infiltrate the gangs."

"I guess the real queen liked a cop."

"And I bet you that our queen runs her dope business the same way the real queen ran Egypt."

7

A PUFF OF CLOUDS FLOATED over the Springfield Boulevard exit of the Long Island Expressway as Jordon Hayes drove his battered '79 van off and stopped for the sign at the end of the ramp.

The dashboard clock read 2:18 P.M.

Twelve minutes later, when he drove off the Horatio Parkway onto Forty-ninth Road in Bayside, Queens, he saw his brick ranch house four blocks away, and his depression deepened. That house was all that was left of his fortune. Life wasn't supposed to have turned out that way for him, not Jordon Hayes, star quarterback of James Madison High School, class of 1969, not the Most Handsome, Most Likely. It had all turned bad when he went to City College and had to compete with all the other Most Likelies, and started dealing marijuana to make extra money to impress everyone on campus. Pushing grass had made him feel like the star quarterback again. He was in his junior year when he'd realized that he could make more money selling dope than he ever could in the straight world. So he'd married his childhood sweetheart, Rachel, bought an expensive home in Kensington, and told everyone he was a stockbroker, which he indeed had become—his job in a large brokerage house made for perfect cover. It had all gone down the tubes when he'd started dealing cocaine. His very first deal had gone down with a cop posing as a Miami dealer. A fucking Spanish-speaking Jew, he thought, ramming the van's accelerator to the floor. Now he had to be content scrounging a living by conning and stealing money from his police and DEA controllers. Today his life options were simple: be an informer or die. He tried to steal a few hours off the street every day to be with his family. It was the only time that he felt human. Perhaps somehow, someday, he'd figure a way out of this mess. Get away from the garbage, someplace where he could start over again.

As his van drew up to his house he noticed a panel truck with the legend "Lake Appliances" on its side, and he cursed silently, thinking that the damn washing machine was on the fritz again. He parked at the curb and, walking up the driveway, glanced idly inside the unoccupied truck. Taking the side entrance, he stepped into the kitchen, and froze. Pop, the family dog, was splayed across the drainboard; its head was gone.

"Rachel? Ira? David?" he screamed.

Running into the living room, he saw Rachel's upended sewing basket on the floor and ran from room to room, calling out their names. He stalked back into the living room and noticed that the basement door in the back of the kitchen was ajar. He jerked it open and flipped the wall switch. The light failed to come on. Poking his head into the darkness, he called out, "Rachel? Ira? David?"

No answers came back.

He wiped the sweat off his mouth with the flat of his hand and slid his foot onto the first step, made his way down the sagging staircase, his scared eyes probing the blackness in front of him. At the bottom he stepped into the dark coldness and whispered, "Rachel?"

An unseen hand screwed up the bulb; the light glowed. Hayes's eyes widened in horror at the sight of the naked bodies hanging from the rafters, the agony of dying forever chiseled into his family's contorted faces.

Jordon Hayes, Most Likely of the class of 1969, sank to his knees crying, unaware of the movement around him.

The Beaux-Arts ornaments and furnishings of the Majestic Theater's lobby on Madison Avenue and 112th Street had long ago been stolen and sold. The Majestic was Manhattan's oldest continuous operating movie house, having been opened amid great fanfare by Mayor Jimmy Walker in 1927. Today the once proud house stood, crumbling and dirty, in ignominious blight in a section of the city now known as Cracktown.

Cracktown's drug lords bought the movie house four years ago to use as a secure meeting place where narco-gangs could straighten out their turf quarrels, fix the price of their product, and negotiate co-op deals to buy in quantity at reduced prices. If some stranger tried to buy a ticket to see one of the schlock blood-and-sex movies that were shown there, he or she would find the show was "sold out." It was a private place open only to drug dealers and their voracious clients, among whom were hookers and transvestites who prowled the aisles plying their trades. Unknown to the drug lords, unarmed undercovers also worked the aisles, making buys, gathering intelligence, painstakingly working their way up the narco networks.

About three-thirty that Friday afternoon, while the credits of *Sisters 'N the Hood* rolled across the screen, a shaft of light speared across the orchestra as one of the exit doors opened and several indistinct figures slipped inside. The door clanged shut; darkness returned. No one paid attention to the six men working their way toward the stage. Three of them carried a rolled-up carpet strung across their shoulders, while the others hefted a large sack.

The dopers continued to deal; the hookers continued to work.

Seven minutes went by before the sound track screeched to a stop and the movie fluttered off the screen, which glowed a dirty, dull ivory. A voice boomed over the speaker, first in English, then in Spanish, "Watch the stage and see how we deal with police informers."

Up in the balcony an undercover slid down as far as she could onto her seat, her heart pounding.

A heavy thud came from the direction of the stage as three men dropped a large burlap bag on the stage and left it with the top open.

The carpet was lifted up off the shoulders of the other three men and unrolled, toppling a terrified and naked Jordon Hayes onto the floor. He was roughly yanked to his feet, his hands untied, and the gag jerked out of his mouth. His eyes moved frantically from one to another of the sullen faces surrounding him, finally locking in horror on the man with a white path of hair down the middle of his head and cold dark eyes almost hidden beneath a thick, overhanging brow.

"I'm going to give you a chance to live," the man with the white streak of hair said softly. "All you have to do is walk across the stage to the other side."

Hayes looked out at the spotlight beaming down onto the silver screen. "I ain't no fucking informer, man," he pleaded.

The man smiled and nodded to the men around Hayes. Three of them took hold of the Most Likely of the class of 1969 and propelled him out onto the stage.

Fumbling to cover up his nakedness, Hayes looked out blankly at his unseen audience and took a few tentative steps, telling himself, Maybe I can make a break. He tried to see ahead of him, but all that was there was blackness and the beam of light from the movie projector. What were they going to do? A sniper out in the audience? Yeah! That's it, they're gonna whack me as soon as I step into the light. I'll duck under it, make a run for it.

He came to the shaft of light and stopped. Remaining motionless, he watched the hundreds of particles swimming around inside its brilliance. Swiftly he ducked into the darkness below the light. A loud hissing came out of the blackness, and some monstrous creature sprang up at him, throwing him to the ground.

The spotlight beamed down; Hayes's terrified screams pierced the silence. An orange-and-green anaconda, as thick as a man's thigh and about fifteen feet long, was coiling itself around his legs, its forked tongue flicking out of its wedge-shaped head and its serpentine eyes fixed on its prey's screaming face. Its coils glided effortlessly around Hayes, sending crushing bolts of pain throughout his struggling body. The more he fought, the faster the coils slithered around him.

Pop-eyed junkies and dopers watched in silence as the powerful constrictor squeezed every drop of life out of Jordon Hayes. Undercovers also watched, helpless to intervene. The telephone inside the movie house had long ago been ripped out of the walls; the dopers' cellular phones and beepers were the new order of the day.

One undercover got up out of his seat and rushed into the lobby. He knew where there was a working phone about a block and a half away.

A narco guard blocked him as he rushed out into the vestibule. "Where't'fuck you goin', man?"

"I don't like no moth'fuckin' snake, man."

"Go back and sit down and close your eyes."

A junkie leaned up over the balcony and shouted, "Way to go, way to go!"

Hayes's left arm stretched out helplessly from the coils. A loud gurgling bubbled from his gaping mouth. A final spasm, and he went limp.

The anaconda uncoiled, positioning its head and the head of its prey. Its mouth opened incredibly wide and clamped over a portion of the dead man's head.

A hooker vomited.

Fiona Lee had just turned twenty-five. As a birthday present to herself, she had her auburn hair cut short, had her nails done at a salon on Washington Street, and bought herself a dress and some silk underpants.

It had been early afternoon on Friday when the Academy's head physical instructor, Sergeant Neary, had approached her on the gym floor and told her to report to him at 1600 today, Saturday, in civilian clothes.

She had thought she was going to be assigned to the barrier detail that was stringing sawhorses along Fifth Avenue in preparation for the president's visit on Sunday. So now she wore jeans, a black T-shirt, heavy black boots, no bra, and no makeup. But as she followed Neary to the fifth floor of the Academy's west wing, she felt a sudden queasiness. This part of the building was off limits to recruits.

Neary moved ahead of her, pushed open the door to one of the rooms, and beckoned her inside, where a tall stranger was waiting behind a desk. Burke motioned for her to take a seat on the chair in front of the desk, as he continued paging through a thick manila folder. "I see you've had a few brushes with the law."

She pulled a defiant face, the way she'd seen Wiseguys do in the movies, and said nothing.

"When you were fourteen you stabbed a teacher in the arm."

Anger filled her tawny eyes. "I stayed after class for extra math help. I was doing square roots at my desk when teacher-of-the-year came over and came on to me."

"Maybe it was an accident."

"Accident my ass. He knew exactly what he was doing. I told him to fuck off, but he just grabbed me harder. Two years later teacher-of-the-year was arrested for sucking little boys' weenies."

"But not before you were adjudicated a juvenile delinquent."

Her eyebrows rose in anger. Stiffly she recited: "A JD adjudication is not a criminal conviction and cannot be used or held against me in any way, shape, or form."

"And who says that?"

"The law says that."

Too Tall Paulie continued to page through the folder, suppressing a satisfied smile. "When you were sixteen you broke a soda bottle across a store manager's face, breaking his nose. He had you arrested, but you were lucky, he withdrew the complaint."

"I had a part-time job after school in the local supermarket. I was in the stock room on my break when he came on to me."

He looked up at her. "Don't you like men?"

"I like 'em fine, as long as they ask first."

He leaned back in his seat and laced his hands behind his head, his long legs stretched out under the desk. "Your language qualification card states you're fluent in Spanish and speak some German. It also states you're a licensed pilot."

"My father had a small air taxi business on Long Island. I've been flying since I was fifteen." Her eyes bored into his suspiciously. "Why don't you tell me who you are and what I'm doing here?"

"I'm Inspector Paul Burke, and I'd like to know why you want to be a police officer."

"It's a job."

"No, young lady, it's more than just a job."

She brushed her hair back. "I want to help people, especially children."

"Do you have any idea how many babies are born crack addicts?"

"A lot. In this city, the highest percentage in the country."

In a low, serious tone he asked, "Would you like to do something to help those unborn babies?"

"Of course. But what can I do?"

He closed the folder with an air of finality. "Care to join the war on drugs?"

A smug smile, a sarcastic answer: "That war's been lost."

"Fiona . . . the *real* war is only beginning."

They talked for three hours. When they finished he was convinced that he'd found the right person. She had all the requisites—she wasn't married or encumbered with any "significant other" in her life.

She looked at him and asked softly, "What's next?"

Burke smiled. "A vacation."

First Deputy Police Commissioner Frank Nagel was puffing antifungal dust on the roses in his backyard in Maspeth, Queens, when Too Tall Paulie pulled into the driveway. The CO of Narcotics had telephoned the first dep at his home as soon as Fiona Lee had left the fifth-floor office in the Academy's west wing. He'd apologized for bothering him on his day off, then said, "I need to see you right away, Commissioner."

The first deputy police commissioner serves as executive aide to the police commissioner and is responsible for the day-to-day administrative business of the Department. But one of his unlisted duties is to oversee all intelligence and counterintelligence operations of the Department.

Nagel had spent forty years in the Job and had been all set to retire at the mandatory age of sixty-two when the police commissioner asked him to fill the recently vacated first dep's slot.

Nagel's pallid skin was blotched with brown age marks, and his tiny green eyes were set too close together. He was wearing khaki trousers that were smeared liberally with paint and oil stains, sneakers, and a worn Seventy-ninth Precinct polo shirt with the logo "Fort Shithouse" emblazoned across the front.

Crossing the lawn, Burke called out, "Afternoon, Commissioner."

Nagel put down his sprayer and stood with his hands on his hips, turning his head to stare at the approaching visitor.

Too Tall Paulie started to say something, but Nagel quickly silenced him by placing his forefinger across his lips. Nagel stepped over to the lawn mower and pulled the cord to the starter. The motor clattered to life, and Nagel adjusted the speed lever until the engine settled into a loud, steady bawl. Pushing the lawn mower over to Too Tall Paulie, Nagel said, "Can't be too careful these days, not with all that fancy eavesdropping stuff the other side has."

Burke looked over the peaceful setting and sighed quietly.

"What's up?" the first dep asked, holding the mower with one hand while he stood in place beside his visitor.

"A recruit class was put in the Academy three weeks ago. What's the lag time before the Job notifies the various city agencies of their names?"

Nagel looked at his visitor. " 'Bout a month, give or take a week or so."

"Our Personnel Bureau notifies all concerned agencies?"

"Correct. They send paper to the City Department of Personnel, Comptroller, the *City Record,* and the health plans."

"What about publishing the list of names in the Special Orders?"

Nagel looked at Burke impatiently; he wanted to finish his chores before he and his wife had to go out that evening. "Orders won't be cut until all necessary notifications are made. Then we predate the list to the effective date of appointment." He smiled at his visitor. "I can see you don't read 'em anymore, do you."

"Not since I made sergeant. Before that I used to read the Special Orders faithfully; I'd check off the vacancies whenever a sergeant died, retired, or was promoted."

"We were all headhunters way back then." He adjusted the mower's speed higher. "Why all these questions, Paulie?"

"I want to put a recruit under, and I don't want to leave a paper trail."

"What about salary and medical benefits?"

"I'll use our cash contingency fund for salary, and ask one of our cop-friendly corporate giants to bury the person in their health plan."

Nagel looked down at the lawn and pulled at his earlobe thoughtfully. "And you want all traces of this person pulled."

"Exactly, including the fingerprints in our files and in Albany and Washington."

Nagel looked at Burke with a suddenly grim expression. "This must be an important caper."

"Levi and DiLeo."

Nagel put his hand on Burke's shoulder and said, "I'll personally take care of it first thing Monday morning."

"Thank you."

Too Tall Paulie took out his pen and one of the phony business cards he always carried around with him, and wrote Fiona Lee's name and Social Security number on the back. The first dep took the card and shoved it into his pants pocket without looking at the name.

Too Tall Paulie ran his finger over the mower's rust-pitted handlebars and asked, "Who runs the Job's deep undercovers?"

A puzzled expression clouded the first dep's face. "I really don't know. I'm not even sure we have any."

"Have a nice weekend, Commissioner," Too Tall Paulie said, and walked off across the well-tended lawn, thinking, The Job's made us all liars.

Thickening clouds were gathering over the Blue Ridge Mountains Sunday afternoon as a Cessna Citation banked for a landing at a private airstrip eighty miles west of Charlottesville, Virginia.

Fiona Lee was the plane's only passenger. She had boarded at the Marine Air Terminal at La Guardia just after one on Sunday. Looking out the window at the unending panorama of uneven mountains, she smiled as she remembered her sham fight with Sergeant Neary. It had been a beauty. Late Saturday she had gotten into her sweats and joined a section of the recruit class in the gym. On cue, Neary had reprimanded her for not wearing a bra and ordered her to go home and change; she would also be subject to command discipline for improper attire. The entire class was stunned into silence when she'd told him, "No." She had expected to be on a work detail where it wouldn't matter. They'd gotten into a screaming match with each other, and he'd marched her before the duty officer, who had told her she had a choice of resigning or being dismissed for insubordination. She'd told them to shove the Job and signed her resignation papers; as she'd stormed out, she had given the finger to both men.

The wheels touched down. The pilot taxied over to a waiting Jeep, where a lean, leathery-faced man with short gray hair and a fine network of wrinkles at the corners of his eyes was leaning against the fender with his arms folded across his chest. There was something youthful about him, even though Fiona placed him somewhere in his early fifties. He was dressed in jeans and cowboy boots and had one of those string ties with a silver clasp on his plaid shirt.

The propeller feathered to a stop. The pilot reached over and opened the door; Fiona climbed out of the aircraft, carefully placing her feet away from the marked NO STEP area on the wing. Someone aboard passed her out her suitcase. She said, "Thank you," and turned to admire the majestic ridgeline looming in the distance. Sucking in the crystal clear air, she became aware of a slight chill and the sounds and smells of the country. She heard approaching footsteps and saw a man out of the corner of her eye. She turned.

"Hi, I'm Ted Porges," said the lean man whom she had seen

leaning up against the Jeep. He reached out and took her suitcase. And you're Mary Beth—"

"No, my name is—"

He interrupted. "Mary Beth. As long as you are on this facility, that is your name."

"Are those the Blue Ridge Mountains?" she asked as he turned and headed back toward the Jeep.

Instead of answering her, he made for the Jeep, leaving her standing on the tarmac. I just get off the plane and the first thing I run into is this guy's attitude, she thought, annoyed, going to the Jeep.

A road spurred off to the west of the landing strip and curved through the lush Virginia hills. "Sure is beautiful," she said, trying to break through Porges's glacial exterior.

"Yep," he answered, his eyes fixed on the road. "We'll be at the Hacienda in a few minutes. After I get you settled in, we'll talk."

The Hacienda was a sprawling complex of one-story farmhouses and barns built around a large ranch-style house that overlooked a verdant valley of peach orchards. There was a soccer field on the stretch of flat land between the main house and the mountains.

Unlike the FBI's groomed training base at Quantico, Virginia, the Hacienda was a secret training facility staffed by DEA and CIA undercover experts and a special Delta Force team whose peculiar mission had won it the nickname "Garbage Disposal Machine."

Fiona's rooms were in the back of the house. They were large and comfortable and afforded a breathtaking view through a floor-to-ceiling glass wall. After checking out the bathroom and closets, she bounced herself on the queen-size mattress and smiled in satisfaction at its hardness.

In the living room she found Porges standing in front of the stone fireplace, looking out at the distant view. He turned toward her and said slowly, "I've been given three weeks to train you. That's not a whole lot of time."

"I'm a quick learner," she said confidently, sitting on the long white sofa without any newcomer awkwardness.

Sitting beside her, Porges said, "The narco-crowd calls the U.S. 'I-95' because their lines of white stretch from coast to coast like the lines of the interstates. In order to protect their highway, they've developed some highly sophisticated techniques to spot undercovers. You're going to have to be good, real good, or else you're gonna be real dead." He crossed his legs and looked thoughtfully at the backs of his weathered, tanned hands. "Most times when the dopers make an undercover they first try and turn him. If that doesn't work, they kill 'im. But when they discover one of their own has turned informer, they murder him slow and painful like. But before they take out the informer they'll murder his entire family, even the pets. Most folks figure they do that to discourage others with similar inclinations. But there is another, more important reason for wiping out an informer's entire family. Can you tell me what that reason might be?"

She crossed her legs, her foot jiggling, eyebrows knitted in concentration. She looked at Porges. "They don't want to leave anyone alive to even up the score in later years."

"And what does that tell you about our macho drug barons?"

"They aren't in a hurry to die."

A grudging smile appeared on Porges's mouth. "You just passed your first test." He turned and looked out the window at the twilight inching over the mountains. "Dinner'll be soon, so why don't I fill you in on the rules of this hotel."

Three days later, a little before nine in the morning, Captain Dave Katz, the XO of Narcotics, walked into his boss's office on the ninth floor of police headquarters and handed him an envelope marked "Personal."

Too Tall Paulie took a pull at his morning coffee, put down the cup, took a switchblade out of the top drawer, and sliced open the flap. The letter was from his niece, Fiona, who was a junior at UVA. She wrote to tell him that she loved her classes in the summer school and was studying hard.

Sliding the note back into the envelope, Chief Burke got up from his seat, switched on the shredder, and fed the envelope into the slot until the growling machine devoured it. Slipping back onto his seat, he asked his XO, "Anything on the leaks?"

"I did backgrounds and currents on all our people, and only came up with two in-house relationships."

"No one driving around in a Lamborghini?"

"Like all good cops, they're deep in hock. And the lovers are all single, and straight, so there's no blackmail card to play. I don't believe that there is a leak out of this office."

Rolling his cup between his palms, Too Tall Paulie asked matter-of-factly, "What do you know about the deep undercovers in the Job?"

Katz was obviously startled by the question. "Only rumors. They're supposedly run by Joey-the-G-Man. Paid lieutenant's money, and covered by medical plans of corporations with Agency or DEA connections."

Adopting a serious expression, Burke said, "Our own undercovers leave a paper trail, don't they?"

"Not much of one. Their records are pulled, and they're given phony legends, including yellow sheets."

"I've been racking my brain trying to figure out how the dopers made our people."

"Me too." Katz's gloomy countenance suddenly lit up. "Well, anyway, I've got some good news for a change. Lloyds of Medellin is going to be making a run off Sandy Hook sometime in the next few days. A freighter left Cuba four days ago, and has been off-loading keys of coke and some heroin along our eastern seaboard. The Joint Task has been angeling off it since she made her first drop."

"Where did their information come from?"

"A DEA subagent in Mexico." A gleeful sparkle glowed in Katz's eyes. "And the mule who is going to make the pickup is Roberto Barrios."

"The Thin Man?"

"The one and only. A Joint Task Force CI named Cupcake has been working Barrios for about a week. He's using a rented cabin cruiser to make the pickup. There should be at least three hundred keys. And when Barrios ties up, our people are going to swarm all over him. The Thin Man is going to have to roll over or spend the rest of his life doing push-ups in a twelve-by-nine cell."

Roberto Barrios slid out of bed and padded into the bathroom. After urinating, he stepped on the scale and frowned upon seeing that he had gained two pounds. He quickly resolved to go back to his own apartment and get on his exercise treadmill. That disgusting weight was going to be burned off by that evening.

Back in the bedroom, he gathered up his clothes and dressed. Buttoning his shirt, he looked down at the sleeping face and thought regretfully, What a waste. Too bad you asked one too many questions about my business, my love, he thought, sliding a tinfoil packet out of his pocket and placing it on the night table. Tenderly brushing a wisp of hair from her face, he bent down and kissed her lips.

Her eyes flashed open. Stretching, she asked, "What time is it?"

"A little after ten."

"Do you have to go so soon?" she cooed, holding up her arms. She was a tall woman with straight, dirty blond hair and small but beautifully shaped breasts and gray eyes.

"Business, my love, regrettably."

She pouted and asked tentatively, "Will I see you tonight?"

"Of course. Why don't we have dinner?"

"Oh, I'd love to." She flopped back on the bed and watched Barrios tie his shoes. "Hey, that was a super party at that club. Thanks for introducing me to Alejandro. He's someone really special."

"Yeah, well, he's a dead fuck."

She sat up, startled. "What do you mean? I thought he was your friend."

"No, chica, he's not my friend. He's Che-Che's friend—and if you fuck him, you're dead." Tapping the packet, he said in a more friendly tone, "I've left you a little present."

She yawned amorously. "Oooooo, thank you, Roberto."

Later that morning, Cupcake would get up and make herself a cup of coffee. While sitting at the kitchen table, she would empty the contents of the foil onto the Formica and, using a razor blade, rake the white powder into a thin line. With her face lowered to the powder, she would press one nostril closed with her finger and with the other suck up the line into her beautiful young body. Six minutes later Cupcake's heart would come to an abrupt, dead stop.

Barrios liked to call his special blend of heroin and cocaine the "Fink's Fizz."

Alejandro and Seaver had long ago developed an elaborate signaling system to arrange a meeting. They had memorized a list of meeting places that were determined by what day the meet was set for. If Seaver needed to see him, he would telephone Alejandro's home and ask for "Frank." The meeting would always be scheduled for 1:00 P.M. when Seaver called it.

When Alejandro needed to see Seaver, he would telephone a

local number cutout and, using his code name, Chilebean, tell the person who answered the day and time of the meet. The day he called the meeting would determine the meeting location.

Early this morning Alejandro had received a wrong numbers call for Frank. He grabbed a sneaker out of the wastebasket on the side of his bed and tossed it across the room.

The wide steps of the Metropolitan Museum of Art were crowded with people, lounging, eating, and taking in the Fifth Avenue view. The air smelled of spring, and the sky was blue.

Alejandro entered the museum and strolled into the Equestrian Court, a great room filled with ornate swords, helmets, and shields; suits of armored figures on horseback; and flags bearing the coats of arms of knights of the Round Table. Taking his time, he studied each exhibit, moving slowly over to the sumptuously and exquisitely detailed parade armor of Henry II; but periodically he would glance around carefully to check out the people around him. After viewing the armor, and seeing nothing to be concerned about, he thought, Now's a good time. Quickly but unobtrusively he left the great court, passed through the rotunda, left the building, and stood under the entrance portico.

Bright early summer afternoon sunlight fell across the avenue, reaching halfway up the museum's steps before the huge building's shadow cast the rest in deep shade.

It was just after 1:00 P.M. when a taxi with a roof billboard advertising Coors Light pulled away from the curb on the west side of Fifth Avenue and drew up in front of the museum.

Alejandro climbed into the rear and told the driver, "Union Square Park."

Andy Seaver reached out and turned on the meter. Watching the traffic, he inched out into the roadway, saying, "The CI who introduced Levi and DiLeo to the Cleopatra network was publicly executed Friday. They used an anaconda to crush him to death on the stage of a crack movie house."

Alejandro slumped back onto his seat. "That'll send a powerful message to the faithful."

"Narcotics had three undercovers inside. They reported that the leader of the assassination team was a tall, well-dressed guy, with pockmarked cheeks and a streak of white hair running down the center of his head."

"So?"

"So after DiLeo and Levi were whacked, Too Tall Paulie had every Ghost assigned to the Savoy caper questioned. No one saw anything, except two female detectives who had been assigned to the lobby. They remembered a tall, handsome, well-dressed man with pockmarked cheeks and a streak of white hair down the center of his head. They watched him get off the elevator around the time of the hit and walk out of the lobby."

Alejandro leaned forward. "What else did they notice about this guy?"

"That's it."

"Did you try and match up the description with anyone in the files?"

"We did and came up with zilch." He stopped for a red light at Sixty-seventh Street. "We have information that Lloyds of Medellin will be making a run off the coast sometime soon, and that Roberto Barrios, the mule from the Savoy, is the one who is going to be lassoing the dope from the sea."

"Is Barrios a mule, a transshipper, or is he in business for himself?"

Seaver cursed softly as he swerved to avoid a jaywalking pedestrian. "Dunno. Barrios and White Streak could be freelancers hired by Cleopatra for specific jobs."

"All the big narco-guys are full of that macho loyalty bullshit; they use only *family* to carry out important jobs. Remember, the real queen demanded loyalty from her subjects and her court."

The light turned green.

Seaver said, "The joint NYPD and DEA task force are angeling off this shipment. They're planning on scooping Barrios up and turning him." His eyes darted up to the rearview mirror. "How do you want to work this?"

"I think me and Barrios should become amigos."

8

ALEJANDRO PAID SEAVER WHAT was on the meter and got out at Union Square Park. Always act normally in public, was one of the sacred tenets taught him at the Hacienda. Porges constantly reminded him of the DEA undercover who was blown in Chicago several years ago because a doper saw him get out of a decoy taxi without paying the fare.

Head lowered in thought, he walked up the steps leading into the commons. There was a farmers market today outside the park's northern boundary, where he could get corn tortillas and beans. He was in the mood for some Mexican home-style food. He thought better with the taste of authentic home-grown in his mouth.

During the ride downtown, he and Seaver had decided to warn Barrios that the Joint Federal Task Force was on to the Medellin shipment. They had figured that it was worth exposing a small part of the operation to the dopers in order for Alejandro to ingratiate himself with the only known link to the Cleopatra network. The problem Alejandro now faced was to think of some plausible way for him to have come into possession of this information and to think of a way of warning Barrios.

He strolled through the park. A big area around the ornate flagpole had been fenced off to keep out the junkies. A large fence also surrounded the children's playground, which formerly had been littered with hypodermic needles. Homeless men, their stolen shopping carts overflowing with their possessions, hogged most of the benches. Schoolgirls from Saint Mary's Academy, sparkling clean in their white blouses and black-and-gray tartan skirts, cast their eyes downward and quickened their steps as they passed the drug dealer stationed at the Park Avenue South entrance. The dealer hissed buzz words at the hurrying girls, "Yo, girls, free golden blow, makes you feel gooood."

Alejandro checked the time: 2:10 P.M. He had a three o'clock call to rehearse new material with the band. Wandering toward the dealer, he looked out across Fourteenth Street at the construction skeleton of a high-rise building, one of many around the city that had been abandoned as a result of the savings and loan debacle.

Moving into the farmers market, Alejandro saw a laborer offloading crates of fruit from a truck. He was a short man with the flat cheekbones and thick lips typical of the people who came from the harsh mountains of Guerrero. Going over to him, he said in Spanish, "You're a long way from home, amigo. How goes it?"

The man slid a crate of grapes onto his shoulder and said, "I was a peasant at home and I'm a peasant here."

"You're making a lot more money here."

"What you make here, you leave here," he said, and walked off with his burden.

Alejandro shrugged and walked over to the mobile restaurant

and ordered his lunch. Biting into a hot tortilla, he became conscious of the conversation of two Spanish women standing a few feet away. They were drinking espresso from plastic cups. One of them was lamenting how she thought her husband was cheating on her because of his sudden need to work late every night. Leaning closer to her friend, she confided, "He hardly touches me anymore." Her friend suggested that she search his clothes for telltale credit card receipts and matchbooks.

Alejandro finished his tortilla and tossed the napkin into the plastic-lined trash barrel. Hurrying out of the market onto Seventeenth Street, he saw that traffic was bottlenecked at Park Avenue South. A jackhammer's harsh rat-ta-ta added to the urban clamor. He looked across the street at an abandoned five-story stately building with rich cast-iron architecture. A lone ventilation fan on the top floor was spinning. He was barely able to make out the fading sign over the entrance: American Drapery and Carpet Company. A dead business in a dying city, he thought, deciding to walk to the club.

The acrid odor of cleaning solvents and disinfectants perfumed the air inside of the Environment.

It was three o'clock, and the club was beginning to stir. Deliveries of food and liquor were being invoiced under the steward's watchful eyes. Two cleaning men mopped, and swept, and polished. On stage Alejandro rehearsed a *bachata,* a pan-Hispanic salsa. The band, which included a *güiro* and a two-headed *tambara* drum, played the rhythm while the trumpeter belted out the melody. Alejandro was next to the conga player woodshedding the lyrics, "Chu, chu, chu, cha, cha, du, du, ba, cha." His lips began swaying to the *bachata*'s propulsive rhythms. Then he sang the words, summoning up the atmosphere of tropical lovemaking. He had just finished making the song fit his style when a familiar voice called out his name. He looked up to see his manager, Josh Budofsky, approaching.

A tall, saturnine man in his early thirties clad in black jeans and a black leather blazer, Budofsky had taken Alejandro on as a client eighteen months ago on the recommendation of Che-Che Morales. "Great lyrics."

"Glad you like it," Alejandro said, sitting at the edge of the stage and dangling his feet.

"I really wish you'd join the twentieth century and buy an answering machine. You're never home, and whenever I need to talk to you, I have to hunt you down."

Alejandro made a dismissive gesture with his hand. "I don't like machines. What's up?"

"I gave your tape and the live video to Paul Belmont at Epic, and he liked it. A lot."

"So when do we sign the contracts?"

"Belmont likes your style, the way you control your audience."

"Cut to the 'but,' Josh."

Budofsky looked down at his black Nikes in embarrassment. "He sees a problem packaging you. Says you're too Latin. Your kind of music gets 'em clapping and shouting in the Caribbean and South America, but it doesn't have staying power in the States. He suggests we repackage you."

"Yeah? What does he have in mind, bluegrass and salsa?"

"More the international type," Budofsky said. "We change you, make a real video that would do for VH-1, and then go back to Belmont.

"Josh, my style of singing is who I am; it's me." Me! he thought. I'm not sure who "me" is. An Irishman? A Mexican? A Tarascan Indian? A singer? An undercover cop?

"The majors have all brought over big-name Latin singers and spent a fortune trying to break them into the American market. Every one of them flopped."

"Julio?"

"European, and he draws big with men and women."

Alejandro shook his head wearily. "I don't know what to tell you, Josh. What you see is what you've got."

"We'll change you, just a little. Maybe hire someone to create a new persona for you, mixing the old and the new."

"I'll think it over."

"And I'll be in touch in a few days."

Watching his manager walk across the dance floor, Alejandro wondered what Josh would say if he knew about his secret life. Getting up, he looked at the band and said, "Let's do it."

Lopez's tire store, on the north side of 119th Street near the corner of Manhattan Avenue, was another dilapidated building on a street that belonged only to the poor. Most of the buildings on the block had all their windows and doors cinder-blocked. But on this street of blight there were three designer jewelry stores, four high-fashion boutiques, and two travel agencies, all of which were fronts to launder drug money. These businesses were the first stop for millions of drug dollars that would go overseas dirty and come back clean.

There was a storage lot on the west side of the tire store's scarred building that was crammed with mountains of old tires. The lot itself was corraled behind a high chain-link fence that was not crowned in concertina wire, nor was the lot patrolled at night by attack dogs. There was no need for such precautions here because every junkie, crackhead, and dealer around knew that Che-Che Morales was the real owner of Lopez's tire store.

Four men gathered around a bridge table in front of the store were playing dominoes when a taxi drew up and Alejandro stepped out. Che-Che Morales glanced up from his line of tiles, looked at the newcomer, and returned his attention to the game.

Summer's twilight had not yet come, and children darted through the spray of an open fire hydrant. Across the street in Morningside Park, a homeless man was sprawled on his back in the grass, an empty liquor bottle clutched in his hands. The man's eyes were partially closed. Without moving his lips, he inched his mouth close to a microphone concealed in his sleeve and said, "Snap the guy who just got out of the cab."

Alejandro walked over and watched the game. Che-Che was absorbed with his tiles. When the game was finished, Che-Che pushed away from the table and walked into the lot. Alejandro followed. Che-Che made his way around stacks of tires.

In the middle of the lot four high mounds of tires were pushed together forming a mountain of rubber with a single, narrow, cavelike entrance. Che-Che squeezed inside the single entrance and waited. Two pigeons flew down and perched on top of the tires.

Twisting to make his way inside the sanctuary, Alejandro said, "I like your office. Who did the decorating?"

"It's safe against laser beams and radio wave penetration, amigo, and all the other shit they use against me." Looking at his guest, he asked, "What brings you here?"

Alejandro dropped his voice to a low, conspiratorial level. "A few nights ago your *compadre* Roberto Barrios introduced me to his latest blond trophy. She was totally fucked up on coke. He goes to take a piss and she starts talking about this big-deal shipment that Barrios is supposed to pick up in his boat. So I can only figure, if this chica knows—who else knows?" Alejandro knew he was going out on a limb, maybe even putting Barrios's lady, the informant, on the chopping block—but he figured that Seaver could arrange to pull her out fast. And this was more than enough to get Che-Che's paranoia going. The rules said that you never, never talked business to civilians, especially ones you were fucking.

Che-Che looked ahead with that impassivity characteristic of Indians, seeing all, saying nothing. When he finally spoke, his tone was calm and flat. "Why are you telling me this?"

"Because you're my friend, and I wouldn't want to see you get hurt."

"I'll pass on your information. Too bad someone is going to lose a shipment."

"What do you mean?" Alejandro asked, puzzled.

"I mean," snarled Che-Che, "that lady was wired in more ways than one. I *know*."

Alejandro brushed a whitish splatter of pigeon droppings from Che-Che's shoulder and looked up at the fluttering birds above them. "It doesn't have to be that way."

Che-Che's mouth drew tight. "Why this sudden interest in my business?"

Alejandro had prepared an answer for this question, too. "I had a visit this afternoon from my manager. Seems all the majors think I'm talented, but much too Latino. They want me to change my style."

"Will they guarantee a contract?"

"They guarantee a maybe. I'm starting to realize that I could spend my life singing in *cuchifrito* joints. I'm thirty-two and I still haven't bought that home for my mother and sister. The way I'm going, I might never be able to."

Che-Che rested his head against the rubber wall, looking up at the patch of blue sky and the two cooing pigeons. "So you figure you'll come with us for a while, do a few deals, and walk away with enough to secure your life."

Alejandro smiled and said, "Something like that."

Che-Che looked him directly in the eyes. "I've known other guys who said they wanted 'in' just to make enough to be able to walk away. But once in, they can't leave. Know why? Because suddenly enough is never enough."

"It will be for me."

"I hope so," Che-Che said, squeezing out of his cocoon. "But sometimes I think nobody gets out of our business alive."

*   *   *

The Department of Parks limestone administrative building on the fringe of Morningside Park had an attached garage with a gable facing Lopez's tire store. The pigeons that had perched on top of Che-Che's tire cocoon flew into their portable coop on top of the garage's flat roof. Their detective handler picked them up one at a time and gingerly removed the miniaturized transmitters concealed in the trained birds' plumage.

In the attic below the roof, two detectives from the Narcotics Division's Unified Intelligence Section manned the static surveillance platform. A tripod-mounted camera with night-vision capabilities and a telescopic lens was peeking out through the gable's ventilation slots, aimed down at Lopez's tire store. The detective standing behind the camera was turning the focusing ring on the eyepiece of the scope, zeroing in on Che-Che and his friend as they strolled out of the lot.

On the other side of the attic another detective sat in front of the portable console. This device contained a digital switching system linked to a voice analyzer that digitally processed the suspect's voice, which had been picked up by the tiny transmitters concealed in the pigeons' feathers. The switching system constantly recorded and scanned conversations, flashing digital numbers across the voice analyzer as it processed the sound of Alejandro's voice.

Lieutenant Sal Elia, the platform's boss, was spying the pair through binoculars. "Get that guy's photo and voice down to Intel right away."

Slowly stirring his espresso later that evening, a man with a swath of white hair glanced at the man sitting across from him and said, "Pussy's going to kill you one day, Roberto."

Barrios laughed lightly. "I'm careful who I screw. Haven't you heard about AIDS?" He picked up his cup, trying to keep his fear from showing on his face. He had been home when the phone call came and the familiar voice had ordered, "Meet me at Billings. Now." Billings was one of Columbus Avenue's upscale diners.

The man with the bolt of white hair was Hector Pizzaro, a well-dressed former Bolivian army officer in his late fifties with large cold eyes, badly pockmarked cheeks. Raising his cup to his lips, Pizzaro said, "Your latest playmate sniffed herself to death this morning. Did you slip her one of your little surprise packages?"

Barrios tried to look surprised. "You sure?"

"Word travels fast in our small world, Roberto. Besides, I have morgue people on the payroll."

Barrios could feel the beads of sweat popping out on his forehead. "Hector, I don't knowingly go out with cokeheads."

"They're security risks, and so are the men who fuck them."

"Hector . . ."

Pizzaro's sternly upraised finger cut him off. "Some guys get off on bragging to women. It makes their come more pleasurable. But in our crew, all it makes them is dead."

"Hector, I swear—"

"Shut the fuck up, and listen." Pizzaro's eyes were as hard and cold as two steel balls. "There *has* been a leak. The DEA knows about our boat."

"Are you sure?"

"Have you forgotten that I'm the head of intelligence? I sent people to the marina where your boat is docked. It just happened to be crawling with gringos wearing thick shoes." His eyes fell to his cup. "They probably planned on arresting and turning you, Roberto."

Barrios leaned across the table to swear, "I'd never roll." Drops of his sweat dripped off his chin.

Hector smiled ironically. "Of course you wouldn't."

Momentarily regaining some of his cool, Barrios asked, "How was the shipment blown?"

Hector shrugged ignorance. "Who knows? If not the

girl . . ." Then he gripped Barrios by the arm. "Tonight I want you to go and talk to Alejandro Monahan. He says he wants to work for us. He's hungry and in a hurry. Men like that are sometimes . . . inventive and useful. See what he has to offer us. But be careful; I haven't checked him out yet."

The trumpeter rifled through the merengue's arpeggio as Alejandro spun across the stage. At the center he stopped, his eyes playing his swaying audience, his hips rolling to the beat. Spreading his arms, he drifted into the lyrics of his theme, "Quierame Mucho."

Song finished, he threw kisses to the audience and ran off stage into his dressing room. He pulled off his sweaty shirt, went over to his cruddy sink, and washed himself. After buttoning on a clean black *guayabera* and combing his hair, he left.

Che-Che was enthroned on his favorite banquette in the balcony. He was watching the dancers on the floor below when he heard women's raised voices and looked around. Alejandro was headed his way when a woman wearing a tight-fitting black jumpsuit with industrial zippers, her hair flaming red, staggered up to Alejandro. Holding a water glass filled with booze, she rubbed herself up against him and said, "I'd love to fuck you."

He looked down into her exposed cleavage. "What are you drinking?"

"Vodka."

"You should mix it with carrot juice. You'll get drunk, but at least you'll have good eyes." He made his way over to Che-Che, slid into the booth, pulled a bottle of champagne from the bucket, and poured some into a glass. Toasting his host, he smiled. *"Salud,* amigo."

Che-Che nodded.

Sipping wine, Alejandro asked, "You got a job for me?"

"I liked your salsa numbers." Watching the people in the loft dancing to the kinetic Latin music, he added, "I have nothing.

But that man might." He pointed his glass at Barrios, sitting alone at one of the tables next to the bar. He was picking at a salad and drinking soda water, ignoring the tumult around him. Alejandro looked at Barrios's familiar evil face. He was a regular and a close associate of Che-Che's.

Bewildered, Alejandro asked, "You trust this guy after what I told you?"

"We're checking him out. Meanwhile, talk to him."

Alejandro went over to Barrios's table, pulled back a chair, and sat, uninvited.

Barrios continued to pick at his salad. "Tell me how you heard about the shipment."

"I already told Che-Che."

"Tell me." His tone was soft, which made it all the more menacing.

Alejandro repeated the story about what Barrios's woman had told him.

"Bullshit. I didn't tell that *puta* anything."

"If you don't want to do me the courtesy of some serious conversation..." Alejandro shrugged indifference, scraped back his chair.

"Sit down," the thin man ordered.

Lowering himself back onto the seat, Alejandro said, "Che-Che vouches for me, and that should be good enough for you."

"Che-Che vouches for nobody." He began sliding lettuce over his plate, making designs in the dressing. I've been told you're looking for a job with us." He arched his eyebrows disparagingly. "We don't need singers."

Leaning forward, Alejandro confided, "I can guarantee the safe delivery of your product into the States."

" 'Guarantee'? That's a big word for a guy who makes his living shaking his ass in joints like this."

Alejandro reached across the table to push aside the other man's salad, and with his finger he outlined the American continent in the salad dressing. Using his finger as a pointer, he explained, "The DEA has all your smuggling routes across the Andes and the Caribbean under satellite and radar surveillance. They have AWACs and Hawkeye radar planes covering your transshipping points in Mexico and Cuba. Here, along the coast, they have radar balloons searching out your low-flying planes and boats coming into the States. Right now you're still winning the war, but they're tightening the noose. Most of your stuff is coming in concealed in cars, lead ingots, sinks, whatever."

Alejandro looked around and lowered his voice during a sudden lull in the music. "Even the *New York Times* knows that Uncle Sam is developing a satellite that will detect the gas emissions given off by cocaine hydrochloride and opiates. Once that thing is deployed you're going to have a serious problem getting your stuff in." He erased the map with his finger, adding, "I can ship your shit anywhere, anytime."

Barrios arched his back, folded his arms across his chest. "Wouldja tell me now a disco singer knows so much about a business he's not in?"

"Look around you, Roberto. All those guys out there on the dance floor dry-humping broads are in your business, and all they ever talk about is dope and pussy."

Barrios seemed bored. He picked up his fork and began idly pushing around pieces of lettuce. "How can *you* guarantee delivery?" He didn't try to hide the contempt in his voice.

"My secret until we agree on the green."

"How much?"

"Five percent of the weight I bring in."

"Is that all?" His voice took on an annoyed edge.

"What was in the shipment the DEA found out about?"

"China White and cocaine," Barrios said reluctantly.

"Heroin from the Golden Triangle. You have to ship that crap all the way from the mountains of Burma, Thailand, and Laos. You can't afford to lose too many of them."

"Five points is too much."

Once again the music started up, and Alejandro raised his voice so he could still be heard. "A kilo of pure costs you around eleven K in Bangkok. You sell that to a broker in the States for between eighty-five and a hundred and a quarter, then it's peddled to a midlevel guy for a quarter of a mil. Five points, amigo, cost you nothing."

They held each other's stares; salsa boomed out from the speakers.

"Two points," Barrios countered.

"Five."

"Show me how you're going to do it, and we'll talk again." He got up and squeezed out from behind the table.

Watching Barrios slip easily through the crowd and disappear down the stone staircase, Alejandro spotted Che-Che watching him.

"How did it go?" Che-Che asked as Alejandro slid in beside him.

"I told him I'd guarantee delivery of his product anywhere in the United States."

Che-Che's brow pulled together. "You told him *what?!*"

Alejandro repeated his statement.

"And how are *you* going to do that?"

"I don't know yet."

Shaking his head with amusement, Che-Che said, "You're a real Tarascan Indian. You charge like a raging bull, not caring what's in front of you. Barrios is not to be taken lightly."

Alejandro flashed a confident smile. "I have something in mind, but I have to work out the details." He looked at Che-Che inquiringly. "Are you and Barrios together?"

Che-Che picked up his wineglass. "No. We work for different firms."

"If this deal works for me, I'll be getting a piece of the weight I bring in. Can you help me sell it?"

"First figure out how you're going to do it, and then we'll talk."

"I'm in a hurry, Che-Che. I don't want to piss my life away in discoville. And believe me, enough will be enough."

Che-Che sipped champagne and said nothing.

Warm night air buffeted Alejandro's face as he raced his Porsche along Shore Parkway. The graceful spans of the Verrazano Narrows Bridge loomed in the distance, and behind it there was an almost imperceptible lightening as the dawn filtered up above the horizon. He had been driving around the city for forty minutes crystallizing his plan for bringing down the Cleopatra network. The car's stereo system rang out with the voice of a new and talented Irish tenor. Whenever he was alone, Alejandro preferred Irish music. It soothed him and helped him think clearly. More important, it did not exhume ugly memories from the past the way Latin music did.

The car sped along the parkway. He looked out at the big ships anchored in Gravesend Bay. Driving past Bensonhurst Park, he glanced at the darkened cars parked in the lovers lane at the water's edge, and he thought of the woman who had so cavalierly tossed her underpants at him and taken him to her bed. He could no longer smell her clinging scent or even remember her name. She was another of the faded memories that added to his loneliness.

He raced the Porsche onto the Gowanus Expressway and a few minutes later was speeding through the almost deserted Brooklyn Battery Tunnel. Once out of the tunnel, he tooled the car through the financial district's eerily deserted streets. He pulled up at the curb alongside a telephone booth across from Trinity Church. Sliding out of his car, he looked at the blackened spire of the venerable old building reaching up into the fading night. He deposited a quarter in the telephone's coin slot, heard the dial tone hiccup; he punched in the number, quickly calculating that it was Thursday morning, June 24.

When the voice came on the other end of the line, Alejandro said, "Chilebean, thirteen hundred."

The voice echoed, "Chilebean, thirteen hundred."

"Are you losing it upstairs?" Seaver demanded as they strolled around the outside of Grant's Tomb. He was obviously disturbed by the turn of events.

"It'll work," Alejandro said confidently.

"You've thought up a lot of crazy things during our time together, and I'll give it to you, most of them have worked. But this one is off the wall."

"Why?"

With some anger, Seaver snapped, "For openers, most of it is against the law."

"C'mon, Andy. We set up scumbags and then fade into the night. There are a dozen dopers doing megatime because of us." He spread his arms in praise. "We're society's unsung heroes. So what's a few bent laws?"

"This one is unusually dangerous. It has too many pitfalls." Seaver was clearly digging in his heels.

"I want Cleopatra."

Seaver heaved a resigned sigh. "How'd you ever think this one up?"

"Last time you sent me back to the Hacienda for training, I got friendly with some of the Delta Force guys. They were demonstrating Parapoint. They explained to me how it worked, and I just filed it away in the back of my head. And bang, I'm talking with Barrios and it popped out."

Seaver lit up a cigar and blew smoke at Alejandro. "I'm familiar with that system, and I know that it happens to have NO-FORM stenciled all over it: 'No Foreign Dissemination.' That includes undercovers of the NYPD. So how the hell do you expect to get your hands on one of them?"

Alejandro's voice took on an urgent, pleading note. "The club is closed Sunday. Early Sunday morning we'll hop a flight to the Hacienda, schmooze around with some of the Delta Force guys, tell 'em what we need, and they'll lend it to us."

Seaver laughed and said, "Bullshit. Those guys won't even give you the time of day unless they get the word in quintuplicate."

"What do we have to lose, Andy?"

"You realize, I guess, that this stunt would more than likely require you to go outside the country, without any backup."

"So?" Alejandro felt the tide was beginning to flow his way.

"So the United States, by treaty, is pledged to notify nations of the insertion of any U.S. police officer on official business into their sovereign territory."

Alejandro brushed aside the objection with a wave of his hand. "Andy, I'm a singer. *'Soy un hombre sincero ...'*" he sang.

Seaver examined the glowing end of his cheroot. "Barrios is playing with you. Before he dances he's going to want to see how you're going to get his stuff in. Then he'll try to steal it from you. Then he'll kill you if he has to. But before any of that, he's going to need answers to questions. Like why the sudden change from singer to doper."

"Greed. 'At's something every doper can bond to."

Seaver still looked doubtful. "And how does a singer of enchiladas know about Parapoint, and how does he manage to get hold of one, or two, or three of them?"

"I read about them in a magazine; then I bribed someone in the military or the Agency to get them."

Seaver shook his head. "Bribery won't work. They'll want to meet your source."

Alejandro scratched his neck, smiled, and told Seaver the legend he'd thought up to explain how he came into possession of Parapoint.

Seaver laughed. "That's good. Those Latinos can't deal with

that. It blows their minds. I'll research and see if Parapoint was ever mentioned in the public media." He dragged on his cigar. "You're going to need a public source for this thing to work." He took the cheroot out of his mouth, studied the glowing ember, and asked, "Is Barrios working for Che-Che?"

"I asked Che-Che that. He told me no. I don't believe him. Recently I saw two Chinese dopers engaged in some heavy-duty conversation with him. And the shipment that they had to turn back was part China White, which the Chinese control. I'm beginning to think that maybe Che-Che has branched out from transshipping to dealing heroin."

"Cleopatra Gold?"

"Could be." He moved close to Mother Hen. "We'd deliver the stuff, let them bring it to their distribution warehouse, and then leak the locations to the good guys. We might even be able to get a line on their money warehouses."

Seaver plunged the cheroot back into his mouth and said, "We could really hurt them."

Alejandro knew he'd just made a sale.

Whiggham Associates was located on the ninth floor of a gray building on Duane Street, close to the city's old butter and egg market.

The reception area's floor and ceiling were laid with a blue acoustical tile, and the windowless room was floored in an orange shag carpet. A painting of Christ on the cross had three plastic roses stuck on top of the golden frame. Two husky men, both of whom needed a shave, were playing dominoes on a low-slung coffee table with an imitation marble top. A burly man with a scar running from his right ear to the edge of his thick lips was sitting at the desk flipping through *Gentlemen's Quarterly*. A short, fat man sat in front of the television, kneading and rubbing his hands as he watched a pornographic movie.

A door led into a large, tastefully furnished office where Hector Pizzaro, the doper with the signature white streak of hair and pockmarked cheeks, spent a good part of his day working behind a rosewood desk on which stood stacks of photographs of NYPD graduation classes. A computer at the side of the desk had intelligence banks that contained copies of the *City Record,* the city's legal newspaper that published the names of all civil servant appointments, and all other information affecting the municipal government, from contracts to the schedule of road repairs. Another file contained the name of every municipal civil servant filed by the department or agency they belonged to, including the NYPD's Force Record File. Another contained the city comptroller's payroll sheets and a complete list of subscribers to the city's various health and welfare plans. There was a special file containing the Police Department's Special Orders, which listed all appointments, promotions, transfers, assignments, resignations, retirements, suspensions, dismissals, and leaves of absence. And deaths.

Most of Whiggham Associates' records came from easily obtainable public sources. The payroll records cost Pizzaro two grams of cocaine and two hundred dollars a month. The police records were more expensive, five grams and five hundred dollars. It was a small price to pay for such high-grade intelligence. Pizzaro brushed a hand through his hair and looked over at the table containing stacks of *SPRING 3100, The Magazine for the Department by the Department.* He pulled out one that had a paste-on attached to its pages and flipped it open to the page.

The seven-year-old magazine had a photograph in the middle of page forty-two of the members of Brooklyn North's TNT Unit, which had recently shut down two warehouses for manufacturing and distributing crack. Money and weapons and bags of glassine envelopes covered a table in the photograph, and behind it stood the members of the arresting team. Levi and DiLeo were in the middle of the group, their arms around each other.

Pizzaro was constantly amazed at the incredible stupidity of the police in allowing its members to pose for pictures in a Department magazine that anyone could subscribe to. He flipped through the pages, looking at grinning faces at picnics and boat rides. "Stupid," he muttered, sitting squarely in front of the computer and inputting "Alejandro Monahan" into the data bank containing the Force Record File. No record. He next ran the name through the Article Two Retirement list. No record. After finding no record of the name in the health plan data bank, he called up the names of all Monahans employed by any of the city's departments or agencies. He pressed the Print button and watched the laser printer churn up printouts. His beeper went off; looking down at the number in its LED display, he grabbed his cellular telephone.

Without ceremony, Morales's voice at the other end asked, "What have you discovered about Roberto and the dead crackhead?"

"She might have been an informer. I'm not sure yet."

"Make sure."

Pizzaro bit down on his lip. "I will."

"Levi and DiLeo got too close to us. I will not want any weak links."

Pizzaro's stomach went hollow. "I understand."

"I hope you do, Hector," Che-Che said, and he disconnected.

Pizzaro inputted the code that admitted him into the Associates File, a data bank that contained the names and pedigree of every person who introduced outsides to members of the crew. These names were then cross-referenced with those of any member of the crew who was later arrested. When Pizzaro had seen that Jordon Hayes had introduced members to someone who had turned out to be a cop, and then the same Jordon Hayes had introduced Levi and DiLeo, he knew that he was dealing with a police informer and a couple of undercover narcotics detectives. The reason he had not caught it sooner was that the Associates

File had been not his idea, but Judith's, and had only recently been opened.

Alejandro's name elicited one response: Alejandro Monahan had introduced banker Franklin Penzer to the network. Hector leaned back, knitting his hands behind his head, staring at the screen. After remaining in that position for several minutes, he arched his finger down on the intercom button and said, "Judith, I need to see you."

A door opened on the side of his office to reveal a console of sophisticated communications equipment and a bank of computers. A statuesque, well-dressed woman in a very short skirt and white silk blouse, fortyish, with dense black hair, high cheekbones, thick lips, and deeply tanned skin, came in holding a white legal pad. She sat on the chair at the side of his desk and asked in a throaty voice, "What's up?"

"One of Roberto Barrios's loves OD'ed. She's being buried Tuesday, and I want you to attend the funeral. There's a good possibility that she was an informer, and if she was, her control will show up for her funeral. Cops bond with their informers. They feel a misplaced sense of guilt whenever one of the pigs is exposed and eliminated. Take some people with you and get photographs and license plate numbers."

"Okay." She crossed her legs.

"A shipment had to be diverted because of a leak. If Roberto's girlfriend was an informer, then our dear Roberto was the source, which means he's getting pussy blind. So he's a liability."

"I'll see to it."

"Mix with the mourners, and—"

She rolled her eyes. "Hector, I know what to do."

"I know you do," he said, looking down at her long, legs. "One more thing. A singer named Alejandro Monahan introduced some of our people to a banker named Franklin Penzer from Tortola in the British Virgins. His bank is in Road Town, the island's capital. We're laundering some of our money with him. I want to send someone to the islands to have a look at the bank and Mr. Penzer, make sure it isn't being run from Washington."

"Want me to go?"

"No. I need you here." Looking down at the shiny black stockings hugging her thighs, he added, "Besides, I'd miss you. Send one of those asshole lawyers we have on the payroll."

"I'll see to it," she said, and got up to leave.

His eyes slid over her body, fixing on her lips. Taking hold of her hand, he said, "Before you go, I'd like you to do something for me."

A smile crossed her mouth, and she slid her pad onto the desk and said, "Don't mess my hair."

— 9 —

A LAZY SUNDAY MORNING hush had fallen over Charlottesville, Virginia. The parking lot of the First Presbyterian Church was filled with worshipers' automobiles. On the campus of the University of Virginia students strolled toward the library. And in the distance a ribbon of puffy clouds drifted over the mountains. Off in the west a Mooney 201 single-engine aircraft skimmed over the gently rolling hills of the Jenkins farm.

Fiona Lee eased back on the yoke, and the craft zoomed up into the sky.

Ted Porges was in the copilot's seat. "You're a natural behind that stick."

"I've been flying since I was fifteen."

"Let's go home."

Four minutes later Fiona Lee eased the yoke forward, cut back on the throttle, and lowered the flaps as she lined up the Mooney 201 with the Hacienda's landing strip.

Porges deliberately watched the avionics as the runway rose to meet them. The wheels touched down as the craft glided to an effortless landing. Fiona taxied over to the Jeep parked on the edge of the tarmac, cut the engine, and watched the propeller come to a complete stop.

During the ride back to the Hacienda, Porges said, "The narco boys are always in the market for pilots." Fiona's face glowed at the understated praise.

A short time later Porges and the woman known to him only as Mary Beth were seated in a timbered room with a large stone fireplace and a glass wall facing the mountains. Porges picked up a remote module and flicked on the VCR. The surveillance film that filled the screen showed two men crossing Manhattan's Canal Street. One of them was carrying a gray cloth bag.

"The guy on the right is Reyes Costas, and the other one is Che-Che Morales. Reyes is the head honcho for the Medellin in the States. Morales is in charge of transshipping their drugs into the States, mainly from Mexico. He also handles shipments for the Calí. He's an inventive guy, it makes him valuable to both cartels. That bag that Reyes is lugging around with him is full of quarters. He only conducts business from public telephones. Now, here are some things I want you to remember about these two men. . . ."

The man standing on the soccer field wearing army fatigues was Sergeant Dave Pollack, of the Delta Force's Garbage Disposal Machine. He, Alejandro, and Seaver were all staring off to the southeast. Alejandro was holding a handset that resembled a portable telephone with an extended telescopic antenna. There were two toggle switches on the handset's faceplate.

The three men watched the sky.

Sixty miles away, flying at an altitude of thirty thousand feet, a "black" Beech King Air 350 with only registration markings banked to the south. Aboard the craft, a Garbage Disposal Machine sergeant wearing an oxygen mask opened the floor hatch in the depressurized cabin and stood back, tugging on a static line. Seeing it was secure, he moved over to the opening and tossed out the parachute.

The bundle toppled to the earth.

The static line went taut, unzipping the pack. The Ram Air canopy streamed out of the bundle and billowed open, the force of the deployment jerking the chute upward before it settled into its graceful glide toward the earth.

"Chute deployed," radioed the sergeant aboard the Beech King.

The men on the soccer field searched the sky. Seaver bit down on the end of his cheroot. Alejandro turned to the Delta Force sergeant and said, "Tell me again how this thing works."

Pollack stuck his thumbs behind his olive-colored webbed belt and said, "The Parapoint delivery system can deliver up to one thousand pounds of equipment onto a dime from sixty miles away and an altitude of thirty thousand feet. The risers—those are the lines coming down from the canopy—are connected to the steering toggles. A black box fifteen inches square and two inches deep is attached to the steering lines, and suspended between the servos. Inside this box is a motor that's powered by a nicad, nickel cadmium battery, and a radio receiver that gets its signals from the homing transmitter in your hand. Those signals reel in and let out the steering toggles according to the messages the black box gets from the homing transmitter; it acts like a magnet drawing the chute to it."

"What about the switches on the transmitter?" Chilebean asked.

"They're only used if you need to operate the system manually. Like if you were in a forest and had to guide the chute through trees in order to prevent it from getting hung up."

Squinting at the speck gliding toward them in the distance, Chilebean asked, "What about wind?"

Pollack said, "The chute must be deployed upwind so that there is no wind resistance. When it's over the homing transmitter it'll automatically turn itself into the wind in order to decrease its rate of descent." Pointing, he said, "Here it comes."

They watched in silence as the white blossom grew larger and larger.

"The revolver is the weapon of choice of narco assassins," Porges was telling Mary Beth. "They like them because they don't jam, they're safe, and they're double action. Now when they have to take out more than one person at a time, they'll use . . ." His voice trailed off when he realized that she had focused her attention elsewhere. He followed her gaze outside to the gliding parachute. "Delta Force must be having a Sunday training exercise."

"But there's nobody strapped in the parachute," she said, getting up and walking over to the glass wall.

The white canopy panels reminded Alejandro of a swan, elegant and princely, gliding smoothly down to earth. It passed directly over their heads, made a hundred-and-eighty-degree turn into the wind, and toppled onto the grass.

Going to the chute, Alejandro, known to Pollack only by his code name Chilebean, asked the sergeant, "Does it work like this every time?"

Gathering up the canopy and enfolding it within its own lines, Pollack said, "Yeah. It's a picture-perfect operation all the time." He stopped gathering the chute and said as an afterthought, "Unless you try to use it in high winds. These babies proved highly effective when the company guys used them for drops in Afghanistan and Pakistan."

Helping him wrap it, Chilebean said, "I need to borrow a few of them for a couple of days."

Pollack went about his work, his brow lowered in concentration. "Well, guess you're going to have to contact someone high in the Agency, DEA, or Army, 'cause sure as shit ain't no one here with the authority to lend 'em out."

Seaver plucked the cheroot from his mouth, spit out a piece of tobacco, and asked the sergeant, "Ever read anything about Parapoint in any civilian magazines or newspapers?"

Anchoring the equipment under his boots, Pollack studied the sky thoughtfully. "Yeah, a while back I read an article in the *New York Times* about how we supplied the Mujahadin. I think there was something in *Aviation Week,* too."

"Parapoint's maximum load is a thousand pounds?" Chilebean asked.

"Yes," the soldier answered, "at least this new model. The early ones handled a lot less."

Chilebean's mental calculations told him that worked out to 2,200 kilos a chute. Five chutes, 11,000 kilos of China White. "Can four or five chutes be deployed at the same time and guided in by one transmitter?"

"Don't see why not, if they're deployed all at once. I mean, shoved out real fast," Pollack said.

Chilebean looked at Mother Hen and asked, "Wanna go into the parachute business?"

Standing at the glass wall, watching the three men gathering up the parachute, Fiona Lee realized that she had never before appreciated just how big a soccer field was. Watching them lugging the clumsy bundle off the field, she focused her attention on the man in the middle and thought, He's got a cute behind.

By three o'clock that afternoon the soccer game between Delta Force and DEA instructors was in its second half. Delta Force was leading 1–0.

Sergeant Pollack led Alejandro and Seaver along a long corridor muffled by floral carpeting. A distant radio played country music, and the agreeable smells of cooking roasts and browning potatoes filtered the air. Pollack moved ahead of them and opened a heavy door, motioning them inside. Once they had entered and the door closed, the sergeant rushed outside to the game.

They found themselves in a rosewood-paneled room decorated with western art and floor-to-ceiling bookcases. Navajo rugs were scattered on the dark wood floors, and the worn leather chairs reeked of the smoke of expensive cigars and the fainter scent of old money.

Ted Porges stood up from the oval table to greet his former student, still known to him only as Chilebean. Shaking his student's hand, he asked, "How goes it out there in the real world?"

"Ain't a day in the sun," Chilebean said, noticing with some shock how much Porges had aged in the last few years. Settling onto a chair, he noticed five flat packets of aluminum foil on the table in front of Porges. His smile lost its warmth, and he asked only half-jokingly, "Are we doing some blow today?"

"Not we, you," Porges said.

Andy Seaver turned on his seat to face Chilebean. "If you're going to get in tight with them, you're going to have to learn how to fake a blow. Because at some point one of the scumbags might insist on you doing a line."

Porges nodded his head in agreement. "That's their acid test to see if you're a cop."

"How come you never taught me before?" Chilebean asked, reaching out and pushing over one of the foils.

" 'Cause you never had the need to know before," Porges said, picking up a remote control from his lap and aiming it at the bookcase. A portion of the bookshelves slid back to reveal a screen. "Now watch closely; and remember—the hand is quicker than the eye."

The screen filled with a surveillance film, across the bottom of the frame the DEA index number, date, and time digitally whizzing by in seconds, minutes, hours. A hotel room; three people were sitting on a sofa in front of a glass coffee table that contained a suitcase full of money. Two of them were black males in their late twenties, well dressed, in a conservative fashion that said middle class and nonthreatening. One of them had a big gap between his front teeth, the other wore a kelly green tie over a brown shirt. The third person was an attractive black woman in her mid-thirties; her hair was cropped close to her head and she wore a Chanel suit and accessories. She was watching Green Tie run a stack of bills through the electronic currency counter. "It's all there," she said.

"But we have to make sure, don't we?" said Gaptooth. Green Tie glanced sideways at her. "You might still be the Man." Gaptooth inched closer to her, reaching out and caressing her breast, saying softly, "I'd be more trusting if I come in your mouth."

Slapping away the offending hand, she said, "If you need reassurance, come in your mother's mouth."

Gaptooth's nostrils flared in anger. His hand moved back as if to slap her.

Green Tie looked up from counting and announced, "It's all here." Staring at the woman, he said, "We could just whack her and take the money."

"You'd never get off the floor alive, and you know it," she said, slapping down the suitcase's lid. "I've had enough of your uptown nigger bullshit. Either we deal now, or me and the green are out of here."

Green Tie flipped the lid back up, contemplating the stacks of money. He slid a silver-foil packet out of his inside pocket and gave it to her, saying, "We never deal with anyone who won't take a hit with us."

She took the foil, looking at it with open suspicion.

Gaptooth got up off the sofa and stood a few feet away, watching her, folding his arms tightly across his chest. "Don't sweat it, sister. It's not a hot shot."

Passing the foil back to Green Tie, she said, "You first. I wouldn't want to blow a slab cocktail."

"You gotta have trust, sister," Green Tie said, opening the foil and tapping cocaine onto the table. He pulled a hundred-dollar bill from one of the stacks in the suitcase, folded it in half, and kneaded the drug into a line. That done, he rolled the bill into a straw.

The woman got up and stood next to Gaptooth.

Bending to the line, Green Tie stuck the rolled-up bill in his nostrils and sucked up the drug. The hit rolled his eyes back into his head. Grimacing pleasure, he smacked his lips and said, " 'At be fine shit, sister." Straightening, he passed the half-closed packet to her.

She tapped the rest of the drug onto the back of her left hand and handed the empty foil to Gaptooth.

Chilebean leaned forward, watching intently.

The woman passed her hand under her nose as if savoring the aroma, at the same time gliding the tip of her tongue around the white line as if she were trying sexually to tempt herself. She danced her tongue slowly over her fingertips and took her three middle fingers into her mouth, sucking them. And then, in one fluid motion, she snorted the drug into her nostril, threw down her hand, tossed back her head, rolled her eyes up into her head, and sighed contentedly.

"She took the hit!" Chilebean exclaimed.

"No, she didn't," Porges said, aiming the remote at the screen and rewinding the film. He fast-forwarded it to the moments before the hit, pushed the slow-motion button, and ordered, "Now, watch closely."

Alejandro noticed that the woman's self-excitation with her fingers had distracted the dopers because it momentarily turned them on. He also noticed that the sniffing sound came at the exact moment that her head snapped back, her eyes rolled, and her hand fell from her face, one fluid motion.

"You get it?" Seaver said intently.

"Let me see it again," Chilebean said.

Porges aimed the remote. After viewing it three more times, Chilebean said, "Instead of snorting it in, she blows air out at the same time she hurls her face back, and throws her hand down."

"You got it," Porges said. "The force of air from her nose, at the exact moment her hand is hurled downward, scatters the cocaine. The granules are tiny so that when they're scattered they're invisible. The dopers see exactly what they wanted to see, her doing a line."

"What happens if she can't stand up and has to do the blow sitting down?" Chilebean asked. "There's no hand motion to scatter the dope."

"Look," Porges said, and did a line sitting down. When done, he looked at his student and said, "You cup your hand around the straw, hiding your mouth. You still do everything in one motion, only you blow the stuff away with your mouth. It's harder to do and takes more practice." He looked at his old student grimly. "Always remember to think of some small diversion to get their attention away from your mouth. The way that undercover grabbed their attention by licking her fingers was perfect. You only need a second or two." Porges pushed the remaining foils across the table to Chilebean. "Now you're going to practice until it becomes second nature." He pulled out a drawer in the table, took a handful of packets, and dumped them on the table.

Unwrapping one, Chilebean said, "This isn't coke."

"Sugar. It's against the law to do dope," Seaver said with a grin.

During the flight from Charlottesville back to New York that evening, Alejandro sat by a window staring down at the shadows creeping over the lush Virginia landscape, thinking of his recurring dream. It was always night, and he was aboard Cleopatra's barge. The purple sails were billowing in the soft breeze, and half-naked slaves, adorned in gold, moved about serving Cleopatra and Che-Che Morales. Huddled on the barge's bow were many of the women he had been to bed with. They were watching him and whispering to each other. Each time the head eunuch would start to pass him and enter the queen's tent, and each time just as he pushed the flap back to step inside, the eunuch's *yataghan* would pierce his heart, and Alejandro would leap up in bed with the cold sweat of fear at his hairline.

Andy Seaver had inclined his seat and was stretched out with his eyes closed, thinking of Wilma Galt, his workaholic banquet manager lady friend who had spent a good part of her life making fancy parties at the Hotel Barrington for rich ladies she despised. Mulling over their five years together, he found it difficult to believe that she totally bought his legend that he was the lead clerical at Pickpocket and Confidence. But, he wondered, did it matter?

"Tired?" Alejandro asked.

"A little," Seaver replied drowsily. "How's your research on Cleopatra going?"

"Okay. She was the world's first feminist."

Seaver opened his eyes, looked over at his undercover. "There's a problem with doing those fake hits." His tone suggested a greater degree of concern than his words.

"You mean I might really have to take a hit."

"Something like that. There are not many rules about what we do, but there are a few written in concrete. First, if an undercover is forced to ingest a narcotic agent, he or she must get themselves to medical attention, forthwith."

"And second?"

"Three real hits and you're out of a job."

Alejandro leaned his seat back. "I'll keep my nose empty."

— 10 —

LIEUTENANT SAL ELIA WAS holed up inside the Unified Intelligence office on the eleventh floor of One Police Plaza. He had listened several times to the tape of Che-Che Morales and Alejandro's conversation. Blowups of the pair walking out of the tire lot were pinned to the cork board that hung on the wall over his desk. The more he viewed the video and listened to the tapes, the more convinced he was that Alejandro was worth getting to know. It was well known within the intelligence community that Che-Che prided himself on being unconnected to the human race. He had no known girlfriends, boyfriends, family, or close friends. The very few semitrusted members of his crew were terrified of him. There were many wiretaps on file of Che-Che's people confiding their fears of him to each other. It was known that many of the narco crowd had imported anacondas from the

Amazon to use as enforcement tools. Elia wondered where the hell they kept the snakes when they were not busy.

Wiretaps had also revealed that Morales did not hesitate to use his constrictors as punishment. Soon after he obtained his pets, stray animals started to disappear from the neighborhood of Lopez's tire store.

Leaning back in his chair, staring up at the photographs, Elia thought, This guy is the only person I've ever seen get close to Che-Che, talk to him as an equal. He listened to the tape again, then shut it off, thinking, Yeah, this guy is most definitely worth getting to know.

Sal Elia was a medium-size man in his late thirties. His thick neck and squat appearance gave him the impression of being fat. He wasn't. Beneath the loose sport shirt and jeans was a broad-shouldered, muscled body as tough as rawhide. Part of Elia's exercise ritual every morning was doing forty push-ups. He had spent all of his sixteen years in the Job working the Junk Squad, as the Narcotics Division was sometimes referred to.

Elia had an abiding faith in his country, the Department, God, and the New York Giants. He was a gentle, soft-spoken man who had set himself a life's mission of putting away as many dopers as he could before he retired and moved his family far away from slime city. His twin sister, Audrey, had OD'ed on heroin two days after her sixteenth birthday. She had taken the drug on a dare. With his sister's death had come a painful emptiness in Elia's soul that was quickly filled with hatred for those who dealt drugs.

After listening to Alejandro tell Che-Che how he had come upon the information regarding the Lloyds of Medellin shipment, Elia picked up the "wet" intelligence report, so called because it was prepared quickly, without an in-depth background investigation into the subject. It was meant only to provide fast intelligence for those in the "need to know" chain.

He read: "Alejandro Monahan, M/H/ 32–36 years. A singer in the club Environment, which is frequented by multikey dealers. Resides at Two Fifth Avenue. U.S. citizen. Utilities listed under A. Monahan. Unlisted telephone listed same name. No record D&B or Personal Credit Bureau. Pays all bills promptly. No credit cards, no savings accounts. No criminal records that name this department. NCIC, no record; FBI, no record; DEA, no record; Narcotics Control Center, no record. Owns 1989 Porsche, registered A. Monahan."

Letting the report fall from his hand, Elia thought, Where does a guy like this get hold of secret information like that to warn Che-Che? A two-bit Latino crooner who can afford a Porsche. Looking up at the photograph of Alejandro, he felt the exciting tingle of the hunter who has sighted his prey.

Sweat glistened on Too Tall Paulie's chest and beads of perspiration sprinkled his hairline as he danced in his office, his lithe body flowing easily to the rhythm of his feet. He had been dancing for almost thirty minutes, venting his anger on the plywood, ranting to himself over and over, They turned the goddamn ship around, and they murdered three of my undercovers. And he knew with cop certainty that the dopers had gotten a line into his office, somewhere.

A knock sounded at the door, and Dave Katz walked in, followed behind by Lieutenant Sal Elia. Not wanting to interrupt their boss, they padded across the office and sat on the sofa against the wall that held the chief's twenty-eight-year collection of police memorabilia.

"What's up?" the boss asked, slipping into quarter time.

Elia said, "We know who blew the Medellin shipment."

Without breaking his time signature, the dancer said, "Talk to me, Lou," using the diminutive of "lieutenant" that was common in the Job.

Elia opened the folder he had brought with him, took out the "wet" intelligence report and the transcript of the roving bug that the pigeons had picked up, index number 93-486-7 UI, and the video of the meeting and placed them on Too Tall Paulie's desk.

"Read them to me," the boss ordered, breathing hard.

When Elia finished reading the boss the reports and showing him the video, Assistant Chief Inspector Paul Burke stepped off the plywood circle and walked thoughtfully into his private toilet.

Listening to the running tapwater, Elia whispered to the XO, "He really looks pissed."

"He is."

Walking out of the toilet toweling himself, Too Tall Paulie looked across the room at the lieutenant and asked, "What do you suggest we do about it, Lou?"

"I've spoken to my undercovers who work the discos. This guy Alejandro is supposedly tight with Che-Che. They're amigos from the same town in Mexico. He's a hot number right now trying to break into the big-league music business. According to my people, he's not in the *business*."

Maybe he isn't, the chief thought, angrily tossing his towel into the bathroom, but he sure as shit appears to have a line into *my* business, and I'm going to make it my personal business to find out how.

Elia continued: "My people tell me he's a pussy hound."

"So?" Katz asked warily.

"This guy is used to rich ladies who get turned on by him, who'll give him a fast blow job in a car, or a one-night stand—and then they're history. I want to insert a female undercover to work this guy."

"I'm against it," Katz blurted out impulsively.

"Why?" asked the boss, buttoning his shirt.

Easing his rumpled polyester suit to the edge of the couch's cushion, Katz began, "Boss, every time we've inserted a female undercover to work a doper one on one we've ended up with a major problem called . . . fucking. They've invariably ended up in bed together, and we've ended up having to shit-can a major case, then retire the undercover on a disability pension because of a bullshit job-related stress syndrome."

"I have female undercovers who he won't be able to seduce," Elia offered.

Katz glared at Elia and said, in an almost pleading way, "This guy isn't going to be turned on by any of your lesbian undercovers, Lou, no matter how much thigh they show." Looking directly at his boss, he added, "I've been burned too many times, Paulie."

Taking his time knotting his tie, Too Tall Paulie said, "Captain Katz is right. We've had too many problems in the past with male-female one-on-ones."

"What do you want me to do with this guy, then?" Elia asked.

"Forget 'im. Your people already told you he's not part of any crew. He probably did overhear the DEA informant running off at the mouth, and hauled ass uptown to warn his fuckin' amigo."

Two hours later Too Tall Paulie crossed Police Plaza and walked under the Municipal Building's vaulted archway. Glancing at the line of Nigerian peddlers hawking designer rip-offs, he thought, A Rolex for fifteen dollars. You gotta be a real schmuck to believe *that*. Once out on Centre Street, he stopped with the rest of the lunchtime crowd, waiting for the light to change. When it did, he dashed across the street and entered City Hall Park. Rows of city limousines were parked in front of New York's center of power. A large, boisterous crowd of Bensonhurst parents were surging up against police barricades, shouting their opposition to the "rainbow curriculum" in their local elementary school.

Leaving the park, he turned north on Broadway in search of one of the city's scarcest resources, a working telephone. He passed several, all with their receivers dangling by their armored cords, all of which had been hurled down by frustrated consumers as a warning to others not to bother. He passed bars and restaurants with telephones. But street-smart cops did not use telephones in bars and restaurants around police headquarters and City Hall. Hurrying along, he found himself dodging the army of panhandlers who left their cardboard igloos to work the noontime crowd.

He finally discovered a working telephone on Franklin Street. Four people were on line ahead of him. He stepped over to the frankfurter peddler and ordered, "The works."

The peddler flipped open a steam tray, speared a frank, and set it into a bun, brushed on a hearty coat of mustard, dumped in a clump of sauerkraut and red onions, wrapped it in a napkin, and said, " 'At'll be a dollar."

Hot dog in hand, Too Tall Paulie joined the line. When his turn came, he inserted a quarter into the slot, made a silent prayer that it still worked, dialed a local number, and said to the woman who answered, "The Cowboy, please."

"The cartels operate through cells controlled by an underboss, five to seven managers, and assorted workers. The underboss is responsible for the safety of the drugs and the money. The two are usually stored separately in two different safe houses," Porges was telling Mary Beth as he stood in front of an organizational chart of the New York branch of the Calí cartel. "All orders for drugs are made through coded telephone calls directly to Colombia. In surveillance films you'll always see underbosses walking around the city lugging cloth bags filled with quarters. Despite what civilians think, these underbosses are not flamboyant characters dripping in gold chains. They live modestly, without attracting attention. And they're not all Hispanic. But all of them are trained in countersurveillance."

He paused thoughtfully, looked at the undercover code-named Mary Beth, and said, "The cartels couldn't operate without the help of lawyers, accountants, bankers. Trust no one, Mary Beth. Play 'em all."

The telephone rang. "Excuse me," he said, and picked up the receiver. "Hello?"

"How's Mary Beth doing?" Too Tall Paulie asked, biting into his frankfurter and dropping strands of sauerkraut on the lapel of his suit jacket.

— 11 —

THE AIR WAS MOIST AND heavy. A thick cloud cover obscured the sun. Thunder occasionally rumbled to the north.

Not many mourners had come to the Tuesday-morning funeral at Saint Gregory's Roman Catholic Church in Hopewell Junction to hear the Reverend John McAllister eulogize Bonnie Haley, the CI registered in DEA files under the name *Cupcake*.

The priest spoke kind, gentle words meant to comfort a grieving family. He spoke of a beautiful, happy girl, growing up in a loving home, and how she had left after graduating high school to pursue her dream of becoming an actress.

The priest did not know that Bonnie had had no intentions of being an actress. She had come to Manhattan because she did not want to squander her beautiful face and body on some boring man from Hopewell Junction, some potbelly slob who plopped down every Sunday to guzzle beer and mindlessly watch television.

Bonnie needed more out of life. She needed a successful man who could give her a life in a duplex overlooking Central Park, winter and summer vacations in exotic places, maids, and nannies for her kids. The priest also did not know that by the time Bonnie was twenty-five the mere thought of having to go down on another man revolted her, causing her to retch. She had discovered that booze and cocaine made it easier for her to open her mouth in her increasingly desperate quest for the perfect husband.

Two of Bonnie's high school girlfriends wept in their pews as their husbands attempted to quiet their fidgety children.

The priest eulogized: "So loving, so full of goodness, that God wanted her at His side."

Bullshit, thought DEA agent Frank Christopher, a tall ex-Marine whose sharply defined features had caused him to be given the street name "Dick Tracy." He had busted Bonnie five years ago on a five-gram buy operation. One night in the Federal Detention Facility for Women had convinced her that life on the inside was not for her. Looking down the aisle at the coffin, Christopher admitted to himself that he had come to like Cupcake. There was a good-natured warmth about her. She never forgot his birthday or Christmas. The few good ties that he had were all presents from her. He felt guilty; he should have pulled her out long ago. The booze and coke had begun to cloud her judgment, making her careless where carelessness meant death. He knew that the guilt pangs he was feeling now would evaporate, because in the world in which he lived, he was a federal agent doing his job, and Cupcake had been nothing more than an instrument helping him to do that job.

Judith Stern took a handkerchief from her black Gucci pocketbook and dabbed her eyes, thinking that she would rather be in bed with Hector tongueing her clit than have to suffer through all this bullshit.

Judith Stern had been named after her grandfather Joseph, who had come to the States from Russia in 1919 and started the family business, G. Stern, Bathing Garments. When Joe died, Judith's father inherited the business and eventually brought in her two brothers, Sam and Jay. Judith had gone to an exclusive Manhattan Jewish school and graduated from Barnard. She had done graduate work in math and economics at Columbia University. After graduation she was expected to get married and have a family. But Judith wanted no part of getting married. She wanted to make money. She had tried to persuade her father to take her into the business. He was adamant; it was unseemly for an educated Jewish woman to go into the rag business. During one particularly loud fight with her father, she had stormed out of their Locust Valley home and never returned. A week later she went to work for one of her father's competitors.

She had met Hector Pizzaro in Bolivia nine years ago. They had quickly become lovers. Once she'd found out what Hector's "business" was, she'd had the idea to start a counterintelligence service for the drug cartels. Quality information for quality money. And this would be a business she could run better than anyone else because of her skills in research and finance.

Tucking her handkerchief into the sleeve of her Chanel dress, she glanced at the man in the pew to her right. He was wearing an expensive off-the-rack suit, properly coordinated with a light blue shirt and dark blue tie. Kneeling forward, she focused on his clasped hands. He wore a large school ring. She smiled to herself, knowing that only the less prestigious colleges sold rings like that, on the assumption that its worth was proven by its massiveness and ornateness. His hair was cut short in an almost military fashion. Stretching her neck, she looked down at his shoes. They were shiny, black, and heavy. Cop shoes. If he'd been on the street making a buy, he'd be wearing Italian loafers. But he wasn't, and the shoes and college ring fit the profile of a DEA agent. Still, she had to be sure. She continued studying him. A bulge at the cuff of his trousers on his right ankle caught her attention: he was wearing an ankle holster.

She felt she could reasonably conclude that the dead woman had been a DEA informant—and that Roberto Barrios had a *mucho* serious problem. Her mind went into overdrive.

"Eternal rest grant to her, O Lord," the priest intoned, leaving the altar to sprinkle holy water over the coffin.

Across the street from the church, two men inside a panel truck with two-way mirrors were recording the scene on video cameras. Three other men were walking the blocks surrounding the church, carrying briefcases with concealed cameras, snapping license plates.

On cue from the funeral director, pallbearers appeared and solemnly gathered around the bier. On signal from the director they took hold of the handles on the casket and rolled it on its wheeled support to the entrance. Mourners left their pews and fell in behind the cortege.

Stopping at the top of the church steps, the pallbearers raised the coffin onto their shoulders and carefully carried it down the steps and over to the waiting hearse. Hector Pizzaro's men recorded the scene, zooming in on the mourners' faces.

Frank Christopher waited at the end of the line, anxious to get back to the office. There was a lot of paper waiting for him. He also desperately needed to find a replacement for Cupcake. Suddenly he became conscious of a seductive perfume and the press of breasts against his back. "Don't turn," a woman whispered. "Wait until everyone is gone before you leave. Che-Che's people are across the street taking pictures."

Christopher didn't hesitate or even look around but peeled away from the mourners and knelt in a pew.

Judith Stern, standing in the shadows, waited until he had

slipped away. She was the last of the mourners to leave the church. Standing at the top of the steps, she pulled her handkerchief out of her sleeve, dabbed her eyes a final, insincere time, and walked down the steps in her spiked heels, thinking, Roberto has become a real liability.

"Well?" Pizzaro asked, looking out from behind his office desk at Judith, who had just returned from the funeral.

She walked across the room and slowly lowered herself onto the chair at the side of his desk. She put her pocketbook on the floor, crossed her legs, and said, "Roberto Barrios's girlfriend was a DEA informer."

Pizzaro leaned back, raking his fingers through his hair. "I'll have him taken care of right away."

"By whom?"

"One of the people in the network."

"But if the project we're working on takes off, we're going to need him."

Pizzaro's expression left no room for argument. "He has to go, Judith."

"Yes, but not right away. Let's get all the mileage we can out of him before we . . . retire him."

He thought about what she said and finally replied, "Okay. But not too long. Pussymen are dangerous."

Reaching into her pocketbook, she smiled at him. *"Sí, jefe."* She took out a gold heart-shaped compact and began fixing her makeup. "And may I suggest that we not use one of our regular people. We don't need witnesses."

"They're all loyal."

She shook her head slowly. "That's today. But what about tomorrow when one of them might be staring at twenty-five to life in a federal prison?"

Pizzaro smiled, a not terribly pleasant sight. "You're always one step ahead, aren't you?"

"That's why you pay me so much money, darling. That, and you know what?" she said, puckering her lips at him.

Lighting a cigarette, Pizzaro said, "I'll give the job to a private contractor."

She smiled back at him. "Why waste the money? I'll take care of it."

Andy Seaver spooned a glob of sour cream and chives out of the silver bowl and plopped it into his baked potato. Looking across at Wade Hicks, the CIA's liaison with the NYPD, he observed, "This place is always crowded."

They were lunching in the Chez Julien dining room of the Barrington, a formal room filled with muffled conversations and careless laughter. Wade Hicks was a big man with a fleshy face and meaty chin; he looked around at his surroundings approvingly and sipped at his Black Label.

"So how's Breckenridge doing?" Seaver asked, slicing into his prime rib.

"I believe he's going to be one of the truly great directors."

"What's going to happen to the Agency people who tried to scuttle his confirmation?"

Hicks's mouth tightened. "Nothing."

"I figured he'd let some time go by and then engage in some Washington-style bloodletting."

Hicks smiled. "That's not his way." Contemplating the red juices oozing out of his filet mignon, he added, "But I imagine there will be some reevaluation of priorities and realignment of positions. Meaning payback time, Andy."

"Naturally." Seaver forked potato into his mouth.

"How is everything in the Job?"

"The faces change, but the script remains the same. When I came in an arresting officer had to make out three blue and four white arrest cards for every collar he made. The Palace Guard streamlined the arrest procedure in '71 and did away with the arrest cards. Guess what?"

"They streamlined it again in '93 and are back with three blues and four whites."

"You got it," Seaver said. Toying with the stem of his wineglass, he confided, "We're training our counterterrorist units in resupplying cutoff police units in the event of a civil insurrection."

"Good idea," Hicks said, slicing another piece of meat.

"Like your outfit, we have to plan for every possible contingency."

"Naturally."

"We were wondering," Seaver said casually, scraping out the dregs of his potato skin, "if you might be able to lend us a Parapoint delivery system. Just for training purposes, you understand."

Hicks's eyes flashed at his luncheon companion. "I'd have to go upstairs with it."

"Of course," Seaver responded in a reassuring way.

They fell silent as the waiter cleaned off their table. They studied the dessert menu. "The raspberry cheesecake is great," Seaver suggested.

"Then the cheesecake it'll be. After all, you're paying." After the waiter had gone, Hicks drank the last of his wine and asked casually, "Do you have many first- or second-generation Cubans in the Department?"

"A few." Seaver braced himself for what was coming.

"We're looking for some good people who know Havana and Ciego de Avila Province."

Seaver took out a small memo pad and made a note on it. "I'll run through the Force Record File and check."

Slicing into the creamy cake, Hicks said, "If we borrowed them, we wouldn't want them leaving a paper trail."

"No problem. One telephone call would transfer them to the Police Academy on a ninety-day temporary assignment; it could be extended indefinitely. And if you liked, we could even black out the message in the telephone log."

"That might be nice," Hicks said, licking his fork. Protocol dictated that whoever called the meeting pick up the tab. So when the waiter presented the bill, Seaver glanced at the total and slid his corporate credit card into the leather billfold.

"Great lunch, Andy. Thanks."

"My pleasure," Seaver said, proffering his guest one of his cheroots.

Hicks took one. Taking his time lighting up, he said, "I understand you paid a visit to the Hacienda over the weekend."

"Yeah, I just love those Blue Ridge Mountains," Seaver replied, wondering how much Hicks had been told about his activities there. And his companion.

He walked his friend outside and saw him into a taxi. Back inside the hotel, he went directly to the banquet manager's office on the mezzanine floor, a large space furnished in reproduction French classical and adorned with arrangements of freshly cut flowers. A couple were sitting at a desk, selecting place settings for their wedding. Seaver stood by a large table, idly flipping through large photo albums of dishes and silverware as well as floral and other decorations. Then he strolled past the manager's glass front office, glancing inside. A woman sat behind an ornate desk. Their eyes met with secret recognition and fell away. He walked out, went downstairs to the registration desk, and said to the man in the morning coat, "Harry Parker, I forget my room number."

Morning Coat input the name into the computer, announced, "Suite fifteen oh six," turned, plucked an antique key from the pigeonhole, and handed it to him.

The suite had a terrace that overlooked the city. Bracing his arms on the railing, he looked out at the view and sighed, wondering if Alejandro was up yet. He heard the door open and turned.

A tall woman dressed in a smartly tailored black dress was rushing toward him. It was Wilma Galt, his workaholic girlfriend, her face aglow with pleasure as she fell into his arms. "I missed you."

The heat of their kisses filled him with a warm glow. Their bodies pressed close; their tongues danced. She ran her hand up his leg, stroking him rock hard. "I love the feel of you," she said, biting his lower lip and at the same time rubbing his bulge against her body.

He began working down her zipper. "Not out here," she said, taking his hand and pulling him into the bedroom.

Later, as they lay in bed exhausted by the fierceness of their lovemaking, she played with his penis and murmured, "How the mighty have fallen."

"Keep doing that and it'll come roaring back."

She turned toward him, leaning on her side and watching his expression. "I miss you a lot, Andy. I want you to know that I don't telephone you at your office anymore because every time I do I'm told you are on patrol." She looked at him. "Why does a clerical man have to go out on patrol?"

Seaver managed a suitably bitter and convincing laugh. "You don't understand the police department. I have the responsibility for keeping the time records—which means I have to go around to all the courts, checking on the appearances of the detectives assigned to the office. I prepare the roll calls for the entire week, which means I have to attend a lot of staffing conferences on the disposition of assets. And, I'm also stuck with the responsibility of visiting complainants to take their statements and forwarding them on to the assigned detective."

"Oh, my," she said, looking down at the erection in her hand.

Stroking it, she asked, "Do you ever think we'll get off this tread-mill we're on and have a normal life?"

"One day," he said, "one day," and rolled on top of her will-ing body.

Research and Analysis occupied the top floor of a seven-story drab factory building five blocks north of the Holland Tunnel. Shortly after three o'clock on that beautiful summer afternoon, Seaver walked into the ratty first-floor reception area decorated in peeling imitation veneer, imitation leather, and plastic flow-ers. The woman sitting behind an old green metal desk looked up at him and asked, "May I help you, sir?"

Seaver looked at the sign on the wall—COPEX INDUS-TRIES—pulled out his credentials, and handed them to her. She flipped open the case and typed his name into the computer. His photograph and pedigree came onto the screen.

"Date of appointment?" she asked.

"January 1, 1962."

"What was your class number in the Academy?"

"Two."

"What was your patrolman's shield number?"

"Five five nine three."

"What is your current assignment?"

"Pickpocket and Confidence."

Seaver rode the freight elevator to the top floor. He thought of Wilma and how their relationship had developed over the years into one of lies that skillfully skirted important questions, like love and a life together. They had met at the wedding of a mutual friend, one of those extravaganzas that seem to go on for days. They'd escaped early from the wedding banquet and ended up in an old jazz club in the Fifties that Seaver had been going to since he was old enough to drink.

He and Wilma were a good fit. He'd never been married. She'd been married to a nice guy who had a big booze problem that had led to a divorce several years ago. He'd known, almost from the first, that he loved her. And when he retired from the Job he was going to sit her down and tell her so. But would she wait that long? he often worried.

Stepping off the elevator, he walked along the concrete corridor toward the computer room, a glass-enclosed area with rows of computer banks, their reel-to-reels spinning and jerking their own strange dances. The black security tag trimmed in silver that Seaver had clipped to his jacket did not have his photograph or his name, only the Roman numerals *IX* in bold silver script. This was the Intelligence Division's top security clearance card with a magnetic strip on the back that opened all doors in the Land of Trick Mirrors. Not many people were authorized to wear the black tag, and the sight of one always caused quick, curious looks at the wearer.

As he entered the computer room he became aware of the soft hum of air-conditioning. There were six rows of data banks and a dozen carrels, tall, partitioned desks with a shelf over the flat, enclosed area. All the carrels faced the data banks, the backs of their chairs flush with a wall, thus preventing prying eyes from seeing the computer screens. There were laser printers on the shelves above the carrels' flat writing surfaces.

Seaver squeezed in behind a carrel's desk and switched on the machine. He signed on by inputting his tax registry number, his special operations identification number, and his mother's maiden name, Slingland. *XXXXXX* flashed in the screen's upper right-hand corner, granting him access to all data banks. Inputting the access code for magazines and periodicals, he typed: "Parapoint Delivery System."

The following scrolled onto the screen:

"The CIA's Secret War in Afghanistan"—*Newsweek* magazine—March 2, 1987, Index, 474–87

"The Covert War"—*New York Times Sunday Magazine*—April 9, 1989, Index, 511–89

"CIA's Secret Army—Delta Force and Navy Seals"—*Aviation Week*—February 1, 1987, Index 173–87

End of List.

He could have gotten that information at any public library by checking out the *Reader's Guide to Periodical Literature*. But after writing down the index numbers of the magazines, he inputted the access code for the Department's secret Force Record File and called up all members of the service, Cuban ancestry, with any connection to Havana and Ciego de Avila Province.

Twenty-three names, shield numbers, and commands appeared. He pressed the Print button, and the laser printer churned out the hard copy. He knew all too well that there were those few in the Job who were authorized to call up the daily inquiries input into all data banks. But he knew how to brush over his electronic footprints. He took the printout, tucked it into his briefcase, and left, heading for the library.

The woman behind the desk wore octagon-shaped glasses, jeans, and a Grateful Dead T-shirt. He passed her the call slips; she looked at his black tag, said, "Yes, sir," and disappeared inside a maze of steel bookcases.

Sixteen minutes later, alone in the duplicating room, Seaver was slipping copies of the articles on Parapoint into his case when his cellular phone went off. He unfolded it and answered, "Hello?"

"That was quick," Hicks said, adding, "I spoke to some of my people. I got those toys you wanted."

"Appreciate it. And I got those names you wanted."

"And it's kosher on both ends, right? See you soon," Hicks said, and disconnected.

Seaver snapped his fingers, remembering that he had one more classified data bank to enter.

Back in the computer room, he squeezed into a carrel and signed on again, smiling to himself at Alejandro's suggestion for a legend to explain his possession of Parapoint. He reentered the

Force Record File and inputted: "Gay male members of service assigned to Intelligence or Narcotics Division."

A minute later he whisked the print out off the printer and tucked it into his briefcase. After doing that, he inputted his personal code, which effectively erased all traces of his log-on and inquiries. He switched off the machine and walked to the elevator with an unlit cheroot sticking out of his unsmiling mouth.

12

S HE SLEPT ON HER SIDE with the sheet molding the curves of her body and her dark brown hair spread over the pillow.

Alejandro turned and snaked his arm under her shoulder, cupping her full breast, gently kneading the nipple.

She moaned and shivered slightly in anticipation.

He pressed his body closer, sliding his other hand up between her legs and nestling it against her mound. Her skin was warm and smooth, and he could smell her perfume. He kissed the tender nape of her neck; for once he felt safe and at peace with himself.

He had finished his last performance around three that morning and had been leaving the club when a hand fell on his shoulder, causing him to turn. "I'm Joanne. And I just had to tell you how much I loved your singing." Her eyes were smiling at him.

He smiled back. "Hi." They both knew what they wanted; and she had ditched her date to get it.

They awoke around noon and made love again. After showering together, they dressed. By one o'clock they were sitting out on his terrace, drinking coffee and listening to the sounds of the city. Lifting her cup to her mouth, Joanne asked in bad Spanish, "*¿Cuandro algo vimos por una vez?*"

He laughed. "Are you trying to ask me when we'll see each other again?"

She flushed. "Yes."

He brushed a ribbon of hair from her forehead. "I'll call you. I really hate to have to cut this short, but I have a two-thirty rehearsal."

She looked at him, her face full of disappointment. She gulped down some coffee, put the mug on the glass top, and opened her pocketbook. She took out her business card, placed it down in front of him, and got up. "This number always reaches me."

He started to get up to walk to the front door with her, but she put her hand on his shoulder, nudging him back onto his seat. "I can see myself out." She stepped off the terrace into the living room, then turned and said, "See ya." She turned away quickly to hide the tears in her eyes.

When he heard the door slam, he picked up her card and, with real sadness, tore it in half. As he stared off at a rising plume of smoke in the distance, his eyes began to well up as he empathized with her loneliness. He sucked in a mouthful of air, tossed the pieces of the card into his coffee mug, and went inside. Something told him that he had to stop living this way, in the country without maps that undercovers lived in, alone and untrusting.

The sky was a soft blue and the breeze warm. A front had pushed through, making New York City's air quality momentarily "acceptable."

Alejandro, dressed in desert tan slacks, light gray sport shirt, and brown tasseled loafers, waited on the northwest corner of Fifth Avenue and Fifty-fourth Street, in front of the University Club.

A woman in her early forties with an elegant carriage walked out of the club to a waiting limousine, casting a sly glance in his direction.

"She liked what she saw," Barrios said, coming up behind him. "Let's walk," he suggested.

They strolled north, past elegant shops and apartment buildings with uniformed doormen. A laughing couple ran from Lucullus's Restaurant into a waiting livery stretch limo. Watching the woman lifting her legs inside, Barrios said, "If your system works for us, I might be able to offer you two points. But first you're going to have to tell me exactly what it is."

"Four points sounds fair to me."

Barrios sucked in his lip. "First you tell me how you're going to guarantee delivery."

"Parachutes."

Barrios's face showed real surprise and clear disbelief. "Parachutes?"

But when Alejandro explained about the Parapoint delivery system, Barrios's doubtful expression changed to one of keen interest. "How many keys a chute?"

"Twenty-two hundred, max."

"We can bring in more weight using other methods."

Alejandro stopped in front of Steuben Glass and looked at the splashing fountain. "But your other methods don't guarantee you delivery. You just had to turn back a boat because of a security leak. With my way, you dump your load sixty miles from a landing zone that you preselected. The chutes won't show on radar, and you don't need a lot of people."

"Our product comes from outside the States."

"So what? You could even file your flight plan with the FAA, fly into the States from wherever, dump your load, and your plane continues on to its scheduled destination. It lands with no drugs aboard. Once the dope is on the ground, it's no big deal to transship it to your distribution centers."

Looking around at the shoppers on Fifth, Barrios asked softly, "Tell me again how this parachute of yours works."

"It has a thing called a Ram Air canopy that looks like a floating wing. Instead of floating vertically down to earth, it glides in a slanting direction, beaming in on a hand-held homing transmitter that resembles a portable telephone."

"Yeah, but what makes it tick?"

"A black box attached under the parachute's canopy has an electronic homing device that's powered by a nickel cadmium battery. This black box controls the chute's steering lines, and directs it right to the transmitter that's sending out the homing signals."

Barrios was still skeptical. "And we can dump the product from thirty thousand feet?"

"'At's right."

"How do you know these things work?" Barrios asked, eyeing a passing woman.

"The CIA used them to supply guerrillas in Afghanistan and Central America. They used to drop their loads over Pakistan and the equipment would slant down to the Afghans."

A sharklike smile came over Barrios's bony face. "Those same ragheads are now peddling those weapons on the open market. Some of our Colombian friends have just bought some Stinger missiles from them."

"Looks like Uncle Sap stepped on his cock again."

Barrios nodded. "It's lucky for us that those assholes in Washington stay dumb."

They stopped with the herd for the light on Fifty-seventh Street. Alejandro glanced across the street at the familiar crestfallen man and little girl sitting on the sidewalk in front of Bergdorf Goodman's holding the tattered sign that read Homeless and Hungry.

The light changed.

Alejandro and Barrios stepped off the curb. Barrios nudged him with his elbow and asked, "You sure you can supply us with this equipment?"

"Absolutely. Everything but the plane and pilot. That'll be your job."

"Will you take part in the drops?"

"Initially, I'll be on the ground to make sure your guys use the equipment correctly. Then you're on your own."

Barrios's lips peeled back in an expression of contempt. " 'Fraid of getting your hands dirty?"

" 'Fraid of amigos with tequila mouths. The fewer people who know about me, the safer we all are."

They continued along in silence. As they were passing the Hotel Pierre on Fifth and Sixty-first, Barrios asked, "Where do you get the chutes from?"

Alejandro stopped suddenly and gave Barrios a cold look. "That's my business."

"Not if you want to come with us."

"We can talk about that later, after we agree on the money."

"We're gonna want a demonstration, and soon."

"Just tell me where and when."

"I'll let you know." He looked at him. "A friend of mine is going to want to talk to you. Seven o'clock tomorrow in the Sapphire Room of the Hotel Versailles."

"Does your friend have a name?"

"Hector."

Alejandro rushed home after his meeting with Barrios and went directly into the bedroom. He slid open the closet door, reached in for his makeup kit, and went into the bathroom.

He put the kit on top of the toilet tank and clicked it open. He took out a tube containing different-colored contact lenses and unscrewed the top. He slipped out a green pair and, after stretching open his left eye, slipped in the soft lens. He did the same with the other eye, then put the tube back in the kit. Next he removed a bottle of clear liquid glue and brushed it on over his chin. He put the bottle down on the sink, took out a neatly trimmed beard, and pressed it on over his chin, thinking, Nobody but Seaver gets to see the real me. He then glued on a mustache. That done, he closed up the kit and returned it to its place on the closet floor. He changed into a faded denim shirt and jeans, took a New York Mets baseball cap out of the closet, and left his apartment, heading for the basement garage.

Precision Industries was housed in four long cinder-block buildings with corrugated roofs along Route 110 in Farmingdale, Long Island, across the highway from a golf driving range. A fifteen-foot fence crowned with rolls of razor wire surrounded the compound, and high-intensity halogen lights were strategically strung out around the perimeter. Security guards manned the double gates, admitting only those whose names appeared on the daily visitors log.

It was late Tuesday afternoon when Alejandro drove up to Precision Industries checkpoint.

"May I help you, sir?" asked one of the guards, holding his clipboard at the ready.

"I'm Mr. A. Brown," Alejandro said. "I'm here to see Jim Hansen."

The guard studied the visitors log. "Who recommended you to Jim Hansen?"

"Mr. Wade Hicks," Alejandro said, wondering if he would ever get to meet the CIA's liaison. Over the years Hicks had arranged many similar appointments for Mr. A. Brown.

The guard said, "Jim will meet you outside of building one."

Hansen was bald and lean, with a hooked nose and a weathered face. He was waiting in the doorway with his thumbs hooked into his jeans pocket. His aviator's ankle boots were old but polished to a deep brown gloss.

Alejandro parked in the designated visitors parking space alongside the building's flower bed and got out, plopping his New York Mets baseball cap on his head.

"Hicks said you'd be coming our way," Hansen said, stepping out of the doorway to shake A. Brown's hand.

Alejandro followed him inside. Rows of parachutes hung limp from the ceiling, reminding Alejandro of ribless umbrellas. Workbenches stretched the length of the building. Workers packed parachutes into their containers, gingerly insuring that the shroud lines were not tangled and were properly aligned. Rockabilly blared from a tape deck on one of the workbenches.

Walking down the aisle, Alejandro asked, "How do these things work?"

"Simple. The canopy offers resistance to air, retarding the descent."

"How long have they been around?"

"A guy named Jacques Garnerin made the first jump in 1797. He dropped three thousand feet from a balloon."

Alejandro stopped to watch a woman packing a chute into its container.

Hansen said, "The people who do this are called riggers, and they're all certificated 'Airman' by the FAA."

Alejandro reached out and felt the canopy.

"It's a low-porosity nylon," Hansen explained, "and the shroud lines are made of polyester or Kevlar."

As they walked toward the rear of the parachute loft, Alejandro said, "Tell me about the Parapoint delivery system."

"It uses a Ram Air canopy that's rectangular. When it's deployed it looks kind of like a flying wing. The air rushes through the front of the chute and gives it an efficient glide ratio, causing it to swoop into the landing zone like a glider." Pausing alongside a rigger, he pointed. "The payload is loaded in the empty space between the shrouds. We call that space the store."

"What causes the chute to deploy?"

Hansen reached across the workbench and pulled over a packed rig. "The container has a row of grommets on the outside that secures it. A curved locking pin runs through the grommets. When the ripcord is pulled the locking pin is disengaged, opening the container, or the rig, as it's called. A pilot chute, which is spring-loaded inside the rig, pops out and acts as an anchor because its rate of descent is much slower than the main chute. As the rig falls away, the anchor remains almost stationary, pulling out what's called the bridle cord, which is attached to the main canopy, pulling it out of its rig, causing it to deploy and blossom."

"What about the guidance system?"

Hansen walked over to a cluttered tool bench that was set in between the workbenches, and after shuffling through tools and equipment, he pulled out a black box and a transmitter. He gestured "A. Brown" over to him.

"This is it," he said, picking up a screwdriver and taking the box apart. He then disassembled the handset. He took a silver pen out of his shirt pocket and pointed to the box. "Here is the power source, and here is the circuit board that receives the signals from the homing transmitter that controls the parachute's flight by reeling in and out the shroud lines." He gave Alejandro a detailed lesson on how the circuit boards worked, looked at him, and asked, "Any questions?"

A. Brown shook his head.

They walked off down the aisle.

Alejandro straightened his baseball cap. "Can anyone walk in here and buy parachutes?"

"Absolutely not. Our industry does a damn good job of policing itself. Not a day passes when some greaser don't walk into one of our showrooms around the country looking to buy parachutes. This industry only sells to legitimate companies, known and verifiable sportsmen, skydiving clubs, and government agencies, including the military, of course."

Alejandro rubbed his jaw thoughtfully. "Suppose someone wanted to set up a sting operation manufacturing Parapoint. What would it take?"

Hansen said confidently, "Couldn't be done. The aerodynamics of parachute manufacturing is not something you can learn in books or take a cram course in. It takes years to learn."

They continued along the aisle. A rigger was tapping a grommet with a ball-peen hammer. A purposeful expression tightened Alejandro's face. "Can you think of any way to set up a phony parachute company so that it would look legit?"

Lighting a cigarette, Hansen said, "You can't manufacture 'em, so you're going to have to buy them." He took a drag on his cigarette, blew the smoke up at a limp parachute, looked at the stranger with the fake beard and mustache and baseball hat with its brim down over his forehead, and said, "I assume you want to retain control over the system, forcing your clients to keep coming back to you."

"Yes."

"Take a cram course in rigging. Learn how to pack them. That way they'll be forced to come back to you."

"Where do I go to learn?"

"There are private instructors, and schools, all FAA certified." He took another drag. "I'm sure Mr. Hicks could make the necessary arrangements for you. That way you could set up a phony skydiving school."

"Would it be possible to buy your product without any identifying manufacturing marks?"

"We do it all the time for certain clients."

"Besides rigging, can you think of any other way I could control the longevity of the system, insuring that they would have to bring the complete system back to me?"

Hansen walked over to a large oyster shell on top of a desk in the corner. He took a final pull on his cigarette and thoughtfully mashed it out inside the shell. Turning, he brushed his palms across his bald head and said, "You could screw up the electronics, causing it to short out every few days."

He walked back over to a tool bench and picked up the black box's circuit board. He took it back to A. Brown and started to trace the circuitry with his pen while talking aloud to himself. "Cross the feeder line here so that it'll short after a few days, then remove this resistor, and . . . that way they'd have to bring it back to be rearmed." A satisfied smile crossed his mouth. "Yeah, that would do it, nicely."

"Couldn't their people fix it?"

"First, I don't know who their people are. But it makes no difference, because if they're not expert on Parapoint, they'd never find the problem. I'd show you how to rig the circuits."

Alejandro took off his cap and waved it vaguely in the air. "If strangers came 'round checking to see if you sold me Parapoint, how would you deal with it?"

"I stick with whatever story we agreed upon. You're not the first of Mr. Hicks's friends we've done business with, Mr. Brown."

"What would ten Parapoints cost me?"

"Three hundred fifty thousand. Since you are with Wade Hicks, your company would save the state and federal tax."

"I'll let you know where to deliver them."

"Let's go into my office," Hansen said, leading the way.

Sunlight speared through the windows of Hansen's corner office. His desk was covered in machine parts, invoices, and swatches of different-colored nylon. Miniature parachutes hung from the ceiling, and a large photograph of a smiling circle of free-falling skydivers was on the wall. Hansen walked behind his desk, pushed some parts out of the way, and lifted his blotter, sliding out a sheet of paper. Passing it to Alejandro, he said,

"Here is a list of my IRS-approved covert accounts. Wire-transfer the money into them, but no deposit can be over thirty-five thousand."

"Okay," Alejandro said, slipping the paper into his jeans pocket. "Now, how about us agreeing on a story for me—and then you teaching me how to sabotage Parapoint's electronics."

A clap of thunder and a flash of lightning splintered the sky Thursday afternoon, causing people to look up and quicken their step.

Alejandro took his time deciphering the old tombstones in Trinity Church's cemetery. He looked at the time: 12:50. He was a bit early for his one o'clock meeting with Seaver.

Traffic was moving freely along Broadway.

Alejandro wore his jeans and a blue T-shirt under a white cotton jacket. Tasseled loafers, no socks.

Tourists walked around the hallowed ground, snapping photographs. A gaggle of schoolchildren gleefully posed in front of Alexander Hamilton's pyramid-shaped monument.

After reading Robert Fulton's bronze bas relief, Alejandro walked over to the fence and looked across Broadway to the corner of Wall Street. A drug dealer was engaged in brief, furtive conversations with well-dressed men holding expensive briefcases. He watched as money was exchanged for packets of foil.

"The free enterprise system at work in the citadel of capitalism," Mother Hen said, coming up behind his deep undercover.

"The resident scumbucket dealing with the resident assholes," Alejandro said. He added curtly, "Let's get out of here."

They walked out of the churchyard, turned west into Rector Street, and crossed Trinity Place, heading for the vertical towers of Battery Park City.

"I'll be meeting with Hector this evening," Alejandro said.

"We believe the shooter in the Levi-DiLeo homicide was a dude named Hector. You can't miss him. He has a streak of white running down the center of his hair. If the Hector you're meeting is that Hector, he probably dyed the white out of his hair immediately after the hit."

Alejandro shook his head in disagreement. "Not necessarily. Most of these macho shooters are so arrogant and overconfident that they never give a second thought to being 'made' at the scene." Alejandro's eyes darted to his control. "I'll probably be 'in play' after meeting Hector. It won't be wise for us to meet again until this is over."

They fell silent, each man occupied with his own thoughts.

They knew that being "in play" was the most dangerous part of the operation for a deep one. It was during this period of time that the dopers' counterintelligence apparatus would be smelling out the undercover's legend, probing for the scent of cop.

"I was careful coming here," Alejandro said. "I rode up and down half a dozen elevators before walking over here."

"From now on only make contact through burst transmissions, unless you find yourself in deep shit, then telephone Control for the cavalry."

Alejandro walked over to the wagon of a pretzel vendor on the corner. After brushing mustard on a pretzel, he broke it in half and handed it to Mother Hen, saying, "I've ordered ten Parapoints."

"How much we talking about?"

"Three hundred fifty thousand." Alejandro passed him the slip of paper with the parachute manufacturer's bank accounts and told him Hansen's instructions regarding wire transfers into the accounts.

Tucking the slip into his pocket, Seaver asked, "What else you going to need?"

"I'm not sure, maybe another two hundred thousand to open a skydiving school."

"Getting you the money is easy, but how are you going to explain your sudden wealth to Che-Che and his crew?"

Alejandro had a ready answer. "I'll borrow on my apartment and car."

"No good," Seaver said, tossing a chunk of pretzel into his mouth. "You have no real credit rating or record, you don't exist. Not even one of *our* banks could justify lending you that much money."

"Then I'll borrow from Che-Che. I'll make him a partner."

"Will he lend it to you?"

"We're blood brothers," Alejandro said, smiling at Seaver. "He'll lend it."

"I'll get the two hundred thousand, anyway, just in case." Tossing the remainder of the pretzel into his mouth and licking a smear of mustard from his lips, he asked, "How you see this thing going down?"

Alejandro stopped walking and thought for a moment before he replied. "We buy duffel bags and install flexible circuit boards the size of credit cards in false panels sewn into the canvas along with thin flexible batteries that we take out of Polaroid film packs. Then we insert two-foot-long pieces of wire for an antenna. Once they float the dope down into the drop zone here in the States, they'll remove the duffel bags from the chutes and ship the entire load to New York. You'll get our electronics people to throw a net over the entire area. When their beepers start chirping the mambo, all you have to do is follow those signals to their warehouses."

Seaver sounded unconvinced. "And if they take the dope out of the duffel bags once they get it into the States, then what do we do?"

Alejandro responded, "We'll spray tiny adhesive diodes inside the duffel bags. These chips aren't powered and do not need an antenna, at least according to the tech guys at the Hacienda."

"How do they work?" Seaver asked, rolling an unlit cheroot across his mouth.

"They're simple unencapsulated diodes that are detected

when a nonlinear junction detector beams a radio wave at them. The diodes return signals that radiate harmonic frequencies back to the detector. All the power to detect them comes from our tracing equipment. The Agency and the KGB used to seed office walls with them in order to confuse bug detectors. They'd give out so many signals that they would mask the real bug."

He scratched the side of his face thoughtfully, looked at Mother Hen, and added, "Andy, it's beautiful. When it all turns to bad, I won't even be around. They'll start blaming each other."

Seaver's eyes fell to the pavement. "I sincerely hope so, my friend." He looked sideways at the undercover. "Besides money, what else are you going to need?"

"I need a crash course in rigging a Ram Air parachute."

"The Garbage Disposal Machine at the Hacienda has riggers. Sanitizing you for a few days, now that you're in play, won't be easy. Getting you down there is going to require some fancy footwork—and more than likely the help of some outside people."

"Use some people from Intelligence."

"I'd never use anyone out of Puzzle Plaza for this kind of operation."

Alejandro smiled at the derogatory reference to police headquarters.

"I'll probably use some people from the Agency's Theater Group. Be ready to go after your last show Saturday."

Walking into Battery Park City's plaza, Seaver paused to light up his cheroot. Alejandro watched him, a flicker of sadness in his eyes. "See ya 'round, *amigo mío*," he said, and walked away.

Biting down on his cigar, Mother Hen watched Chilebean walking across the plaza, repressing an inexplicable urge to call him back.

*　*　*

The Second Federal Reserve District is housed in a sandstone-and-limestone fortress at 33 Liberty Street, three blocks north of Trinity Church. It took Seaver three minutes to walk there after having ridden skyscraper elevators for half an hour.

He showed his police credentials to the guards inside the vestibule and was escorted by one of them into a side office, where a dour little man sat behind a big desk. The man looked up, nodded recognition to Seaver, and dismissively thanked the guard. Getting up and walking out from behind his desk, the man asked, "How have you been?"

"Good," Seaver said. "I need to go downstairs."

"Of course," the man said, and without another word led Seaver out into the corridor and to a heavy wooden door in the middle of the passageway.

The man unlocked the door with his key ring and held it open for the police lieutenant. They stepped inside. The man closed and locked the door. Black surveillance cameras were bracketed on the wall. The dour man flipped through his key ring and inserted one into the elevator lock. The door slid open; they stepped inside. Behind the latticed grille that formed the false ceiling of the elevator, Seaver caught the gleam of a lens. The door closed automatically under their weight. There were no floor indicator buttons on the panel, only six unnumbered keyholes. The man inserted another key into one of the locks, and the elevator descended four stories below the ground.

They stepped out into a cavernous subterranean chamber with seven tunnels radiating off a central hall that was just beyond the floor-to-ceiling steel gate that separated the chamber from the elevator.

Grottos had been cut into the walls of the tunnels, and each one was filled with pallets of gold bricks and paper money. Five levels below the street, gold belonging to many nations moved from one space to another, according to the ebb and flow of the balance of trade, without ever leaving the building. Miniature surveillance cameras were mounted inconspicuously in the corners of each grotto and along the tunnels. Electrically powered forklifts hummed through the tunnels with pallets of gold and money resting on their steel fingers.

Half a dozen armed Treasury Department guards were on station on both sides of the steel gate. Seaver took out his credentials and handed them to the sergeant in charge, who scrutinized them and then passed them through the bars to another sergeant, who took them and disappeared into an office to the left of the gate. The sergeant came out shortly, holding a photograph of Seaver along with his official pedigree.

After comparing the photographs to the face on the other side of the gate, the sergeant holding the credentials asked Seaver, "What was your mother's maiden name?"

"Slingland."

"What was your maternal grandmother's maiden name?"

"McGovern."

"What's your wife's name?"

"I'm not married."

The sergeant motioned for the gate to be opened.

A guard pulled open a gray metal wall box and worked the levers. The steel gate slid back, allowing Seaver and the man to walk inside the chamber. The two men continued along one of the tunnels until they came to a hingeless steel door that had a chrome plate beside it that contained a cipher lock pad, a miniaturized camera lens, and a handprint pad.

Seaver punched his code number into the cipher pad and stood in front of the camera lens. A red dot glowed inside the lens, and an automaton's voice ordered, "Place. Your. Right. Hand. Into. The. Handprint."

Seaver did this, and the steel door slid up into the wall.

"Okay. Take care," the man said, and walked off.

The room that Seaver walked into was crammed with all sorts of sophisticated consoles and equipment. He was inside the most secret P Room, an abbreviation for Police Room, used by each of the twenty-four Federal Reserve Districts to transfer federal monies to police departments for use in undercover narcotics operations that were beyond the financial resources of the local agencies.

Ray Kinnahan, a stocky man with a ruddy face, wearing gray trousers and a black shirt with the collar open, was waiting on the other side of the door. Going up to Seaver and pumping his hand, he said, "Thanks for getting my nephew transferred out of that Six-seven shithouse, Andy. The kid was going ape having to deal with those Rastafarians."

"How does he like the Nineteenth?"

"All sunshine and roses." Kinnahan was the Federal Reserve District's liaison with law enforcement within the second district's jurisdiction. He led Seaver along a wide aisle between the consoles. A large translucent plot board on the wall had a flat map of the world on which was marked the worldwide clandestine transfers of federal monies out of the second district.

Kinnahan's windowless office had an American flag in the corner and a photograph of the Kinnahan family on his desk that included his wife and their six sons and their wives and children. The family posed around a Christmas tree.

After lowering himself onto his chair, Kinnahan reached into a side drawer and took out a packet of forms, which he then pushed across the desk to Seaver. The forms requested covert funds from the government, and each one had TOP SECRET stamped across its face.

Seaver pushed across the list of bank accounts that Hansen had given to Alejandro. "These accounts belong to an authorized vendor." He outlined how the wire transfer of funds was to take place.

Looking over the list, Kinnahan asked, "How much?"

"Three hundred fifty thousand to play, and a coupla hundred thousand walking-around money."

Leaning back in his chair, Kinnahan asked, "Usual terms?"

"Yes. Uncle gets his back first, plus half of all confiscated assets."

"Done."

Seaver tore off the paper ribbon around the packet and separated the pages. Each one had a warning across the top advising that any false statement was perjury under the U.S. Code. On the back of each form was an abridged explanation of the Internal Revenue Tax Code, which required all cash transactions over ten thousand dollars to be reported on Form 4787, except as provided for under Section 4e of the code, which gave congressional authorization for the secret transfer and laundering of federal monies to be used in covert law enforcement operations. This provision of the code also approved the secret transfer of government funds into the private accounts of vendors and manufacturers who supplied police agencies with the necessary "tools of the trade," as long as these secret accounts were not "offshore" and were registered with and had the approval of the Internal Revenue Service.

Watching Seaver fill out the forms, Kinnahan asked, "A big operation?"

"They're all big, Ray, you know that. But this one, yeah, it's important. It's what we in the trade call personal."

Kinnahan took the forms and stacked them neatly in a pile. "You going to want to take the two hundred grand with you?"

"No. I might get mugged."

Kinnahan laughed. "You gotta gun."

"A cop's gun don't mean shit in this town. Last week in the Seven-nine two rookies were patrolling their beats together. At Fulton and Nostrand, a gang of drug dealers surrounded them, shoved TEC-9s in their faces, took their guns and shields, and told them that if they see them again, they're gonna be dead meat."

Shaking his head with disbelief, Kinnahan asked, "What did the cops do?"

"They went into the station house and resigned."

The Sapphire Room, on the second floor of the Hotel Versailles, was a gilt-trimmed cobalt blue room with a custom-designed cherrywood bar, dark blue carpet, high ceilings, and soft lighting.

Alejandro, wearing a dark blue cotton sport jacket over a yellow polo shirt and jeans, walked into the cobalt blue room just before seven o'clock.

The bar was crowded, every banquette taken save the one that the maître d' led Alejandro directly to. They were saving this one, waiting for me, he thought, watching the man avert his eyes and grab the ten-dollar tip at the same time. Classy joint for a meet, he thought, sliding onto the booth and motioning for the waiter. "Johnny Black and soda."

Sipping his drink and glancing around the room, Alejandro wondered who the dopers were and where they had stashed their cameras. He assumed that the leather booth was wired.

At precisely seven-thirty, Roberto Barrios appeared in the entrance and, without bothering to look for him at the bar, walked directly over to his booth. "Let's go," he said quietly.

Alejandro motioned for the check.

Scratching his chin, Barrios said, "It's taken care of."

A black sedan with tinted windows was idling at the curb when they walked out of the hotel. A well-dressed man with a tight face that suggested a recent lift, hair dyed black and teeth capped white, stood on the curb in front of the car.

Barrios looped his arm around Alejandro's and steered him over to the man.

"My card," the stranger said, handing it to Alejandro.

It read Carlsen, Thromberg, Stassen, and Peach, Attorneys at Law.

Tossing it into the gutter, Alejandro asked, "So?"

"I am John Courtney Carlsen, and I am now informing you that my clients, Messieurs Robert Barrios and Hector Pizzaro, are not independently predisposed to engage in criminal conduct, and that if you are a police officer, or a federal agent, you are now directed, by me, to cease and desist your entrapment activities against my clients. I am also advising you that if my clients are the subjects of a criminal investigation, you are required to read them their *Miranda* warnings. And furthermore . . ."

As the lawyer talked on, Alejandro edged closer to him, his jaw rigid, his hand stealthily unzipping his fly. He reached inside his pants, fished out his penis, and urinated on John Courtney Carlsen's leg.

"Wuuuuuhhaaaa!" the lawyer howled, stumbling backward and falling against the car. "You son of a *bitch!*" he screamed.

Alejandro zipped up, looked at Barrios, and said, "Let's get on with it."

"I like your style," Barrios said, opening the door. He looked at the lawyer. "We'll be in touch."

Once the singer was inside, Barrios slammed the door and walked back inside the hotel.

Hector Pizzaro, dressed immaculately in a light tan suit, sat on the far side of the seat, appraising Alejandro. His white swath of hair reminded Alejandro of a ski slope in a coal field. Pizzaro leaned forward and tapped on the partition. The car drove out into Park Avenue traffic.

Pizzaro took a plastic laundry basket off the floor and slapped it down on the seat next to Alejandro, ordering, "Get undressed."

Alejandro looked at the orange basket, shrugged, and began struggling out of his clothes, folding them and depositing them in the basket.

A few minutes later Alejandro said, "Okay."

Pizzaro turned his attention from the passing street scene and said, "Skivvies, too."

Alejandro worked down his briefs and tossed them in with the rest.

Pizzaro pressed a button on his armrest, and the tinted partition whisked down. He handed the basket to the olive-skinned man on the passenger seat, and the partition slid back up.

Pizzaro scoured Alejandro's body for a concealed transmitter. "Face me and lift your arms over your head," he ordered.

Alejandro complied.

"Lay back and spread your legs."

Alejandro complied.

After examining his body, Pizzaro said, "Lift your balls."

Alejandro did that.

"Get up and turn around."

Alejandro did as he was ordered.

Satisfied that there was nothing strapped to his back, Pizzaro ran his hand through Alejandro's hair and ordered, "Get doggie style and spread your cheeks."

Alejandro struggled onto all fours, resting his forehead on the armrest, and reached behind to spread the cheeks of his buttocks.

Pizzaro examined his body. Seeing no transmitter, he said, "Okay, you can sit up."

Alejandro unwound himself and sat. Pizzaro moved close to him and again raked his fingers through his hair, gliding them around and behind his ears and under the lobes. That done, and finding nothing, he yanked a bath towel off the car's rear shelf and tossed it at the singer. "In case you're the modest type."

Spreading the towel across his lap, Alejandro said, "You're a very careful man, amigo. Mind telling me what that bit with the lawyer was all about?"

Pizzaro looked at him with a contemptuous expression. "If you turn out to be a cop, anything we might do together or say to each other would not be admissible in court."

"You think of everything."

Pizzaro leaned his head back against the cushion. "Tell me about your friend, Franklin Penzer."

"The banker? I hardly know the guy. I met him at the club. He liked my music. He's one of the honchos in a bank in Road Town in the British Virgins. He's a big spender, and he likes the ladies, a lot. I introduced him to Che-Che a while back. I think they're doing some business together."

"You don't vouch for him?"

"I vouch for no one but me. For all I know, Penzer could be a cop." He began to shiver from the air-conditioning in the car.

Pizzaro's cunning glance swept over him. "For all I know, you could be a cop."

They stared at each other for a moment.

Pizzaro broke the spell by looking out the window. "Your Parapoint delivery system is interesting. How did you learn about it?"

"I read about it in the Sunday *Times*. I don't remember when."

"The *Sunday Magazine,* 'The Covert War,' April 9, 1989."

This guy is not one of the field hands, Alejandro thought. "You're obviously a man who likes to get his facts right," he said.

"I was in Bolivian army intelligence, and was trained by masters."

"How did you end up in New York?"

Pizzaro ignored the question. "How do you see Parapoint working for us?"

Alejandro repeated what he had told Barrios, then went into greater detail, explaining the security advantages of Parapoint.

"The remote transmitter can only control five chutes at a time?"

"Yes. But I can get you as many transmitters as you need to bring in your heroin."

"And who told you that we're talking about heroin and not cocaine?"

"Barrios."

Brushing an imaginary speck from his trouser leg, Hector said, "He did, did he?" He looked out the window, an unpleasantly thoughtful expression on his face. He turned and looked at the singer. "Are you prepared to deliver all the systems we can use?"

"Eventually, yes. I have two systems for the demonstration, and ten on order from a manufacturer."

"A growing business, is it? I want to know how you managed to get your hands on the Parapoint system."

"Through a friend."

A nasty smile crossed the doper's face. "That answer is not good enough, amigo. Try again."

Alejandro raised his eyes upward. "My friend is a major in the Air Force Reserve. He's stationed in the office of the quartermaster, in Bush Terminal, in Brooklyn. I asked him if he ever heard of the system, and he told me that they have them in stock. So I asked him to lend me two for a while. I promised to get them back to him."

"If you have to return them to your friend, how are you going to let us use them for our business?"

Alejandro pulled the bath towel around him more closely. "I brought them to a parachute manufacturer on Long Island who has a very expensive nose candy habit. For cash, he's making me ten copies."

"Junkies are bad people to do business with."

"He doesn't know who I am. As far as he's concerned I'm a guy named A. Brown."

"What's the company name?"

"Precision Industries."

"What did you use for money?"

"Che-Che made me a present of thirty thousand, and I had some of my own, enough for a down payment."

"Where you getting the balance?"

Alejandro hugged himself against the cold and sat forward on the seat cushion. "I'm going to borrow it from Che-Che."

Pizzaro looked at him and smiled. "Che-Che?"

"Yeah."

"You must realize that we could buy our own Parapoint systems."

"Maybe, but then you gotta have your own riggers to repack the chutes. That lengthens your security chain, makes you even more vulnerable to the DEA and the rest of them." He glanced at Pizzaro. "Besides, I work cheap. It wouldn't pay you to get your own systems. I'll rent 'em to you and repack 'em for you."

"Where did you learn to pack chutes?"

"My friend taught me."

Pizzaro thought it over for some time. Then he said suddenly, "We'll pay you three thousand dollars a drop for every chute we use."

"Barrios and I agreed on four points."

"Roberto was not authorized to agree to anything. And, for your own information, we don't pay points."

"Five thousand a chute," Alejandro said.

"Thirty-five."

"Forty-five and you pay the cost of transporting the system back for repacking."

"Four."

"Forty-five and costs," Alejandro said.

"Done." Pizzaro pressed a button on the armrest and the partition slid down. He gestured to the man on the passenger seat, who passed the laundry basket through to Alejandro. Watching him pulling up his briefs, Pizzaro asked, "Why would a U.S. Air Force major risk going to jail in order to smuggle you a classified system like Parapoint?"

Tugging up his jeans, Alejandro said, "He likes me, a lot."

Pizzaro shot him a look, his face creasing with disbelief.

Seeing his look, Alejandro said, "Hey, amigo, whatever it takes to get you through the day." He reached back into the basket, took out his polo shirt, and yanked it down over his head.

"What's your friend's name and address?"

"Jeff Scott. He lives on Cornelia Street in the Village."

Staring straight ahead at the tinted partition, his face a blank, Pizzaro asked softly, "Do your mother and sister still live in Zihuatanejo?"

Alejandro's heart thudded in his chest. "What does my family have to do with any of this?"

Pizzaro did not bother to reply. The car stopped and the driver held the door on Alejandro's side open without speaking. The message had been passed on; no further words were necessary.

A bank of thunderheads rolled across the sky as Che-Che Morales walked from La Bandera restaurant on Roosevelt Avenue and Sixty-sixth Street in Jackson Heights, Queens, toward the black sedan that had just drawn up at the curb.

He looked up at the threatening clouds and wondered if they were omens sent to him by the great god Quetzalcoatl.

One of the bodyguards, who preceded Che-Che out of La Bandera, rushed ahead to open the car door for the drug lord.

Sliding inside, he looked across the seat at Hector Pizzaro and asked, "Well?"

Pizzaro pressed a button on the armrest, and his recent conversation with Alejandro played out of the rear speakers. When the tape concluded, Pizzaro opened his mouth to say something, but Che-Che rushed a silencing finger across his mouth.

The sedan, convoyed by a van full of bodyguards, whisked through the Queens streets. Staring out the window, Che-Che watched the working-class neighborhood of attached frame houses meld into the industrial hodgepodge of Long Island City. The convoy drove west on Roosevelt Avenue to Skillman Avenue, where it streaked into Thirty-fourth Avenue, passed the

Ravenswood Houses, and drew up at the curb on Vernon Boulevard in front of Rainey Park.

The pushers and junkies who inhabited the park heard the squeal of tires, looked out to see the van disgorging its cargo of mean-looking men, and shuffled off with their heads bowed in supplication to the dopers. A bodyguard rushed to open the sedan's door. The drug lord climbed out in his sandals and jeans, followed close behind by his impeccably dressed chief of counterintelligence.

The few people still inside the park vanished as Che-Che entered.

They walked to the water's edge. The tide lapped against the bulkhead's boulders. Evening was descending over the city, and ribbons of lights were strung across the Queensboro Bridge, silhouetting its fat cables against a purple sky.

Pizzaro gripped the railing, looking down at the shroud of mist gathering above the water. "Why do we need this Alejandro?"

Che-Che gripped the railing and leaned back, looking up at the Manhattan skyline. "Because the parachutes will save us a lot of money and trouble—and because what he told you and Roberto about security is true. The more people involved in our transportation, the greater our risks." He looked at the side of Pizzaro's face. "What does it cost us? Pennies. And my blood brother has an inventive mind. We need new thoughts; they help prevent us from getting careless."

Pizzaro stuck his hands in the pockets of his trousers. "I haven't fully checked him out yet."

"He's no cop. I knew his family in Zihuatanejo."

"But his father was a gringo."

"So what?"

"We can't be too careful, Che-Che."

"True," Che-Che said with an element of suspicion in his

voice. "Check out that Air Force friend of his. Make sure he is what Alejandro says he is."

Across the street from the park an oil truck pulled up in front of one of the Ravenswood Houses. The driver climbed down and walked over to the plot of grass along the side of the building. He took the top off the oil fill pipe and walked back to the truck. After pulling a hose off the rack, he tugged it over to the pipe and secured its nozzle there by clamping it. He walked back to the rear of the truck and pressed a button on the automatic delivery system, and the meter began spinning out the gallons of fuel being dispensed— only no oil was being pumped out of this truck.

The sign on the side of the oil tank read Matarazzo and Sons. Welders of the NYPD's Motor Transport Support Unit had constructed a metal platform along the bottom of the oval mobile surveillance vehicle so that the detectives of Unified Intelligence could stand upright when they aimed their lasers and cameras out of the concealed portholes.

Lieutenant Sal Elia, the thick-necked, squat boss from Unified Intelligence who had first spotted Alejandro with Che-Che Morales at Lopez's tire store, stood at the far end of the platform behind the driver's cab, peering through a telescopic tube, studying the two men standing at the water's edge. He called out to the detectives strung out along the parapet, "Aim those lasers at the railing."

Two detectives inside the tank aimed their laser transmitters at the embankment's black wrought-iron railing. The cross hairs zeroed in on the area of the fence near the dopers' hands and bodies. The laser beams bounced off the wrought iron, picking up the vibrations from the sound pressure generated by the dopers' voices. These vibrations caused a shift in the laser's wavelength, modulating what was reflected back to the laser receiver on a tripod platform inside the oil tank. The laser receiver concentrated the modulated beam's infrared signal onto a photomultiplier, which transformed it into a series of electrical impulses. These impulses were then fed into an amplifier and a computerized demodulator, which separated vibrations from audio, recovering the original voice signals and allowing the output to be recorded.

Pizzaro, holding on to the railing with both hands, pushed himself back and forth several times in standing push-ups, looked at the side of Che-Che's face, and asked, "How the hell can we trust this friend of yours if he goes with fags?"

Che-Che withered him with an expression of impatience; sweeping his hand behind him at the bodyguards, he said, "You think none of them ever had their cocks sucked by a man?"

Pizzaro did not answer him.

"I want this network airtight," Che-Che said. "Any problems, you get rid of them. And speaking of problems, what did you find out about Roberto and his dead junkie girlfriend?"

"Judith checked it out. Her name was Bonnie Haley, and she was a DEA informer."

Che-Che's mouth went tight. "Get rid of Barrios."

Pizzaro looked across the river. "We're going to need a plane and a pilot for this."

"We have plenty of both."

"I don't trust any of the pilots. Most of them are gringo drunks without honor."

Che-Che made a gesture of impatience. "Then get a new pilot, someone reliable."

"I'll take care of it. What are you going to do when he asks you to borrow the money?"

Morales smiled slowly and replied, "I'm going to lend it to him and become his partner."

Brushing down the side of his hair with his hand, Pizzaro said, "Our Colombian friends might not like us going on our own, competing with them for control of the heroin market. We could get ourselves killed."

* * *

Alejandro arrived home from Environment shortly after four Friday morning. Driving his car down the underground ramp, he felt frustration gnawing at him. Che-Che had not shown up at the club that night, so he had been unable to ask him for the money; and he still had not told Seaver about his car ride with Hector Pizzaro.

After driving into his assigned parking space, he turned off the ignition and, reaching under his seat, flipped the toggle switch, killing the car's electrical system. He looked over at the surveillance cameras scanning the garage and walked toward the elevator. Seeing the telephone strapped to the support column, he reached into his jeans and fished out a quarter. Maybe he'd risk one fast call to Control to set up a final face-to-face with Seaver. He lifted the receiver off the hook, took a quick look around, then plunked the receiver back down. He walked over to the elevator, knowing that if he was Pizzaro, he would have put a wire on that phone and on every other available telephone in the neighborhood.

His terrace door was open, and the fresh smell of rain blew across his darkened living room. Out on the terrace, he breathed deeply, then looked down at the breakfast dishes, hoping that the woman Joanne did not think too badly of him. He gathered up the dishes, went into the kitchen, and washed them, leaving them on the drainboard to dry.

He crossed the living room, closed the terrace door, drew the curtains, and switched off the lights, then sat on the sofa. Stacks of books he was using in his research on Cleopatra were on the stone-topped coffee table. Running his finger over their spines in the dim morning light, he thought, Queen Cleopatra, what would you do now?

He looked down at his wristwatch, saw it was 5:22 A.M., and went over to his breakfront. He picked up the turquoise-shell head of the Aztec warrior, its plumed headdress decorated with the visage of the god of war, and carried it into his bedroom.

He went into the bathroom and closed the door. Sitting on the toilet seat, he counted the shells on the bottom row below the left ear; when he came to the twelfth one, he turned it counterclockwise until a concealed door on the base sprang open and a small bundle wrapped in plastic fell into his waiting hand. He snapped a towel off the rack, placed it on the bottom of the tub, and carefully set the Aztec head on its side.

Inside the plastic was a pocketbook-size satellite radio with burst transmission capabilities and a collapsible dish antenna fifteen inches in diameter. He unfolded the antenna and plugged it into the radio. A tiny green light glowed when he turned on the unit. He began whispering into the handset. He described Hector Pizzaro and said that he matched exactly the man seen leaving the scene of the Levi-DeLeo homicide. He went on to give a succinct report of their conversation, adding that Pizzaro was ex-Bolivian army intelligence and possibly high in the Cleopatra counterintelligence network. He warned Seaver that the banker in Road Town should be told to be on the lookout for unwelcome strangers. Finally he mentioned Pizzaro's veiled threat against his family and requested that Seaver give them "eyes and ears."

As he spoke, his thirty-second message was encoded automatically inside the radio. He looked at his watch: 5:28. There were two minutes to his assigned window of transmission. He got up, switched off the bathroom light, and, standing on the toilet seat, lowered the frosted window. Orienting the antenna to the southeast, he waited until the second hand had swept around to 5:30, then pushed the burgundy button on the front panel, causing his thirty-second message to be compressed into a burst less than a second of transmission time. His signal bounced off a joint CIA/DEA law enforcement satellite orbiting high above the earth's atmosphere.

Chilebean's transmission was picked up by the satellite's antenna, filtered through an encryption device, and burst back to earth, where it was snagged by one of the huge dish antennas of the CIA Counter-Narcotics Center's secret communication compound sixty miles northwest of Knoxville, Tennessee.

At nine o'clock that Friday morning a woman wearing a kerchief on her head pushed a baby carriage into Yeshiva Beth Chaim's school yard.

A Brownsville detective slam-dunked one into the net.

The woman with the baby carriage made three walk-arounds of the yard before one of the secretaries from the Board of Education's Manhattan Maintenance Unit stepped out to grab a smoke. The secretary played with the cooing baby. The women exchanged pleasantries, agreeing that it had turned into a beautiful day.

Eleven minutes after the woman with the baby carriage walked out of the school yard, Deputy Chief Joseph Romano was sitting alone inside the Room, smoking a cigarette and reading the CNC flash transmission that had been passed by CIA's morning courier in the school yard. He looked up from the flash message when he heard the beeps of someone accessing the cipher lock.

Andy Seaver tugged open the heavy door and stepped inside. Grinding out his cigarette in the battered ashtray, Joey-the-G-Man said, "He's in play, and we need protection for his mother and sister."

"Shit!" Mother Hen said, angrily grabbing the back of a chair.

13

DETECTIVE BOB TOBIN OF the Tenth Narcotics District arrived at 14 Cornelia Street around ten o'clock Friday night wearing the uniform of an air force major.

Tobin had been working a day duty when the Whip called him into his office to inform him that Intelligence had a party going down that evening, and that he had been selected as one of the players. "Your name is gonna be Jeff Scott on this playbill," the Whip had said.

A tall handsome man in his mid-forties, with deep blue eyes and sandy hair, Tobin had just walked into the vestibule of the Cornelia Street tenement when he saw the shadow of a man looming under the staircase.

Retired police captain Frankie "No Chin" Vitalie, who had spent his thirty years in the Job working in the Land of Trick

Mirrors, and who had retired in 1986 to devote all his time to his budding real estate business, stepped out into the light.

No Chin's umbilical cord to the Job had never been severed. He was now high on the Land of Trick Mirrors list of "special friends" who could be counted on to "do the right thing" and then amnesia it. Vitalie provided safe houses and legend apartments for the Special Operations Section.

"You had a couple of visitors," Vitalie said to the man in the air force uniform. "Two dopers oozing Penzoil outta every pore came 'round checking on your legend."

"Did 'Jeff Scott' hold up?"

Vitalie spread his arms in self-praise, exposing a mouthful of capped teeth, and said, "I'm still the greatest."

"I picked up a tail when I left Bush Terminal tonight. They're parked down the block."

"They're sniffing out your legend. Any idea what's going down?"

"Haven't a clue. I've only got a walk-on in this one. But if you want to catch a few laughs, get over to the Palm Tree. We're going to put on a floor show for our friends."

The Palm Tree, a tastefully decorated cabaret with plants filling its windows, was located on Grove Street, a pebble's throw from Sheridan Square. It was after eleven o'clock when "Jeff Scott" walked in, dressed in khaki slacks with a dark green webbed belt and a lime green polo shirt snug around his trim body.

Men huddled together on the banquettes and crowded around the bar. A drag queen was holding court with two fag hags, one of whom was talking loudly in an exaggerated French accent. They were sitting in one of the corner booths. Tonga, the Palm Tree's pet chimpanzee, was perched on the branch of a large indoor tree above the fag hags, looking down at them, intrigued by the strange accent. Streisand was singing "Evergreen" over the stereo system.

No Chin Vitalie had squeezed into one of the booths and was sipping at his drink and watching Jeff Scott make his way through the crowd over to the bar.

Detective Hank Johnston, from the Major Case Squad, sat at the bar, drinking dark rum and Coke. He wore canvas shoes, no socks, white chinos, and a sleeveless tropical shirt with its tails out. He was in his early thirties and had one of those nondescript faces that no one ever bothered to notice.

"Hi, Hank," Jeff Scott said, edging up to him. He called out to the bartender, "Jack and soda."

The bartender, a wide-shouldered man, picked up a water glass, tossed in ice cubes, poured in a long stream of Jack Daniel's bourbon, added a splash of soda, and set the glass on a pink bar napkin in front of Scott.

Sipping the strong drink, Scott said, "This'll blow your skirt up."

"Whatever it takes."

They smiled and touched glasses.

Two dopers swaggered into the Palm Tree. They were short men, both wearing raffish shirts open low with gold medallions, diamond-studded nugget wristwatches, and gray plastic shoes. They had just gotten past the entrance when they froze in place, taking in their new surroundings, their eyes growing wide and their mouths falling open at the sight of men shuffling around the dance floor in close embrace, kissing, and others at the bar, holding hands, laughing. They looked at each other with open surprise and uneasiness.

No Chin Vitalie sipped his drink, relishing the unfolding scene.

The dopers slowly made their way over to the bar but were unable to bring themselves to push through the crowd for dread of brushing up against one of *them* and catching whatever it was that made them fags. So they remained back of the crowd's fringe, shooting disgusted looks at Jeff Scott and the other fag.

Seeing them standing back, Hank Johnston smiled and turned, seeking out the bartender's eyes and then pointing at the dopers. The bartender caught the signal, looked out over the heads of the crowd, and, seeing the uncomfortable men, shouted, "Make way for my friends."

A path opened, and the dopers, mustering as much machismo as they could, swaggered up to the bar.

Leaning over the inlaid copper, the bartender puckered his thick lips and asked, "What'll it be, ladies?"

"Champagne," the taller one barked with as much authority as his hoarse voice could muster.

"A glass or a bottle, dear?" asked the bartender.

"A fucking bottle," the shorter one snapped, tossing two hundred onto the bar.

"Whatever you say, sweet lips," the bartender said. He turned his back to them and bent to open the small refrigerator under the bar, craning his neck and wiggling his ass. "Now, don't you boys get fresh and grab my cheeks."

The men standing in the immediate area of the dopers turned away, laughing.

After moving several bottles around inside the refrigerator, the bartender pulled out a bottle of champagne, held it up to his customers, and said, "Extra Brut, you brutes," and began working off the cork.

The dopers kept glancing over at their quarry.

"Here comes the best part," the bartender singsonged just as the cork popped, sending a geyser of foam shooting out of the bottle.

"Just pour the damn wine," the taller one ordered, "and leave the bottle."

The dopers guzzled the champagne; they dumped more into their glasses and gulped it down, then dumped in more.

Tonga had climbed farther down the tree so that she might

better hear the strange accent. She was crouched on a branch directly over the laughing French fag hag.

No Chin Vitalie ordered another drink.

"Let's dance," Scott said to his friend.

The detectives slid off their stools and, holding hands, made their way onto the dance floor. As they were gliding around the crowded circle, Johnston searched for their backup. He spotted them sitting at one of the cocktail tables scattered around the dance floor.

The detectives' eyes met in secret recognition. Johnston nodded to the backups. The two detectives at the cocktail table got up and began edging through the crowd to the dopers. The detectives slid up next to them and waited until they had gulped a mouthful of wine before placing their hands on the dopers' thighs and asking, "Would you like to dance?"

The dopers spit out their wine across the bar and began to gag and cough uncontrollably.

"Honey, you all right?" one of the detectives asked, patting the taller one's back.

"Lemme alone," the taller one gasped, shoving the hand away and rushing out of the bar. His gagging friend followed.

"Was it something that I said?" one of the detectives shouted after the departing men. At this point Tonga decided that she did not like the French accent and pissed on the fag hag.

A single sheet wrapped Judith Stern's body as she lay on the round bed, watching Carlsen admiring himself in the dresser's mirror. He was wearing his boxer shorts with the monogram *JCC* on the right leg. "That damn Spick pissed on my leg. I should have smashed him right in his ugly face," he said, patting down the sides of his layered hair.

"They're all animals, darling. Don't bring yourself down to their level."

Looking at her reflection, he asked, "Did you enjoy it?"

"Need you ask? I'm going to take out a patent on that tongue of yours." She beckoned him with her arms.

Smiling smugly, he came to her and sat on the bed. "I love you, Judith."

"I love you, too," she said, pressing his head to her chest. "You make me feel like a complete woman."

He kneaded her nipple between his teeth.

"That's not fair. You have an eleven A.M. plane to catch, so don't get me started."

"When I come home, I'll expect to find you waiting right here."

"I'll be here with my engine running."

"Good." He got up, yanked his trousers off the back of the chair, and thrust his leg through.

She sat up, pulling the sheet up across her chest and tucking it in under her arms. "John, be careful in Road Town. That place is loaded with intelligence people from all sides of the equation."

"I know what I'm doing. If Penzer, or that bank, is Agency or DEA, I'll know it." The light went out in the lawyer's eyes. "Hector would kill us if he ever found out about this apartment."

"I know. He's suspicious of everyone. That's why it's important that you report directly to me when you get back. Don't tell anyone else what you found out; don't telephone, and don't send a fax." She looked down at the sheet, noticing how it formed a valley between her legs. "Do you think we'll ever have a life together, John?"

Knotting his tie, he turned and looked at her. "That would require a lot of money, Judith. I've three children to see through college. Bunny would not leave the marriage empty-handed. Under the law, she is entitled to half my income. I'd come out with almost nothing."

"What about Hector's money?"

"We wouldn't be able to count on that, it could stop anytime."

She looked up at the highboy on the other side of the room and said softly, "We could take off one of their money warehouses."

His jaw fell. "Have you gone crazy? They'd hunt us down and skin us alive, literally, skin us. They slice off a sliver at a time until there's nothing left."

Judith pulled the sheet around her more tightly. "But suppose we could pull it off without them ever knowing about it? Think of it, darling, thirty, forty million dollars in untraceable bills, stored in some musty old warehouse just waiting to be laundered."

He shook his head and said in an angry voice, "Do you have any idea how bulky that much money is, and how difficult it would be to transport it away from the warehouse? Not to mention how hard it would be to get our greedy hands on it. The locations of those warehouses are known only to Hector and a few others, and they're guarded day and night."

"We wouldn't have to launder it, darling. Just spend it!"

"You're serious!" He crossed the room, his expression deeply worried. He brushed a tendril of hair from her forehead. "Your mother is dead. Your father is in an old-age home, and you intensely dislike your brothers for dumping him there. I, on the other hand, love my children, I even like Bunny, and I am not about to do anything that will guarantee their deaths, or my own."

She gave him a peck on the mouth. "Hurry, darling, you'll miss your plane."

14

A FLUFFY WHITE RABBIT STOLE adorned the neck of the life-size cutout of Madonna standing against the stage at Environment. At two o'clock Sunday morning the booming music and swirling colored lights began to fade, and the shimmying dancers rushed up to the darkened stage, chanting, "Alejandro! Alejandro!"

Che-Che Morales put down his champagne glass.

A beam of light speared down out of the blackness. The audience cried out in anxious anticipation when Alejandro walked into the circle of light wearing faded blue jeans and a black shirt open at the collar, holding his trademark rose up to his mouth. He remained motionless, his head bowed, accepting their adulation. Women pressed up against the stage, their outstretched arms straining to touch him.

He brushed the flower's cold petals across his lips, kissing it good-bye, walked over to the edge of the stage, knelt on one knee, just beyond the reach of his fans, and tossed the rose to a woman who was shouting her love for him. She snatched the flower out of the air and scrambled on all fours up onto the stage. She threw her arms around him and began kissing him. The audience roared their approval.

Alejandro tried to break her grip around his neck. The marimba player ran over to help him. Two bouncers joined him and gently led the woman, still clutching her precious rose to her face, off the stage and back to her seat.

Alejandro backpedaled to the center of the stage, throwing kisses to his fans, then spreading his arms wide. At last he hit the air with his hip and broke into "El Pájaro Chogui," a raucous song set to a samba-reggae rhythm that propelled him across the stage, his body gyrating to the beat, sending his fans into a hand-waving, dancing frenzy.

Ninety minutes later, his body soaked with sweat, Alejandro closed with "Quierame Mucho," and as he always did whenever he sang his theme song, he stared forlornly out into the blackness, searching for a face that was never there.

Running off stage, he could hear the boisterous demands for an encore but he hurried into his dressing room and got out of his clothes. Standing naked at the sink, he turned on the faucet, waited for the rusty water to clear, lathered a washcloth, and began washing himself.

After toweling himself dry, he dusted himself with baby powder, stepped into fresh briefs, and tugged on his jeans. After pulling a tan polo shirt over his head, he gathered up his dirty clothes and stuffed them into his canvas overnight bag.

Looking at his watch, he saw that it was almost four in the morning; Seaver had instructed him to be ready to leave for the Hacienda after the last show. He was curious how Mother Hen planned to sanitize him.

Combing his hair, he heard someone behind him and turned to see his manager, Josh Budofsky, pushing past the curtains. "You're up kinda late, Josh," he said, putting down his comb.

"I brought Belmont along. The guy who liked your tape." He lowered himself onto a metal folding chair. "He had to run or else he'd be here with me now. After watching you tonight, he and I agreed that we could maybe break you through into the major leagues."

"I don't have much time, Josh."

Budofsky stood up and almost shouted, "What the hell is the matter with you? I'm your damn manager, and all you ever do is fight every move I make to get you to the top. Look, Alejandro, if I'm wasting my time, let me know. I'll look around and find a real wannabe."

Alejandro felt a tight band of anxiety grip his stomach. Budofsky was a nice guy, a sincere person who really wanted to help him get to the top of the music business, but his dreams exceeded Alejandro's own realistic estimate of his abilities. And now Seaver was waiting outside someplace. "I'm sorry, Josh. I'll do whatever you think is necessary."

"OK. We'll go into the studio, work on some new songs. I got a good writer for you. We'll work on your image, too, something a little less Latin the majors could deal with. After that we'll do a video. Shouldn't take more than a month."

"Sounds good." Alejandro said, stealing a look at his watch. "Why don't we meet in the middle of the week?"

"Okay. I'll be in touch. Got time for a drink?"

"You caught me at a bad time. I've got some friends waiting."

"Hanging around that crew could prove injurious to your health and your career."

"I'm a big boy, Josh," he said, firmly leading his manager over to the stage exit.

"And a wise one, I hope," Budofsky said, waving good-bye over his shoulder.

Alejandro climbed the staircase to the balcony and was greeted by back-slapping fans. He made his way through the crowd over to the banquette and slid in beside a smiling Che-Che Morales.

"Good show," Che-Che said.

"Thanks." Lapsing into Tarascan, Alejandro told him the details of the Parapoint delivery system and his need to borrow money for the purchase of ten of the parachutes and their homing transmitters.

Che-Che held up his glass to the swirling lights, studying the colors dancing inside the crystal. "Go speak to Roberto and Pizzaro. They're over at the bar."

"Are they your money guys?"

Che-Che did not answer him, merely stared down at the action on the main floor.

"You'll lend me the money?" Alejandro asked.

"*Sí.* We'll be partners." He saw the frown on the singer's face and asked, "You're not happy with that arrangement?"

"I thought I'd just be able to repay you the money."

"This is business, my brother."

"It's going to take me longer than I thought to buy that home for my mother."

"As I told you before, once you're in the business you learn early that enough is never enough."

"I'm going to have to keep my overhead down."

"Yes, that's always a problem. The golden rules are to keep the operation simple and trust no one."

Alejandro leaned back against the banquette and stretched his arm above his head to relieve the ache of tension he suddenly felt. "I was going to set up a phony skydiving school, but on second thought, I don't need it. A loft somewhere in the city where I can repack the chutes and service the transmitters—that's all I really need."

"You're learning."

Tracing the beads of moisture on one of the champagne bottles, Alejandro asked, "Why haven't you trusted me enough to tell me that Pizzaro and Barrios work for you?"

"I knew you'd work it out by yourself."

Alejandro looked Che-Che in the eye, wondering if *he* was really the number one man after all.

Che-Che met his stare and said, "Pizzaro and Barrios are waiting for you at the bar."

Skirting around the crowded dance floor, Alejandro headed for the busy bar. Squeezing in between Pizzaro and Barrios, he said, "So, when do we do it?"

"Want something to drink?" Pizzaro asked.

"I loved your show, Alejandro," said Jasmine, the Chinese barmaid with the yellow ribbon tied around her pigtail.

Letting his eyes smile back at her, Alejandro said, "Thank you."

"Johnny Black over rocks?" she asked.

"Please," said the singer, and watched her pour a stream of scotch into a water glass.

Pizzaro nudged Alejandro. "She likes you."

"It's my honesty," Alejandro said.

She looked up from her task. "It's that, and your beautiful hands."

Alejandro measured his hands. "I don't see anything special about them."

"You're not a woman," she said, placing a cocktail napkin on the bar in front of him and setting down his drink.

When she'd drifted off to serve another customer, Pizzaro leaned into Alejandro and whispered, "I want you and two delivery systems waiting in front of your apartment at nine A.M. day after tomorrow."

Quickly realizing that it was going to be a close call getting back from the Hacienda in time to make the meet, Alejandro said, "I'm off Monday, but I have a show to do Tuesday. I gotta be back for that."

"You'll be back when you get back. Che-Che'll take care of this end," Barrios said, sipping his soda water and leering at the barmaid.

Che-Che came over to them, accompanied by three bodyguards. The other dopers standing at the bar melted away into the crowd.

"Is everything arranged?"

"Yeah," Pizzaro said.

A woman's hand fell on Alejandro's shoulder. She was gracefully tall and slender with thick black hair that tumbled over her shoulders. She wore a black dress hemmed slightly above the knees, and she had a Gucci tote bag slung over her shoulder. "Would you like to dance?"

"No thanks," he said.

"I'm a great dancer," she said, shrugging the tote bag off her shoulder and handing it to Che-Che, saying, "Hold this, would you?" and slithering backward onto the dance floor, shaking her body to the music's beat, caressing herself with her hands, beckoning him with her body.

Watching her exhibitionistic dance, Alejandro deepened his smile to one of simulated sexual interest. Could she be Seaver's messenger?

Her body taunted him. The crowd took up the chant. "Alejandro . . . Alejandro." Jasmine came up behind Alejandro and said, "I bet you're a great dancer."

"Go ahead," Che-Che said.

The woman's fingers were calling to him. Alejandro began swaying to the rhythm. He slid his glass onto the bar, threw his hands on his hips, and swaggered out onto the floor.

They circled each other cautiously, dancing closer and closer until their bodies touched and locked, grinding as one to the fierce beat of the music, their fiery eyes welded together.

Some of the crowd watched them; others danced around them.

"What's he got that drives women wild?" Barrios asked Pizzaro.

"He's not a pig like you," Jasmine said.

Barrios gave her a nasty look, started to say something, and then saw Che-Che watching him.

The woman draped her arms over Alejandro's shoulders, licking his lips with her tongue.

"What's your name?" Alejandro asked her.

"Jackie," she answered, then ground into him purposefully, sucking on his ear, whispering, "A mutual friend sent me."

"Let's make it look good," he said, gnawing on her bottom lip.

After several minutes of dancing together, he asked in a voice loud enough for the dopers to hear, "Why don't we get out of here?"

"Let's." She broke away from him, walked over to the bar, snatched up her tote bag, said coolly, "Thanks," to Che-Che, and slipping her hand into Alejandro's, she walked off toward the stairs.

After watching them disappear, Pizzaro fixed his gaze on Barrios. The thin man caught the urgent message in the look and motioned to four crew members to follow him. They all took off after the pair.

Holding on to her hand, Alejandro led her through the club and out into the lobby, edging around the noisy crowd and out into the night. People milled about. They slipped deftly through groups of revelers.

"There's my limo," she said, lifting her chin at a double-parked stretch job. She opened the door, and he climbed inside.

Barrios and the four men came rushing out of the club and began to force their way through the crowd.

"Who the fuck you shovin', asshole?" a burly youth shouted into one of the dopers' faces, and began pummeling him with his fists.

A free-for-all broke out around the metal detector. Security guards rushed into the melee. Barrios and one other crew member broke through and came running up to the limo. The crew member ran out into the street, blocking the limo from driving off. Barrios yanked open the door and froze.

Alejandro was sprawled across the seat, his eyes closed, a low moan coming from his partially open mouth. Jackie was on her knees, sucking rapturously on an erect phallus.

Barrios brightened; he watched for a few seconds, then quietly closed the door. He gestured to the man blocking the car to step aside. The limo drove off.

Jackie pushed herself off the floor, dropping the dildo into her tote and straightening out her clothes and hair. She reached back into the large pocketbook, took out her lipstick, and began painting her lips.

Alejandro sat up, brushing back his hair with his hands. "Thank you."

"Not to mention it," she said, blotting her lips together. "The Agency recruited me in my senior year in college. An exciting, challenging career, my political science professor told me. Giving fake head is not my idea of a challenging career."

He smiled at her. "Thanks anyway."

She tossed her lipstick into her bag. "My husband occasionally gets on my case about what it is that I do at night."

"And what do you tell him?"

She winked at him. "The same bullshit you men tell women!" Pulling the tote's drawstring closed, she said, "If you ever need an orgasm, call me. I do great orgasms."

"I'll remember that."

*   *   *

Across the street from the club, Andy Seaver leaned across the leather seat and lit Wade Hicks's cheroot. They were sitting in the front seat of an Agency flash car, a 1993 Jaguar. Soft music flowed from the speakers as the silent climate control system sucked up the offending cigar smoke. Seaver asked, "None of your 'players' knew my boy?"

"They're professional, Andy," Hicks said, watching the glowing ember at the end of his cigar. "They only want to know what they need to know to carry out an operation. The female agent was given a description of her mark and told where she'd be able to find him. The others only knew to slow up anyone who followed them out."

"Where are your people dropping him?"

"Fifth and Seventy-ninth, where one of our vans will scoop 'im up and drive him to La Guardia; one of the Company's planes will fly him to the Hacienda." He looked at the man across from him. "Think the bad guys'll be looking for him?"

"Naw." Seaver made his voice sound more confident than he really felt. "They're going to believe he's busy with his newfound love. They relate to that." Rolling his cigar in small circles in his mouth, Seaver wondered if Wilma might still be up.

15

A RIBBON OF WHITE SMOKE drifted up from a camper's morning fire on the side of the Blue Ridge Mountains as a dirty pickup with dented doors sped along the road leading from the Hacienda's airstrip, its wheels throwing up clouds of dust behind it. Sitting in the pickup's passenger seat with his window down, Alejandro sucked in the sweet, clean country air and glanced at his driver. He had been surprised to climb out of the aircraft and not find his teacher there to greet him. Porges had always been there in the past. Was it a bad omen?

Eight and four-tenths miles outside of Charlottesville, a tongue of winding dirt road branched off I-64 and snaked through a shaded tunnel of heavy foliage until it burst into a large clearing, where a white clapboard church rested on a cinder-block foundation. Automobiles, vans, and pickups were parked haphazardly across the untended lawn. Many of them had bumper stickers that read "Keep on Truckin' for Jesus."

The church's double front doors were tied open with string. All its windows were down, and the congregation was singing, clapping, and hallelujahing the glories of God.

Fiona Lee, the undercover in training known at the Hacienda as Mary Beth, wearing a floral print cotton dress and no bra, stood on the aisle of the first pew, singing and waving her arms over her head. Porges was standing next to her, frowning as he tried to deal with his student's astonishing religious fervor.

Mary Beth had sprung her need for religion on him late Friday afternoon. They had been inside the communications training barn on the east side of the soccer field. He had just finished field-stripping a new transmitter that had been manufactured to resemble a Tampax and was worn internally by female agents. After explaining the device's flexible power source, he had just finished with, "The pull string is the antenna," when Mary Beth had taken the transmitter out of his hand, reassembled it, and, twirling it around by its string, announced, "I need to go to church on Sunday."

His brows knitted together. "We have chaplains here."

"What kind you got, Teddy?"

"Catholic, Protestant, Jewish."

"Got any evangelical Protestants?"

"The Protestant chaplain can conduct standard Protestant services."

"No offense, Teddy, but I'm not into generic religion, and I'm no lace-curtain Protestant. I'm a foot-stomping, fire-and-brimstone-shoutin', glory-to-God Protestant."

"Mary Beth, you'll just have to do your foot stomping here, not in town."

Slapping the gauze-sheathed transmitter on the metal workbench, she'd announced, "I'm outta here," and stormed off toward the barn door.

Porges had looked down at the advanced communications device and called, "Wait a minute. Let's talk." He'd been trying frantically to remember what the personnel guide said under the heading "Freedom of Worship."

On Sunday morning when Porges had driven the pickup under the portico of the main house and seen her running toward him with her breasts bouncing, he'd sensed immediately that he had made a mistake in agreeing to take her to church.

Now the preacher shouted out, "Glory to God!"

Suddenly Mary Beth was sashaying out into the aisle, clapping and singing with all the others. She followed them around the church in a singing, clapping revival line. Porges felt the skin on his face and neck tighten. He slumped down into his seat, his knuckles clenched white with anger and embarrassment. He hadn't been in any church in forty years, and he'd never been in one like this.

Thirty-six minutes later the pickup raced along the thin road and lurched onto I-64. Porges snarled, "I ought to ground you for the duration."

"Chill down, Teddy, what harm did it do? I needed a little R and R from that reform school." She looked at him. "The preacher liked my tits."

A begrudging smile. "I saw."

As Porges sped the pickup along the interstate, heading back to the Hacienda, Mary Beth stared out the window. They had just zipped past Lee J's Gun Shop when she spotted the spur off the interstate that ran up to a large dirt parking lot in front of a long flat-roofed building. It reminded her somewhat of the roller-skating rink on 179th Street and the Grand Concourse in the Bronx. The sign on top of the building read TEXAS TWO-STEPPIN' EVERY NIGHT.

Her head turned to the window. She allowed herself a smile and said, "Don't worry, Teddy, I'll behave myself from now on."

Sergeant Ambrose J. Mayhew had the blackest skin Alejandro had ever seen and a booming voice that was a strange mixture of southern easiness and military authority. The barn that they were in was behind the main house, a few meters to the right of the motor pool, and it had bales of hay stacked along its outer walls. The barn served as the Hacienda's armory and parachute rigging center.

Mayhew and the undercover known as Chilebean were standing together alongside a rigging table. "Ready?" the instructor asked his student.

Alejandro looked at the man in the army fatigues and said, "Yes, sir."

"Just 'Sergeant' will do fine, son."

Mayhew yanked the ripcord of the Ram Air parachute, opening the container. He pulled the canopy out of its silken sleeve and extended it the full length of the table to the cotter pin that held the canopy in place at the apex. "First thing you do when you start is check for short lining to make sure that the suspension lines are unaltered, and none of the lines are crossed through any of the canopy's panels," Mayhew said as his big hands carefully patted each panel, searching for any that were blown or burned, pressing each panel by hand and smoothing away any curls or folds.

It took a long time. Mayhew wasn't in any rush. When that was done, he unhooked the canopy's apex and slid the sleeve back over the canopy and down the suspension lines and then, pulling the line toward him, S-rolled them up inside the skirt. He looked at his student. "Y'all getting this, son?"

"Yes."

Mayhew nodded and began S-folding the canopy into the

pack tray. Taking his time, he spring-loaded the pilot chute on top and, closing the pack, carefully replaced the pin through the grommets. Resting his arms across the top of the rig, he looked his student in the eyes and asked, "Y'all got it?"

"I think so."

Mayhew plunked the rig down in front of Chilebean, saying, "Have a go at it, son. Take ya time, we got plenty of it. When you pack a chute, you're *never* in a hurry."

The dew-covered grass had that freshly cut smell. Stars filled the sky. At a little after eleven o'clock Sunday night Alejandro walked out of the main house, cut across the lawn, and sat on the edge of the soccer field, hugging his knees to his chest. His fingers were stiff from the hours spent unpacking and repacking parachutes.

Porges had shown up at the armory around three that afternoon and had spent the rest of the day with him and Mayhew. The three of them had had dinner together. Over dessert and coffee, Alejandro had paid fascinated attention as Mayhew explained the aerodynamics of parachutes.

Staring off at the twinkling lights that dotted the distant mountainside, he wondered about the kind of people who lived such reclusive lives and decided that they must be as he'd like to be, peaceful and one with nature. Stretching back over the knoll, he breathed deeply, trying to identify the different smells that honeyed the air.

He looked up at the heavens and traced the constellations, wondering if somewhere out there in the boundless universe, many, many light-years away, Cleopatra, the last queen of Egypt, the greatest of all queens, might not be staring down at him, wishing him well in his quest to destroy the evil usurper of her royal name.

Hearing the crunch of a footstep behind him, he raised his head off the ground to look.

"Comfortable?" Fiona Lee, the undercover known as Mary Beth, asked, lowering herself onto the grass next to him.

He shot up into a sitting position. The moon's reflection caught her face, her eyes bright with its fullness, and revealed her mischievous smile. The air brought her scent to him; he smelled jasmine and juniper. He stared at her, shocked out of his reflections. Who was this woman? he wondered, aware of increasing discomfort.

Bracing her hands on the ground behind her, she asked, "Are you staff or one of the inmates?" When he did not answer her, she eyed him up and down and said, "An inmate. Tell ya what. This meeting never happened, okay? I need someone from the real world to talk to. I've had about all the hut-two-three-four-double-time march I can handle."

Scrambling to his feet, he said, "Lady, we shouldn't even be talking."

"Loo-sen up, guy. A hundred years from now our little indiscretion won't mean diddly."

"But it might a week from now," he said, walking away.

"How'd you like to go Texas two-steppin' with me tonight?"

He spun around, beginning to get angry. Who the hell was she? A security test? Or a gal who liked to break rules? He decided to find out. "How do you propose we get into town?"

"We use our ingenuity and steal a car from the motor pool."

He glanced in the direction of the main house. There was a light on in the second-floor recreation room. An owl hooted, a good sign. He bent, he scooped up blades of grass and tossed them into the air, watching them waft back to the ground. His grandmother used to tell him that it was important to learn how to read the grass because it was Atzel's way of helping mortals to make correct decisions. The blades pointed to the motor pool. He surprised himself by extending his hand to her and saying, "Let's go."

*   *   *

A neon sign in the shape of cowboy boots glowed on top of Harvey Lee's Texas Two-Steppin' Parlor. Alejandro parked the stolen van in the lot behind the dance parlor, and they got out. Looking around, he was surprised not to see Porges leading a detail of Hacienda security guards toward them. He found it hard to believe that they had been able to sneak into the motor pool and get away with a van without being detected. He took Fiona by the hand and led her off across the dirt lot toward the dance hall.

"What are we going to call each other?" she asked.

"I'm going to be Jesse James."

"I like it. And I'll be Belle Starr."

They shook hands, an unspoken understanding passing between them not to mention their work or their assignments, or to give up anything that might identify them or the Agency. They walked in the lobby and looked around curiously.

A four-sided video screen hung down over the center of the large dance floor. Hank Williams, Jr., was picking on his guitar and wailin' 'bout his daddy's naughty ways. Most of the men inside the dance hall wore cowboy hats and jeans. Many had on boots, some street shoes or sneakers. The women were dressed mostly in jeans, too; some of them had on dresses; and a few wore fringed cowgirl outfits, the backs of their jackets glittering with rhinestones.

There was a raised area around the floor where people could watch the dancers and the screen. There was also a scattering of pool tables and a horseshoe-shaped bar of knotty pine that was decorated around the top with old wagon wheels. On the inside of the hall, just to the right of the ticket taker, there was a glass display counter where Western crafts were sold and where patrons could have their names cleated into the backs of their belts so prospective dancing partners could know who it was they were approaching. Knowing a person's name helped break the ice of a first meeting.

"Let's get our names put on our belts," she said, and led him over to the counter. They pulled their belts out of the loops and handed them to the cowgirl.

As the woman behind the counter slid one of the belts into the stamping machine, the make-believe Belle Starr gave her dancing partner a sidelong glance, quickly recognizing his adorable butt from the time she had seen him at the Hacienda, lugging a parachute off the soccer field.

Alejandro looked around the dance hall and realized that for the first time in many years he was with ordinary people, doing ordinary things. For a brief period in his life he was just going to be the make-believe Jesse James, and he was going Texas two-steppin' with a beautiful woman who got off on breaking the rules.

This was the first time he'd seen her in decent light. Her short hair was auburn, her skin smooth and golden. Her body was slight, but when he first put his hands on her he could feel the coiled strength. Her neck was long and graceful, her mouth at once firm yet impish.

Dwelling on his various code names and his recently acquired make-believe name, he realized that he was a make-believe person living a make-believe life in a real slime-pool world. He also knew with absolute certainty that the longest trip he was ever going to make in his life was getting from his brain through to his blocked emotions. He ached to be a whole man, to be able to reach deep inside himself and rescue his authentic self.

"Here they are," the cowgirl said, handing them back their belts.

After sliding her belt through her jeans loops, the make-believe Belle Starr took hold of his hand and said, "Let's go dance, podner."

Johnny Cash was singing about Folsom and truckin' and cheatin' on a good-hearted woman.

Jesse James and Belle Starr two-stepped around the floor. She pirouetted under his arm. He reeled her back into his embrace, enjoying the warmth and resilience of her body, aware of some current passing between them.

She felt his hand at her waist, then was acutely conscious of her own body. Occasionally his hand would glancingly touch her breast; her breath caught involuntarily every time that happened. "You're a great dancer," she said, avoiding his eyes.

"So are you," he said, feeling strange, unfamiliar stirrings in his chest. Part of him felt like a kid at his first high school prom.

Ted Porges slipped onto a barstool and motioned to the cowgirl bartender. "Wild Turkey, rocks, water on the side." Mashing his cigarette into the cartridge case ashtray, he watched his two AWOL students lining up for a quadrille and thought, Look at those assholes making a spectacle of themselves. Sipping the Kentucky straight bourbon, Porges felt the throbbing pulse of gathering rage in his neck and cursed under his breath, trying to decide what he was going to do with them.

They had just broken the Hacienda's sacred commandment: Thou shalt not knowingly become acquainted with, associate with, talk to, or above all go to bed with another undercover lest you unwittingly give up yourself and the other undercover during the course of an operation. There were never more than a dozen undercovers at the Hacienda currently undergoing training. Each instructor designed his student's schedule so that it would not cross with that of any other student. The undercovers ate their meals alone in their rooms or, on rare occasions, with one of their instructors. They were not allowed to talk to any unauthorized person, especially other students.

He gulped down his drink and motioned for another, studying them as they bowed to each other, laughing. Not for the first time in his career, he admitted to himself that no matter how many he trained, no matter how close he came to feel to them, he could never really appreciate their desperately lonely existence or their consuming need for the love and affection that was denied them. Everyone needed a hug, his wife was fond of telling him in the morning. A touch of kindness brought a glow to most people, but to a deep one, that touch might burst a well-fortified dam of suppressed human emotions that could prove fatal. He'd seen too many of them over the years succumb to emotions that put them on a morgue slab. They looked happy out there dancing around with the civilian types. They looked as though they were one of them.

Willie was singing "Quierame Mucho." Chilebean was holding her close, dancing with his eyes closed. Porges gulped down his drink, slapped a twenty on the bar, and left the dance parlor.

The moon was well down behind the mountains when Alejandro drove into the Hacienda's motor pool and parked. They remained in their seats, not talking, listening to the sounds of a country morning. He slid his hand across the seat and found hers waiting. "Thanks, Belle Starr. I needed tonight."

She chucked open the door, turned, and traced his face with her fingers. "When will you be leaving?"

He looked out at the misty mountains. "This morning."

"Good-bye."

Watching her run away across the motor pool, he became aware of the awful burden of loneliness sweeping back to settle on him in a way all too familiar.

At noon Porges ground the Jeep to a stop alongside a two-engine jet aircraft. Their ride from the house had been made in icy silence. His teacher was not pleased with him, and Alejandro had a good idea why.

"See ya," he said, opening the door.

Porges looked at him. "During the years you've been coming here, have you ever seen a guardhouse or a sentry?"

"No."

"Lemme tell you something, 'Jesse,' they're all around. All the roads leading into this place are seeded with cameras; there are camouflaged surveillance platforms manned by people day—and night!"

Chilebean looked out at the plane.

"Do you have any idea of the gravity of your security breach?"

Alejandro faced him, flushing slightly in embarrassment. "I'm sorry. I should have known better. It's been a long time since I felt human."

Porges's knuckles were white around the steering wheel. "You'd damn well better stay battened down if you have any intention of staying alive in this business. You don't have a personal life." He breathed hard, trying not to lose it. "You can't fucking *afford* a personal life."

Alejandro let go a repenting sigh. "I'm sorry, Ted."

The whine of the jet's engines winding up broke the silence between them. The teacher spoke. "Tell me everything you learned about her."

"She's fun to be with, she likes to dance, and I enjoyed her company. That's all. No names, no memories."

"Get outta here. And, Chilebean, last night never happened."

16

WHEN BURKE ARRIVED AT his office at One Police Plaza on Monday morning, he found Lieutenant Sal Elia, the Whip of Unified Intelligence, sitting in the anteroom flipping through a clipboard of legal bulletins.

"Morning, Chief," Elia said, quickly returning the board to its wall hook.

Too Tall Paulie grunted, "Morning," and gestured to the lieutenant to follow him into his office.

Inside, Too Tall Paulie strode into the toilet and came out with a soda bottle full of tapwater. He took it to the windowsill and proceeded to water the plants. While he was doing this, his lead clerical came in, placed a mug of coffee on his desk, and left.

Done watering, Too Tall Paulie put the bottle on the windowsill, turned and picked up the mug, and stood at the window sipping his coffee, studying the scurrying people nine floors below. "Ever notice how the city's beat is a little faster on Monday mornings?"

Opening his accordion folder, Elia said, "Everyone is trying to work up enough steam to get them through the week."

"Yeah, I guess that's it." Turning from the window to face his lieutenant, he asked, "What's up?"

Elia went over to the VCR and inserted the surveillance cassette of Che-Che Morales and Hector Pizzaro standing at the water's edge in Rainey Park. Digital numbers showing the date and the time in hours, minutes, and seconds spun across the bottom of each frame. The dopers' conversation that had been laser-recorded from inside the mobile surveillance platform had been sequenced into the sound track. When Too Tall Paulie heard Pizzaro say, "We're going to need a plane and a pilot for this," he thoughtfully raised his eyes to the ceiling.

The film played out. Too Tall Paulie snatched the remote module off the top of the VCR and pressed the Rewind button. They watched the film a second and third time.

"What do you make of it?" Too Tall Paulie asked.

"I believe that Che-Che is going into the heroin trade, direct and in a big way. I also think that he's trying to get an exclusive franchise on China White from the Golden Triangle warlords."

Burke put both hands to the small of his back, stretched, yawned, and then asked, "You think he's running the Cleopatra network?"

"If he's not, he's damn close to number one, whoever that is." Elia got up, dragged the chair over to the side of his boss's desk, and sat. Leaning forward with his elbows resting on his knees, he said softly, "Why don't we fly a few birds into the Colombian camp and have them dump a load of disinformation bullshit on Che-Che? That could rip up a good chunk of the entire network for us. It'd save us a lot of wear and tear."

Too Tall Paulie stood up and took off his shirt. He went over to the closet, took out his dance board and his tap shoes. The plates of the shoes were worn and silky-looking.

Elia got up and went and stared out the window.

After putting on his tap shoes, Too Tall Paulie stepped onto the board and sprang into four-four jazz time, his hands forming into fists as he reflected on how many times over the years he had leaked disinformation to the other side and ignored the carnage he had caused. He truly believed that was how you fought the drug war—without rules or quarter. I've really come to hate the Job, he thought, breaking his time signature and noodling, letting his tapping feet reflect his emotions. "What about this Pizzaro guy?" he asked, slightly out of breath.

"Our Ghosts definitely make him as the guy they saw walking away from the Levi-DiLeo homicide. More'n likely he was the shooter."

"And the Judith they talked about in the video?"

"Not sure. The only Judith on file is listed as a coyote, with no known pedigree. But this one is obviously part of Che-Che's crew."

"Where do you think Pizzaro will go looking for a pilot?"

Elia peered past the verticals at a slice of downtown real estate. "Does the name Lyle Caswell do anything for you?"

Noodling, Too Tall Paulie said, "Agency guy who trained ragheads in how to blow up things. Lured back to the States in a sting operation and sentenced to max time in a federal dungeon. That was sixty or sixty-one."

"Sixty," Elia confirmed. "He's out on parole; runs a fancy employment agency catering to the drug trade. Guarantees his people aren't drug users or boozers. He recruits only top talent."

"Caswell must be getting up there."

"He's in his early seventies."

"Where is his operation?"

"Right here in New York. Calls his company Executives Unlimited. Pizzaro's been a customer in the past."

"Fancy title for a scumbag operation," Too Tall Paulie said, still noodling.

Elia was warming to the idea of putting a disinformation scam on the rails. "Want me to let a pigeon loose?"

Burke held up a calming hand. "Not so fast. I think our best bet is to wait until we're sure of all the players."

"And Hector Pizzaro?"

"One way or the other he's going to take the long count." Breaking his time signature, Too Tall Paulie slipped into four-four jazz time, his arms loose and dangly.

17

ON TUESDAY, NINE O'CLOCK eastern time, Alejandro waited in front of his Fifth Avenue apartment with two Parapoints stuffed carefully inside nylon suitcases. The homing transmitters were packed away inside his overnight along with a change of underwear, a couple of polo shirts, a toothbrush, hairbrush, after-shave, and a throw-away razor. He had arrived home from the Hacienda around nine Monday night and had gone to sleep. Before dozing off, he'd set the alarm clock for four in the morning and tossed an old sneaker into the middle of the bedroom to remind him to burst a message to Seaver during his five-thirty window of transmission.

The burst transmission would tell Mother Hen that the demonstration was set for Tuesday—and that he hadn't a clue where it would take place.

At nine-forty Tuesday morning a dirty green van drew up at the curb in front of his apartment. Barrios was driving; Pizzaro sat in the passenger seat. The side door slammed open, and two men jumped out and rushed to grab the suitcases. They jumped back into the van with them.

Alejandro picked up his overnight and climbed into the body of the van, asking, "Where we off to?"

Nobody bothered to answer his question.

At eleven-forty that morning a Grumman Gulfstream gathered speed as it hurtled down the five-thousand-foot runway at La Guardia Airport's Marine Terminal.

Alejandro, sitting by himself across the aisle from Pizzaro and Barrios, looked out the porthole at the murky waters of Flushing Bay. To his west he could see the razor-wire perimeter of Riker's Island Penitentiary and South Brother Island. As the private jet reached up into the sky, a spark of concern ignited inside Alejandro. This plane can go for distance, he thought. Where are they taking me? He glanced to his right and saw that Pizzaro and Barrios had their heads together, whispering. The two men who had rushed out of the van to gather up Parapoints were strapped into seats in the rear of the plane.

Alejandro looked back out the porthole. All he could see was clouds. The plane continued to climb. When it reached its cruising altitude, which he guessed was at least twenty thousand feet, it leveled off and flew in a westerly direction.

The minutes melted into hours; Alejandro's uneasiness grew. He continued looking out the window, trying to see through breaks in the clouds, searching for some recognizable landmass. Every now and then there would be a break, but all he saw was water, an endless bowl of water.

They had been flying for about five hours in a west-southwest direction. Suddenly the cloud cover broke, and they flew into a boundless blue sky. Below he could make out the familiar shoreline of Baja on the Gulf of California. A cold blade of fear sliced through his heart. *Do your mother and sister still live in Zihuatanejo?* They were making the ultimate threat against him and his family. He felt the rage begin to rise in his throat but forced it back down. Willing an expression of calm on his face, he looked across the aisle at Pizzaro and said, "It will be good to get home for a short visit."

Pizzaro smiled.

At two o'clock in the afternoon central time the Grumman Gulfstream swooped in across the mountains and landed in Zihuatanejo's airport. The aircraft taxied to the part of the tarmac where the civilian, military, CIA, DEA, and dopers' aircraft were ecumenically parked with the tacit understanding that "if you destroy my plane, I'll destroy your plane."

There were no passport or immigration controls for the new arrivals from the States. A black sedan bearing the ornate emblems of the judicial police on its bumpers, and with curtains stretched across the windows in the rear, was parked near the space the Grumman Gulfstream taxied into. Two big men wearing mirrored sunglasses and *guayabera* shirts lounged up against the car. Pizzaro climbed out of the plane first and walked over to the two men. After a brief conversation, he turned and beckoned the others.

With the two judicial cops in the front seat and Pizzaro and Barrios on either side of him in the back, Alejandro realized that he was way out on a limb without a safety net. He glanced behind him and through a gap in the curtain saw his suitcases containing the Parapoints being off-loaded from the aircraft.

As the sedan sped out of the airport, Alejandro calculated that it had been eight years since he'd been home. But as the car sped through villages, he saw that nothing had changed. Housewives still trudged behind their husbands along sunbaked paths, their burdens balanced on their heads, while the men rode on the family burro, legs dangling, straw hats tilted forward rakishly, machetes stuck through their rope belts. He also noticed that the arrogant children of the arrogant rich still raced their expensive cars along National Highway 200, while women and children waited for rickety, overcrowded buses that were notoriously late and slow. Pushing aside the curtain on the side window and looking up, he saw that many of the ramshackle huts clinging to the hillside now had satellite dishes; he wondered if the peasants' good fortune was due to hard work or drug money.

When the official car sped around Kyoto Square, Zihuatanejo's only traffic circle, and he looked out and saw the Japanese shinto arch, he wondered, as he always had whenever he passed the circle, what were the town fathers smoking when they'd built it and named it for a city in Japan?

The sedan sped over the dried-out canal cluttered with trash and headed out on the beach road that ran the length of La Playa Ropa. Seeing all the condos under construction on the mountainside made him realize that the sleepy fishing village of his childhood had been discovered by the outside world, and he wondered how much of that world included *traficantes*.

When the sedan passed the Bay Club and Kon-Tiki restaurants, Alejandro reached across the seat, parted the curtains, and looked to his right at the glorious vista spread out before him. Below, the lagoon's aquamarine water filled the space between the two mountains. A cruise ship rode at anchor; yachts crowded the harbor. Lowering himself back into his seat, he asked Pizzaro, "When are we going back to New York?"

"Tomorrow afternoon," Pizzaro said, parting the curtain and watching a van drive out of the Sotovento Hotel's cobblestone driveway and fall in behind them.

Just past the Hotel Catalina, the sedan suddenly swerved left and sped up a long curving driveway, passing posted signs proclaiming government property and prohibiting entry.

They were driving up to the Parthenon, a multimillion-dollar replica of the Parthenon in Athens, Greece, built on a chunk of Zihuatanejo's most expensive real estate by the police chief of Mexico City, whose monthly salary was $350 U.S.

The caravan drove up onto the heights and stopped. Men lugging automatic weapons poured out of the van and rushed to take up strategic positions around the hilltop. Barrios went over to the van, reached inside, and came out with a pair of binoculars; he crossed to the bluff and began scanning the road. Watching him do this, Alejandro thought, We're on their home turf, where they have most of the umpires on their payroll, and they're still paranoid. The good guys must be starting to get their attention.

Walking over to Pizzaro, who was leaning up against the van, Alejandro asked, "When and where is the drop?"

Pizzaro ignored his question. "Since we're in your hometown, why don't you invite us over to your mother's for a home-cooked meal, and introduce us to your sister. Her name is Maria, isn't it?"

Alejandro glared at him. "When I see my family, I'll see 'em alone, not with any of your goons."

They remained there for three and a half hours, until the sun touched the ocean, sending shimmering pink rays skimming across the water. The ocean told him it was almost sunset, and he knew that all along La Playa Ropa people were drifting out onto the beach to enjoy it and the brief "green flash" that followed.

At the northwest end of La Playa Ropa—a section of beach the locals called "Gringo Gulch" because the Canadian and American dropouts and holdover hippies lived there—people were gathering for the ritual of sunset watching at Rossy's, a two-story beach restaurant built on columns and open to the air.

Grim-lipped, Alejandro watched the huge ball float down out of the sky, its hue so furious a blazing orange that a golden aureole sprang forth around the ball, lighting up the sky and the ocean. He snapped a look at the others. Everyone was watching the sight.

The sun slipped down behind the line, pulling the day with it and replacing light with darkness.

Alejandro had never felt more alone.

A man leaned out of the back of the van and shouted in Spanish, "The plane just left."

"Where's the landing zone?" Alejandro called to Pizzaro.

"We're going to be moving out in a few minutes," the doper said, and looked over to Barrios, who was scanning the road with the binoculars.

The flight of stone steps lifted out of the sands of La Playa Ropa and rose up to a narrow footpath that clung to the mountain's steep side. The footpath spiraled upward, weaving higher and higher above the ocean; at the top an abandoned lighthouse stood sentinel over land that had been baked into barrenness by the sun.

The night was black, the moon full and the breeze cool, laced with the day's leftover heat. Alejandro glanced south at the lights of Zihuatanejo. They looked like a hodgepodge of twinkling campfires set into the shadows of towering mountains.

The sound of Pizzaro talking on the walkie-talkie caused Alejandro to look over his shoulder. Barrios was leaning up against the lighthouse, watching him. Their eyes locked. The caravan had driven down from the heights of the Parthenon twenty minutes earlier and had driven out the beach road, stopping a little beyond Rossy's. The bodyguards jumped out of the van and spread out around the foot of the small mountain while Alejandro, Pizzaro, and Barrios trudged up the stone steps to the lonely lighthouse.

Alejandro gazed down over the beach, where the sands were thick with his past. At night the sands belonged to the tree rats, and to the packs of emaciated dogs scavenging for food, and to the lovers who copulated under thatched roof *palapas* with the rising tide lapping at their feet. He saw himself as a barefoot boy trudging from hotel to hotel, hawking his jewelry. "Silver necklace, señora? Pure silver bracelet, señora?" He smiled when his thoughts resurrected his dognapping days, when he would snatch tourists' pets and turn them over to Bill Trout, La Playa Ropa's king of the dognappers, to negotiate the ransom from the animals' hysterical owners.

He was remembering the good times he used to have with the gentle expatriate from Chicago's South Side when Pizzaro shouted, "The chutes have been dropped."

Alejandro extended the handset's antenna and walked backward to the middle of the bluff, holding the homing device in front of him, its beacon reaching far out into the darkness.

Pizzaro and Barrios moved about, peering off the bluff, searching out the surrounding light.

At first Alejandro thought they were birds gliding at him out of the moon. As the birds grew in definition, however, a spark of excitement grew in his chest. He aimed the transmitter in their direction and said, "There they are."

Pizzaro and Barrios hurried over and stood beside him, their gazes following the transmitter's line of sight.

Gliding gracefully out of the night, the parachutes looked like prehistoric birds of prey riding the thermals down to earth with their bundles of misery secured in their talons, and at that moment Alejandro was glad that he was a cop working to put a gang of evil people out of business.

The Ram Air chutes glided closer and closer, growing in size until they were a few meters away from the mountaintop. Then they slowed and appeared to stop, hovering on their pillows of air, as the computerized guidance system adjusted for wind direction. Pizzaro wore a satisfied smile; Barrios kept glancing from the homing device in Alejandro's hand to the parachutes, as if anxiously awaiting the finale.

The parachutes veered off to the left, made a hundred-and-eighty-degree turn around the mountain, cut across the flat bluff, and crumpled to the ground behind them, their canopies blossoming down over the shroud lines and their cargoes.

Sticking the transmitter into his waistband, Alejandro walked over to the parachutes and kneeled on one knee to toss the canopies off the duffel bags. Looking around at Pizzaro, he asked, "Do we have a deal?"

"Impressive," Pizzaro said, coming over and placing his foot on one of the duffel bags, "but what guarantee do we have that Parapoint will always work, and be on target? If we lost our product during the delivery mode, we'd be out a lot of money. After all, we're a small company trying to compete in a hostile environment."

"Hey, amigo, get down off the cross, the natives need the wood. Martyrdom don't look good on you," Alejandro said.

Pizzaro made a small gray laugh. "You're right."

Alejandro did not notice Barrios drifting off behind him, nor did he see the thin man's bony fingers slip under the tails of his shirt and come out with a nine-millimeter automatic pistol. A beam of moonlight reflected off the chrome-plated weapon and tinged the corner of Alejandro's eye at the same moment he saw Pizzaro's face cloud and heard the crunch of a footstep behind him.

They're going to take me out! he thought, leaping off the ground, digging his heels into the dirt, and propelling himself backward at the sound. He collided with Barrios, smashing into the doper's face with the back of his head. They toppled to the ground, with Barrios bleeding from his nose and mouth and pummeling Alejandro about the body with his weapon.

Pizzaro rushed over to the struggling men and threw a headlock around Alejandro's face, yanking him to his knees with such force that a bolt of pain speared down his neck and into his arms. The undercover dug his teeth into Pizzaro's arm, and the doper cried out in pain. Alejandro's head was forced backward by the powerful vise.

Barrios scrambled off the ground and, angrily gripping the nine-millimeter by its barrel, smashed the weapon across Alejandro's head. The undercover's rage dulled the pain; he dug his teeth deeper, tasting the coppery flow of blood. With both hands he grabbed Pizzaro's ankles and jerked his feet out from under him, at the same time arching his own body back and sweeping his feet upward, catching Barrios in the testicles, *whoosh*ing the air from his lungs, and crumpling the doper to his knees.

A scream exploded from Barrios as he toppled sideways to the ground, crunched up in a fetal position and hugging his groin.

Alejandro leaped for the weapon Barrios had dropped. Pizzaro grabbed one of his legs and twisted him away from the nine-millimeter.

Alejandro back-kicked Pizzaro in the face and then, as he broke free, hurled himself at the weapon. Barrios leaped on top of him, wrestling for control of the gun. Alejandro struggled his finger through the trigger guard. Pizzaro ran over to them and began kicking Alejandro about the body. A shot rang out. The bullet *thunk*ed into the side of the lighthouse, sending shards of stone flying. Alejandro heard the sound of running feet. Gathering all his strength, he yanked the weapon free and was firming it into his hand when the blow came and blackness swept over him.

─── 18 ───

The lines were blurred. Alejandro became aware of them at the same moment he opened his eyes and felt the pounding in his head and the awful ache in his back and shoulders. He was sprawled on a cold cement floor. He blinked several times, trying to focus on the vertical lines; they were bars set high into the wall in front of him.

He sat up. He hurt more. If they had wanted me dead, I'd be dead. He grimaced from the terrible smell. His eyes explored his cell. The sink and toilet were caked in excrement and humming with flies. He retched from the stench. Graffiti written in feces was scrawled on the walls. Names and dates. Curses directed at the mothers of the police, *hijo de una puta.*

Hearing incongruously happy music wafting in from the outside, he forced himself to get up, stood under the wall with the barred window, and turned his face up, trying desperately to suck in some fresh air. He noticed black patches across his fingertips. Holding up his hands to the dim illumination that came from the streetlights outside, he saw that they'd fingerprinted him. The bastards had flown him there to test Parapoint, deliver their not-so-veiled threat against him and his family—and then have their tamed policemen fax his prints to the FBI, NCIC, and probably the CIA's Counter-Narcotics Center, too.

They're clever and cautious, he thought, stretching for the bars and then leaping to try to grab hold of them. He needed to know where he was. He figured he'd been out for at least an hour and hoped he didn't have a concussion or worse. His hands just missed the bars, and he fell back down and squatted, looking around his cell. There was no cot, nothing nearby to stand on to help him reach up and grab hold of the bars. The toilet and sink were on the other side of the cell. He hunkered down and sprang upward, stretching up for the bars. This time he caught hold of them and scrambled up the wall.

The razor-sharp fronds of the palm trees lining Avenida Moreles were swaying in the gentle breeze. Across the street was the post office and, to its right, Plaza Cuauhtémoc. A line of frightened people had gathered on the street in front of his prison, awaiting their turn to be summoned inside the town headquarters of the judicial police.

His ears pricked up when he heard the heavy metallic scraping of the lock on his cell door. He dropped down as the door was pushed open. Two guards, both around five feet tall, wearing ill-fitting, mismatched uniforms with dirty undershirts showing under their open collars, strutted inside. They would have been comical were it not for the pump shotguns cradled in their arms.

"*Venga,*" one of them barked.

Alejandro gathered himself up and walked out into a dingy passage lit by the glow of a single bulb hanging by a stretch of black wire from a hole in the ceiling. The air was heavy with the stench of human sweat, shit, and fear. Both sides of the passage were lined with steel doors. The absence of sound from behind them suggested the ominous silence of the helpless. One of the guards shoved him forward, toward a wooden door at the end of the corridor.

The largest rat he had ever seen scurried between his legs. It went ahead of them, up to the wooden door, and attempted to squeeze under it. But it couldn't get its fat body through, so it pulled out its head and scurried back up the passageway. The shotgun blast almost burst Alejandro's eardrums. The rat exploded into a crimson mass of fur, cartilage, and body parts that splattered over the walls and ceilings. Some of the mushy mass hit Alejandro in the face. Wiping off the mess, he turned and glared at his guards. They were grinning at him, showing their decaying and missing teeth. The one who had fired the round ejected the spent cartridge from his smoking weapon and jabbed the barrel into Alejandro's back, making him stumble forward.

The paneled office behind the wooden door was air-conditioned. The man standing behind the big desk in the center of the room had on pleated white slacks, a designer polo shirt, an automatic pistol on his hip, and an expensive gold watch on his wrist. He was a little older than Alejandro and wore his black hair slicked back without a part.

He waved the guards out and pointed to the single battered chair in front of his desk. When the door closed, he said in perfect English, "I'm Major Hernandez y Hernandez."

"Why am I here?"

The major's hands flew up in a broad gesture of dismissal. "Possession of cocaine, resisting arrest, destroying property, et cetera."

"I want to telephone the American embassy's hot line in Mexico City."

Hernandez y Hernandez's thick lips curled into a sarcastic grin. "We can dispense with that formality. Since you're a Mexican citizen."

"I'm an American citizen."

"I'm afraid not, Mr. Alejandro Monahan. Your parents did what all gringo-Mexican parents do. They took out an American and a Mexican passport when you were born. Dual citizenship; illegal, but common."

Alejandro sat up rigidly on the chair, his body now aching all over. "What do you want, Major?"

Hernandez y Hernandez picked up a single sheet of paper from his otherwise clean desk, read it, and said, "We faxed your fingerprints and photo to the States. You have no criminal record; you are unknown to the drug intelligence community. And"—the major stared at him—"you have never been a member of any law enforcement agency." He let the paper fall from his hand.

"The wonders of modern communication. You get to know all that in a matter of hours." Alejandro started to get out of the chair.

"Sit down. You're not out of here yet. It's not often we get to arrest a major drug dealer."

"That's because they all have you on their payrolls."

Hernandez y Hernandez laughed. "You have *cojónes*. Most people who sit in that chair tremble when I look at them."

"How much?"

Hernandez y Hernandez pulled out the top drawer, took out a calculator, and began punching in numbers. "My personal expenses . . . damage to government property . . . and then there was your private accommodations . . . That will be two thousand U.S."

"Two thousand for a ninety-minute stay in that shithole? Amigo, put some real into your life."

The major looked up from the calculator. "If we had put you

into a holding cell with the general population, I don't think you would be able to sit right for a long, long time. Amigo."

"What's the total?"

Hernandez y Hernandez pressed the button, looked up at him, and said, "Since you're a friend of a friend, we'll round it off to an even five thousand U.S."

"Tell ya what, amigo, send the bill to our mutual friend, I'm fresh out of cash." Alejandro heaved himself out of the chair, making for the door.

"Open it and you're dead."

Alejandro grabbed the doorknob, pulled, and found the same two guards lolling up against the wall with their shotguns nestled in the crook of their arms. He closed the door quietly, walked back, and lowered himself onto the chair, saying, "Amigo, we got a problem."

"I have no problems."

"We're both businessmen who work for the same people. We both know that you were well taken care of for your speedy fingerprint check to Washington. And now you're trying to sweeten your mango by scoring me. The people we work for wouldn't like to hear that. I'm important to them, very important. If anything happened to me, you'd be in deep shit."

Hernandez y Hernandez's easy smile vanished. He regarded Alejandro in wary silence.

"I don't have any money with me, and even if I did, I wouldn't give it to you," Alejandro said, feeling the icy flow of adrenaline. "My friends are waiting."

Hernandez y Hernandez bit down on his lower lip, walked over to the door, threw it open, and told the guards in Spanish, "Let him go."

Alejandro walked out of the police station and darted across the avenue, quickly melting into the crowd of strollers in Plaza Cuauhtémoc, relishing the sounds and smells of home. He didn't know where Pizzaro and Barrios were, but wherever they were, he hoped they hurt as much as he did. He looked at his watch: 9:10 central time. He did not know what plans had been made to get them back to New York, but he did know that now that he was here, there were things that needed doing and not much time to do them.

Rosa's ice-cream store was crowded, and all the outside tables at Pollo Loco and La Sirena Gorda were taken. Many families were out for their evening stroll through the plaza. Hurrying along, he happened to glance into Coconuts restaurant, and there, sitting under a palm tree inside the open-air part, was his old dognapping partner, Bill Trout. His beard was white now, but he still had his trademark boar's tooth around his neck on a silver chain that some lost love had given him. By the look of things, he was trying to calm a frantic couple from the States. Another disappearing pet caper, and Trout to the rescue. Alejandro was tempted to go in and say hello, but he didn't; there was no time.

He hurried to Benito Juarez Avenue, where he turned left and gingerly navigated the broken sidewalk past stores without any doors, just curtains stirring in the gentle evening breeze.

Crossing Antonia Nava Street, he saw his destination spread out in front of him: El Globo, the town's boomerang-shaped market that was open until eleven every night, except on Sunday, when it was closed. El Globo would be a good place to lose anyone who might be following him. Once in the market, he made his way down the aisles, pausing now and then to glance around, looking for clouded eyes that refused to meet his.

Farmers stood behind their stalls, hawking fruits and vegetables. Lamb and pig carcasses lay across the tops of display cases boiling with flies and crawling with insects. Housewives plied the aisles searching for bargains, negotiating with merchants. Going into the children's aisle, Alejandro was glad to see that the toys were still made the old way, by hand.

He moved from aisle to aisle, always pausing to look. After

slipping into the area where sandals were sold, he ducked outside and leaned up against the wall, waiting to see if anyone came out after him. Again he was struck by how little things had changed. Animal bones were still overflowing from El Globo's sole Dumpster, which was swarming with all sorts of flying things and surrounded by packs of dogs fighting over the spilled scraps. Across the street, housewives waited patiently in line outside Tortillaria Daniel to buy their morning's tortillas. The groaning old conveyer belt still crept along, carrying the disk-shaped bread out of the clay oven.

Satisfied that he had not acquired a tail, Alejandro pushed away from the wall, walked out into the street, and hailed a taxi. Settling into the vintage Volkswagen's passenger seat, he wished the driver "Good evening," then said, "Galería Zonya."

On the way through town, Alejandro saw that the locals still removed their license plates whenever they parked illegally in order to prevent the traffic police from removing them and ransoming them back.

Galería Zonya was in the middle of Cuauhtémoc Avenue, a street lined with tourist shops and restaurants. The *galería* was known for its Indian clothes, handicrafts, and artifacts. Zonya was renowned among the local Indians as a *mentirosa,* a storyteller. A full-blooded, free-spirited Tarascan, she had dedicated her life to keeping alive the oral history of her people.

She was sitting in a corner of her empty store, listening to a tape of songs from the Andes, when Alejandro entered. A willowy woman in her late fifties with dark hair cascading down her back, she was wearing an ankle-length red-and-black cotton dress made of a coarse Guatemalan cotton tartan. She wore no shoes and had on necklaces and bracelets made of shark teeth. She looked across at him, and a smile curved her full mouth. She went to him, threw her arms around him, and kissed both his cheeks, asking in Tarascan, "What are you doing here in Zihua? I heard you were becoming a famous singer in New York."

He took her hands in his and smiled warmly into her large gray eyes, noting the flecks of black in the irises. "I'm here on a short visit to see my mother and sister, and to ask you some questions about our Indian heritage."

"There are no Indians left in Mexico, they traded their heritage for pickups and polyester."

He smiled. "You'll never change. Have you married?"

Now she smiled back as she said, "Marriage is an evil white man's institution meant to enslave the female spirit." She locked the front door and switched off the lights. "Let's go into the back, I have some homemade mescal."

She led him past the curtains into the back room. Cartons of handicrafts were stacked about. A large hand-carved table of brazilwood was centered under the ceiling fan. She poured them "shooters," tall thin glasses of mescal. They banged the bottom of the glass on the table and downed their drinks.

" 'At'll get your insides' attention real quick," he said.

She poured them another round. He cocked his head to one side, listening to what sounded like distant gunfire. "Someone must be celebrating."

"Or some mestizo found his woman with another man," she said in a bored tone.

"Zonya, I don't have much time," he began. "My grandmother used to tell us a story about a queen who sailed across the great waters in a straw boat, and landed here with a great treasure, and married a Tarascan king. Are you familiar with that story?"

"That queen was Cleopatra." She scraped her chair back, got up, and went over to the armoire on the other side of the room.

Watching her rummage through the bottom of the cabinet, he said, "Cleopatra would have had to sail that boat down the Red Sea into the Indian Ocean, across the South Atlantic, and around Cape Horn into the South Pacific, and up the coast to here."

Zonya came back holding a clay figure, which she put on the

table in front of him. It was seventy centimeters high and depicted a stately woman wearing a Tarascan queen's headdress with a cobra and a viper coiled around the parrot feathers. The serpents had almost human grins. The woman's face bore a striking similarity to Cleopatra's profile on ancient coins dating from her dynasty. Around her neck was a silver chain holding a miniature of a solar bark or boat with the symbol of the Egyptian sun god, charms of dung beetles, and baboons worshiping beneath a crescent moon. Ibex heads decorated the bark's bow and stern. "This is part Tarascan and part Egyptian," he said.

"This is a replica of a bust that was excavated on Ixtapa Island in 1962. The original is on display in the National Museum of Anthropology in Mexico City."

Alejandro was so fascinated that he forgot his still-aching body and his anxiety. "I've never seen snakes like these in any Tarascan art."

"Because you'll never find them in Mexico."

"What makes you say that the queen was Cleopatra?"

"My grandmother's great-grandmother said it was Cleopatra."

"Was the original carving dated?"

"The classic era, somewhere between 40 B.C. and A.D. 10."

Alejandro thought for a moment and then said softly, "Cleopatra was supposed to have died August 30, 30 B.C. How did the archaeologists explain Egyptian myths on a piece of Tarascan art dating from the classic era?"

Zonya smiled triumphantly. "They couldn't. Some of them speculated that it was coincidence. My grandmother's great-grandmother said that after the queen married the king, he gave her Ixtapa Island as a wedding present. The queen used the island for herself and her ladies, allowing only women on the island. There is a letter in Madrid from Cortés to Carlos Primero reporting that Ixtapa Island was populated only by women."

She toyed with her glass of mescal, making wet circles on the brazilwood tabletop. She looked past him, her eyes focusing on the ancient past. "The world believes the queen died of an asp bite."

"I don't," he said in Tarascan, gulping mescal and looking at her. "Asp venom attacks the blood. It's a slow, agonizingly painful way to die. It swells and discolors the body. The ancients weren't toxicologists, but they knew the effects of different snakebites. Women do not kill themselves by disfiguring their bodies. Cleopatra was too beautiful and vain to do that."

She nodded vigorously in agreement. "What do you think really happened?"

Alejandro said, "Cobra venom attacks the central nervous system. It's a painless death, and it does not disfigure. We both have reason to believe that the queen escaped. Vanished from Egypt. I think Cleopatra ordered that a slave with a similar build to hers be dressed in her royal robes. She then had this slave bitten by an asp. Then she ordered her two loyal servants, Iras and Charmian, to stick their hands into a basket containing a cobra. When the Romans battered their way into the throne room, they found a disfigured corpse in royal robes, and the two servants. Charmian was still alive; that's a historical fact. She told Octavian that 'it was a fitting death for a princess descended from so many royal kings,' and died."

"Wouldn't the Romans have wondered why she allowed herself such a painful death?"

Alejandro went on with growing assurance. "I believe that the Romans saw exactly what they wanted to see: a dead Cleopatra. Again, historical fact; she knew the end was near and had five ships built for her escape. Cleopatra was a direct descendant of Ptolemy and guardian of the Ptolemaic treasure. When the Romans went to the treasure rooms the cupboard was bare. Archaeologists have been searching for the treasure for centuries. Recently a royal Mayan tomb was unearthed in Campeche, Mexico." He leaned close to the *mentirosa* and said softly,

"They discovered some of the treasure in that tomb."

Her eyes fell to the table as if she were studying the grain of the red-and-purple dyewood. "You appear to have spent a lot of time studying the queen's life." Her eyes met his. "Is that because someone named Cleopatra killed your father?"

Holding her gaze, he shifted on his chair, aware that she had gone to the very heart of his secret, the real purpose of his entire life.

A profound silence fell between them.

Finally he broke it by asking quietly, in English now, "Did you ever know or hear of anyone in or around Zihua using the name Cleopatra?"

She poured more mescal into their glasses. "Your journey has been long and painful, hasn't it, Alejandro?"

"Yes."

She downed her drink. "Years ago I heard of a Medellin assassin who used that name. But she was not from Mexico."

Alejandro picked up the effigy of the stately woman wearing the Tarascan headdress; the serpents coiled around the parrot feathers seemed to be laughing at him.

19

T HE HORIZON WAS A DIS-
tant line where black met
black and the stars disappeared.

A thatched-roof house stood on the side of the cliff overlooking La Playa Ropa. There was a porch in front of the house that afforded a breathtaking view of the entire lagoon. A brick path ran down from the ocean road and was lined with avocado and coconut trees. The path ended at the rear door of the house; it led inside, into a large kitchen floored in rust-colored tiles.

Alejandro had taken a taxi from Zonya's and now stood in the shadows of the trees, listening to the pounding surf. He was home.

He stood there for a while, gazing at the darkened house, and then made his way out of the shadows and walked down the lane. The family's several dogs shattered the midnight air with barking.

"Who's there?" his mother's voice called in Spanish.

"Mama, it's me, Alejandro," he shouted, running into the creaking house.

His mother's hair was white in the light of the single overlight in the kitchen, and it cascaded down her back. She wore a cotton nightgown, and despite her wrinkles, her beauty was still much in evidence. She flung herself into her son's arms, crying, "My baby is home!" Smothering him with her loving kisses, she said, "Why didn't you let me know you were coming? Look at you, you're too skinny."

He hugged her close, savoring her love. "I love you, Mama."

His mother was so excited at seeing him after a lapse of eight years that she was trembling and almost in tears. "What are you doing here? Are you home for good?"

Still holding her in his arms, Alejandro told her, "The hotel association wanted me to do a show in one of the hotels in Ixtapa. I'm only going to be here for a few more hours." He looked around, savoring the changeless comfort of home, relishing the familiar smells. "I love you, Mama."

Her tone changed. "Let's go outside and look at the stars together."

They walked between the coconut and avocado trees, holding hands, not talking.

"Why do you lie to your mother? Do you think that my son could appear in any hotel in Mexico and that I would not hear about it?"

"Mama . . ."

"No, Alejandro. I fell in love with an Irish cop, and married him. I married him because he loved me. But he also loved that damn police department. There was not a day that passed in our lives together that his mistress did not break my heart."

"Mama—"

"Listen to me! Seaver and Romano, the one they call Joey-the-G-Man, were always talking their secret talks with your father when they visited on vacation. They'd go off so I could not hear what they were saying. I didn't have to hear; I only had to look at them to know what they were talking about. And then your father retired, and we lived here in paradise, and I was happier than I'd ever been." She paused, memories crowding in on her. "One day much later, Seaver came alone. He and your father sat under that avocado tree, talking their secrets, and my heart broke. The *traficantes* had come to Zihua, and then Seaver came, and two weeks later your father was dead. . . ."

"Mama—"

"Listen! When you were twenty years old Seaver came here again. You sat with him under that same avocado tree talking secrets just like your father did, and my heart was torn with fear for you. I knew what they wanted. And then you left; and my life left with you."

"Mama, a man has to do—"

She slapped her son's face. "Don't you ever say that macho nonsense to me! Your father used to say the same thing. A man doesn't have to do anything he doesn't want to do."

Alejandro rubbed his stinging cheek. "You don't understand."

"That's the problem, I do understand."

He kicked a fallen coconut across the ground. "I never meant to cause you any pain."

She placed the flat of her hand consolingly on her son's cheek. "I know. It's time you came home and got married, had a family. I need to see my grandchildren before I go to God."

A physically painful feeling of immense guilt shot through him. "Mama, please don't talk like that."

"When will you be coming home?"

"Soon, Mama, real soon." He looked back at the house. "Where is Maria?"

"Your sister is out with friends."

"At one o'clock in the morning?"

She laughed. "You're not home thirty minutes and you're already the Mexican brother. Your sister is a woman; she doesn't have to account to you."

He smiled in embarrassment. "I'm sorry, Mama."

They continued walking. She looked up at her son and asked, "Is it true that some apartments in New York rent for as much as ten thousand dollars a month?"

20

HEADLIGHTS PIERCED THE night. A car drew up to a stop on the ocean road in front of Alejandro's mother's house. He ran to the window in time to see his sister Maria lean across the passenger seat and kiss the driver. Alejandro went out the rear door and ran up the path, calling, "Maria!"

She broke free of the embrace, turned, saw her brother, and called out his name as she rushed from the car to his arms.

The driver of the car got out, leaned over the roof, and said, "I'll call you tomorrow, Maria."

"Juan Carlos, this is my brother, Alejandro."

"Hi," he said nervously, then quickly got into his car and drove away.

Their mother ran from the house and embraced her family. Tears came to Alejandro as he stood in front of the house, kissing his mother and sister, telling them how much he loved and missed them. The Monahan family was together, and that made him feel human again.

Juan Carlos sped his car down the ocean road. When he came to the statue of the four dolphins, he turned left and drove down the winding street and parked in front of the police substation across from La Villa del Sol Hotel. He glanced at the police blockhouse, saw all the lights were out, and thought, Our protectors are asleep. He looked up at the antennas on the roof of the police building and reached into his shirt pocket, taking out a pack of Fiesta cigarettes. He shook one out into his mouth, pushed in the lighter, and, holding the package on his lap, pushed in the tiny button concealed on the right side of the package. He pulled out the lighter, lit the cigarette, and said, "The brother's come home." His voice message was encoded automatically into a scrambled digital code inside the miniature burst transmitter. After tucking the package of cigarettes back into his shirt pocket, he tilted it toward the antennas on the roof of the blockhouse and pushed the Send button on the top.

He remained parked for a few minutes, enjoying his smoke. Then he tossed the butt out the window and watched it hit the ground in a shower of sparks. Time to go home and see what was on CNN.

21

T HE ROW OF ATTACHED ONE-
story garages strung across
the back of Yeshiva Beth Chaim's schoolyard was in darkness,
save for the Special Operations Section Communications Unit
that fronted West End Avenue, where a fluorescent ceiling fixture bathed the room in a soft white luminescence. Detective
Mary Reddington, a leggy strawberry blonde in her middle thirties, sat at the communications console doing needlepoint. She
glanced up at the digital clock in time to see the wheel turn to
"0430—Wednesday." Three and a half hours of her tour remained, and then she and her husband were off on a twelve-day
cruise to the Canary Islands. She heard a rustling noise from
outside and leaned up out of her swivel chair to look out the
window.

The bread man was making a delivery to the bodega across the street on West End Avenue. Reddington watched him stack the long brown bags inside the doorway and push the squeaky accordion gate closed. Lowering herself back to the worn leather seat of the chair, she noticed that a haze of smog thickened the faint morning glow over the city. She looked back at the clock: 0433. She went back to her needlepoint.

The night supervisor at the CIA's Counter-Narcotics Center, sixty miles northeast of Knoxville, Tennessee, read Juan Carlos's decoded cryptogram.

"How do you want us to send it?" the cipher clerk asked, glancing out the window at the string of dish antennas.

Handing the message back to the clerk, the supervisor said, "Coded fax. Get it right out."

Detective Reddington pushed the needle through the canvas and glanced up at the clock: 0450. The fax machine began to clatter. Reddington put the canvas and the needle on the ledge of the console. Remaining seated, she walked her chair over to the machine. She tore off the coded fax, switched on the cryptoanalysis machine, fed the message into it, and watched as the jumble of numbers spun across the display window. After reading the decoded message, she wheeled herself over to the computer, inputted the access code for the "Mother Hen Data Bank," and typed in "Chilebean." Andy Seaver's name scrolled across the screen. She telephoned him at home; after getting no answer there, she accessed the "Significant Other" file and typed in Seaver's name. Wilma Galt's name and telephone number appeared on the screen, followed by Seaver's official legend.

By 0526 that morning, Joey-the-G-Man was losing his private battle as he lit his third cigarette of the day. He looked across the table at Seaver, and asked, "Why the fuck do you suppose they flew him to Zihuatanejo?"

Seaver shrugged and speculated, "Probably to test Parapoint

on their own turf, and to let him know that they know where his mother and sister lived."

"If the demonstration went okay, Che-Che'll want to get right to it. Are the chutes ready?"

"I'm collecting them from Hansen today."

"And the money to pay for them?"

"It's already been transferred into Precision Industries' covert accounts." Seaver took the cheroot out of his mouth, laced his hands behind his head, and said, "Hansen had a visit from a woman with DEA credentials. They checked out phony. She wanted to know about Alejandro. Hansen said she was a looker, well dressed, with thick black hair and deeply tanned skin."

Romano looked very worried. "What did Hansen tell her?"

"He stuck to the legend Alejandro and him made up."

"She buy it?"

"He thinks she did."

Joey-the-G-man took a deep drag on his cigarette, blew the smoke up at the ceiling, and said, "We'd better arrange to give Chilebean's family more eyes and ears. Can you ask Hicks to have his people down there ready to scoop them up and stash them in an Agency safe house if things start to get messy?"

"I've already taken care of that."

"How are you guys going to make contact when he gets back?"

"Burst transmissions."

"And what if he's in a hurry?"

"In an emergency he can always call Control. And we've developed a few alternate ways for him to pass me information by making contact at night between his performances."

The sound of the cipher lock being keyed caused them to look up. Detective Reddington walked inside and closed the door behind her. She handed her boss a decoded fax from CNC that read "Chilebean's aboard aircraft that entered US airspace 0649 central time this date. Destination per flight plan filed is New York La Guardia." He put the message on the table, looked up at Reddington, and said, "Have a good cruise, Mary."

In another part of Queens, other passengers were deplaning at JFK. John Courtney Carlsen's suit was wrinkled and his tasseled loafers scuffed when he walked out of Customs and into the crowded airline terminal, carrying his designer carryall. The American Airlines flight from Tortola had stopped in San Juan, Puerto Rico, where he had restudied his notes on the Kingscross Bank of Road Town, a brass-plate financial institution without security guards that trafficked in a worldwide network of electronic debits and credits. He had been relieved to see that the real owners of Kingscross were veiled behind an interlocking pyramid of European and Middle Eastern companies and was particularly delighted that many of them were Pakistani and Saudi. This reassured him that Che-Che was laundering money through a perfectly unscrupulous bank free of any CIA or DEA shenanigans.

Walking out past the bank of frosted-glass doors into the gauntlet of waiting friends and relatives, he spotted a man in a chauffeur's cap holding up a cardboard sign with his name crayoned across the front. He walked over to the man. "I'm Mr. Carlsen."

"I'm saposta drive ya to da Hotel Madison."

"And who told you to do that?"

"Some guy named Leon. He wants ya to call him at his hotel, here's the number. Ask for room 708," he said, passing Carlsen a folded slip of paper.

Carlsen walked over to the bank of shiny telephones, deposited a quarter, and when he heard the electronic hiccup, dialed. The phone was snapped up on the first ring, and Judith Stern's gleeful voice came over the line. "Welcome home, darling."

"What's with the Leon routine?"

"Would you want the help to know you're about to have an assignation? He'll drive you to a hotel."

He smiled. "Why there and not the apartment?"

Her voice got serious. "Hector's been acting strange lately. Why take chances?"

"I'll be right over," he said, and slowly replaced the receiver. He hadn't been able to stop thinking about the money warehouses during his trip down to Road Town. All that money, just sitting in some stinking building waiting to be shipped out of the country. He kept asking himself over and over again, Could we really get away with ripping one of them off?

The Madison was an inconspicuous hotel on Forty-ninth Street, two blocks west of Ninth Avenue. Carlsen walked past the desk clerk and took the elevator up to the seventh floor. The carpet had a faded floral design, and four of the wall sconces that lined the wall were out.

Judith opened the door the second he knocked on it, pulled him into the room, and threw herself into his arms. Kissing him passionately, she kicked the door closed.

Finally he stepped back, looking at her. "I missed you," he said, and hugged her.

She took him by the hand and tugged him over to the bed. He pulled her down on top of him. "Not so fast, lover," she insisted. "Business first. Tell me what you found out in Road Town."

"I can report that Alejandro's friend, Franklin Penzer, runs a perfectly dishonest bank. And I can also tell you that Penzer is greedy and has expensive tastes."

"And the ownership of the bank?"

He told her about the financial setup and principals, adding, "Penzer assured me of the bank's regulatory flexibility, which translates into a bank with little or no regulations, strict confidentiality, and an enlightened money-laundering policy."

"No Agency or DEA types lurking around the boardroom?"

"No." He sat up, taking her hand in his, and his face grew still as he asked, "Do you really love me, Judith?"

An expression of dismay washed over her face. "How can you ask me that?"

An ominous quiet fell between them. He began rubbing her hand. Avoiding her eyes, he said, "I've been thinking a lot about what we talked about before I left."

Unnoticed by him, her eyes became cheerless and cold. "What was that, darling?" she asked, curving herself into him and slipping her arm around his shoulder.

He kissed her head. "Those money warehouses. Do you really think we could get away with it?"

"Yes, I do," she said, nibbling on his earlobe.

"Are you sure?"

"Do you think I'd jeopardize my life or yours if I wasn't?"

"I guess not."

"It's only a matter of erasing one of them from a disk, and then arranging it to look as though Hector did it, if the loss should ever be discovered."

Mumbling into the curve of her neck, he said, "I love the idea of putting the weight on Hector."

She kissed him, cupped his face with her palms, and got up. She went to the dresser and picked up her pocketbook.

"Where are you going?" he asked.

She lowered herself next to him, pocketbook in hand, and said, "To the bathroom, silly. We don't want any little John Courtneys right now, do we?" She kissed him as her right hand crept into her pocketbook and came out with a .32-caliber Magnum revolver chambered with six hollow-tipped rounds. She brought the barrel up to his temple and fired, exploding the left side of his head in a red mist that splattered chunks of brain and skull across the dirty fleur-de-lis wallpaper. She dropped the revolver back into her bag, looked down at the twitching body, and said, "You failed your security test, John."

*   *   *

Dressed only in his underpants, Roberto Barrios worked his bedroom StairMaster as he gazed out his eighth-floor window at the roofs of brownstones clustered along West Ninety-ninth Street. His body still hurt from the fight with Alejandro on the top of that damn mountain. Hector had wanted to put on some real muscle to instill fear into the singer, let him know that he couldn't count on his friendship with Che-Che to protect him. That Bolivian prick is big on handing object lessons out to others, he thought, increasing the speed of the exercise machine, feeling the sweat trickling down his armpits. Hector had me worried there for a while with my girlfriend from Hopewell Junction. The bitch really had me fooled.

The doorbell rang, and he stumbled on the treads. He'd only arrived home from Zihuatanejo an hour ago and wasn't expecting anyone.

It rang again.

Switching off the machine, he stepped down, then grabbed his robe from the bed and tossed it around his shoulders as he made for the nightstand. He slid open its drawer and took out a nine-millimeter automatic pistol, pulling back the receiver until he saw the glint of a chambered round. Then, letting the slide snap forward, he picked his way out of the bedroom and padded carefully across the living room to the foyer. Standing to the side of the door, he asked, "Who is it?"

"It's me, Judith."

Weapon in hand, he unlocked the door, slid the chain lock out of its restraining bar, and stepped back. He aimed his weapon at the opening. "Come in, Judith."

She stepped inside. He grabbed her pocketbook out of her hand and tossed it across the room, spun her around, and slammed her up against the wall, at the same time kicking the door closed. Pressing her up against the flocked wallpaper, he put the barrel of the automatic to her head and snarled, "I just got back from Mexico, and Hector's whore pays me an unexpected visit. I gotta think, Why?"

Careful not to move, she said in an aggrieved tone, "This is not the greeting I expected, Roberto."

"Cut the bullshit, and keep your hands flat. How did you get by the doorman?"

"I walked through the service entrance like I owned the place. We need to talk, Roberto."

"Spread your legs, and move back. I want you leaning on your fingertips."

She complied with his order, complaining, "This is uncomfortable."

"Dead is more uncomfortable," he snapped, running his hand over her body, searching for concealed weapons. Stepping back, he leveled the nine-millimeter at her and said, "Turn around."

She faced him.

"Take off your clothes."

She kicked off her shoes angrily, reached behind and unzipped her dress, and stepped out of it. Glaring at him contemptuously, she asked, "Satisfied?"

"Everything."

Staring at him, she worked off her panty hose, rolling them down one leg at a time, then tossed them aside. Next came her bra and underpants.

"Turn around slowly," he ordered, scanning her body for a weapon. "Lift your tits."

She complied. Seeing nothing taped to her body, he moved up to her, looked directly into her eyes, ran his hand up between her legs, and thrust a finger inside her body.

She grimaced from the intrusion and said, "You fucking pig."

Stepping back, he motioned her farther inside the living room with his pistol. Four white sofas were set around a glass-topped coffee table on a bamboo frame in the middle of the room. He walked behind one of the sofas and waited for her to sit; then he lowered himself on the one directly across from her. "Tell me why you're here."

Angrily, she snatched up two pillows to try to cover her nakedness. "Your dead girlfriend was an informer for the Drug Enforcement Agency," she said in a strangely neutral tone of voice. She grabbed two more decorative pillows off the sofa and piled them on her lap.

Barrios gave her an icy smile. "You're becoming paranoid like your boyfriend. You both see DEA lurking everywhere."

Pushing the pillows against her body, she leaned forward, spitting out her words. "Hector had me check out her funeral. Her grieving parents were there. So was her DEA handler. Bonnie Haley died from one of your Fink's Fizzes, which means you knew damn well what she was. Che-Che would order you killed if he knew."

"You got no proof of any of that."

There was a clear note of fear in his voice, and she picked up on it. "I lied to Hector and told him that she wasn't working for anyone. I saved your miserable ass, Roberto."

Staring at her with open skepticism, he asked, "And why did you do that for me, Judith?"

She sat back, moving the pillows with her. "Have you ever noticed how most of the people in our business die young?"

"I've noticed."

"The smart money leaves young and rich."

He stared uncertainly at her for a long moment, his pistol loose in his hand. "You're going to take out a money warehouse."

"I can't do it alone."

Barrios looked at her as if she had just offered him a rattlesnake sandwich. "It's never been done, and the few assholes who've tried it have been skinned alive. No, thank you, I think I'll skip this little dance."

"I know most of the access codes to the data banks."

"All except the locations of the warehouses. Right?"

"I'll have that information soon."

"And if you do get it, then what?"

She told him her plan, the same one she had told Carlsen.

He leaned back. "Why me?"

Judith became more confident and pressed her argument. "Because most people in the network know that we don't like each other, know our natural distrust of each other. So they would figure that there was no way we would work together on anything."

"You're an arrogant bitch, but you're smart. So I have to figure you just might even be able to pull something like this off." He looked past her at the wall. "If you did get hold of the locations, what about the guards?"

"They're driven there every day by one of Hector's people. And they're not assigned to the same warehouses two days in a row. All we'd have to do is eliminate one team of guards from the disk, and no one would be sent to guard it. We'd have it all to ourselves. The problem would be trucking the money out of there."

Obviously beginning to accept the idea, he responded, "And laundering it."

"We wouldn't have to," she said, smiling at his sudden interest.

He inched forward, focusing on her cleavage, so visible above the pillows she was clutching to herself. "Does Hector satisfy you?"

Her eyes grew cold. "That's none of your business. May I get dressed?"

"I thought maybe we'd go into the bedroom and talk this deal over."

"You are a pig," she said in genuine disgust.

"But a pig you need. Sex makes me trust people, Judith."

"It's not the sex, it's the power it gives you." She held his eyes, her face set in a thoughtful expression. "Oh, why not?" she said, pushing the pillows away and stretching out over the sofa. "We'll do it here."

He got up and slipped off his robe. He sat down next to her and began kneading her nipple with his left hand while the right still held the nine-millimeter automatic. "You're a very beautiful woman."

She moaned. Demanded, "Harder."

He kneaded the long nipple between his fingers. She slid her arm around him, pushing his head down to her mouth, and she kissed him, drilling her tongue deep. He began kissing her body, making his way slowly down her body.

Breathlessly she asked, "Can you please put that damn gun away? It's hard for me to concentrate on the moment with that thing staring at my head."

He smiled, put the automatic on top of the coffee table, and resumed caressing her body. She groaned, nudging him lower with her right hand as the left sneaked up under her wig and pulled out a flat piece of metal about two and a half inches long with one dull edge and one razor-sharp edge. Moaning and thrashing while his face was pressed against her body, she delicately held the lethal blade between her thumb and middle finger, with her forefinger braced on the back of the dull edge. She moaned, "Roberto, I want you to look up at me."

His face lifted up, and he saw the blade coming down at him. His eyes grew wide in terror, but before he could react, she had slashed the razor edge across his face, slicing open both his eyes.

"Ahhhhhhh! Ahhhhhhh!" he screamed, slapping his hands across his bleeding eyes. He leaped off the sofa and stumbled over the table, toppling himself and the gun onto the floor, where he writhed in incredible pain.

Judith sprang up, grabbed the automatic from the floor, and tried to aim it at his head but couldn't because he was twisting and thrashing about violently, screaming as the blood poured out between his fingers. She tracked his jerking head movements with the gun until he stopped for the merest second. Then she shot him in the head.

She cleaned the blade by wiping it on the sofa and returned it to its hiding place under her wig. She went out into the foyer and began gathering up her clothes.

The stubborn haze that had clung to the city during the night and early-morning hours had been burned off by the sun and replaced by a cloudless blue sky as Judith drove a rented Ford off the Queens Boulevard exit of the Long Island Expressway, with Tina Turner's sassy voice booming out of the tape deck.

Eleven blocks south of the exit, on the west side of Sixty-eighth Street, there was an oasis of garden apartments overlooked by the condos of Forest Hills. The long gravel driveway that cut in from the boulevard emptied into a residential community of manicured lawns and hedges. The sign at the driveway's entrance read The Jacob I. Fine Community.

It had taken her almost seventy minutes to drive there in the afternoon traffic from Barrios's West Side apartment because she had taken a detour through Cocaine Alley, as Roosevelt Avenue in Woodside was known. When she stopped for the light on Sixty-ninth Street, she had reached under her seat and pulled out the brown paper bag containing the carefully cleaned and wiped guns she had used to kill Carlsen and Barrios. Just before the light changed, she cracked the door on the driver's side and dumped the bag into the street; she knew that some crackhead would find them and suck them up into the netherworld of narcotics. Eventually some junkie would get arrested with one or both of them in his possession, and the police would try to tie him in to both murders. She liked playing mind games with the cops. So far she had won every time.

After easing up the graveled driveway, she parked and locked the car. Standing in the small visitors' parking lot, she watched an old man wearing green-tinted sunglasses with chartreuse frames, a designer sweatsuit, and a Walkman plugged into his ear bobbing along with his walker. "That's the spirit," she said to herself, walking down the curving pathway to an apartment whose brass nameplate read "Sol Stern."

She saw her father sitting in his wheelchair on the small patch of lawn in front of his apartment, staring blankly off into space. His nurse, dressed in jeans, sneakers, and a blue cotton blouse, was sitting on a folding chair next to him, reading a paperback.

"How is my father?"

The nurse slapped the book closed and got to her feet. "The same," she said, obviously surprised by the unexpected visit.

"Leave us for a while," Judith said, adding, "I pay you way above the going rate, and for that I expect you to dress more appropriately. My father likes well-dressed people around him."

The licensed practical nurse started to say something, but she was cut off by Judith, who said, "If you have a problem with that, tell me, and I'll replace you."

"No problem, Miss Stern," she said, and walked off along the pathway. In a tough economy even nurses were looking for work.

Gazing tenderly into her father's rheumy eyes, Judith found it hard to believe that this was the tall, handsome, robust man she had so loved as a child. How could he turn into this shrunken shell with ugly brown spots all over his face and gnarled hands? Was this really her father, the man who had built G. Stern Bathing Garments, from a storefront operation on Hester Street into one of the largest dress manufacturers in the country?

She took her handkerchief out of her pocketbook and wiped food particles from the corners of his mouth. Then she took out small scissors and began to cut his nose hairs and then the tufts of hair in his ears.

This done, she sat next to him, took his unresponsive hand in hers, and kissed it. "I love you, Daddy. I always remember how you used to sit me on your lap when I was little, and tell me how beautiful and special I was. I remember the secret game we used to play." Her tone became curiously remote. "You broke my heart when you brought Sam and Jay into the business and wouldn't let me come in. I've always been smarter than both my brothers. When Mama died I really expected you to come to me and tell me that there was a place for me in the business." Her voice trailed off. She watched a black squirrel darting up the trunk of a golden maple tree. Her mind snapped back to the present. "I'm making a fortune in *my* business, Daddy. I wish you didn't have this damn Alzheimer's. You'd be so proud of me, I just know you would. . . ."

As his daughter's soft tones washed over him, Sol Stern's lips began to tremble as though he were struggling to get words out. Faint recognition dawned in his otherwise cloudy eyes.

"Uhhhhhhhh. Uhhhhhhhh. Uhhhhhhhh."

She moved closer. "What is it, Daddy? Tell me."

"Uhhhhhhhh. Uhhhhhhhh. Martha, make sure you clean the damn chicken this time."

"I'm not the goddamn maid!" she shouted. But she was too late. He had vanished, slipped back into the echoing emptiness of his mind.

22

THE SLENDER FIVE-MILE-LONG landmass of Thomas Cay was shaped like a harpoon. It was one of the seven hundred islands that made up the Bahamas, and it lay one hundred and fifty-six miles northeast of Miami, Florida. A five-thousand-foot concrete airstrip cut through the scrub vegetation and sea grapes that covered the cay. The western edge of the island was fringed with three miles of golden sand that curved along an expanse of turquoise water known as Pirate's Cove, where sleek inboard-engined speedboats, Cigarette boats and steel-hulled motorboats powered by five three hundred–horsepower engines lolled at anchor.

Che-Che Morales had effectively bought control of Thomas Cay five years ago through one of his dummy offshore corporations. It was rapidly transformed into a marshaling area for the transshipping of drugs into the United States. At night, pit bull terriers and Doberman pinschers patrolled the shoreline along with their handlers, while Jeeps fitted with pedestal-mounted twin M-60 machine guns patrolled the cay around the clock. A communications tower that also held the antennas for the latest navigational aids rose up from the island's center; a sophisticated, formerly Soviet radar searched out the sky and sea. Six prefabricated barracks, each with its own Laundromat, were clustered on the eastern side of the cay and camouflaged revetments of reinforced concrete abutted the runway's western edge and housed the network's small fleet of jet aircraft and high-performance twin-engine turbo-props.

Alejandro, dressed in khaki shorts, Top-Siders, and a short-sleeved unbuttoned cotton shirt, knelt inside a hangar on the southern edge of the runway, strapping a duffel bag filled with packets of heroin to the "store" of a Parapoint delivery system. Che-Che, Pizzaro, and Judith stood over him, watching. There was a row of nine other parachutes on the floor and a tightly packed pallet of four-kilogram packets of Cleopatra Gold alongside a pile of empty duffel bags.

It was eleven o'clock Monday morning on the sun-drenched cay. Alejandro had finished his last set at Environment on Sunday around four in the morning. He'd been up in the balcony, complaining to Che-Che about the treatment he had received from Pizzaro and Barrios in Mexico, when he'd seen Pizzaro, accompanied by a dark-haired, statuesque woman carrying a small overnight bag, making his way over to them. The duo had stopped in front of them and stood there, saying nothing. Pizzaro had worn a tight smile. Che-Che had finished his champagne and put down the glass, looked at Alejandro, and said, "We're all going on a short trip."

Alejandro had had her eyes for a moment, then deliberately

and slowly had looked her over, particularly noticing her very full red lips and her deeply tanned skin.

"I'm Judith," she had said in her husky voice. "Hector and I will drive you home so that you can pack."

Getting up off his knees, Alejandro noticed Judith watching him. He met her eyes as he bent to pick up another duffel bag. He spread open the top and began taking packets of heroin off the pallet and stuffing them inside. As he did this his eyes studied the canvas, trying to see if he could spot the false panels that contained the credit-card-size flexible circuit boards and the thin flexible batteries that powered them. He felt relief each time he tried and failed. Stretching his arm inside to stack the dope, he felt around the sides, seeing if he could detect any of the adhesive diodes. He couldn't. After filling the bag, he folded the flaps over the top, pushing the eyelets over the curved locking pin. This done, he held out his hand to Pizzaro, who took a padlock out of the cloth bag he was holding and handed it to him. Alejandro snapped it through the locking pin, securing the folds in place.

Forty-six minutes later Alejandro looked over at Che-Che and announced, "That's the last of 'em."

Judith, who was dressed in white shorts, beige espadrilles, a brown cotton blouse with three buttons on the top, and a wrap-around tie waist that displayed her flat stomach, looked Alejandro in the eye and asked, "Did you check the guidance system in each of the black boxes?"

Alejandro noticed that Che-Che was standing by passively, allowing her to run the show. Where does this dame fit into all this? he thought. One minute she's a worker ant, the next she comes on like the queen bee.

He looked at her and said, "I tested each nicad battery, all the receivers, the circuitry, and each homing transmitter. I also made sure that all the transmitters were set on the same frequency."

She asked, "What about the parachutes, you check them out, too?"

"I packed each one myself," Alejandro said. He looked around and asked, "Where is Barrios?"

"He retired," Pizzaro said. His tone of voice did not welcome any further questions.

Judith moved along the row of parachutes, studying each one. Offhandedly she asked Alejandro, "How are you opening the chutes?"

"Static lines," he answered, hiding his sudden concern behind a bland smile.

She knelt down and began kneading a duffel bag. "Why not use barometric pressure releases?" she asked, moving to another one.

"They're only used on vertical drops when you want to deploy at low levels," Alejandro replied.

Running her finger over the duffel bag's seams, she glanced over her shoulder at Alejandro and said, "You appear to know a lot about parachutes, for a singer."

Alejandro said a silent thank-you to Sergeant Mayhew for his intensive hours of lessons on the aerodynamics of parachutes. Next time he got to the Hacienda he was going to take Mayhew a bottle of scotch.

Pizzaro looked across the hangar at the van parked up against the ribbed steel wall and said, "I'm glad this island is only a short hop to Florida."

A disingenuous smile pinched Alejandro's mouth. "No way you're dropping this load in Florida."

Che-Che's eyes flashed to Alejandro. "Why do you say that?"

"Because it would be moronic to drop this stuff into the government's nerve center for drug interdiction. You'd have to deal with AWACs, and tethered aerostat radar balloons."

"You told us that Parapoint was undetectable," Pizzaro said.

"It is," Alejandro said, "but the drop plane ain't invisible. The DEA just added radar balloons in Florida that are tethered ten thousand feet up and provide look-down coverage that detects planes trying to sneak in below the beams of their land-based radar."

"We know all that," Judith said, not looking at him but continuing to examine the systems.

Pizzaro looked at Alejandro and said slowly, "We're filing flight plans with the FAA. We're going to be legit flights."

"Bullshit," Alejandro snapped. "Look, you guys do whatever you gotta do, but don't look to con me."

Judith looked surprised. "And what makes you think we're trying to con you?"

"You're a New York operation; you're too smart to waste Parapoint on a drop way outside your territory."

Judith's eyes grew larger. She walked up to Alejandro and with her polished nails slowly made white tracks along his arm. "Why don't you tell us how *you* would make the drop?"

Alejandro stared at her for a long beat and said, "I'd load the dope aboard one of those Lears you have parked outside. I'd take off at night, and wave-hop without navigation lights to New York. Thirty minutes out from the drop zone I'd turn off the plane's transponder to cut the odds as low as possible. Then I'd climb to twenty thousand feet, throttle back, have the guy in the cabin drop the load, dive back down to the floor, and head for home. I'd be in and out without being spotted."

"Very good," Judith said, slowly clapping her hands in mock applause.

Che-Che brushed down the sides of his long hair and asked Alejandro, "Why wouldn't you deploy the chutes sixty miles out from an altitude of thirty thousand feet?"

"I'd look to get the stuff on the ground as fast as I could," Alejandro answered. "Darting up from the floor forty miles out would give you enough distance so that the Ram Air chutes would have sufficient glide ratio to make it to a landing zone close to the coast."

The dopers exchanged blank looks. Judith asked Alejandro, "Where along the coastline would you make your drop?"

Alejandro shrugged. "I don't know."

Pizzaro peeled away from the others and walked across the hangar to the van. He climbed inside. The engine coughed and the vehicle moved in reverse, jerking to a stop alongside the rows of parachutes. Making his way back into the body of the van, he navigated the rows of metal rollers that had been welded to the floor, shoved open the double side doors, and stood on the van's chrome running tube.

Judith got up into the forklift that had been used to deliver the pallets of heroin. After starting up the engine, she drove over to the line of parachutes. Alejandro reached into a cardboard box that was on the floor next to the remaining stack of duffel bags and took out a handful of webbed harnesses that had loops at each end. He handed some to Pizzaro; they each strapped harnesses around the parachute containers.

Che-Che watched, saying nothing, seeing all.

Alejandro slipped the loops that were strapped around the first container over the forklift's twin forks. Judith hefted up the delivery system and tooled over to the van's open side doors. Alejandro and Pizzaro climbed into the van. Leaning out the door, with one foot firmly planted on the running tube, Alejandro stretched out his arm and, motioning to Judith, guided the load inside the van. Parapoint and its load crumped down onto the rollers. Alejandro and Pizzaro pushed it to the back.

They repeated this until all the systems were stored inside the van. Pizzaro climbed back behind the steering wheel; Che-Che got onto the passenger seat.

Judith called out to Alejandro, "Come ride with me."

Alejandro climbed into the forklift and shared the worn leather seat with her.

The hangar door slid open and the van drove out into the bright afternoon sunshine, followed by the forklift. Two bare-chested Oriental men wearing sandals and white shorts were walking toward the hangar. Alejandro recognized them from Environment. They were the same guys he'd seen huddling there with Che-Che. The van stopped; Che-Che climbed down and ran over to them.

"Who are those guys?" he asked Judith.

"I don't know."

"I bet they're his suppliers from the Golden Triangle."

The skin around Judith's eyes got tight. "I wouldn't know. I take orders just like you do."

For someone who only takes orders, you shove a lot of your weight around, lady, he thought. Che-Che shook hands with the two men and ran back to the waiting van.

The minicaravan drove onto the airstrip. About fifty meters west, six Quonset hurts were drawn up next to each other. Narcotics were being off-loaded from a turboprop aircraft and fork-lifted into the huts, while bare-chested men with grim, unshaven faces and carrying an assortment of automatic weapons guarded the area around the buildings and the turboprop. A Jeep fitted with pedestal-mounted twin sixties was parked on top of a nearby sand dune.

The breeze felt good on Alejandro's face. Looking around, he could not see any containers of chemicals or plastic mixing barrels or any drying shacks where coca leaves were dried before being processed into paste. Nor could he find any of the telltale signs of cocaine production. He was sure that this was mainly a transshipping point for Cleopatra Gold. "This is no two-bit operation Che-Che's got going here. . . ."

She smiled. "Che-Che is one smart hombre."

The van drove off the runway and along a spur that ran in front of a row of camouflaged revetments.

Alejandro lifted his face to the breeze.

"You must be tired," she said.

"Not really. The adrenaline's going."

"You get off on living on the edge, don't you?"

"Yeah, I do," he said, sliding his hand up her naked leg.

She slapped his hand away. "The last guy who tried that ended up snake meat."

"It might be worth it."

"Don't count on it."

He looked at her profile, with its sharply defined nose, and asked quietly, "What really happened to Barrios?"

"I don't know," she said with a shrug of her shoulders, and then, looking at him, added, "Maybe he got sick and died from an acute case of running-off-at-the-mouth disease."

They drove behind the end revetment. A Boeing 767 was parked under desert netting. The van stopped alongside the plane's open door. Judith stopped the forklift between the van and the planes.

Pizzaro climbed out and, walking around the front of the van to the side doors, motioned to Judith. She nudged Alejandro off the forklift and drove over to a baggage handling conveyor that they positioned between the van's door and the loading door of the airplane. Pizzaro pointed at Alejandro and said, "You climb up into the plane and I'll send 'em to you."

The seats had been removed and steel rollers welded to the plane's floor. Static lines stretched the length of the aircraft; an on-board oxygen console was fastened on the right side of the door.

"Ready?" Pizzaro called over to Alejandro, who was standing just inside the plane.

"Send 'em up," Alejandro called back.

Che-Che and Judith were standing by the van, talking in hushed tones. Just before Alejandro began to slide the packed chutes into the plane, he saw a flash of gold between Judith's breasts. An oversize medallion on a chain was revealed by a puff of wind that ballooned her shirt out for a moment. Something about it was very familiar, but he couldn't put his finger on it.

Pizzaro pushed a Parapoint system onto the conveyor, which deposited it inside the plane. Alejandro moved it to the rear. A bit of a race between the two started; it stopped when Che-Che warned them sternly to be more careful. Bending at the knees, Alejandro pushed forward one system after another, until the front of the aircraft was full. Then, without warning, the cockpit door swung open and Fiona Lee stepped out. Their eyes met and fell away; in obvious confusion she whirled back inside, closing the door behind her.

Another Parapoint plopped into the aircraft. He rushed over to it and began pushing it toward the others. His eyes were riveted on the cockpit door, his thoughts echoing Seaver's long-ago warning when he was first sheep-dipped: "Be careful of entanglements with women. Their knowledge of you can prove deadly."

Another system dropped inside.

Sitting in the cockpit, Fiona Lee gripped the yoke until her knuckles turned white, thinking, Jesus, what do I do now?

After the transfer had been made, Alejandro climbed out of the plane, trying to sort out the jumble of thoughts whizzing around his head. Who was she working for? What the hell am I going to do about her? I can't tell Seaver; he'll yank me out and I might never get another shot at Cleopatra.

Che-Che was waiting for him by the van. "You have a show to do tonight," Che-Che said. Glancing at Judith, he added, "She'll be going back with you."

Alejandro replied in Tarascan, "What about the drop? I wanna be there to see this thing works for real."

"Kee dah mee oo nah koh dah yeh vah," Judith said in Tarascan—"The drop will be taken care of without you."

Alejandro stared at her in surprise. "Where did you learn the language?"

"I taught myself," she said, looking into his eyes. "I'm a smart lady. I'd have thought you would have figured that out by now."

23

A VERY EAST SIDE CROWD showed up at Environment Monday night, adding a touch of class to the joint. Alejandro had arrived early for the first show and was sitting alone in the balcony, watching the dancers below. The loft seemed empty without Che-Che and his crew. He assumed that they were still in Thomas Cay, but he had no way of knowing that for sure.

His gut was churning with frustration over what to do about the woman he knew as Belle Starr. There was no sense in playing the "I shouldn't have" and "what if" mind games with himself. Now he had to figure out how he was going to handle it. His survival instincts told him to tell Mother Hen, but he knew what would happen if he did that. He'd be yanked and resurfaced somewhere in some nothing job in the police department. He couldn't live the life of a regular cop, not after so many years of his high-wire existence.

He had to get close to Belle Starr and talk with her, find out who she was with, get her to forget about him and not report him to *her* Mother Hen. He felt himself getting more and more antsy, a bad sign for an undercover.

They'd been keeping him on a short leash, but he had resolved to get in touch with Seaver tonight after his first performance. It was risky, but he had to let him know that the drop was imminent so Mother Hen could get his electronic eyes and ears ready.

He had been tempted to telephone Control but had decided against doing that because Pizzaro might have sicced one of his lip-reading teams on him. He'd heard how the Bolivian had trained them by having them sit in front of a television set for hours, watching programs without sound, concentrating on the actors' lips. Those damn lip-readers could be anyplace. And for all he knew, the Cleopatra Gold might have already been air-dropped. He glanced around the loft. The Chinese barmaid, Jasmine, was standing behind the bar, cleaning glasses. Seeing him look in her direction, she asked, "Where is everyone?"

He shrugged indifferently. "Want something?" she asked, holding a rocks glass up to the light.

"A glass of soda, please."

"You got it, handsome," she said, and tossed ice into the glass. She came out from behind the bar, walked over to him, and set the glass on a cocktail napkin, asking, "Would you like anything else?"

He looked into her big dark eyes and said, "No, thank you." Noticing her bow, he asked, "Do you always wear that yellow ribbon?"

Her easy smile vanished as her finger glided over the back of his hand. "Not *always.*"

He watched her slither back behind the bar. Sipping at the soda, he saw his manager, Josh Budofsky, climbing up into the loft. Holding his glass to his mouth, he watched him approach. Budofsky tossed a slip of paper onto the table.

"Here is the address and suite number of where we're meeting to work on your new act. I'll meet you there tomorrow at three P.M. Please be there, Alejandro."

Pushing back his chair, Alejandro tucked the slip of paper into his pocket and said, "See you tomorrow."

"I'll catch the show from here," Budofsky said, and, looking across at Jasmine, he ordered a stinger.

The music stopped. As the lights dimmed, the crowd on the dance floor rushed up to the stage, chanting, "Alejandro, Alejandro." A spotlight beamed down to reveal him standing motionless, head bowed, his trademark rose held loosely in his right hand.

Seventy minutes later he ran offstage with the cries for "More!" echoing behind him. As he rushed into his dressing area, he was brought up short by the sight of Judith sitting on a folding chair, filing her nails. "You're very good," she said without looking up at him.

"Thanks," he said, getting his first really good look at her long legs, which were exposed by her short black skirt. "I have to change now."

"Don't let me stop you," she said, still not looking up from her task or showing any sign of leaving.

"I won't," he said, and unbuttoned his shirt. He took it off and tossed it into the overflowing plastic laundry bag on the floor, aware of the impatience swelling inside him.

Filing a nail, Judith glanced down at the smelly clothes. She wrinkled her nose. "When do you clean that stuff?"

"When the bag gets full," he said, kicking off his shoes, unzipping his trousers, stepping out of them, and tossing them into the pile on the floor. As he stood in his briefs at the sink, washing himself, she looked up at him and her lips parted slightly. She lowered her eyes when he pulled off his briefs and stepped into a fresh pair. He got dressed: jeans, short-sleeved paisley shirt, brown loafers, no socks. Facing her, he asked, "Why are you here?"

"I thought we might spend some time together."

"I'm going out to get something to eat."

"I'll go with you." It was more of a command than a suggestion.

A light rain had come and gone, leaving behind warm, balmy city smells and the light freshness of a brief summer shower. The Emerald Pub was an Irish hangout on the east side of Second Avenue, a few storefronts south of Fifty-first Street. Heavy doors inlaid with frosted glass in the shape of shamrocks swung open to reveal a long bar on the left and a small bandstand up against the right wall where the bar area ended and the dining area began.

The bar was crowded when Alejandro and Judith arrived shortly after one A.M. The Emerald Pub was one of the few remaining Manhattan joints where live bands played music from the old country; guest artists appeared nightly to play the music of rebellion and lament that evoked Ireland's rich and troubled history.

They edged their way through the crowd into the dining area and stopped in front of the bandstand to look for an empty table. A big thick-necked man with a pudgy face was up on the stage singing about the "troubles." Alejandro looked up at him and nodded as he made eye contact, rubbing the left side of his nose with his right thumb.

The singer nodded back.

Booths lined both walls of the dining room, and there was a double row of tables cramped into the space between them. A waiter came over and led them to a booth facing the stage. They squeezed in next to each other, facing the three-piece band.

"I've never been in an Irish pub before," Judith said.

"Then your education has been sadly neglected, lass."

She laughed. "My teachers at Ramaz wouldn't approve of a nice Jewish girl going into any bar. They even kept us separated from the nice Jewish boys at school."

"You'd have been perfectly safe." He was surprised at his own defensiveness. "We Irish are a warm, kind, gentle people with a great love of life and literature."

She looked at him quizzically. "What a strange man you are. You really are completely at home here, aren't you?"

"And why shouldn't I be, lass, I'm a Monahan, aren't I?"

She laughed. "You're no more an Irishman than I am. You're a Mexican, an American, a Tarascan Indian. I bet you're the only man in here not wearing socks or oversize boxer shorts."

"You peeked."

She dropped her eyes.

He looked at her, not saying anything for a moment. "And what about Judith? Does she know who she is?"

"She knows."

"I don't know her last name."

Her face grew cold. "That's not important. You don't need to know."

A waitress came over, and they ordered shepherd's pie. The singer gripped the microphone as the drummer beat out a roll for attention. "Ladies and gentlemen," he began, "I'd like you to put your hands together and help me ask an old friend to get up here and sing us a song." He swept his big paw out to Alejandro. "Al Monahan, will ya give us a tune?"

Alejandro looked at Judith, shrugged helplessness, squeezed out, and walked up to the stage, accompanied by a smattering of polite applause.

Two men sitting at the bar exchanged odd looks. One leaned close to the other and said, "He doesn't look like a Monahan."

After talking briefly to the band, Alejandro turned and faced his audience. He stood with his hands at his sides, his eyes searching out the distant past, and began singing "The Ballad of Willie McBride," a haunting song that told the story of a nineteen-year-old boy killed in the trenches in 1918. Alejandro's light baritone had an Irish lilt and was filled with heartfelt emotion as he sang the refrain about a boy turned man in the desolate trenches, a young soldier who had his life snuffed out in a great conflict that was not of his making. Slowly a hush descended over the pub, and most eyes moved to the singer. The few patrons who continued to talk were shushed quiet by the others. The man at the bar who had been skeptical looked at his friend and said, "He might not look like a Monahan, but he sure as hell sings like one."

Judith felt slightly breathless watching him and listening to his moving rendition of the old song. She became conscious that she was squeezing her thighs together. Wrapping her hands around her water glass, she focused on his beautiful hands with the long, sensitive fingers.

Andy Seaver mashed his cheroot in the copper ashtray, slipped off the barstool, and slipped out of the Emerald Pub. "Willie McBride" was the piece Chilebean was to sing if the drop was imminent. He hurried along Second Avenue and turned onto Fifty-second Street, then ducked into the shadowy doorway of a vacant store and unfolded his department-issue cellular phone. He punched in a number and, when the voice answered, pressed the scramble button and said, "It's going down."

Alejandro finished the song. The audience surged to its feet, clapping and shouting for more. He stood there, graciously accepting their praise. Then he turned and shook hands with the singer, jumped off the stage, and went back to his seat.

"You're quite the actor," Judith said as he moved in next to her.

"I'll take that as a compliment and say 'Thank you.' "

After they had finished eating, Judith picked up her fork and began to break off the remaining crust of her pie. "Why don't you get the check? It's time for us to leave."

"I've got forty minutes before I have to get back."

"Che-Che canceled your last show. He wants you to come with me, now."

24

A CARGO HELICOPTER RE-sembling some prehistoric bird lifted off the pad at the uptown heliport and flew north. Alejandro and Judith, the only passengers, sat on seats that pulled down off the bulkhead. Rows of rollers were welded to the floor. Looking out the window at the sleeping city, Alejandro followed the lights of the few cars beneath them on the Franklin Delano Roosevelt Drive. Then the helicopter veered west. They were flying over Harlem's battered streets.

He looked down at the tenement roofs, block after block of abandoned buildings. In his mind's eye he could see small groups of sullen men congregated on street corners, exchanging glassine envelopes for crumpled bills. Then they were over Spanish Harlem, the broad shining path of the Hudson just beyond. He looked at the tanned face beside him and asked, "Where are we going?"

"*Vamos a hacer dinero,*" she said in flawless Spanish—"Let's make some money."

The helicopter suddenly turned to a northwest heading. The Bronx was sprawled out below them. Soon the city's brilliance gave way to the scattered pinpoints of light from the suburbs. After thirty minutes had elapsed, they were flying over the indistinct shapes of low mountains. Judith kept peering out intently, obviously looking for a landmark. Alejandro decided that they must be somewhere over the Catskills.

Suddenly she thrust her hand into her tote bag and brought out a pair of night-vision glasses, which she strapped around her head. She made her way to the cockpit and shouted something to the pilot over the roar of the rotors. The helicopter swooped into a hundred-and-eighty-degree turn as she checked out the terrain. Satisfied that the landing zone was safe, she ordered the pilot to land.

The helicopter came down in a small clearing of low-lying level grassland completely surrounded by trees that showed only a darker shape against the darkness. A single faint light winked up from the clearing.

"Quickly, outside," she ordered as the copter settled to earth. Grabbing her tote bag, she left the aircraft and motioned to Alejandro to follow her. They ducked under the blades that were slowly spinning down. A sudden, almost deafening silence came over the area.

Alejandro smelled the forest and heard the night sounds but saw no signs of life. Judith stood in the secluded meadow, searching out the trees through her night-vision glasses. She turned and called to the pilot, "Radio Hector we're ready."

The Boeing 767 that had been skimming the deck, flying without lights, suddenly climbed up into the darkness, leveled off at thirty thousand feet, and throttled back to a near stalling speed.

Tethered to a safety line, with an on-board oxygen mask

strapped to his face and a radio headset, Pizzaro bent over the last of the Parapoint systems he had lined up facing the open hatchway of the now depressurized cabin. With his hands planted firmly on top of the first Parapoint, he waited expectantly. Hearing a single command through his earphones, Pizzaro pushed the last system up against the others. They rolled smoothly over the aircraft's floor and toppled out one by one into the night. All ten systems fell free until they were jerked by the static lines, making the pilot chutes pop out and the Ram Air parachutes deploy and blossom. He and another doper struggled to get the door closed against the roaring force of the wind. Pizzaro had not been prepared for the almost impossible task of securing a door on a large plane in flight. He finally closed and locked the door, snapped the intercom out of its wall niche, and, panting with exhaustion, said, "Let's go home."

Throttling up, Fiona Lee headed the plane back toward the sea and her uncertain future.

Alejandro paced nervously up and down the meadow, looking off into the star-filled night, holding a homing transmitter. Judith also had one, its antenna extended in front of her, and was waving it about like a conjurer trying to make magic.

Behind them the helicopter pilot, a wiry little guy on the long side of fifty with hard miles on the clock, wearing an old flight jacket, jeans, and sneakers, stood in the cargo passenger door. He pressed the external cargo mechanical release button and extended the hoist cable down to the ground.

Alejandro spotted them first swaying down silently and gracefully toward the clearing. "There," he called, aiming his transmitter at them.

Judith gave a little gasp and ran over to stand beside him, raising her transmitter up at the gliding parachutes. They watched them grow larger and larger. One by one they glided in, skimming over the treetops, their duffel bags thudding into the soft dirt as the Ram Air canopies blossomed down over the riggings. One almost snagged in a tree, then fell free with a snapping of branches that broke the silence like gunfire.

"Get the cable," she ordered him.

Alejandro ran back to the helicopter. The pilot handed him a pair of work gloves, which he pulled on quickly. Holding the end of the cable, he ran over to the nearest duffel bag and snaked it under the folded-down flaps where the eyelets were pushed down over the locking pin and secured with a padlock. He bent the steel rope and secured it to the other side with a pressure clamp she had handed him. That done, he turned and waved to the pilot, who pressed a button on the side of the cargo passenger door. The hoist cable began to rewind, pulling the duffel bag over the grass and hoisting it up and into the helicopter. The pilot released the pressure clamp, pulled the cable out from under the folds, and pushed the cargo along the casters to the back of the helicopter. It took them another thirty-three minutes to get the remaining nine duffel bags stored aboard. Alejandro began gathering up the parachutes and their rigs.

"Leave them," Judith ordered.

"We can't abandon this equipment," he shouted over the whine of the copter's engine and the swish of the rotors winding up.

"Get on board the helicopter!"

He stood his ground defiantly. "I'm not leaving this stuff here. Are you crazy? These things don't grow on trees."

She ran over to him, shouting, "Don't you think we know what we're doing? The dope is what's important, not these things. Now hurry up and get aboard."

He climbed into the craft while she waited below. After he was aboard, she took a portable radio out of her tote and, turning her back so that he could not read her lips, made a transmission.

The helicopter lifted out of the meadow, leaving the parachutes billowing in the night breeze. Once again Alejandro began thinking about her place in the network. As the craft flew out over the mountains, he spotted what appeared to be a truck, using only its parking lights, stopping just inside the clearing they had just flown out of. So they have a cleanup crew, he thought. Then he felt a stab of anxiety—what if they discovered the transmitters hidden in the duffel bags? He decided finally that the risk was minimal, and his thoughts turned again to Judith. She was standing in the front, just behind the pilot, staring at some kind of map or chart in the faint illumination of a small navigator's spotlight. As she turned to speak to the pilot, her medallion slipped out of her blouse. Alejandro could see it clearly for several seconds as it caught the light.

When she came back aft and sat down next to him, he put his lips close to her ear so that she could hear him over the noise of the copter and, pointing to the medallion, said, "That looks like the profile of someone I know."

She looked at him in the darkness and said, "I doubt it. She died in Egypt a long time ago. You might call her our good-luck charm."

"Are all our people on the street?" Romano asked Seaver.

"Yeah, they're all on station," Seaver said, sounding more confident than he felt. He removed the ever-present cheroot from his mouth and studied the transparent sheet of plastic with horizontal and perpendicular lines that was above a large console inside Special Operations communications room. Bright dots of internally projected light were interspersed between the lines. Pointing his cigar at the plot board, Seaver said, "Each dot represents one of our mobile units. The grid takes in the city's five boroughs, Nassau, Westchester, and Suffolk counties. It also covers New Jersey on an arch line from Bayonne to Fort Lee. Once those duffel bags come within a hair of this town, our electronics will be on them, and we'll triangulate them to their destination."

Romano asked in a worried tone, "And if they take the dope out of the bags?"

"Then our units will beam in on the adhesive diodes."

Romano continued to worry. This was a totally untested operation for which the rule book hadn't been written. "Suppose they make the drop outside the grid, maybe Philadelphia—and leave the dope there."

"I'm gambling that they won't."

Romano persisted. "Let's say they do."

"Then we lose."

Looking at the detectives bunched around the console, Joey-the-G-Man asked, "Shit. Anyone got a cigarette?"

The helicopter's nose rose slightly as it landed back at the East Side heliport. Not a word had passed between its two passengers for the last twenty minutes.

Judith looked at him and asked in a not terribly concerned voice, "Tired?"

"A little," he said.

She smiled. "You better get used to long hours, amigo." The helicopter finally came to rest on the pad.

"Are we off-loading the stuff here?" he asked, astounded that the dopers would make a transfer in such a public place.

"That's not our department," she said, getting up and making for the door.

They climbed out of the helicopter and walked over to a waiting sedan. Climbing into the back, Alejandro recognized the driver as one of Che-Che's crew. He glanced back and saw a windowless black van pull up by the helicopter's cargo passenger door.

"You know," he said to Judith, "you might as well do this in Times Square."

She gave him a cool glance. "You don't get it. The more open you are, the less suspicion you'll attract. We just off-loaded sacks full of computer printouts—if anybody asks." Turning away to look out the window, she asked, "Where do you want to be dropped off?"

"Home. I want to crawl under the sheet and sleep."

She slid her hand on his thigh. "I'd like to go with you."

"I don't think so," he said, looking out the car window.

The black, windowless van drove up the ramp leading out of the Sixtieth Street heliport and turned north onto York Avenue. Above it a tram glided effortlessly across its cables, making a routine transit from Roosevelt Island to its station on Second Avenue.

Day was breaking through the night.

At Sixty-third Street the van made a hard right into the southbound entrance of the FDR Drive. The ten duffel bags containing the packets of Cleopatra Gold were stacked in the back of the van, guarded by two men armed with mini Uzi machine guns and a third armed with a LAW rocket launcher. The driver was a broad-shouldered man with a short ponytail held together by a rubber band. He had a diamond chip stuck through his left earlobe.

Jasmine, the bartender from Environment, her yellow ribbon tied around her long queue, sat in the passenger seat, wearing brown pleated slacks and a brown silk blouse with tiny whales and seals on it. Her Kelly bag with a brown-and-gold Hermès scarf tied around its handle rested on her lap. Inside the pocketbook, its checkered handle upright for easy access, was a nine-millimeter S&W automatic pistol.

Throughout the city mobile surveillance platforms disguised as commercial and recreational vehicles beamed in on the signals being emitted from the transmitters hidden inside the seams of the duffel bags.

Deep inside Mobile Control One—a hollowed-out soda truck with an exterior facade of stacked soda cases—Detective Kathy Herer sat at the cramped control console with her headset snug over her blond hair, watching the beeping signals of surveillance units converge on the black van.

"Mobile One to all units," she transmitted, keying up a tight shot of the FDR Drive on the screen, "Lucifer is going south on the FDR. Angels three and five cover Bowling Green exit in case Lucifer does a spin-around on us."

Watching the clear plastic plot board inside the Special Operations communications room, Joey-the-G-Man glanced over at Seaver and said, "Looks like we got lucky."

"Yeah, maybe," Seaver said, gnawing at the right corner of his mouth. He was sure that Chilebean was not out of harm's way yet.

Romano got out of his chair and looked directly at Seaver, then walked over to the window. Seaver took the cue and followed him.

Staring out across the empty school yard at the net of the basketball goal, Joey-the-G-Man said, " 'At's a lotta heroin they just dumped on us. I'm thinking we oughta grab it." He hitched up his trousers and muttered, "We'd make a major league score on this one."

"If we do, we'll end up with their junk and some of their front-line people—but risk losing the head of the network."

"Hey," Romano objected, "Pizzaro ain't horseradish. And we can tie Che-Che into a conspiracy to import narcotics."

"Chilebean is not positive that Che-Che is the head guy," Seaver said, taking out his box of cheroots and shaking one out. "I'd really like to burn this Cleopatra. She must have been the one who gave the orders to hit our three undercovers."

Romano pressed his argument home to the thing that was really bothering him. "If we don't grab that dope, and they somehow manage to slip it through our electronic net, we could have a heavy-duty problem."

"What dope?" Seaver asked, lighting another cheroot and glancing at his boss through the smoke.

— 25 —

THE CAR HAD BARELY pulled up to the curb in front of Alejandro's apartment when Judith slipped her hand in his and asked, "Are you sure you wouldn't like me to come upstairs with you?"

Sneaking a look at the dashboard clock and seeing that there were only seven minutes left to his transmission window, he said, "I'd love it, but I'm really beat. Another time, okay?"

She leaned across the seat and raked her fingers through his hair. "I hope that I wasn't too bossy out there."

Alejandro gave her a reassuring smile. "Hey, you had a job to do and you did it. I understand that."

She looked directly into his eyes. He leaned across the seat and met her waiting lips. Her skin was smooth and hot, and her breasts swelled against his chest. He put his hands on her shoulders and pushed away from her.

"I hope we can be friends," she said, grabbing one of his ear-lobes playfully.

"So do I. I've thought of another way for Che-Che to wash his money."

Her hand fell to his groin, and she whispered, "Would you like me to suck you off? Now! Right here!"

He groaned. "I'd bloody love it, but next time. I want to be at my best." He looked at the driver, who was staring out the windshield, seemingly oblivious of them. He also saw that another minute had passed. He jerked open the door. "See you soon."

"I certainly hope so."

He walked slowly along the crescent driveway toward the building's white portico.

Judith sat back and crossed her legs, jiggling her left foot. To the driver she ordered, "Take me to Che-Che." Looking at Alejandro entering the lobby of his building, she muttered, "You'll be seeing me sooner than you think."

Joggers were making their early-morning circuits around Washington Square Park. Once inside his lobby and out of view from the street, Alejandro dashed for the elevator. He threw open the door to his apartment and let it slam shut behind him, running into the living room to grab the head of the Aztec warrior. He slipped quickly into his bedroom, shaking the pocket-size satellite radio out of its hiding place. He tossed the head onto his bed and entered the bathroom, pulling the radio out of its plastic sheath. He unfolded the tiny dish antenna and plugged it into the radio.

Standing on the toilet seat, he pushed down the frosted window, aimed the antenna, and whispered hurriedly into the microphone, "Heroin chuted over Catskill region around 0230 today. Urgent you ascertain pedigree and background of the white female between forty and forty-seven years of age who left the Emerald Pub with me. First name, Judith; surname unknown. Fluent in Spanish, English, and Tarascan. Known to have attended the Ramaz school. I need a meet with Mother Hen. I'll be leaving my apartment around 1445 to keep appointment with Budofsky."

He checked the time. The second hand was sweeping around to 0530. Watching the swift-moving hand, he thought of the lion-colored mountain just outside of Zihuatanejo, with the heap of stones piled up as a memorial to the honest policemen and journalists murdered by the drug lords, and he recalled that sunny day long ago when he had added his personal stone to the cairn. The hand swept to six; he pressed the red button, compressing his message into a second of energy that hurled his transmission to the orbiting law enforcement satellite.

Out on his terrace, Alejandro gazed off into the pearly lightness replacing the fading night, aware of the anxiousness surging through his body. Somewhere out there police units were closing in on a drug warehouse. He worried that the dopers might spot the cops, or that one of the bags' seams might come undone, or the dopers might somehow slip through the net.

I've got the undercover blues, he thought. He felt it would be different if only he could be out there with them. But then he knew down deep that not a thing would be changed if he was.

Grabbing the railing tightly with both hands, he thought of how good Judith felt in his arms and of her almost insistent offer of sex. Suddenly he was very tired and walked back inside to get undressed and take a long, hot shower. He had barely crawled into bed and pulled up the sheet when the telephone rang.

"Yeah?" he mumbled sleepily into the mouthpiece.

"*Ahee es lo key koo ahn'doe,*" Che-Che said, and went on in Tarascan, telling Alejandro that he wanted to see him that night before his first show. Morales would send a car to pick him up at seven in front of his apartment. He ended the conversation by adding, "Don't mention this call to anyone. *Por la seguridad.*"

"*Sí,*" Alejandro said, and slowly slipped the receiver back into its cradle. Che-Che had never before telephoned him at home. He reached over the side of the bed, picked a sneaker out of the basket, and tossed the reminder into the middle of the room. Rolling onto his side, he pulled the sheet over his neck and closed his eyes, knowing that sleep would not now come easily to him.

Lines fore and aft secured the four-masted schooner *Peking* to the dockside capstans of the South Street Seaport. The black van containing the Cleopatra Gold had exited the FDR Drive at Front Street and continued south along South Street.

Jasmine looked out at the massive suspended iron canopy of the Fulton Fish Market. The majestic interior was a beehive of early-morning activity as store owners and restaurateurs negotiated over the day's catch. She watched a man wearing fisherman's boots and a bloody white apron toss a bucket of crushed ice over a bin full of flounder.

"Make the next right," she told the driver sharply.

The van turned into Burling Slip, then made a quick right into Plaza Prudential and Bache, continuing north to Water Street. It halted at the three steel traffic stanchions rising vertically out of the ground at the intersection of Water and Beekman streets, preventing vehicles from continuing north.

The driver steered the van onto the sidewalk and around the barricade, drove west onto Beekman, again rolled up on the sidewalk, and then stopped in front of a restored Georgian-Federal warehouse with a high-pitched roof. This part of the South Street Seaport had nineteenth-century lampposts and Belgian block street pavements punctuated with slabs of granite, all designed to evoke images of the horse-drawn era. Abutting the west side of the warehouse was an abandoned five-story box-shaped building that had a hip roof and all its windows boarded up with plywood that was decorated mostly with painted blue anchors.

Jasmine slid off the passenger seat and walked over the bluestone sidewalk to the corner, examining the area for anything suspicious. Seeing nothing amiss, she looked at the driver of the van and nodded. He jumped down and knocked twice on the steel accordion door of the warehouse.

The television cameras bracketed on both sides of the door's header zoomed in on him. The door clattered up. The driver got back in the van and drove it inside, where the duffel bags were off-loaded.

Jasmine stood by, supervising the unloading of the duffel bags. After the two men who had done the unloading stood the bags upright, Jasmine went from one to the next, unlocking the pad-locks. The ground floor was divided into aisles by tall metal shelving racks filled with dolls and toys, fake amphorae, differ-ent-size sailing ships, and stuffed toy animals.

Jasmine walked out, supervising the workers, watching the heroin being removed and stuffed carefully inside the cavities in the dolls and animals.

"A few of the packets broke," one of the crew shouted across to the van driver.

"Pour the loose stuff into the dolls," Jasmine ordered.

"What do we do with the duffel bags?" another of the crew asked.

"They go back into the van," she said, her voice trailing off when she saw one of the men licking some loose heroin off his finger. Walking slowly over to the van driver, she lifted her jaw at the finger licker and asked, "Who is that guy, Juan?"

"Manny Rodriguez. We brought him up from the cay a few weeks ago."

"Kill him," she said quietly, and walked away.

A plumbing truck with lengths of different-size pipe strapped to its side drove down Beekman Street. The plumber in the pas-senger seat was talking to the driver just loudly enough for the transmitter concealed in the sun visor to pick up his words. "Mo-bile Four to home base. Lucifer has unloaded. Do you want him taken out? K."

Inside the Special Operations communications room, Seaver felt his heartbeat quicken. He looked over at Romano, who was sitting on a chair staring at the toes of his shoes and smoking another bummed cigarette.

"What do we tell him?" Seaver asked the boss.

Joey-the-G-Man tapped the ash off his cigarette, letting it fall on the floor, and ordered firmly, "Tell 'em to maintain their distance and observe and report."

A taxi with a rooftop billboard showing a beautiful woman in a swimsuit advertising a suntan lotion drew up at the curb in front of Alejandro. Getting into the cab, he told the driver to take him to 1049 Broadway. Seaver turned on the meter and edged the taxi out into the Fifth Avenue traffic and around Washington Square. He asked, "How are you doing?"

"What happened with the drop?" Alejandro asked anxiously.

"It's in a warehouse on Beekman Street, behind the Fulton Fish Market."

Alejandro gave a satisfied nod of his head as he saw Seaver watching him in the rearview mirror. "And the duffel bags?"

"They hauled them away in the van," Seaver said, turning east. "We tracked them back to your loft."

Alejandro nodded thoughtfully. "Now I know why Pizzaro insisted that I give him a key. Now that he knows it works, Che-Che is not going to waste any time exploiting Parapoint."

Seaver swerved to avoid a pedestrian jaywalking out from between parked cars. "I wish there was some way we could maintain control over those damn bags."

"They'll kill me real quick if they ever discover those transmitters. The longer we wait, the more we risk."

Seaver nodded in unhappy agreement and changed the subject. "Any ideas on Cleopatra?"

"Not really, just some vague feelings."

"Who's this Judith you want a make on?"

"Her piss would etch glass. Other than that, apart from what I gave you earlier, I know nothing."

"Where's she in the pecking order?" Seaver asked.

"I've seen her throw her weight around like she was pretty far up."

"And Che-Che?"

"I just don't know, Andy. I don't see a swinging-dick Latino like Che-Che taking orders from any woman. But the funny thing is, I've never once seen him with a woman."

"Just because you haven't seen one doesn't mean there isn't one. This guy keeps most of his life closed off, even from those closest to him. So maybe Judith fits in there."

"Maybe. Something else has been bothering me. I don't see Che-Che with the smarts to put this network together." He paused, thinking. "How long will it take you to get a line on Judith?"

"I've got my best people working on it. When I know, you'll know."

Alejandro pressed harder. "How will you get the word to me?"

"Read your junk mail," Seaver said, again looking at the undercover's reflection in the rearview mirror, noticing the signs of aging in his face, new lines at the corners of his eyes. Alejandro had requested this meeting, yet he had not revealed anything important to justify it, which he would have done had he come up with anything solid. Seaver suspected that he needed a "personal," a contact with someone who cared for him, knew him. Seaver served as Alejandro's only contact with the real world, where people led lives that made some sense. "Do you need any equipment to repack the parachutes?" Seaver finally asked.

"I got everything I need in the loft. In a little while I'm going to need some more adhesive diodes."

"I'll get them to you." Then he suddenly asked, "Do you remember the lawyer, Carlsen?"

"I remember him," Alejandro said with a grim edge.

"Carlsen and Barrios were whacked on the same day. We think a woman took both of them out."

"Why?"

"The crime scene boys discovered female pubic hairs on the sofa near Barrios's nude body." Seaver shuddered involuntarily as he reported, "Both of his eyes had been sliced open. And the lawyer had lipstick on his lips."

Alejandro shook his head and observed glumly, "Female shooters have become a growth industry in the dope business."

Seaver stopped for the red light on Twenty-third Street. Staring out the windshield, he asked, "Why do you stay at it? And please don't tell me because of your father. There has to be more to it."

"I'm a believer, Andy. My dad fought *traficantes* and other scum all his life. They killed him in the end. My mother's people have been exploited for centuries. These scumbags are using them, poisoning them."

"Don't you think you've done enough?" Seaver asked just as the light changed and he raced the taxi ahead of the rest of the herd.

His tone drenched in sarcasm, Alejandro continued, " 'Say no to drugs'—that was this country's big public relations answer to the war. If anyone wants to know about the war on drugs, tell 'im to look at Colombia, where the *traficantes* have murdered half the judiciary. They've killed hundreds of policemen and journalists, thousands of civilians. Those people know what the drug war is really about."

Seaver waited until Alejandro's passion was spent and said quietly, "I'm worried about you."

"I'm okay, Andy," Alejandro reassured him. "But I'm more convinced than ever—the only way we're going to win this thing is by covert operations against the networks; destroy their infrastructure, take out the leaders."

"We're putting a lot of them inside for life."

Alejandro gestured impatiently. "Bullshit. The criminal justice system is paroling Nicky Barnes after he was sentenced to life without parole. How many people did good ol' Nicky murder when he was operating?"

"A lot." Seaver sighed. "But Nicky gave up a lot of people in order to win that parole."

"He gave up Harlem brothers who in the normal course of events wouldn't have lived to see thirty-five anyway. Name one *traficante* or pinky ring he gave up. They're the movers and shakers in this business."

Seaver's jaw muscles began to pulse. "What's your next move?"

"I told Judith that I thought of another way for Che-Che to wash his money. Suddenly he telephoned me, said he wanted to see me. He's sending a car for me at seven tonight."

Seaver turned around and looked at Alejandro in surprise, demanding, "Do you know enough about money laundering to pull it off?"

"They teach us well at the Hacienda."

"What do you have in mind for Che-Che?"

"Using Parapoint to launder their money."

"We're helping this network import heroin, now you want to help them wash their money. There are some who would say we're facilitating drug traffic."

"Us? 'Om'on, Andy. I'm a singer and you're a file clerk."

"Keep your hands at your sides and your hips in neutral, and sing 'Stardust,' " Scott Hart said.

Hart, Alejandro, and Josh Budofsky were in a nineteenth-floor rehearsal studio that Budofsky had rented. Alejandro was alone on the stage, standing in front of a pleated maroon curtain that had faded into a creamy gray color. An anxious Budofsky was sitting on the aisle in the last row alongside Hart, a thin black man in his middle sixties, with sparse gray hair and big brown eyes.

Without accompaniment of music, Alejandro began to sing.

Keeping his eyes focused above the heads of his two-person audience, Alejandro sang for the stranger who was to help change his musical personality. He was nervous. After all the crap I've lived through these past years, I get nervous singing for this guy, he thought.

Hart rested his chin on the back of a seat, his eyes and ears evaluating the man on the stage. When Alejandro finished the song, Hart told him to sing "What Is This Thing Called Love?"

Alejandro began to sing, and without realizing it, he started to move the tempo to a Latin beat.

"No. No," Hart said. "Sing it the way Porter wrote it. And I want to hear perfect phrasing—every word clearly enunciated."

When Alejandro finished singing that song, Hart told him to sing anything he liked.

Sucking in a deep breath and staring off at the verdant hills of Ireland that his grandmother had told him so many stories about, Alejandro pulled out all the stops, singing a beautiful, but, compared with Porter, somewhat sentimental, Irish ballad.

Hart's hands dropped to his lap, and he sighed.

Budofsky leaned close to him and whispered, "What's the matter?"

"I think you got yourself a voice that can't be trained," he said, rising out of his seat. "What you heard is all you're ever going to get." He squeezed out past Budofsky, walked down the aisle. "Okay, young feller," he said. "Let's you and me see what we can do."

Barchester Towers, a luxury thirty-story glass condominium with several tiers of setbacks, was situated at Seventy-seventh Street and the East River. The spacious lobby had marble floors, burnished wood walls, and large, somewhat worn tapestries.

When Alejandro got out of the car that Che-Che had sent for him, he was met by one of the drug lord's crew and escorted past the doormen and the concierge to a waiting elevator. His escort said nothing as the two of them rode up to the penthouse.

Che-Che had the entire top floor. The apartment had a wrap-around terrace and a glass-walled living room. In the foyer Alejandro was met by a huge man with a boxer's battered face. He was wearing a butler's white jacket, jeans, sneakers, and a bulge on his hip.

"Mr. Morales is waiting for you inside," the man said, and led Alejandro into a large room with five seating groups, mostly quite good French and English antiques. In contrast there was a pool table in one corner of the room and many video games scattered about. There were large groups of stuffed animals, including an enormous giraffe, an elephant, and a lion, toys for the children of giants, all standing on the floor. There were three buckets filled with ice holding bottles of Dom Pérignon and silver bowls holding crystal containers of Beluga Malossal caviar.

Walking inside, Alejandro was somewhat stunned by the quality of the antiques, with their carved and painted wood, silk brocade coverings. No way Che-Che put that stuff together, he thought.

Morales, dressed only in his briefs and straw sandals and a shark-tooth necklace, was playing a space war video with total concentration.

"Who's winning?" Alejandro asked, coming up behind the drug lord.

"Me," he said, adding without looking away from the game, "I want you to repack the parachutes. Have them ready to be picked up tomorrow afternoon."

He walked away from the game, over to a bowl of caviar. After scooping up a glob on a knife made of horn, he licked it off the blade and flipped the knife back into the black mass. He picked up a manila envelope from the same table that the silver bowl was on and handed it to Alejandro. He said, "Fifty thousand dollars for doing a good job. Parapoint was smart, real smart."

"Thanks," Alejandro said, holding the envelope in his hand and wondering if it would fit inside his shirt.

Che-Che went over and embraced a giant panda, snuggling close, brushing his cheek against the soft fur. "When I was a kid, I never had any toys. Now I buy whatever I want. I got these stuffed animals in all my apartments to remind me that I wasn't really shit when I was a kid." He let go of the panda and pointed to a glass door. "Let's go out on the terrace and talk. My enemies have lasers that can pick up the vibrations of our conversation."

The city was spread out beneath them, the lights, the roadways, the majestic bridges, the broad ribbons of water dividing the land. Looking off the edge of the roof, Che-Che said, "I feel like the serpent god Coaticue with my body coiled around it all."

Alejandro stared at him in momentary disbelief. "I hope you don't expect me to call you 'my lord.' "

Che-Che laughed. "You're the only one who would dare talk to me like that."

"That's because we are brothers."

A fierce, almost savage expression came over Che-Che's face. He turned to face Alejandro and said thoughtfully, "When I was a boy pimping in Ixtapa, I used to run women back and forth between the fancy hotels. They gave gringos cut-rate blow jobs while their wives took cha-cha lessons. Over the years I've grown to hate the gringos. They're all pigs; they look down on our people, treat them like shit." He looked away from his friend. "We *traficantes* are the only ones who really do for our people. We build them soccer fields, hospitals, we get them doctors when they need them."

Alejandro nodded agreement. "The gringos hate us because they didn't invent the drug trade."

Che-Che flashed a bitter smile at him. "All that stuff about you wanting to come in with us in order to buy your mother a house was bullshit, wasn't it? You came with us because you wanted the money, the excitement."

"No, Che-Che." He looked away off in the distance, selecting his words carefully. "You and me are sons of Cortés and Cuauhtémoc, we're mestizos. Down deep all our people have a secret pride that the *mestizaje,* the mixed-blood Mexicans, control the drug business. It's our revenge against all of them."

Che-Che embraced him, kissing both his cheeks. "It's lonely sometimes. I'm happy you're with me." Moving his mouth close to Alejandro's ear, he whispered in idiomatic Tarascan, "Trust no one, and don't ever mention this conversation to anyone—especially Pizzaro and his whore, Judith."

"Okay."

"Let's walk."

They strolled along the terrace.

"I might have come up with one or two things that could wash your money more efficiently," Alejandro offered.

Che-Che looked openly pleased. "That's good, because my money is starting to be a real problem. Not enough washing machines, amigo."

"What about Road Town?" Alejandro asked casually.

"The green has to be transported by hand; that limits the amount we can wash at any one time. BCCI, the Bank of Credit and Commerce International, used to wash as much as we gave them for two points. They'd wire-transfer my money into my accounts in Luxembourg and Panama. Since they went out of business, we've been forced to go back to using cells of five or six 'smurfs' who travel around the country buying just short of ten thousand dollars' worth of cashier and bank checks to get around the reporting requirements of the Bank Secrecy Act. . . ."

Listening to the drug lord's litany of complaints, Alejandro thought how much like the CEO of a large corporation he sounded.

". . . we don't leave a paper trail. But smurfing means we gotta spend a lot of time breaking down the money to under ten K, and then getting it to our smurfs. All this is expensive and dangerous. Recently a couple of our smurfs were taken off."

"You need inside knowledge to rip off money people."

"Pizzaro is checking on it."

Running his finger along the ledge of the terrace, Alejandro said, "And who is checking on Pizzaro?"

Che-Che shot him a sharp look but said nothing. Walking on down the terrace, he said, "Tell me what you've come up with to help me wash my money."

Alejandro didn't respond immediately, and then it was with a question rather than an answer. "The purpose of washing money is to sneak large amounts of dirty money into the banking system, right?"

"So?"

"So the fastest way of doing that besides wire transfers is to load up a plane and fly it to a friendly offshore bank. Only problem is that the DEA, Customs, and the CIA have a net over this country and spot your money planes. They try to force them to land; sometimes they even shoot them down. But when they don't, they follow them to their destination and radio ahead to have the local police waiting for them. Then the locals take a big chunk of your cash to allow your money in."

Che-Che nodded unhappily. "The fucking DEA gets off on helping other cops to steal our money. The DEA tipped off the Bolivians a few weeks ago. When a money plane landed, the cops and the army were waiting, the vultures. They grabbed eight million dollars of our money, called it an 'import tax.'"

Judging that this was the right moment, Alejandro suggested, "Why don't we use Parapoint to drop bags of money on the deck of a boat just outside the territorial limits? The boat can dock in some offshore country with a friendly banking system. They'd wire-transfer the green anywhere in the world for you."

Alejandro looked at Che-Che, watching his expression as he considered the idea for a long, thoughtful moment.

Staring off at the clouds gathering in the north, Che-Che asked, "What do you want for yourself out of all this?"

"I want to swim where there are no sharks."

On Thursday morning, Alejandro completed his last show a little before four. Returning his audience's applause after his encore, he looked up in the loft and saw Che-Che, Jasmine, and the two Oriental men from Thomas Cay looking down at him.

He ran off the stage, went into his dressing room, and changed, tossing his sweaty clothes onto the swelling heap on the floor. He pushed open the metal door and stepped out into the parking lot.

During his drive home, he kept repeating the name *Jasmine* over and over. What the hell was she doing sitting up there with those guys? he kept asking himself. Then he remembered seeing a familiar yellow ribbon in an ashtray in Morales's apartment. His mind suddenly made the connection, and he pictured Jasmine—always with just such a yellow ribbon in her queue.

Back at his apartment he undressed and took a shower, continuing to review all the occasions he had seen Jasmine and Che-Che together. His instincts told him that there was more to the relationship between the two. Now the yellow ribbon clinched it. Wearing only briefs, he walked into the living room. He took down the Aztec head from the shelf and went back into the bedroom. Sitting on the mattress, he took out the burst transmitter and then reached back inside the cavity. Using his fingers, he peeled off the badge taped to its roof and pulled it out. He stared at the NYPD detective shield, turned it over, and read the plaque on the back: "Detective Endowment Association. Presented to Detective First Grade Eamon Monahan on his retirement July 2, 1963."

After studying the plaque for a few minutes, he picked up the radio and encoded, "Ascertain ID of female Oriental named Jasmine. Works as bartender at Environment. Age twenty-seven to thirty-three." As he spoke into the transmitter he suddenly remembered something that had puzzled him at the time, early one morning when everyone had been smashed on booze. It was the sight of Morales casually untying the ribbon from Jasmine's hair and winding it around his finger.

26

T HE TWO FABRIC-CUTTING
tables inside the Thirty-sixth
Street loft were fifty feet long and five feet wide. There were big
empty spaces where racks of ladies' dresses awaiting shipment
once lined the concrete floors. Glued to the cinnabar-colored
cinder-block walls were peeling travel posters and old advertising layouts showing models wearing out-of-date dresses.

When Alejandro arrived at the rented loft on Thursday morning, carrying a container of coffee in a brown bag, he found the
duffel bags strewn over one of the tables. He switched on the
overhead lights. Sipping at his coffee, he meandered about
through the loft, attempting to locate any bugging or surveillance that Pizzaro might have left behind. Finding none, he
gulped down the remainder of his coffee and tossed the container
into the wire wastebasket, then walked over to the utility closet.

Just because he hadn't found anything, he couldn't assume the loft was free of bugs.

The tiny space smelled of disinfectant. A black sponge lay stiff on the floor. A mop was stuck into an orange bucket, and a plastic jug half-filled with a pea-green cleaning solvent was on top of the shelf, along with coarse brown paper towels and six spray cans with labels that claimed they were air fresheners.

He reached up and took down the cans and went over to the table with the duffel bags. He put down the cans and picked up one of the bags, checking its seams for any sign of wear or tampering. Seeing nothing suspicious, he picked up a spray can, gave the nozzle a three-quarter turn counterclockwise, and sprayed the inside of the bag with a liberal dose of adhesive diodes. As he sprayed each bag, he kept wondering about the head of the Cleopatra network. Whoever it was, he had enough self-confidence to allow his identity to remain hidden. Maybe it was someone who had a need to remain hidden. Someone in the public eye? Every working network that I've ever heard of had a boss who was known to everyone, he thought. Maybe Che-Che is the boss after all. The sound of the freight elevator stirred him out of his reverie.

The elevator's tin-plated door clanged open. Pizzaro and three crew members wheeled in a large dolly covered with a tarpaulin that was tied around the bottom of the dolly. Alejandro's heart quickened when he spotted the woman he knew as Belle Starr walk in with the others. When did they get back from Thomas Cay? he wondered, waving at them.

"How ya doin', amigo," Pizzaro said, coming over to him and giving him a hug. "You did good, real good."

"Thanks, he said, his eyes staying almost too deliberately away from hers until he realized that ignoring her so obviously was in itself a possible giveaway. So he looked directly at her and said, "Hi. What's your name?"

Fiona was helping the others untie the tarpaulin. She glanced over at him and said, "None of your business."

"Is that your new head of public relations?" Alejandro asked Pizzaro.

"Yeah. She's cute, isn't she?"

"If you like the type."

"Can you repack the chutes by tonight?" Pizzaro asked.

"I'll have 'em ready," Alejandro said, watching them throw the tarpaulin off the dolly. The Ram Air canopies and their shroud lines were wrapped around their rigs and secured there by webbed belts. The men lifted them up off the dolly and put them on the table containing the duffel bags.

"Put them in a line," Alejandro told them.

Pizzaro asked Alejandro if he had the two homing transmitters.

"Yeah, I have 'em."

Pizzaro then looked around the loft with an almost proprietary air and ordered, "When you get all the chutes repacked, stack them back on the dolly, and leave. We'll pick them up."

"Okay," Alejandro said, noticing Fiona edging back behind the others and looking at him intensely as she tucked a stick of gum into her mouth. "I hope your guys were careful when they tied up those chutes. We don't need any rips or holes in the canopies," he said to Pizzaro.

Pizzaro didn't respond, merely walked off toward the freight elevator, followed by the others.

Alejandro lifted the first rig in line over to the other table, untied the belt, and began unsnaking the shroud lines and the canopy from around the rig. After bridling the lines through his fingers, untangling them, he stretched them down the table, aware that Pizzaro and the others were still there.

When he heard the elevator door open and close, he made sure that they were gone and then walked over to where the female undercover had been standing. He searched the floor thoroughly for the gum wrapper. Unable to find it, he bent down and looked under the table. He spotted it lying among dustballs and used coffee containers, a balled-up yellow wrapper with a fringe of silver sticking out of its fold.

Stretching his arm under the table, he fingered it closer so that he could grab it. Then he stood and unraveled the paper, pressing it out on top of the table. With his thumb and forefinger he pried it open along its seam.

The message "16 Alice" was written on the inside. He balled it up again, took it into the filthy bathroom, and flushed it down the toilet.

Back at the table, he worked the lines of the Ram Air canopy to their full length and secured the canopy's apex to the cotter pin that he had inserted in the table's top. Patting each of the panels to see if any were blown or burned, he smoothed out the curls and folds, then opened the black box that contained the power source for the steering mechanism that reeled the shroud lines in and out, checking the nickel cadmium battery with a meter. That done, he S-rolled the canopy and its lines into the skirt and spring-loaded the pilot chute on top of the canopy before closing up the rig and inserting the curved locking pin through the rig's grommets. He took the rig over to the dolly and went back to the table to get another one.

A simple code that could be used when they wanted to set up a meet was taught to the students at the Hacienda. Unscrambled, it consisted of an odd name, preferably the only one, of a person or place listed in the local telephone directory; that was to be preceded by the first two numbers of the appointed hour stated in military time.

Alice Tully Hall was located on the northwest corner of Broadway and Sixty-fifth Street. Posters in glass cases announced that Helen Whitehead was giving a piano recital at 4:00 P.M. that included Schubert's Piano Sonata in A Major.

Alejandro arrived at the hall eight minutes before four o'clock in the afternoon. He was informed by the woman in the box office that the recital was sold out. When he asked her if a ticket had been left for him in the name of J. James, he watched as she began flipping through a handful of windowed envelopes.

"Mr. J. James," she said, passing the envelope through the slot.

Inside the crowded lobby, he looked around until he found her standing in the far right corner. She had changed out of her jeans and was wearing a tailored black-and-white-checked suit with black pumps. Making his way over to her, he realized that she was almost as tall as he was. Once he was standing beside her, he said, "What's your name?"

"Fiona, and yours is Alejandro."

"How do you know that?"

"I asked one of the crew."

"Who are you working for?"

She looked at him askance. "Not even a 'Hello,' or a 'Nice to see you again'? You really do get right into it."

"We don't have time for pleasantries. You and I broke rule numero uno by exposing ourselves to each other. And now we have to try to fix it, and maybe even stay alive. So why don't you tell me who you are with?"

Her expression became serious. "NYPD Narcotics Division. And you?"

"We work for the same people," he said, deliberately leading her to believe that he was an undercover working for the junk squad. "Did you tell your control about me?"

"No. I've been waiting until we had a chance to talk. This assignment is important to me, I don't want to be pulled out."

"If our controls find out that we know each other, that is exactly what they'll do," he said, surveying the faces about the hall. He felt deeply uneasy about being there with her. Moving closer, he asked, "How did you manage to work your way into Che-Che's crew?"

"I was told to apply for a pilot's job with a company named Executives Unlimited. It's run by a renegade CIA guy named Lyle Caswell who did heavy time with Uncle for dealing high-tech weaponry with the camel drivers."

"Caswell sees you and puts you on the payroll?" he said with a tone of disbelief.

"Not exactly. He took me on a checkout flight out of Newark Airport. But it was mostly timing. I walked into his office the same time he was shopping around for a pilot who still had a working liver."

Alejandro folded his arms across his chest, noticing her fine, silken hair and the scent of her perfume. "Working together, we might be able to get the job done sooner."

"I'm for that. But we'll need a cover that will allow us to be seen together. Sneaking around like this won't work."

"We'll become lovers."

Her lips formed a knowing smile. *"Pretend* lovers works for me."

"That's what I meant," he said, but he was surprised to find himself feeling a definite sense of disappointment. "Have you gotten close to any of their crew?"

"No, but two of the assholes have come on to me."

"Try and get close to them, especially when they're sloshed on tequila. Find out if Pizzaro or anyone else maintains an office, or a business front of any kind."

"It's important?"

He nodded. "Very. They wash a lot of their money in Road Town in the British Virgins—and they smurf some of it. But this is a network with a large cash flow, and it doesn't all add up, in my mind."

Fiona thought for a moment, then suggested, "Maybe they're warehousing it until they can get it out of the country?"

Alejandro looked unconvinced. "You were down in Thomas Cay. You saw those facilities. This is a sophisticated network.

They tell everyone that they store it, but I think that's disinformation. They're getting a large part of the money washed somehow."

"I'll check around."

She made a move to leave, but Alejandro asked her, "What do you know about Judith?"

"Only that she's supposedly Pizzaro's girlfriend."

Again letting his eyes check out the faces of people nearby, he said, "She's more than a girlfriend. Any idea when they're going to bring in the next load?"

"No. I'm on standby." She opened her pocketbook and showed him a beeper. "Pizzaro gave me this. Whenever he buzzes me, I'm to call and be ready to go on another trip."

"Pizzaro gave you that?"

She saw the concern on his face, then quickly got his point. "Don't worry. I took it apart, there's no transmitter hidden inside."

"I hope you're positive, because if you're not, we're both dead."

She put a reassuring hand on his arm. "I'll see you tonight at Environment. I'll introduce myself to you; then we can begin our big romance."

Chimes rang; people began moving out of the lobby and to their seats. "Are you going to stay for the recital?" she asked him.

"No," he said, and walked away.

Fiona sat through the program until intermission, then left to keep her appointment.

Too Tall Paulie stared at the surveillance photographs for a long time, saying nothing. The vertical blinds made sun strips across his desk. Looking up at Lieutenant Elia, he finally asked, "Where were they taken?"

"Across from one of Che-Che's known pads on East Seventy-seventh Street."

Too Tall Paulie looked back at the shot of Alejandro walking into Che-Che's lobby. "So? We knew they were amigos."

"Boss, I believe that this mutt is a worthwhile subject of an investigation."

"Is there any evidence, circumstantial or otherwise, linking this Alejandro to the dope business?"

"No. Our informants tell us he's just a singer."

Burke shot him an exasperated look. "So why the hell do you have a bug up your ass over him?"

"A feeling," Elia responded. "Something about this Alejan-dro"—he pronounced the name with a mockingly exaggerated stress on the "han"—"just isn't kosher."

"We don't have assets to squander on *feelings*. It's the policy for this division to work the major networks and leave the nickel-and dime-baggers to the local precincts to take care of."

Elia persisted despite his boss's resistance. "I dug up some more background on him. Wanna hear?"

Too Tall Paulie sighed in resignation. "Okay, tell me."

"Alejandro Monahan. His father was a senior noncom in the U.S. Army. Retired to Mexico with his Mexican wife. The father was killed in an ambush with the town's chief of police."

Too Tall Paulie's eyes opened wide in surprise; he looked away from Elia and asked in apparent indifference, "What town did all this happen in?"

"Zihuatanejo."

An icy chill gripped the boss of the Narcotics Division. "What was his father's name?"

"Eamon Monahan."

Those bastards, they're using Eamon's kid, he thought, con-cealing his feelings by keeping a bored expression on his face. "Forget this guy, Lieutenant. He's nothing. *If* we had extra as-sets, I'd humor you and let you do him, but we don't. So do me a favor and shit-can this guy and get on with the important stuff."

"Okay," Elia said, leaning up out of his seat to retrieve the pile of photographs from the desk.

"Leave them," Too Tall Paulie said, "in case any more photos of him come across my desk."

After Elia was gone, Too Tall Paulie slipped one of the photographs of Alejandro into a manila envelope and walked grimly out of the office.

The esplanade of Battery Park City fronted Hudson River, directly across from Jersey City. The tide was high. Walking west on Public Place, Burke spotted his undercover leaning against the railing watching a container ship making for the open sea.

"She sure is big," he said, standing beside her.

"There is something romantic about a big ship rushing to meet the hazards of the sea."

"Almost like your job."

"Not quite," she said, pushing away from the railing and carefully sweeping the area around them with her eyes. A young man wearing a shiny black-and-chartreuse bodysuit, his arms flailing in front of him, sped past them on Kelly green roller blades.

"Talk to me, Fiona."

She told him about how she had flown the doper's plane to Thomas Cay, then went into considerable detail describing all the activities she observed on the island, along with a description of the facilities. Almost as an afterthought, she added, "They're dropping dope somewhere outside the city by parachute."

Too Tall Paulie cursed under his breath. "Where are they making the drop?"

"I'm not sure, someplace west of the city up in the Catskills, I think. The settings in the on-board navigational computer were preset, so once I left New York TAC I didn't have a specific destination, just coordinates." She smiled at Burke and said, "They're as paranoid as we are."

27

A CUBAN MAMBO BLASTED over Environment's speaker system as Alejandro climbed into the balcony Friday morning after his last show. Che-Che and Pizzaro were huddled in a banquette talking to the same two Oriental men he had seen on Thomas Cay. Fiona, along with three other dopers and their girlfriends, was sitting at a table near the bar. She was laughing at something one of the other women had just confided.

Seeing her with the dopers and their girlfriends made Alejandro stiffen involuntarily. Ignoring her, he went over to the bar.

"What'll it be, handsome?" Jasmine asked.

"Club soda," he said.

Jasmine put the glass in front of him and, as she was turning to leave, smiled and trailed her fingers across his hand.

Sipping his drink, he turned to watch the dancers on the loft's tiny dance floor, but out of the corner of his eye he focused on Che-Che's table. One of the Oriental men was emphasizing his words to Pizzaro with vigorous gestures. A few minutes later the two Oriental types got up abruptly and left. Che-Che saw Alejandro watching and waved him over.

"What was that all about?" he asked, sliding in next to the drug lord.

"Nothing important," Che-Che said, picking up his glass of champagne and staring at his two guests as they disappeared down the stairs.

"Che-Che tells me you want to drop our money onto boats," Pizzaro said, pouring more of the golden wine into his glass.

"Why not?" Alejandro said. He picked up his empty glass and signaled a waitress for more club soda. "It works the same at sea as it does on land," he explained confidently. "At sea you could drop the chutes directly into the cargo hatches."

Pizzaro looked at Che-Che and nodded in agreement. "It's clean and it's simple."

"The problem is that every time we come up with something new, the cops or the DEA eventually find out about it and screw it up for us. Someone either talks or is turned, or some wise-ass cop gets close to us," Che-Che said, watching a woman dancer wearing a dramatically short skirt.

"It doesn't matter with Parapoint, Che-Che," Alejandro said. "Even if they should find out about it, there's nothing that they can do to stop it. There's no way they can know when and where you're going to use those parachutes."

"Unless someone tells them," Pizzaro said, his attention being drawn to one of the women on the dance floor.

They fell silent.

Fiona and the women at her table had their heads together. They burst out laughing.

Alejandro had focused on Fiona and was watching her. Che-Che noticed his stare and, moving his head closer to the singer, asked, "You like?"

"Yeah, I like. Is she with anyone?" Alejandro asked.

"Not so far," Pizzaro said, smiling at one of the women on the dance floor.

"Excuse me," Alejandro said, sliding out of the booth.

Approaching the table, he saw Fiona and the other women watching him. One of the women whispered something, and all three laughed. Alejandro felt as if his fly were open. "Hi," he said to Fiona, nodding a lukewarm hello to the other dopers at the table.

"Hello," Fiona said, beaming at him. "These are my girl-friends Chus, Arlene, and Laura. Chus is with handsome Juan over there, and Arlene is with adorable Tito, and Laura is with—"

"Everyone," Laura burst in.

The women laughed again.

Alejandro glanced at all the empty wine bottles and asked Fiona, "And who are you with?"

"I'm with myself. I've got a double-headed vibrator that works better than any man."

"Maybe I can change your mind? Why don't we dance and talk about it?"

"Why not?" Fiona said, getting up.

Watching Alejandro dancing with Fiona, Pizzaro leaned close to his boss and said, "When are you going to give me the word to take that guy out?"

"Hector, you're too anxious to kill people. Who would repack our parachutes and recharge the guidance systems?"

"We could train one of our people."

"The devil you know is better than the devil you don't know. Besides, I like the way he sings."

Pizzaro scowled in anger. "I don't trust him. He's not one of us. He could give up the whole thing."

"I trust him," Che-Che said flatly, watching Fiona shimmying her body against Alejandro. "You check that one out?"

"Yeah, she's okay. I got her from Caswell."

Che-Che looked at Pizarro, a flicker of concern crossing his face. "I was surprised when they let him out."

"Hey, Caswell did a lot of hard time."

"But not all that he was supposed to do. He could have rolled over to get out. Maybe you should pay him a visit, check her out again. I don't sleep good when I see a new face mixing it up with our crew."

"I'll take care of it," Pizzaro said.

Che-Che grabbed his wrist, anchoring it to the table. "Ramón and Conrado were two good shooters, but they let two cops get close to us and they had to pay for that mistake. I hope you never get careless."

"I won't," Pizzaro said, jerking his wrist free, his mouth suddenly dry.

With his hands planted on Fiona's swaying hips, Alejandro ground his body into hers, whispering, "Let's make this look good."

"Not *that* good," she said, dancing away from him with her body and hands swaying to the music's beat.

Andy Seaver was inside the body of a big RV that was parked in the South Street parking lot, directly across the street from the Fulton Fish Market and a block and a half away from the warehouse where the Cleopatra Gold was stored. He was watching the four television monitors that were inset above the communications console. The radio crackled with reports from the various surveillance platforms strung around the warehouse.

"I hope our net is good and tight," he said to Detective Kathy Herer, who was handling the radio traffic.

"Lou, a mouse couldn't sneak through the stuff we threw up around that place. We even put static observation platforms in the high-rise office buildings."

"What about that boarded-up building abutting the west side of the warehouse?"

"Deserted as far as we can tell."

"Anyone inside our warehouse?"

"Those that went in together came out together. They drove off in a van."

"Did our Break and Enter people do a survey?"

She handed him an official report. He read it, folded the sheet into quarters, and stuck it into his shirt pocket. Studying the monitors in front of him, he said, "Zoom in on those padlocks on the sliding door."

The detective pressed a green plastic button on the console; the video cameras that had been concealed in nearby streetlights focused on the steel accordion door.

"Those padlocks are Rugers. I want one of our people to do a walk-by and get the numbers off them. Once we have them we can order keys from the company."

Alejandro and Fiona left the club arm in arm. Turning on the ignition of his sports car, he looked at her and put his finger to his lips.

After driving the car down the ramp leading into his apartment's underground garage, he parked in his assigned space, got out, and locked the car. Walking toward the elevator, he slid his hand in hers and asked, "Scared?"

"A little bit. And you?"

"I'm always scared," he said, turning the elevator call key. "Only I don't let it get in my way anymore. I'm in a state of perpetual numbness." He looked at her with an expression of sincere concern. "We have to assume that Pizzaro will put some of his goons on us, to make sure we're really an item. So from now on whenever we're together we're going to have to act like we got the hots for each other."

"I understand," she said, looking down at her shoes.

Walking into his apartment and looking around, she asked, "Do you usually get to take women you just met home with you?"

"Sometimes."

She wandered aimlessly around his living room, getting a better sense of him from his possessions. Stopping by his breakfront, she looked at the spines of his books. She admired the Aztec head. "This is lovely."

"Thank you. Let's go out onto the terrace and talk."

There was a slight coolness in the air, and the twilight was splashed with purple and pink. He slid his arm around her waist as they looked out over the city. "Do you ever think about our one night on the town, Texas two-steppin'?"

"Sometimes," she said softly, looking down at Washington Square.

"I saw you gabbing with some of those women. Find out anything?"

Fiona gave him a sly smile. "Girlfriends know a lot more than their boyfriends think they do. It seems that Señor Pizzaro maintains an office on Duane Street. The cover name is Whiggham Associates. None of his crew like to go there because Judith also has an office there—they're all afraid of her." Her expression grew serious; she looked at him and said nervously, "According to Chus—one of the women at the table tonight—they've come up with a way of fingering undercovers."

"How?"

"She didn't say and I didn't ask. But Chus did tell me that Judith's office is loaded with all sorts of high-tech communications gear; no one is allowed inside her office, even Pizzaro."

"I thought that Pizzaro was her boss."

"Che-Che gave that order."

Alejandro considered what she had told him and then asked, "Are Pizzaro and Judith lovers?"

"Yes, according to the women. But it's nothing heavy."

"What about Jasmine?"

"They didn't mention her."

Concealing his disappointment, Alejandro pressed on. "What did they have to say about Che-Che?"

"They're all terrified of him. And from the little I've heard, they should be."

"What about the Oriental guys from the cay who were talking to Che-Che tonight?"

"Chus made an offhand remark that one of the 'money men' at Che-Che's table looked pissed off. She figured that was because he hadn't gotten . . . had sex."

"The money men?" He was puzzled by this reference.

"That's what she said."

"Anything else?"

A smile crossed her mouth. "No, nothing, really."

"What? Tell me everything, you never know what's important."

"Well, it seems Juan isn't circumcised, and that his thing is bent. Chus gets grossed out whenever they do it."

A flush came to his cheeks and he said, "Let's go inside."

He closed the terrace door behind them and led her into the bedroom. She sat up with her back against the headboard and her legs crossed at the ankles.

"Why is this job so important to you?" he asked.

"My father was pissed off that I wasn't a boy and spent most of his life taking it out on me. I'm a better pilot than he ever was, yet he'd tell everyone that I couldn't fly. I guess I still have a need to prove that he was wrong." She turned her face to him. "So how did you get into this business?"

He opened his mouth to say something, but the truth wouldn't come. No matter how much he wanted to, he was unable to say it, so he slipped into a variation of his "legend" about his past.

When he finished he saw her looking at him with an irritated expression. "I don't believe a word you've just told me." Before he could protest, she placed a silencing finger across his lips and said, "It's okay. You don't owe me the truth."

At that moment her beeper went off. They both jumped, startled. She looked at the device clipped to her belt, and rolling across his body, she grabbed the telephone off the night table and started dialing.

He liked the way she felt on top of him.

Her call was answered before the first ring was over.

"Where are you?" Pizzaro asked.

"With Alejandro in his apartment."

"Get dressed and meet me in front of the club."

"Right," she said, and thoughtfully replaced the receiver. "It was Hector. He wants me to meet him right away. Looks like they're making another drop." She studied the design on the sheet and added, "He thinks we were fucking, of course."

"Good."

The gray building on Duane Street looked like a squat, flat-topped box with a high-rise smokestack. It was early Sunday morning, and the streets and roadways in this industrial part of the city were largely deserted. Most of the buildings housed factories and warehouses, mostly companies that handled machine tools and automobile parts. An occasional truck broke the silence, speeding along Hudson Street.

Each one of the eleven floors of the gray building was dark. The front entrance had a locked revolving door and two other doors on either side of it. The lobby was dimly lit. There was a security desk inside, but no guard was in sight. Alejandro had been standing in the shadows of a doorway across the street for the past fifteen minutes, watching the lobby of the gray building.

Before leaving his apartment Saturday night to do his first

show, he had gone into his bedroom and taken the shoe rack out of his closet. He had peeled up the carpet carefully, then, using a kitchen knife, he'd pried up a floor hatch. From a hidden compartment he'd taken out the state-of-the-art burglary kit that he had been issued by the Hacienda's "Technical Services" section. After looking down at one revolver and two automatic handguns hidden there, he had decided against going armed.

Now he darted across the street, looked into the lobby, and, seeing no sign of the guard, took out a flat black pouch from the cloth knapsack slung over his shoulder. Then he shook out a tension wrench, a flat band of tempered steel, and a diamond-tipped lock pick.

He inserted the wrench into the keyhole of the door on the left of the revolving door and turned the wrench to the right, creating a turning pressure on the cylinder the same way as a key. After slipping the diamond pick into the lock, he skillfully began to feel for the tumbler pins that were housed along the cylinder's sheer line. He found the first one and pushed it up slightly to slide the pick under it, snaking for the next pin in line. The pick operated the same way as the serrated edge of a key, by relieving the spring tension and allowing the cylinder to turn.

He got the next three pins up and was inching for the next in line when the sudden squeal of brakes made him flinch and lose his grip on the pins; they slipped back into their holes. He turned to see a sports car swaying along Duane Street. Damn! He started over again. It took him another four minutes to work the lock and get inside.

The lobby reeked of alcohol; he figured the guard must be someplace sleeping it off. He saw from the building's directory that Whiggham Associates was in suite 900. He hurried over to the stairwell—elevators made noise, he'd been taught at the Hacienda. He paused on the ninth-floor stairwell and cracked the door, sweeping his eyes up and down the deserted corridor. He slipped out into the hallway and padded along the dimly lit horseshoe-shaped corridor, looking for suite 900.

The entrance to Whiggham Associates did not show any signs of being wired for an alarm system. Kneeling, Alejandro looked into his kit and found the tiny television camera with the long cord and the fiber optic lens at the tip. He should snake it under the door and take a look at what was on the other side, but he did not want to take the time to do that. Even though today was Sunday, he was concerned that some of the companies in the building might have some people working on the weekend. If there were, they'd probably come in late morning. He looked at the time: 3:48. He took out the pouch, shook out the wrench and lock pick, began working the cylinder.

Standing inside the waiting room, gazing with amusement at the acoustical ceiling tiles, the garish orange shag carpet, the painting of Christ on the cross, and the plastic roses stuck into the top of the frame, he thought, One of Hector's crew must have been the decorator. After examining the door that apparently led into Pizzaro's office and seeing no alarm system, he turned the knob and went in.

In contrast with the other room, Hector's office was tastefully furnished. He concluded that a different decorator had done this job. He went over to the big rosewood desk and started rummaging through the stacks of SPRING 3100, the magazine for policemen by policemen, piled high along with other publications. Many of them had different-colored Post-it notes stuck onto the edges of their pages.

He slipped one magazine out of the pile and began flipping to the flagged pages. On one there was a photograph of a beautiful woman dressed in a red, white, and blue sweatsuit, smiling and holding a soccer ball in her hand. The caption under it identified her as a police officer from the 108th Precinct; she had spent last July in Barcelona, Spain, as part of the U.S. Olympic handball team.

The next photograph on the page identified the valedictorian of the graduating class of July 3, 1992. There was also a photograph of a Queens Narcotics Unit standing behind a table loaded down with ninety-seven kilos of seized cocaine. Each of the officers was identified by name.

Quickly shuffling through more of the magazines, he came to one with photographs of the murdered undercovers DiLeo and Levi. There was a handwritten notation that the undercovers had been introduced into the network by Jordon Hayes.

He put that *SPRING 3100* back in its place in the pile and flipped through the stacks of the *City Record*. The first one he opened had the names of every member of the latest class of recruits to enter the Police Academy. Hector really knows his business, he thought with begrudging admiration.

After carefully rearranging the *City Record* stack, he sat down at Pizzaro's computer terminal, switched it on, and called up the menu. The machine beeped, and "PASSWORD REQUIRED" flashed in the upper left-hand corner of the screen. He glanced at the time and looked across the room, fixing on the door with the cipher lock. That's gotta be Judith's office, he thought. From the looks of that lock, that's where the family jewels are stored.

He turned off the machine, returned Hector's chair to the exact position in which he had found it, and, lugging his kit, padded over to the door with the cipher lock.

From inside the knapsack he took out a four-by-five-inch electronic black box with a viewing window across the top. A wire with a suction cup at the end protruded out of the top. The box had an on/off switch on the faceplate and a thin magnet on the back. He had used this device many times over the years but still didn't have a clue how it worked. Once he'd asked Porges but had been told that only a few of the weirdos in Technical Services understood how it worked.

He attached the box to the faceplate of the cipher lock and suctioned the cup to the lock. He flipped on the switch. The viewing window glowed red, and six digits began spinning rapidly as the machine searched out every possible combination number. The first digit locked in place; the five remaining parts of the combination continued spinning. The second number locked, then the third and fourth. Within eight minutes he had the combination. He punched the number into the cipher lock's keypad.

The windowless room was long and narrow and packed with communications equipment, including a radio console with a large-screen computer terminal, two fax machines, and a shredder. The cramped space was scented faintly with Judith's perfume. A box of tissues sat on the console ledge, along with a doll dressed in a frilly spring dress, holding a parasol. There was a row of drawers under the console. He opened them and found boxes of pencils, paper for the laser printer and fax machines, unopened boxes of tissues, a spray bottle of perfume, and an unopened package of panty hose. After looking around, he decided that whatever treasures were there were locked up inside the data banks.

Lowering himself into her chair, he switched on the terminal and called up the menu. "PASSWORD REQUIRED" flashed in the middle of the screen.

Rolling his eyes, he thought, What password would Judith use to protect her data banks? She'd use something different, not easily thought of or known. Not something easy like her birthday or her Social Security number. No, she'd use something no one would think of, something few people even knew anything about. He thought of her gold Cleopatra medallion and smiled. Yeah, that's what she'd use. Slowly he typed in the name, Cleopatra. PASSWORD REQUIRED. Cleopatra VII. PASSWORD REQUIRED.

Next he entered the names of Cleopatra's handmaidens, Iras and Charmian, both separately and together, and was denied entry. Her birthday? 69 B.C. PASSWORD REQUIRED.

I've spent a lot of time reading about this lady, so *think,* he thought, frustration gnawing at him. What was the name of the guy who smuggled her into Caesar's apartment rolled up in a rug? He input the name, Apollodorus. PASSWORD REQUIRED. Think! Damn it, think.

Mark Anthony had written to Octavian that she was a fascinatingly beautiful woman with a prodigious sexual talent, he recalled. The men she loved? He typed in Caesar and Mark Anthony together and separately and was again denied permission to enter.

What other man did she love? Her father. He typed in Ptolemy XII. PASSWORD REQUIRED. Watching the flashing words on the screen, he felt like putting his fist through them. Instead he told himself to think harder and asked himself what her father's nickname was. He typed in Auletes and was denied entry. Shaking his head with frustration, he thought of what Auletes meant in English and typed in, The Flute Player. The program's menu scrolled across the screen. He punched the air in satisfaction.

One of the menus listed "Corporation Accounts." He called it up. The network had a string of expensive clothing boutiques and jewelry stores and restaurants, along with an assortment of wholesale business across the country. Four to six stores formed a corporation that fed into an out-of-state parent corporation. Money was wired to the out-of-state parent companies, where it was wired out of state into the account of another corporation. The money was bounced around the country until it was wired to accounts in Montevideo, Uruguay, or Milan, Italy, where it was again wire-transferred into numbered accounts in Luxembourg and Panama.

On paper all these transactions appeared to be legitimate business activities. There were also invoices for the sale of zircons and lead bars. They would ship zircons that on anything but expert close inspection looked like real diamonds and lead gilded to look like gold bars, listed on phony invoices to justify the transfer of large sums out of the country to pay for the imitation diamonds and gold.

There were also account records showing the smuggling of large sums out of the country and the washing of staggering amounts in Road Town. There was no time to go through the entire program; he had seen enough to know that the Cleopatra network had washed over thirty-five million dollars over an eight-month period.

He switched on the laser printer. When the printer finished, he took the pages of printout and stuffed them into his knapsack. Looking anxiously at the time, he wondered if he should take a look at another data bank.

Don't get greedy and careless, he told himself. Looking around the office, making sure everything was as he'd found it, he pushed Judith's chair against the console and left, locking the door behind him.

On Monday morning Alejandro shut off the alarm clock and sat up in bed, looking at the computer printouts spread over the floor. He had spent all day Sunday holed up in his apartment, studying the records.

Friday's mail had contained a junk ad that had been sent first class in a large beige envelope that informed him that his official entry number may have already been selected to win a new BMW 850i or $100,000 in cash. No purchase was necessary, but he must enter the contest to win. The envelope had a large window across the top containing his entry number: E 3125517M. That number translated into a meet with Mother Hen at a safe house located at 312 East 55th Street, at 1700 Monday.

He popped off the bed and gathered the printouts, rolling up the pages and stashing them in the hidden compartment under the floor of his closet. Then he showered and washed the sleep out of his eyes. He lathered his face, took the throwaway razor out of the soap dish, looked up into the mirror dangling from the shower caddy, and shaved. After dressing and gulping down a cup of coffee, he left. Outside, he hailed a taxi and told the driver to take him to the Thirty-sixth Street loft.

The duffel bags were waiting for him, stacked neatly on one of the long tables. That makes three drops, he thought as he began checking the seams. Seeing that they were okay, he started taking the parachutes off the dolly. It was after two o'clock in the afternoon when he finished repacking the delivery systems. He was lifting the last one onto the dolly when the elevator door clattered open and Pizzaro led three of his crew, including Fiona, into the loft.

"They ready?" Pizzaro asked sharply.

"Just finished," Alejandro said, noting the fatigue lines around Fiona's eyes and cheeks. The strain of the repeated round-trip flights, and being out there alone, was beginning to show. She gave him a weak smile and started helping the others spread the tarpaulin over the rigs. When that was done, Pizzaro led them toward the elevator.

Fiona dashed over to Alejandro and gave him a fast kiss on the cheek. "Let's go, Fiona," Pizzaro barked impatiently.

Alejandro waited five minutes after they left before locking up the loft and leaving. Walking out of the building, he spied the black sedan parked at the curb. The back window slid down. "Hi," Judith said.

Climbing into the backseat, Alejandro noticed that her left foot was tapping on the carpeting; something had her all wound up. "You and I have some unfinished business," she said, sliding her hand in his.

"I've been looking forward to it." Alejandro smiled, thinking, Now she's looking to cash in her rain check.

* * *

Fiona was sitting on the jump seat in the back of the van, day-dreaming about that first time she had seen Alejandro, on the soccer field, when the sudden squeal of brakes snapped her back to the here and now. As she leaned up out of her seat to look out the windshield, her stomach turned over in fear.

They were parked in front of the lower Madison Avenue address of Executives Unlimited. Pizzaro jumped out and shoved open a side door. "Let's you and me go visit an old friend," he said to her.

She climbed down and walked with him into the dilapidated building, her pulse rapid and her knees shaking.

Executives Unlimited had its dingy office on the fourth floor. Pizzaro let her lead the way along the curving hallway to a door with peeling gold letters. They entered without knocking and stood in a small anteroom with a green plastic sofa and an end table of pressed wood that held a large brown ceramic lamp with a balloon base and black shade. The sound of galloping horses and gunfire came from the inner office. Pizzaro threw open the door.

Lyle Caswell was watching an old western on a portable television on the edge of his desk, sipping coffee from a container; from the smell, the coffee had been spiced liberally with booze. Pizzaro pulled a sour face.

"Hey, Hector, how are you?" Caswell said, looking at Fiona. Caswell was lean and bony with sunken cheeks and deep wrinkles nestled around the corners of his eyes. He didn't look very happy to see his unexpected visitors.

Pizzaro sat down on the only available chair, leaving Fiona standing. "You remember Fiona?"

"Sure," he said, opening a side drawer, putting the container inside, and pushing the drawer closed. "How are these guys treating you?"

"Just fine," she said, trying not to show any nervousness.

Pointing a finger at her, Caswell said, "You be careful of this Hector, he's a real ladies' man, always looking to stick it to the bearded clam."

Looking down at the yellow-and-blue design of the silk tie he was wearing, Pizzaro said, "Some of your friends are wondering how you got your parole."

"I got my parole by doing hard fucking time," Caswell said resentfully.

Pizzaro looked away from him at the television. One cowboy leaped onto a horse and went galloping off after another cowboy who was shooting at him. "There are some people who are worried that you might have rolled over in order to get out."

A vein on the right side of Caswell's neck began pulsing. "What are you stuffing up your nose, Hector? They cut me loose early because they needed my bunk. Don't you guys read the newspapers? All the prisons in this country are bursting at the seams."

Pizzaro looked back at him coldly. "Yeah, I remember hearing something about that." He looked up at Fiona. "She's a good pilot."

Caswell relaxed. "I only send my friends top talent."

"Did you know she was a cop?"

Caswell's weak smile turned instantly to an expression of terror. "I checked her out. I swear I did." His hands came up as if he were praying.

"I'm no cop, you bastard!" Fiona shouted at Pizzaro.

"I checked her; she came up clean," Caswell pleaded, the unmistakable stink of fear rising from his body.

"I'm no damn cop!" she shouted again.

Pizzaro slid out a .38-caliber S&W Chief from his waistband and shot Caswell in the face. The hollow-tipped bullet plowed in just under the right eye and blew out his skull.

Fiona recoiled in horror. She grabbed Pizzaro by the shoulder and began shaking him. "I'm not a cop!"

"I know that," he said calmly. "But he wasn't sure enough, and he should have been sure. That made him a risk." Jamming the barrel against her stomach, he asked, "You got a problem with any of this?"

She glared at him. "The only problem I have is that my period is two days late."

His lips smiled; his eyes stayed cold. "I like you."

"I like you, too. You're a great humanitarian."

Pizzaro took out his silk pocket scarf and, walking around the desk, wiped the revolver clean of his fingerprints. Then he planted it in the dead man's hand.

"You don't think that the cops'll fall for that phony suicide routine, do you?" Fiona asked, fighting to keep her voice from shaking.

"Of course they will. They got so many unsolved murders in this city that they jump at any excuse to solve one."

Leaving the building, Pizzaro said, "Even if you were a cop, it'd make no difference. Now you're an accessory to murder."

28

JUDITH'S AMPLE BREASTS were soft, her nipples erect. She had hooked one leg over his and was biting his shoulder, none too gently, while he brushed his finger through her thick pubic hair.

"Was I as good as Fiona?" she asked, rolling her eyes to his.

"There was no contest. You're a woman, she's a child."

She took hold of his hand and guided a finger inside her. She groaned in delight and opened her legs wide.

They made love again, then lay on their backs, staring up into their own private spaces. Glancing over her bronzed body, staring at the gold Cleopatra medallion around her neck, he asked, "What's the story with you and Hector?"

"We have an arrangement; but it's not an exclusive one." Rolling over and propping herself on her elbow, she attempted to change the subject of conversation to him.

Eyes showing only contentment under her gaze, he slipped easily into the familiar myths as he told her about his make-believe life and past. He concluded with the true story of how he got his gig at Environment. "Now what about you?" he asked.

She told him that she was an only child and how disappointed her father had been when she'd decided against going into the family business. "I wanted to make it on my own."

"Where did you meet Hector?"

"We met in Bolivia years ago."

"And Che-Che?"

"I met him here in New York, about three years ago," she lied smoothly.

"Where the heck did he ever come up with the name 'Cleopatra Gold'?"

She arched one brow, surprised he would ask. "I thought you knew that. According to Tarascan myth, Cleopatra escaped from Egypt and sailed all the way to Ixtapa."

"I heard that story when I was a kid, but I never believed it."

She rolled off the bed and began gathering up her clothes. She padded into the bathroom and closed the door. When he heard the shower, he leaped up off the bed, picked up his briefs, and stepped into them.

"How did you like being with an older woman?" she called seductively from inside the bathroom.

"Very much," he called back, realizing as he answered that he really meant it.

She came out of the bathroom dressed, to find him sprawled on the bed.

"Will I see you again?" he asked, getting up and taking her in his arms.

She gave him a long good-bye kiss. "Yes. But not *this* way. Today was a one-shot deal. I don't mix my money with my pleasure."

"What about Hector?"

"That's different."

After she was gone, he quickly showered and dressed, reflecting on his time alone with Judith. He concluded that she was probably as big a liar as he was.

Alejandro got out of the taxi at Fifty-seventh Street and Second Avenue. It was the third cab he had taken since leaving his apartment, to insure that he was not being followed. He crossed the avenue to the pizza parlor on the northwest corner and ordered a slice. Standing at the counter, he swept his eyes over the street, searching out any break in the normal rhythm. Students from the High School of Art and Design congregated on the corners. People waited patiently by the bus stop. Women pushed baby carriages; a dog walker led her charges down the street. He tossed the crust of pizza into the plastic-lined garbage basket and left, strolling south on Second Avenue, taking his time window shopping.

The nameplate on the door read "J. McMahon." Alejandro admitted himself with a key.

"Wanna drink?" Seaver asked, standing at the bar.

"Scotch." Walking over to the window, Alejandro added, "This is definitely not cool, meeting here while I'm in play."

"We have to talk," Seaver said, handing him a glass filled almost to the top.

Peering out the window, Alejandro noticed that the fountain was not working. He turned and handed Seaver a shopping bag containing the printouts from Pizzaro's office. "Some of their money records. You'd better get them to the accountants."

Seaver put the shopping bag on the floor without looking at the records. "What does it look like?"

"Like big bucks. They have all these different kinds of stores throughout the country that are nothing more than shells that siphon money from their drug deals. They get it into the banking system by funneling it through phony corporations until it eventually ends up in the accounts of overseas shell companies." He sipped at his drink. "What did you find out about Judith and Jasmine?"

"Judith's last name is Stern. She was born on Long Island, June 3, 1942."

"She's fifty-one," Alejandro said, sounding curiously remote.

"Her father built up the family business; he inherited it from *his* father. They manufacture women's swimwear. The old man is in a nursing home in Queens now, and the business is run by her brothers. Evidently she wanted into the business, but big daddy said no way, so she told them all to go to hell; and went to work for a competitor. Two years later she was running the damn place. Then all of a sudden she drops out of sight and resurfaces south of the border." He handed over a transcript of her college records.

Reading it, Alejandro observed, "She's no dope. She's got a fucking MBA."

Seaver continued to read from notes on a piece of paper. "She met Che-Che in Ixtapa, and started working for him. It's not clear whether or not she was one of his hookers. But she took a collar in Mexico for selling phony time shares to gringo tourists. Che-Che bribed her out of it." Leaning forward and looking directly at him, Seaver said, "I had Wade Hicks run a check on her passport files. She *was* in Mexico when your dad was murdered. That does not mean that she was the shooter, or had anything to do with it."

Alejandro put his glass on the coffee table, dawning comprehension spreading across his face. "They're partners, Andy. Che-Che had the connections with the major Colombian dopers, and she had the business know-how. They make a good team."

"And Pizzaro?" Seaver asked.

Alejandro rubbed his jaw thoughtfully. "As I see it, Pizzaro is only a hired stone killer with an extra fringe benefit—Judith fucks him so she can keep an eye on him and his ambition. What did you get on Jasmine?"

"Her name is Jasmine Sa Kee." Seaver was looking again at his notes. "Daddy is one of the world's biggest heroin dealers. He operates out of the Golden Triangle."

Alejandro snapped his fingers. "That's it—that's where we connect in the China White. Jasmine's daddy provides the shit, and Che-Che and Judith package and sell it."

"The question is, does Che-Che or Judith know who Jasmine is?" Seaver said in a low voice.

"What's your guess?"

"I don't think they know who she is."

Alejandro nodded. "I agree. My bet is that Daddy sent Jasmine to the States to learn the retail and wholesale end of the business so he can build his own white interstate across this country. I also think she's fucking Che-Che!"

Seaver leaned back, his eyes fixed on the thin crack running across the ceiling. "We have a big problem."

"What?"

"The boss had to go before the Intelligence oversight board and give his semiannual report. He gave them the skinny on this operation. They freaked out when they heard how much heroin we were sitting on. They want arrests made, and the dope seized . . . or . . ."

"Or what?" Alejandro growled angrily. "Andy, I didn't work this network to see these scumbags walk in court. Most of the evidence we have is not admissible, like those financial records. I don't want to see this bitch Cleopatra get away."

Seaver held up both hands in a calming gesture. "I agree with you. I wanna see them go down the tubes, too; but we gotta take out that dope."

Alejandro began to pace around the room, his mind going at full speed. "Why don't I sneak into the warehouse and destroy it? *That* would throw them into a panic. I could even plant a cloth bag full of quarters so they'd think one of the Colombian animals did it. The queen just might make a major blunder if all that dope was turned to mush."

Against his better judgment, Seaver began to warm to the idea. "How would you do it?"

"Pyranol."

" 'At'll do it, all right. But we don't have any of the stuff."

"Our CIA friend Wade Hicks will give you whatever we need," Alejandro said confidently.

"You seem sure of that."

Alejandro looked at his hands. "Andy, you visited my father five days before he was killed. You told me that you had asked him to keep an eye on the *traficantes* in and around Zihua. For who? The NYPD? No way. You asked him to do that as a favor for Hicks. That's why Chilebean and Mr. A. Brown get whatever they need from the Agency. Hicks is trying to make amends for what happened to my father."

For several long minutes Seaver looked out the window. Then he said, "Maybe you're right." He took out a cheroot and lit it up, blowing smoke across the room. As if this small bombshell had never gone off, he asked, "What else will you need?"

Alejandro just stared at him for a moment. Then he shrugged and responded in a matter-of-fact way, as if he were making a shopping list, "Igniters for the Pyranol. Digital timers with watch faces powered by camera batteries." He slipped into a momentary silence, then added, "This could get hairy. Get me a Heckler and Koch MP5 nine-millimeter submachine gun, and four or five magazines loaded with Glaser rounds."

"Why an MP5?"

"Because it comes equipped with a sound suppressor. It weighs four pounds, has almost no muzzle recoil or jump, and its barrel is 4.5 inches long."

"You realize that those damn Glaser rounds have thirty lead pellets packed into their noses."

"That's why I want them. They make a wound the size of a saucer, yet they won't go through walls and kill innocent people."

Seaver suddenly grew cautious. "I don't know if the boss will go along with this. Your job is to lie, entrap, facilitate, suborn, conspire, whatever. What you're *not* supposed to do is give Rambo imitations."

Alejandro's eyes blazed with anger. "You tell Romano that I want to do this. If he gives you a hard time, tell 'im that I have something he wants real bad."

"What?"

"I know how those undercovers were blown."

29

CALVIN JONES WAS A SE-
nior police administrative
aide in the office of the deputy commissioner, management and
budget. He was a lanky man with oversize ears, slightly protrud-
ing eyes, and steel gray hair. SPAA Jones was a man fatally ad-
dicted to nose candy. For the past two and a half years he had
been Pizzaro's main source of information within the NYPD. He
had been badly shaken up by an unexpected late-morning telephone call from Pizzaro. "Meet me downstairs. Now."

Walking out of One Police Plaza, he spied the man who owned
his soul, the stone killer with the white strip of hair, sitting on
one of the wooden benches that lined the wide walkway leading
into the plaza. As Jones approached, Pizzaro got up and walked
through the Municipal Building's archway; Jones followed. Pizzaro crossed Centre Street into City Hall Park, going on to

Broadway, where he bought an ice-cream sandwich from a sidewalk vendor. Walking north, Pizzaro waited for his informer to catch up and then asked pleasantly, "How are you, Calvin?"

"Good. I've been wanting to talk to you about our arrangement."

Pizzaro raised his eyebrows in mock surprise. "How's that?"

"I take a lotta chances getting you that information, so I figure that I should get a lot more money—say, double what you give me now."

Pizzaro smiled acquiescence, but the skin around his eyes tightened imperceptibly. "Whatever is fair, amigo. You're an invaluable source." He offered him a wintry smile. "The day policemen are sworn in is the day that most of their personal records are made out, correct?"

"Hector, we've been over that landscape many times."

"Humor me, amigo."

"Yeah. They fill out insurance forms, they choose a medical plan, fill out tax withholding forms, and they sign their oaths of office."

"No other Department records?"

"Not that I can think of."

"Who is at the swearing-in ceremony?"

"The mayor usually shows up, the top brass in the Department, family, friends. All the paperwork is completed before the invited guests arrive."

"Before they arrive, who is there with the rookies?"

Jones thought carefully before he replied, ticking each off on his fingers. "Representatives of the various medical plans to explain them to the rookies, someone from the pension bureau to tell them their different pension options, someone from payroll to explain what's going to be taken out of their paychecks. Oh, yeah, and the CO of the Police Academy to lay the law down to them and tell them what's expected of them, and . . ." His voice trailed off as something struck him.

"And what, Calvin?" Pizzaro said, jamming the last of his ice cream into his mouth.

Jones's eyes drifted uneasily over to the rows of official cars parked in front of City Hall, and he confessed reluctantly, "Representatives of the various religious, line, and fraternal organizations are there to sign the rookies up even before they really start training."

"I see them mentioned all the time in *SPRING 3100*. So what?"

"So they're not part of the Department. They're all private organizations, and none of their records are part of a cop's folder. See these outfits are there to look after cops, like a union would."

"Why the hell didn't you tell me that before? I assumed they were part of the Department."

"No, they're not," SPAA Jones said sheepishly. "I never thought of them before because they aren't officially part of the department."

"How many of them are there?"

"Around thirty."

"Can you get me a list of them?"

SPAA Jones reached behind and took out his billfold. He flipped it open and took out a blue-and-green plastic card with an embossed blue-and-gold shield in the center and passed it to Pizzaro. "This is the Centurion Foundation's 1993 card."

"Who are they?" Pizzaro asked, studying the card.

"Businessmen who give out scholarship awards to the various religious, line, and fraternal organizations. A list of them all is on the back."

Pizzaro looked over the names. "New York cops appear to be big-time joiners. Where do these outfits have their offices?"

Jones was eager to cut this fascinating conversation short. "All over the city. The PBA is across the street in the Woolworth Building. A lot of them have their offices there. But they're all listed in the phone book."

"If they were going to put a cop undercover, would they pull his membership records in these organizations?"

"No. They only pull his fingerprints and his folder. I guess no one ever thought to ask these organizations to destroy their records."

Dumb gringos, no wonder they're losing their war, Pizzaro thought. He slipped the Centurion Foundation's card into the pocket of his soft cotton shirt, saying, "You did good, Calvin."

Jones's back stiffened. "Thanks."

Pizzaro made a move to pull out his silk pocket scarf containing a few packets of his own version of the Fink's Fizz, then thought better of it. He'd wait until he got a replacement for Jones before letting him sniff himself into hell. Mañana, pig.

Tito, the dapper doper who, of all the crew, was most trusted by Pizzaro, stood in front of his boss's desk looking at the blue-and-gold laminated card the counterintelligence chief was holding up in front of him.

"I want you to get the address of every one of these organizations. Then take some people and break into them. I want a copy of their membership lists."

Tito looked perplexed. "Am I looking for something special?"

"Yeah, you are. If you come up with the name Fiona Lee or Alejandro Monahan, you let me know real fast."

Tito reached for the card. Pizzaro yanked it back just beyond his reach. "No mistakes."

A basketball swished through the tattered hoop in Yeshiva Beth Chaim's school yard at the exact moment Joey-the-G-Man's brow wrinkled in consternation. He was looking at the surveillance photograph that Chief Burke had slid across his desk. "Am I supposed to know who this guy is?"

"I think you do."

"Refresh my memory."

"It's Eamon's son."

Holding the picture up in front of him, Romano said, "Now that you mention it, there is a resemblance. What's he doing in one of your photos?"

"He was observed by one of my teams paying a visit to one of Che-Che Morales's hideaways."

"Really? The last time I heard of him he was slinging tacos in his mother's restaurant."

Looking with disdain at the Intelligence chief, Too Tall Paulie said, "You're the perfect man for your job. You trust no one, you're a state-of-the-art liar—and you don't give a shit who you have to hurt to get the job done."

Their angry eyes locked and held for a moment.

Joey-the-G-Man pushed the photograph back across the desk. "I think you'd better leave."

"He's Eamon's son."

Joey-the-G-Man swept his hand at the window. "All those boys playing basketball are someone's son." He leaned forward. "You're a sanctimonious prick, you always have been. For years dopers have been icing each other because of your disinformation, and you walk away clean. Holier-than-thou Paulie, facilitate a homicide? Never," he added in a tone dripping with sarcasm. Then, making an obvious effort to calm down, Romano said almost apologetically, "Paulie, all I can tell you is that I don't know anything about Alejandro. I didn't even know he was in New York."

"Why is it that I don't believe you?" Burke said, getting up and walking out of the office without closing the door behind him.

Driving back to police headquarters, Too Tall Paulie pressed a button on the side of the steering column. The concealed door panel snapped open. Keeping his eyes on the road, he reached down and switched on the radio. The squawk of police calls filled the car. Taking out the handset, he transmitted, "Narcotics CO to Central, K."

"Go CO, K."

"Have the Whip of Unified Intelligence ten-two my office forthwith, K."

"Ten-four."

Sal Elia was waiting calmly when Too Tall Paulie stormed into his office twenty-three minutes later. Going behind his desk, Burke said, "I want you to go sick."

Elia looked astonished. "Why?"

"I have a job for you; I don't want you working any charts." Paulie unlocked the bottom drawer that held the confidential telephone, took it out, and set it on the floor. From the false bottom panel, he took out an envelope and passed it to the lieu- tenant. "The photograph inside belongs to Police Officer Fiona Lee. She is currently on assignment flying dope into the country for Che-Che Morales."

Looking at her smiling face, Elia asked, "Is she experienced?"

"I snatched her out of recruit school. She's smart and she's tough, but she's out there all by her lonesome."

"Why me, why now? And whatcha want me to do?"

"I want you to baby-sit her. I planted outside Environment the other night, and I saw her leaving with Alejandro. I now think that the singer might be working for Che-Che—or, worse, for Joey-the-G-Man."

"What a way to fight a fucking war," Elia said, shaking his head sadly.

Alejandro and Fiona were exhausted when they arrived at his apartment early Wednesday morning. "Let's make it a quick evening," she said. "The hell with whether or not they're watch- ing us."

"Stay a little while and then go," he said, throwing himself across the bed.

They lay on opposite sides of the mattress. She spread her skirt over her legs and tucked the pillow under her head. "Maybe I'll snooze for a minute or two," she said, and closed her eyes.

He fell asleep, too. He dreamed of a mango sculpted into the shape of a flower, and he heard the surf of La Playa Ropa pounding against the rocks, and he saw Indians hawking rugs and serapes along the Paseo del Pescadero. He opened his eyes and found himself next to her. Her skin was warm, and her scent reminded him of lilacs. He brushed a strand of hair away from her face; her closeness excited him. Suddenly she opened her eyes, and they shared a longing stare. He kissed her; she caressed his face with her hand and kissed him back. He caressed her breast; she pressed her body closer. He felt the heat from her face and slid his hand under her dress.

Suddenly she grabbed his wrist and tugged it away from her body. Sitting up, she said, "I don't want to do this. Not now, not here."

"Fiona—"

"Please. Don't say anything, Alejandro. We both know that it would be stupid."

"You're right. I got carried away. I don't want it to happen this way, either. I want it to be different with us. If it happens . . ."

"Me too," she said, and kissed him.

"I'll go downstairs with you and put you into a cab."

She smiled. "If any of those dirtbags saw you doing that, they'd really get suspicious."

He took hold of her hand. "Be careful, please."

"You too."

30

THE PARAPOINT DELIVERY SYS-
tems were stacked on the
dolly inside the loft. Alejandro was standing at one of the long
tables looking at the photographs of the dopers' warehouse that
Seaver had included in the shopping list Federal Express delivered to his apartment late Wednesday afternoon. Included with
the Pyranol and the nine-millimeter submachine gun were keys
to the padlocks that secured the warehouse's accordion door.

Alejandro had the shopping list and his burglary kit packed into
an overnight bag, along with a .38-caliber detective special from
the stash in his closet. He loaded it with lethal Glaser rounds.

Hearing the elevator coming up, he thrust the photographs
into the overnight, pushed the bag well under the table, and ran
into the toilet. He waited until he heard the elevator gate clatter
open before he flushed the toilet and walked out, zipping up his

fly. "Hey," he said, going over and giving Fiona a peck on the lips, noticing how tired she looked.

"What about a kiss for me?" Pizzaro asked.

"You're too ugly," Alejandro said.

Pizzaro's beeper went off. After looking at the number, he took out his cellular telephone and walked off by himself, unfolding it. Standing with his back to the others, he spoke briefly, disconnected, and made two additional calls before he folded up the phone, turned to the others, and said, "Let's get those parachutes out of here."

Fiona helped wheel the dolly onto the elevator.

Sal Elia had parked the Jeep Cherokee on Fashion Avenue four blocks away from the Thirty-sixth Street loft. When he saw the dopers' van being loaded, he started the engine. He wanted to be able to drive right out after them. Normally he would have put many different kinds of vehicles on a tail job like this one, but he did not have the luxury of any help this time. Elia had decided that he would have to take a risk and stick close. He didn't want to get himself gridlocked behind a bus while Fiona and her friends disappeared.

Pizzaro told the van driver to cut across town and take the West Side Highway north.

"I thought we were gonna—"

"Do what I tell you," Pizzaro snapped, half turning in the passenger seat and looking intently in both side-view mirrors.

Elia fell back another car length. He felt more secure on the overhead parkway because of the distances between exits. He switched on the radio concealed inside the door panel and listened to the crackle of the police transmissions. If something unpleasant is going to go down, I want that handset on my lap, he thought.

*   *   *

He was almost relieved to see that the Jeep Cherokee had just scooted back behind the beer truck and was tailing. There you are, my policeman, Pizzaro thought. Looking at the driver, he said, "Get off at the next exit and cut across to Fifth Avenue." Glancing at Fiona in the back, he asked, "How you feeling back there?"

Fiona's heart skipped a beat at the doper's sudden concern for her comfort. "Just great, Hector."

Crowds of people ebbed and flowed across South Street. Pier 17 and and the Pier Pavilion were filled with afternoon tourists. The temperature had soared into the nineties. Children gazed with awe at the steel bathtub square-riggers *Wavertree* and *Peking*, and they waited their turns to climb up the gangplanks.

Seaver was inside Mobile Control One, in the parking lot across the street from the Fulton Fish Market, with a headset on, watching the video monitors. It was 3:03 Thursday afternoon; Alejandro was late. He was supposed to have been inside the warehouse by three and be out by four. He had just crushed out his cheroot in the ashtray when he spotted Alejandro, carrying an overnight bag and strolling past the warehouse. The undercover was wearing jeans, a short-sleeved shirt with its tails out, Top-Siders, and a Mets baseball cap pulled down over his brow. Seaver noted the transmitter pen sticking out of Alejandro's shirt pocket.

Alejandro walked to the corner and turned to walk back past the warehouse. "Now," Seaver said into his headset. One by one, per his instructions, the video cameras on all the surveillance platforms were switched off. It would never do to have a film record of Chilebean breaking into a dope warehouse bereft of a search warrant.

Alejandro took out the set of keys that Seaver had gotten from the Ruger Lock Company, unlocked the padlocks, and rolled up the door. Standing in the doorway with his back to the street, he slid the wrench and lock pick into the cylinder and skillfully raked open the door. He hurried inside, closed the door, and leaned up against the wall, getting his bearings. The interior was cool and silent, the only sounds filtering in from the bustling seaport and the summer afternoon.

Outside, one of Seaver's detectives in an Izod shirt rolled down the door and slapped the padlocks back on.

Alejandro looked at the rows of racks lining the floor. Their shelves were crowded with dolls and toys. There were rows of large stuffed animals, pandas, lions, apes, elephants, and giraffes. Some of those strikingly large, inanimate creatures were still wrapped in protective plastic for shipping. There were pallets of lead bars stacked one on top of the other. Other stacked pallets were covered with large canvas overspreads. There were large cardboard cartons stacked neatly on the floor. Three forklifts were parked to the right of the entrance. A balcony ran around the interior, and there was an overhead crane on a track that cut across the middle of the warehouse. He heard barking and, looking in the direction of the sounds, saw cages holding stray dogs that had been snatched from the streets.

Inside Mobile Control One, Seaver transmitted the signal for all platforms to switch their cameras back on.

Alejandro darted over to the pallets covered by the overspreads. After taking the nine-millimeter submachine gun out of the overnight, he knelt on one knee and lifted up the bottom of the overhang to see what looked like gold bars. Using the gun barrel, he scraped off a thin layer of gold paint to reveal the bluish white metallic dullness of lead. I bet they keep shipping this junk all over the world, he thought.

He hurried up the steps onto the balcony. Gallons of gold paint and cases labeled "Zircons" were stored there. Leaning over the railing of the balcony, he surveyed the warehouse. The spooky quiet of the vast space made him uncomfortable. The walls were all brick except for the west one, which appeared to be plasterboard that had been painted black. There were pyramids of wooden crates along the entire width of that wall.

He climbed back down to the main floor. Walking down the aisle between the racks, he surveyed the merchandise stored in the shelves. He stopped at a row of pandas and began prodding the furry toy animals, trying to feel what was inside. The stuffing felt lumpy. He turned one panda on its back, checking out the seam. It appeared to be stitched flush. Trying to pull it apart, he was startled when the Velcro seam ripped apart to reveal packets of white powder. He didn't need a testing kit to figure out he'd found the Cleopatra Gold. He took down a doll and tore off its head; it was packed with heroin.

He opened the overnight and took out a handful of stainless-steel containers that looked like hockey pucks. They were filled with Pyranol, an incendiary that ignited for only a few seconds but produced extremely high temperatures, heat intense enough to burn through a half inch of steel in two seconds.

He began placing the Pyranol disks on the shelves next to the stuffed animals. That done, he reached back into his overnight, took out a handful of igniters, and began inserting them into the detonation holes in the container's faceplates. He went around connecting the wires extending from the igniters to eight digital timers. When the timers reached the preset time, the circuit would close and the current from the battery would fire the igniters. The ensuing fire would spread quickly, burning with enough intensity to melt all the racks and vaporize the heroin. Checking the time, and seeing that it was 3:25, he decided to set the timers for 4:05. Seaver was supposed to unlock the sliding door at precisely four o'clock. That would give him just enough time to snoop around and see if he had overlooked any goodies.

*   *   *

Pizzaro kept his eyes on the Jeep Cherokee in the two side mirrors throughout the van's circuitous ride through the city.

Fiona's instincts told her something had gone dreadfully wrong, and she was scared. Unarmed, she felt naked, totally exposed. She recalled the parting words of her close-combat instructor: "When all else fails, run." She glanced at the back door.

"It's locked, chica," Pizzaro said.

Sal Elia was trapped in the gridlock of Park Avenue's northbound lane one block away from the Waldorf Astoria. The traffic lights were out of sync, and there were triple-parked limousines lined up in front of the famous hotel, forcing the traffic to squeeze past slowly. Horns blared and tempers flared as Pizzaro's van inched its way through and sped across Fiftieth Street.

Elia could do nothing but creep along with the rest of the traffic, frustration gnawing at him. He hated these secret one-man jobs. He should have at least half a dozen other vehicles on this tail. He was shocked when he saw Pizzaro's van draw up to the curb between Fiftieth and Fifty-first and stop.

Smart bastards, he thought, an ironic smile forming in the corners of his mouth. They're waiting there to see if they're being followed; I'll have to drive on past them. He inched the Jeep up, next in line to enter the bottleneck.

The clouded back window of one of the triple-parked limousines purred down, leaving a six-inch opening. Jasmine leaned her delicate shoulder into the stock of a small-bore rifle as her finger tightened around the trigger. Her eyes focused on the cross hairs of the sniperscope, zeroing in on the side of Elia's head.

Let's get going, Elia was thinking at the moment the bullet tore into his head.

Jasmine thumbed the window control to Up and leaned back against the cushioned seat. Che-Che was sitting beside her. "It's done," he said into his cellular telephone. "I'll meet you at the warehouse."

Pizzaro's van sped away from the curb.

Alejandro's attention had been drawn to the warehouse's black wall. The more he looked at it, the more he realized that it somehow threw off the dimensions of the building. He decided to take a closer look. Lugging his overnight with him, he walked over and squeezed in alongside one of the crates. Casting his eyes down the aisle separating the crates from the wall, he figured that there was about a three-foot space between them.

To his right, four pyramids over, there was a wooden door concealed behind the boxes. He ran over to it and pressed himself between two stacks of crates to reach the door. It was a hollow door with cheap hardware, and it was unlocked. He opened it. There was about four feet between the brick wall and the plasterboard.

Stepping into the space, he confronted a steel fire door; on it was a cipher lock with a handpad. No way I'm getting past that, he thought. He bent down in the cramped space and took out the television camera that had a fiber-optic cord with a video lens set into its tip. He switched on the tiny television monitor and began snaking the cord underneath the steel door. Sweat rolled down from his armpits. He wiped his forehead dry with one arm, checked the time, and saw that he still had twenty-seven minutes until detonation.

Judith Stern had been working in her office inside Whiggham Associates when Pizzaro's telephone call came. After listening to him, she slammed the phone down angrily, opened her alligator pocketbook to make sure her automatic pistol was inside, and hurried from her office, cursing "those stupid fucking Latino assholes."

*   *   *

Burke was at his desk, trying to keep his mind on an Unusual Occurrence report he was reading from the duty captain of the Seven-eighth Precinct, about a shooting that had gone down earlier that morning involving two members of one of his Buy and Bust teams in Brooklyn. He felt immense satisfaction when he read the paragraph that explained how after the arresting officers identified themselves to the suspects, the three mutts reached for their TEC-9s and were shot dead by the undercovers. Three less scumbags, he thought just as Captain Dave Katz came bursting into his office.

Too Tall Paulie's eyes fixed on his XO's ashen face. "Shit," he muttered. He'd seen that expression too many times over these past years. "Who?" he asked in a barely audible voice.

"Sal Elia was ambushed in front of the Waldorf. He's dead."

Burke's lips trembled and he buried his face in his hands.

Katz brushed his own eyes dry, sucked in a deep breath, and asked, "Do you want to go to the scene?"

Too Tall Paulie's hands fell to his desk. With a tone of awful calm, he ordered, "Get me Romano on the line."

Alejandro stared with openmouthed fascination at what he was seeing on the tiny television screen. Mountains of money were stacked on pallets, filling the concealed space behind the fire door. He felt as though he were dreaming. During all his years working in the slime pool he had heard stories about the legendary money warehouses, but never had he seen one.

Moving the lighted probe under the door, going from one green mountain to another, he thought that there was just no way any criminal justice system could withstand the corrupting seduction of so much money.

Putting his mouth down to the transmitter pen in his shirt, he whispered, "The back of the warehouse is packed with their money." He was snaking the cord farther inside the concealed room when he heard the outside accordion door being rolled up.

He quickly checked his watch: there was plenty of time left before Seaver was due to let him out. He hurriedly pulled the snake out from under the door and stuffed the television monitor into his knapsack. "Don't come rushing in," he radioed to Seaver. "Maybe they'll just be here a few minutes."

"Bullshit," Seaver said, listening to the transmission, while he watched more of Pizzaro's men climbing out of the van.

Alejandro hunkered down behind the crates, his hand firm around the nine-millimeter's pistol grip, his finger flexed on the trigger. He slid the selector to three-burst rounds and noticed that his hand was shaking. He told himself to be calm, then brushed his arm across his brow, wiping away the sweat running into his eyes. He looked at his watch; eighteen minutes until detonation. Hiding behind the crates, making himself as small as he could, he peeked out and watched the dopers coming in.

Juan, the one with the short ponytail and diamond chip in his ear, was the first to enter. Fiona and Pizzaro were next, followed by three other dopers. The door was pulled down with a bang and locked; Fiona felt her knees go weak and a chill creep up her spine.

As he walked over to her, Pizzaro's expression turned deadly. "Why don't you explain to me why you joined the Saint George Association and the Policewomen's Endowment Association?" he asked calmly. Then, without a flicker of warning, he punched her in the mouth, sending her to the floor.

"I don't know—" She broke off when Pizzaro brutally kicked her in her stomach, bending her double in agony.

Alejandro's natural instinct was to come out of his hiding place firing; but common sense stopped him. He'd be able to take out Pizzaro and maybe two, or even three, others, but not before one of them killed Fiona. The wise thing was to wait for the explosion. When the dopers were thrown off guard, he could lay down a field of fire from his hiding place. With the sound suppressor and the heat and smoke from the fire, the dopers might not even be able to locate him.

Peeking out from behind his hiding place, he saw Fiona take another kick in the face that slapped her head backward. Hold on, Fiona, he prayed silently.

Two of the crew pulled her up from the floor. Pizzaro grabbed her chin. "You're a cop."

"No I'm not," she mumbled through the blood streaming from her nose and mouth. "I was only a cop for three weeks. They fired me because I kicked one of the instructors in the balls. I told all this to Caswell. Didn't he tell you?"

Pizzaro punched her in the stomach. "No, he didn't tell me, because you didn't tell him." He started to walk away, turned suddenly, and kicked her in the groin. She collapsed, sagging between two dopers.

"Pull off her jeans," Pizzaro ordered, taking out a butane lighter and turning up the flame. Grabbing her hair, he held the hissing flame up to her face and said, "I'm going to burn your pussy with this, and then you're going to tell me whatever I want to know."

She lashed out with her legs, fighting to prevent them from removing her jeans.

The warehouse door opened and Che-Che and Jasmine came in, followed by four of Che-Che's bodyguards.

"What is all this?" Che-Che demanded, watching the struggling woman.

"She's a cop," Pizzaro said.

"I'm not a cop," she said, glaring defiantly at her tormentors.

Che-Che went over to her and looked into her eyes. "Maybe she's telling the truth."

Pizzaro shook his head in violent disagreement. "Che-Che, they pulled all her records, but forgot about the membership in the cops' religious and fraternal clubs," he said.

"Maybe, maybe not," Che-Che said, watching Juan yank her jeans off, "but I can't take that chance." He motioned to Pizzaro to continue his interrogation.

"Want her underpants off?" Juan asked Pizzaro.

"Naw, leave 'em on; I'll burn my way through. Get her down on her back and spread her legs," Pizzaro ordered.

Alejandro could wait no longer. He slid the barrel of the nine-millimeter submachine gun along the ledge of one of the uneven crates and began drawing a sight on Pizzaro's back as the doper slowly moved the flame up between Fiona's thrashing legs.

"Don't do that," Judith called, slamming a side door of the warehouse behind her and locking it.

"Who the fuck do you think you are, telling me what to do?" Pizzaro shouted as she approached.

"I'm your boss, Hector. Kill her if you have to, but don't do that," she said, her glacial expression leaving no doubt that she was ready to kill if he disobeyed her.

Pizzaro's mouth fell open; he looked to Che-Che for orders.

Che-Che's smile had a hint of delight as he looked at Pizzaro and said, "Do what Judith tells you. She and I got a private thing going."

Pizzaro quickly recovered his composure. "Whatever you say."

Alejandro crouched back down, cradling the nine-millimeter submachine gun in his arms, aware of the sweat coursing down his temples and the loud thumping of his heart. Hang on, Fiona. Hang on, he prayed.

Judith walked up to Fiona. "Let her get dressed," she said, handing her her jeans.

"Thanks," Fiona said, taking them and turning away from the others while she put them on.

* * *

"Shit," Romano said, hanging up the phone. He had just been informed by the front desk that the commanding officer of Narcotics was on his way in to see him.

The door to his office burst open; Burke seemed to fill the entire doorway, rage visible in his flushed expression and throbbing temples. Romano had never seen Burke like this before. The sheer ferocity made him rise slowly out of his seat and ask in a shocked voice, "What?"

"Che-Che just had Sal Elia whacked in front of the Waldorf. Another one of my people is dead because of your goddamn lies."

Romano began to regain some of his composure. "What are you talking about?"

"I'm talking about Alejandro Monahan." He slammed the door behind him and stormed over to the desk. "He's either with you, or he's with Che-Che, and you're going to tell me."

"I'm sorry about Elia, but what the hell does that have to do with Alejandro?"

"Elia was baby-sitting Fiona Lee when he was killed."

"Who the hell is Fiona Lee?" Romano shouted.

"She's my undercover, who is flying the planes that are parachuting heroin into this city!" Burke shouted back.

Romano sank into his seat, his lips pressed together tightly.

"Sal Elia's murder means that her cover was blown. If we don't get to her fast, they'll kill her, too. I don't want to lose another one of my people, Joey."

"Paulie—"

"No more bullshit! Get on that fucking horn to your spies and find out where my Fiona is. If you don't, I'm going to plant disinformation bombshells all over this town on the nonexistent Special Ops Unit of the NYPD. I'll send all those ACLU liberals into a feeding frenzy that will make Knapp look like a love-in."

"You wouldn't do that," Romano said uncertainly.

"Try me."

* * *

Andy Seaver was chewing nervously on his tenth cheroot of the day and staring at the monitors inside the recreational vehicle when the radio crackled. "Control to Mobile One, K."

"Mobile One standing by, K," Seaver transmitted.

"What is happening? K," Joey-the-G-Man asked.

Seaver told him that Pizzaro and the rest of the crew had turned up at the warehouse.

"Was there a woman with them?" Joey-the-G-Man asked, and gave Fiona's description.

"Affirmative, she arrived with Pizzaro."

"She's a narc undercover. Her cover's been blown."

"You're so young and beautiful," Che-Che said, caressing Fiona's face. "Does Alejandro know you're a cop?"

"I'm not a cop," she insisted.

"Of course you are," he said, walking away from the others and crossing the warehouse to a large cardboard box near the cages that housed stray dogs. He pushed the carton aside to reveal a deep pit that had been dug out below the floor. "Bring her over here," he ordered.

Pizzaro and another doper dragged the struggling undercover toward the pit.

Hiding behind the crate, Alejandro inched his way up into a kneeling position, tightening the machine gun's short stock against his shoulder and sighting in on Pizzaro.

Fiona, both arms gripped tightly by the dopers, looked down into the pit. A brown-and-green anaconda about fifteen feet long was coiled up at the bottom. It lay motionless, silent; its serpentine eyes glowed like dark emeralds.

"Isn't he pretty?" Che-Che cooed.

"It's as obscene as you are," Fiona said, looking away, her eyes darting frantically toward the west wall and the stack of crates lined up in front of it. Suddenly she caught a glimpse of a man staring down the barrel of a submachine gun with a bulbous snout. She quickly looked away, unsure if it was Alejandro but hoping to God it was.

"May I talk to her?" Judith asked Che-Che.

"Yeah. Try and talk some smarts into her."

"They'll kill you if you don't let me help you," Judith said. "Is it worth giving up your life?"

"I'm not a cop. I can prove it."

Judith began to say something, but her mouth froze open as her eyes went wide; staring across the warehouse, she had just noticed the exposed igniter wires strung across the storage racks and around the necks of the stuffed animals. Almost as if she'd been dazed by a blow, she walked stiffly toward the racks.

At that moment a thunderous fireball exploded across the warehouse.

At virtually the same instant, Alejandro fired a three-burst round into Pizzaro's chest, killing him instantly.

Two fast kicks delivered by Fiona to Che-Che's groin doubled him over, and the third toppled him down into the pit. The anaconda struck with lightning speed, slapping its thick coils around the screaming man.

Fiona jabbed her fingers into Juan's eyes; his shirt was in flames. She made a zigzag run over to the crates stacked in front of the black wall. Tito, who had suffered least from the fireball, fired a burst from his Uzi at her. Alejandro exploded his head with another three-round burst. The surviving dopers fired their guns wildly, spraying the warehouse with bullets, unable to see who was killing them.

Fire raced along the racks; the stuffed animals ignited like flaming dominoes and filled the warehouse with smoke and the noxious stench of burning fur and heroin.

One of Che-Che's bodyguards began spraying shots at the crates along the western wall. Alejandro took him down with a burst to his stomach.

Jasmine ran over to the pit and tried to draw a bead with her gun on the anaconda's swaying head. Che-Che was struggling feebly against the overwhelming power of his pet's coils; the pit echoed with his screams. The awful sounds of his snapping bones replaced his screams as the air was crushed out of his body.

Andy Seaver and the detectives inside Mobile One ran out of the van and over to the warehouse door.

Jasmine fired two rounds into the anaconda's head, killing it. Its coils unwound slowly from around Che-Che.

Andy Seaver ran inside. Jasmine whirled around in a combat stance and fired three rounds at him. Seaver hit the floor and rolled left, firing two rounds that plowed into Jasmine's chest, pitching her backward into the pit.

The surviving dopers threw down their weapons and raised their hands over their heads.

The melted racks had collapsed into a pile of twisted, smoldering junk; the flames and heat had turned what remained of the heroin into globs of oozing black mud.

The dead anaconda's coils lay slack across the body of Che-Che, who was bleeding from his eyes, ears, and mouth. The powerful snake had spiraled his body, crushing his ribs and piercing his lungs with shards of bones. Suddenly his glazed eyes opened and he saw Jasmine's body. He managed to get one hand free of the snake's weight and inched it over to touch Jasmine's shoulder gently. I don't want to meet the Spirit God alone, he thought as he died.

During the confusion of battle, with smoke filling the inside of the warehouse, Judith had managed to run unnoticed behind a stack of pallets and make her way over to the forklifts parked by the door. Hiding behind them, she waited for her chance to duck outside. Firemen were dragging thick, rigid hoses inside the warehouse and beginning to water down the smoldering mass of junk. Crowds of tourists were congregating in the street.

Policemen struggled to establish a "frozen zone" around the warehouse.

Alejandro and Fiona both remained hidden behind the crates.

Burke and Romano arrived together; they were soon in a huddle with Seaver, concocting a poor excuse for a plausible story. Detectives were handcuffing prisoners and reading them their rights.

"I wanna call my lawyer," one told his arresting officer.

Fiona looked down the aisle between the crates and the fake wall. Alejandro was stuffing his machine gun into the overnight. Looking up at her, he mouthed, "Are you okay?"

"Yes," she whispered.

Ambulance attendants rushed inside to treat the wounded and remove the dead.

"What's happening, Officer?" Judith said to one of the firemen as she walked out from behind the forklift.

"You can't come in here, lady," the fireman said angrily, and led her outside.

Alejandro had been peering out from his hiding place, watching the police brass and not really paying much attention to what else was going on inside the warehouse. Suddenly he caught sight of Judith leaving.

"Andy, I'm coming out!" he shouted.

Seaver ran around to the detectives, shouting, "He's one of us! Don't shoot! He's one of us!"

Holding his overnight bag in front of his face to conceal his identity, Alejandro ran for the entrance, aware of the .38 Colt detective special jammed into his waistband in the small of his back. He dashed outside in time to see Che-Che's limousine, engulfed by the crowd, inching its way through to South Street. He plunged after it, pushing and shoving, shouldering his way.

Judith heaved a big sigh of relief as she drove Che-Che's limousine through the crowd and turned into South Street.

Alejandro collided with a baby carriage, toppling the baby out. He picked up the baby and handed it back to its screaming mother, then plunged back into the crowd. He reached the street in time to see the limousine driving south.

Looking around, he spotted a man getting out of a taxi in front of the Fulton Fish Market. He raced over to the cab, climbed into the back, and said, "I want you to follow that limo up ahead."

"Are you kidding?" the driver asked.

Alejandro slid a hundred-dollar bill through the security partition to the driver. "Stay with her and there's another one at the end for you."

"Whatever you say, mister."

Judith looked up into the rearview mirror and did not see any cars that seemed to be pursuing her. She had been lucky to extricate herself from that mess and had no intention of bringing herself to the attention of the police now by driving recklessly. She had more than enough money stashed in her numbered accounts in Luxembourg to allow her to live out her life like a queen.

She continued driving south until she reached Whitehall Street, where she made the U-turn and drove back north on the FDR Drive. She exited the highway at the Midtown Tunnel and drove through to Queens. Slowing to pay her toll, she opened her pocketbook and pushed aside her automatic pistol to take out her wallet. After paying, she drove onto the Long Island Expressway.

Alejandro's cab stopped while the driver paid the toll. From his seat in the back, he watched the limousine disappear over the rise in the overhead highway.

The nurse was dressed more appropriately today, in a pleated white skirt and black blouse. Judith didn't particularly care for her sneakers, but this was not the time to bring up that subject. Looking down at her father sitting on his wheelchair, she said to the nurse, "Please leave us alone for a few minutes."

She draped herself over her father and began sobbing. "I have to go away for a while, Daddy. I'll come back as soon as I can. My business here is over. How I wish you knew how successful I've been. I'm famous."

She pressed him close, savoring his old man's smell, the roughness of his skin, dipping into her well of memories, remembering the times they used to play their secret game. "Do you understand anything I'm telling you?" she asked despairingly, then kissed his cheek.

"Judith."

She froze at the sound of Alejandro's now familiar voice. Remaining draped over her father, she slowly turned her head toward the sound as she inched her hand down into her pocketbook. "So you were a cop after all. I have to give you credit, you were really good." Sliding her hand around the pistol's grip, she added, "Did I ever tell you that your father was just unlucky enough to get in my way?"

She whipped the pistol around from behind her father's head and fired two rounds. One of them tore into Alejandro's shoulder, spinning him around and splaying him on his back on the grass. The second one thudded into a maple tree.

Writhing from pain, aware of his bleeding, he tried to turn over to crawl behind the tree, but she was much too quick for him.

She ran over to him and knelt down, placing the barrel of her automatic against his temple. "Too bad it has to end like this. I thought you showed real promise. But you were just another fucking cop."

Grimacing from his pain, he slowly wormed his good hand under his hip, searching for the revolver tucked into the small of his back. "I don't believe you killed my father."

"You better believe. I killed him, and now it's your turn."

Alejandro's fingers slid around the checkered pistol grip.

She leaned down and kissed his lips. "Your daddy tried to play soldier."

He grimaced with pain. "My daddy wasn't a soldier, he was a cop," he said softly, and fired a round into her stomach. With a shocked expression on her face, she toppled on her side, exposing a gaping hole where her stomach used to be.

Sol Stern's eyes came to life; he looked with horror and recognition at the woman lying on the bloodstained grass. His gnarled hands groped for the chair's wheels, and somehow he began to push his way over to the woman. Suddenly he hit a bump and lost control, dumping himself on the ground. Crawling over to his daughter, he said, "My beautiful Cleopatra, what have they done to you?"

Judith felt the cold flowing over her body. Everything was getting dark and fuzzy. Looking at her father through the mist, she cried out, "Daddy!" and closed her eyes forever.

Sol Stern felt himself slipping back into the unforgiving void of his mind. His last thoughts were of their game—he was the Flute Player, and she was the most beautiful girl in the world. She was truly and eternally Queen Cleopatra, Queen of Kings and Goddess of Goddesses.

ACKNOWLEDGMENTS

I would like to thank the following people for their help in writing *Cleopatra Gold:* Paul Evans for teaching me about the music business; Annete Meyers for leading me into the world of finance; Judy Green of Bankers Trust Security for taking the time to teach me about money laundering; Captain Joe Lesi, NYPD, for sharing his expertise on the undercover operations of the Narcotics Division; Robert Mason for teaching me about "electronic" tailing methods; my agents, Knox Burger and Kitty Sprague, for *always* being there for me; James O'Shea Wade for his tremendous help with editing the manuscript; Paul Boccardi of Crown Publishers for his many kindnesses; Mary Higgins Clark for her insightful suggestions; Sally R. Sommer for the pleasurable experience of learning about tap-dancing. A big thank-you to my friend in Delta Force and my buddy in the Agency for teaching me about the Parapoint delivery system and other high-tech wonders. Wyatt Sprague of the band Urban Blight for taking the time to teach me about the music business and the club scene. A special thank-you to all my friends in Zihuatanejo for giving me the flavor of Zihua: Bill Fish, Tanya, Juan Carlos, Don, Dan and Dennie, and Rex.